DOCTOR PLAYBOY

J. SAMAN

Cover Designer: Lori Jackson

Photographer: Rafa Catala

Model: Jorge Del Rio

Editing: My Brother's Editor

Editing: Emily Lawrence

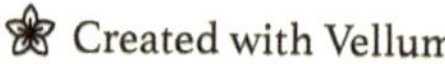 Created with Vellum

PART I

1

The wood planks of the steps leading from our private beach up to our Martha's Vineyard home dig into the soles of my bare feet. But it's got nothing on my shoulder that's twinging and kicking up like a bull at a rodeo. I've been so miserable since I got here, I hardly recognize my own reflection and the pain isn't helping to improve my mood.

Neither is how weak I still feel.

They talked about this in med school.

Patients going into depression after a major injury or illness.

I have no illusions that's what this is. I just never considered it would happen to me. On either of those accounts.

My shoes dangle from two fingers. My other hand brushes back the windswept strands of my chestnut hair that cling to my face. It's too long, but finding the energy to do something about it isn't high on my priority list. At least not until I can get the green light to go back to Minnesota.

Tonight was fun, though. Kinda monotonous, same old shit as it always is, but fun. My brothers and baby sister all flew out to the island, and I would be a fool to believe it wasn't because

I'm here for the foreseeable future. They're worried about me. *I'm* worried about myself, and it shines through.

What will I do if I never fully recover? If I can't go back? If I can't continue and finish my residency?

If I can never operate again?

And as if fate enjoys the kick to my ass, my shirt sleeve catches on a random nail that's sticking out of the wood railing and my shoulder jerks.

"Fuck," I hiss as I rub over the barely healed scar, aggravated with just how tender the wound and the surrounding tissue still are. "Heal. I command you to heal."

I snicker, a little buzzed and a lot annoyed that I'm still hurting despite the joint I smoked and the two strong drinks I nursed tonight. Carter stayed at the bar. So did Kaplan and Oliver. Landon didn't even attempt it, having gone to bed likely when his nine-year-old princess Miss Stella—my favorite girl on the planet—sacked out for the night.

He doesn't know how to leave her, and that's an entirely different matter.

So different from my reason for being banished to our parents' estate on The Vineyard in the middle of my goddamn neurosurgery residency at the Mayo Clinic.

Which brings me back to my aching shoulder.

And the music I hear, a lulling distraction luring me away from the break in the path where it diverges between the main house and the pool, tennis courts, garages, and staff residences. For a moment, I freeze, unsure exactly what I'm hearing. A violin? Cello maybe?

But from where and from whom?

I amble toward the music, too depressed to go to bed with my thoughts and too bored to bother trying to fuck one of the local chicks.

Boring. So boring. It's not even their fault. It's purely mine.

But that sound. That achingly, mournful, exquisite sound.

It rattles my bones in the best of ways. It calls attention to my muscles, urging, begging them to follow it. To capture it. To listen more intently. I've never heard this song before—though far from a classical music expert. This feels more modern.

The sound leads me to the garage. All five bays are closed, but there is a light glowing through the upper windows and no matter how high I jump, I can't quite make out who is there. Trying the side door, I find it unlocked and, as quietly as possible, I turn the handle, slipping inside and shutting it behind me with a soft click.

The air in the garage is thick, heavy with humidity, and I roll my sleeves up to my elbows.

The music is coming from the other side of the garage, and I weave my way around the large Jeep, Tesla, and Mercedes convertible only to stop dead in my tracks for a second time, my breath stalling in my lungs at the sight before me.

Hot damn.

A woman is sitting on a folding chair, her black-as-night hair hanging over the back of it, her face flushed and tacky with sweat. From this angle, I'd swear the only thing she's wearing is the large cello sitting between her spread thighs, but as I edge closer, I notice a paper-thin, gauzy white, flowy top that stops just below her ample breasts and matching tiny shorts.

Her eyes are closed, her head bowed as one hand moves swiftly and fluidly up the long neck of the instrument while the other gracefully drags the bow along the strings. Carefully, I keep to the shadows along the doors, angling for a better position to watch her. She hasn't heard me yet and though I feel as though I should know her, that I've seen her before somewhere, I'm coming up at a loss.

Another step and then I stop, standing here like a creeper as she plays the cello in a way I've never heard or seen any instrument played before. The way she draws each note from it, coaxing its exquisite moans like a lover, has me entranced.

Or maybe that's the woman.

Because just looking at her has my dick hard as steel when it hasn't shown interest in anything or anyone in over a month. Calling her simply beautiful is practically an insult. Words haven't yet been invented to describe her, and she hasn't even opened her eyes yet.

Or looked up.

But I need her to. The urge to see her face and what she looks like when she discovers me here is oddly compelling. Then I might need to fuck her. Work whatever bizarre magic she's weaving out of my body. Unless she's Rina's friend or something. Shit. She is at my parents' estate and judging by the way she's dressed and her comfort playing cello here, she belongs.

I clear my throat, but she doesn't catch it. In fact, she's so lost in her music she doesn't notice me until I grab a random old deck chair and drag it over to sit beside her. Then she startles. Almost violently, she practically falls off her chair as her head flies up and her gaze snaps over to me.

Startling blue-green eyes land on mine and something strange and foreign stirs in my chest, squeezing ever so slightly. She blinks rapidly—her eyelashes a thick, black fan across her creamy cheeks—as she adjusts herself on her chair and licks her pillowy lips nervously.

"Luca."

Now it's my turn to blink. "You know me?"

A flush of crimson creeps up from the top of her cleavage to the roots of her hair. "Well, yes, sir. I mean, it's been a while, but I... of course. That is to say, I knew you weren't Dr. Landon."

She shakes her head, flustered. Clears her throat. "Did I wake you with my playing?"

Sir. She called me sir. And Dr. Landon? *The fuck?*

I study her closer. Raven hair. Caribbean-ocean eyes. Knockout body.

Shit. Raven hair. Raven. How could I have not recognized our house manager's daughter? Double shit. Morgan Fairchild has been with our family since around the time Kaplan was born. He and his wife both, but she died shortly after Raven was born. If he knew the thoughts I was just having about his daughter, he'd kill me. Literally, since the man is former MI6.

"Raven."

If possible, her blush deepens.

"It's been..."

A long time. I swear, she was all braces and big glasses and looked nothing like this the last time I saw her. She was also—

"Four years," she answers for me, gently setting her large black cello down along with her bow into an open case beside her chair. "Since you and Dr. Landon graduated medical school. At least, that was the last time we spoke." Embarrassment consumes her features, and she looks down. But I'm caught on that four years ago thing.

"Raven, how old are you?"

"Eighteen."

Her answer rocks something inside me and I lean forward, my elbows hitting my thighs as I pin her with a stare I can't explain.

"And how long have you been eighteen?"

Her head tilts at my odd question, but I wait her out, needing to know just what level of depraved son of a bitch I'm hitting.

"Three months."

My gut sinks.

"I turn twenty-nine in two weeks."

Why am I telling her that? I'm nearly eleven years older than her. She's a teenager. Essentially part of our staff, who are more like extended family. I shouldn't feel this sort of... disappointment? Is that what that is?

"I know when your birthday is, Luca, and I know how old you are."

A smirk hits my lips at the "duh" way she says that. "Is that right?"

She stares innocently at me, but there is something else there. A glimmer in her eyes. Something that tells me she likes how thrown off I am by our age difference. Almost as if she can see my ill-placed desire for her and wants to play with it, twirl it around her fingers.

I'm Luca, but Landon is Dr. Landon. I lean back in my chair, rubbing a hand over my mouth as I consider her. If she's at all embarrassed about her blatant lack of clothing, she's not showing it as she cautiously waits for my next move while not removing her gaze from mine.

Such a gorgeous contradiction—shy and brave—I find my smirk growing against my better judgment.

"You're a lot younger than I am. Does our age difference bother you?" The way it bothers me.

She laughs now, the sound a sexy rasp. Her voice is like those sea salt caramels Rina made me eat earlier with her. Smooth and creamy, yet with a zinging coarseness at the end.

"Should it?" She laughs harder at my expression. "I've been told being eighteen is considered a legal adult. I can vote and fight for our country and..." She leans forward, cupping her hand around her mouth as if she's about to tell me a secret. "I don't even have to ask for my daddy's permission before I want to go do something I shouldn't."

My dick jumps excitedly at that proposition, but I tamp it down. She's bold. Beautiful. And impossible. The first woman to get my dick stirring in over a month is as forbidden to me in just about every way a woman can be. Gotta love that irony, but that doesn't mean I'm getting up and walking away either. She's a winless game I can't help but want to continue playing.

"Is that what has you out here? You no longer need permission to be up past midnight?"

A shrug of her shoulder, her hands twining up in her hair, lifting the heavy strands off her dewy neck. It also lifts the bottom of her crop top and I catch the hint of the heavy undersides of her breasts. Holy damn, that's insanely fucking sexy.

"Are you flirting with me?" I tease when she doesn't answer.

"Possibly. Does that bother you?" she asks, throwing my question back at me.

I chuckle under my breath. It fucking should. "Not even a bit. I'm just glad you've stopped calling me sir and haven't referred to me as Dr. Luca. But you never answered my initial question."

She tosses her hands up, the strands of her hair falling around her. "I couldn't sleep. What's your excuse?"

My eyes snap back up to hers. "I decided I was done for the night and didn't feel like going to one of the parties my siblings were headed for."

"No woman for Luca Abbot-Fritz to end the night with? Has such an atrocity ever occurred before?" She gives an exaggerated gasp, covering her mouth as her eyes widen.

"You mock me, Little Bird, thinking you know me so well. You knew it was me and not Landon, as well as my birthday, age, and evidently my fuck habits. What else do you know?"

Aqua eyes sparkle, lit with challenge as she matches my position, crossing her legs at the knee, her arms across her breasts forcing them up just a bit and revealing a hint of more cleavage. Cleavage I have absolutely no business looking at, but her rare and exquisite form of beauty makes it impossible not to notice.

"I know you sleep shirtless, only in your boxer briefs. I

know you like to run ten miles before the sun comes up because your eyes are sensitive to light, and you don't want to run with sunglasses."

"Wait, wait, wait," I interrupt, holding up a hand. "How do you know I only sleep in boxer briefs?"

She winks at me without answering. "I know you take your coffee with a touch of cream and no sugar because you prefer hazelnut coffee and feel that's sweet enough. I know you know every line from the original three Star Wars movies and likely all the newer ones, even if you hate one, two, and three. I know you also have a coveted secret stash of Star Wars figurines but brought only five of your favorites with you when you left for college. I know your heart shifts as quickly as your eyes, favoring a new woman every week. I know your greatest love is your family and that you'd give your life for any of them without a second's hesitation."

I stare at her. Utterly floored. "Raven Fairchild, how long have you been stalking me?"

"Nearly all my life."

A laugh bursts from my chest. "And why is that?"

"If you're looking for someone to pad your ego with compliments and batting eyelashes as they throw themselves at you, you're talking to the wrong girl."

"You know, you're nothing like the girl who stuttered at the sight of me, saying sir and Dr. Landon."

"That was all before you looked at my boobs."

I choke out a cough, hacking up my lungs. "Christ, woman. You're going to kill me."

"What are you doing here, *Luca*?" She emphasizes my name. "Looking for a quick, easy lay?"

"If I wanted that, I'd be at the party right now. Instead of here with you. But the fact remains, you know an awful lot about me when I know so little about you."

"You mean like how you didn't even recognize me tonight?"

"Caught that, did you?"

She raises an eyebrow.

I shrug contritely. I should have recognized her. Maybe I wouldn't be sitting out here with her then. As close as I am. Intrigued and unable to force myself to get up and walk away as I should.

"You saved my life once. Do you remember?"

I rack my brain for a moment and then answer, "When you fell in the pool, and I jumped in after you?"

She nods, staring down at her lap, her fingers twirling an errant string on her tiny shorts. "I was running back to the staff house and tripped over something in the yard. I sprained my ankle and fell into the pool at the same time. I was in so much pain I could hardly swim and was struggling to reach the side. You jumped in. Dragged me out."

"Then I spent the rest of the afternoon watching Disney movies while you were bundled up under a blanket in front of the fire. I think I also made popcorn and ordered pizza."

A smile lights up her face. "You did."

"What does that have to do with the stalking?"

Her head falls back, her long hair along with it, and I admire the column of her neck. How graceful she is. She doesn't look or act eighteen. That's for damn sure.

"I developed an adolescent crush that day." She rights herself. "But don't worry, old man. I gave up that ghost a long time ago."

My hand hits my chest. "Old man?"

She scrunches her nose. "So old."

"I'm wounded."

"I've been told."

Any warmth or amusement I was feeling instantly dies inside me as ice runs through my veins, making my body shudder and my shoulder ache as if to remind me of the real reason I'm on this island. She leans forward, her fingers stroking over my hand, a tender look in her eyes, along with a soft smile. No pity and it's a relief.

"Walk me home."

It's not a question, but I stand all the same, swallowing thickly. I flip my hand around, grasping hers and helping her up. She doesn't release me as she goes for the massive cello, nor does she allow me to take it from her when I attempt. Instead, she silently holds my hand as we exit the garage, the warm, salty wind hitting us with its briny tang, blowing our hair and clothing about.

And when we reach the front door of the staff quarters at the back of the estate, she gives my hand a squeeze, meets my eyes for a flicker of a second, releases me, and walks inside, shutting the door behind her. No good night or see you around.

I chuckle to myself, rubbing my hand over my mouth.

Well, that was unexpected as hell. Kind of fun. A lot dirty— at least my thoughts were. Raven Fairchild. Yes, definitely unexpected. And inappropriate...

I have no idea what that was. All I know is I can't do it again. Not with her. No matter how much I want to.

The sun is not even up when I hear the knock on my door. I groan, squinting my eyes open a millimeter, only to snap them shut again just as quickly. "Dad, I practiced all last night. I'm not behind."

"Well, that's good because I was thinking I'd take you for a run and then breakfast."

I shoot up, half falling out of bed before I catch myself with a hand on the hardwood. Righting myself, I search all around my room. "You're not in my room, are you?"

He laughs and that laugh...

"Is that an invitation?"

"My father will crush your balls in a vise until they pop."

"Now that's some imagery to wake up to."

My eyes collide with my nightstand, with the alarm clock I have on there. Fuck, it's five a.m. Too early. Way, way too early. Oh, and the smell. That's obviously me. I should have showered last night after I came back here. I cup my hand over my mouth and breathe out, only to immediately inhale. And wince.

Dammit.

"Luca, what are you doing here?"

"How do you know I'm not Landon?"

Because Landon knows I exist, and you didn't until last night. Hell, I babysit his daughter Stella three days a week when we're not here on the island. And Landon Fritz would *never* come knocking on my door before dawn. If at all.

"I'm rolling my eyes at you for that question."

"Very childish. Now get up. It's nearly dawn and as you know, I don't like to run when the sun is already up."

"I'm not a runner. Go find someone else to torture."

Truth. I roll over onto my side, yanking the blankets over my head.

"No."

"I'll only slow you down."

"I don't care about that. I'm not up to form anyway. Come with me. Spend the day with me. Before I can talk myself out of it."

Oh. That gets me. My eyes snap open beneath the blanket and before I can stop it, I'm smiling. Like a giddy schoolgirl, I'm smiling. I'd do a spastic dance in my bed if I wasn't positive he'd hear it.

Luca Fritz—*Luca freaking Fritz!*—is here against his better judgment and he's right on that. If I wasn't so determined to be different from the women he takes to his bed, I would have jumped him like a Vegas streetwalker jumps a drunk high roller. Accidental marriage and all. But, yeah, I don't want to be every other girl to him and I'm already at a disadvantage.

Hello, could he have brought up the age gap a few more times?

But he's here and I'm... fuck it.

Clamoring out of bed, I swing the door open and faint to the floor in a pile of mush. Or more accurately, I drool. A lot. Luca Fritz is standing here, hovering in my doorframe, his hands gripping the top edge, making his biceps bulge and his triceps pop as he angles in. He's wearing blue gym shorts, a gray sports shirt, and sneakers that likely cost more than my performance cello, and I want to drop to my knees and take him in my mouth.

A compulsion I've never had before, but there it is, folks.

"You're not dressed."

"Huh?"

A smirk curls deviously up his lips as he gives me a slow once-over that makes my toes curl with the dark look in his eyes. "Little Bird, you're as naked as a baby jaybird."

"What?"

I glance down. I'm not naked. I mean, I'm sorta naked. I'm wearing the white linen crop tank top I was wearing last night and my panties, which are boy shorts so, not a thong or anything.

My head snaps back up. "I wasn't exactly expecting you."

Certainly not after I brought up his injury. Something that had me up for more than a few hours after I said good night to him.

"I'm going to wait outside for everyone's safety. Change into workout stuff and let's go run—"

I slam the door in his face before he can finish that thought. I wasn't lying. I haven't been running in forever. I do HIIT (high intensity interval training), yoga, and more yoga. Sometimes ballet and Pilates too. It's good for my posture and back muscles, which I need in order to play cello for hours a day.

But running?

"I hope this means you're changing?"

"You said you were going outside."

He laughs and then I hear his heavy footsteps head down the stairs and oh my God, this is actually happening. Luca motherfucking Fritz wants to run with me and then take me to breakfast. After I made him frown like he just watched The Patriots get smoked in the Super Bowl. And before you go all rolling your eyes, try being a Boston sports fan and then talk to me.

Still, I do the squeal and jump up and down about ten times before I get my shit together and put on my hottest yoga pants —the ones that make my butt look like a Kardashians'—and a sports bra that shows an awesome amount of cleavage—not difficult with my girls. No shirt because why would I do that?

I have no shame.

I know who he is, okay? I'm not stupid or delusional. He's an Abbot-Fritz. Luca Abbot-Fritz at that. Billionaire playboy who charms and swoons a new girl off her feet every week. And I'm the daughter of his father's house manager and head of security. I'm staff. And nearly eleven years younger as we established last night.

He's not interested. Not really anyway, and I know that.

But when you've wanted something your whole life and you're presented with a chance, you take that chance. You don't squander it and you don't second-guess it. I put on deodorant to hide the stink and brush my teeth using the small bathroom I have in here. I give myself a once-over in the mirror, staring at my reflection as I try to pump myself up while talking myself down.

"No regrets. Even if all he wants is to be friends."

Ugh.

"You're going to get your heart broken."

I flip myself off and leave the smarter half of me behind, heading outside into the freaking blackness of no dawn in sight.

"You're crazy, right?"

"I haven't run in the five days I've been on this island. Not the five days I was in the hospital before that because I was unconscious and intubated in the ICU and sure as hell not in the weeks prior to that after my injury or my surgery. We're talking about over a month here, baby girl. You reminded me last night that this is my thing and now you're beholden to follow through on rehabbing me."

My hands hit my hips. "Don't you pay people for that?"

"I do. But they're not nearly as fucking hot as you are. Damn. Are you trying to make running beside you painful?"

"It's going to be painful for me. Might as well be for you too."

He chuckles, running his hand through his hair as he almost begrudgingly takes me in. "You look different than when I saw you last at fourteen."

"Thank God for braces, contacts, and puberty."

More laughter, a head shake, and then he waves me to go ahead of him, only I have no clue how to start this. Do people just start running? Feels almost silly. I should pay attention more.

"Come on, Little Bird. Let's hit the sand."

"How many nicknames do you have for me? Or is this just what you call all your girls so you don't have to remember their names?"

I get an ass swat that has me grinning like a psycho but start off anyway, jogging like I have a clue what I'm doing.

An hour later, I think I've died a thousand deaths. I had to stop no less than five times because of the excruciating splint in my side. I nearly collapsed twice. Tripped over my own feet at least eight.

But Luca is all light bouncing feet and adorable smiles and damn... childhood crushes suck sometimes.

"I haven't felt this good in so long. I was worried I wouldn't be able to run but look at me. Not as weak as I thought." He fist pumps and I flip him off, my hands on my knees as I try to drag in air, sweating like a sinner in church.

We've somehow managed to make it to the outskirts of Edgartown. Martha's Vineyard if you don't know where the Abbot-Fritz summer home is. Well, the one they visit the most frequently. Dr. Fritz senior volunteers his time at the local hospital here on the island and also on The Cape during the summer months.

And for my entire life, I've spent my summers here while he does that and his wife, Octavia Abbot-Fritz—she insists I call her Octavia—does whatever billionaire mothers of six children do. She runs charities and the Abbot Foundation and chases after her little monsters.

Only her monsters are very grown now.

One in particular turning into a predator who stalks women with their eyes.

"You're staring at my ass. Again," I wheeze.

I bend down to pick up a seashell that's not all that impressive, if only to drive and encourage that point home further.

"I'm not."

"You're a terrible liar."

"Only when I don't care about getting caught."

I grin stupidly, knowing he can't see it. Then I give my ass a shake and he laughs, reaching out and swatting it. Again. That's two ass spanks before dawn.

I flip around, cocking an eyebrow, but his eyes are already locked on the turbulent sea, his expression matching its wrath. Unsettled. Disturbed. All playfulness evaporated.

"Yet another miserable, gray, sunless day," he declares, his tone flat and all wrong.

I stop, frowning at his suddenly sullen tone. I had heard the rumor. The mentioning under breaths of depression, only seeing it now for the first time on him. Maybe a bit last night, but this is different.

His gaze now casts heavenward at the dull, gray sky.

"You sound like you're quoting *The Rainy Day* by Henry Wadsworth Longfellow."

He doesn't reply, but a quote from the poem hits me. 'Be still, sad heart! and cease repining;

Behind the clouds is the sun still shining...' I look up too. "The sun is always there, Luca. Always shining down. Even when it's hidden behind the clouds."

He cuts sharply to me. "But how do you know that if you can't see it?"

I shrug. "Faith. Science."

"Such an easy bullshit answer that offers no reassurance and zero help."

Oh, the venom. The accusation, as if only he knows what pain feels like and there is no sun because he can't find it and he sure as hell can't feel it.

I take a step in his direction, dropping my crappy shell into his hand. "I can feel it. She tries to break through, fights like hell, but sometimes those clouds aren't having it. It's like when you're flying and you hit the space above the clouds and boom, sunshine. But we have to work for it. Don't you feel this?" I pan my hands around us. "All this energy surrounding you? The waves and the sand and yes, the clouds too? But if it's the sun you need, even if you can't see her, she's there. You just have to be patient."

His hand meets my jaw, pretending to wipe sand or grit from my skin as an excuse to touch me. I let him, stepping into his fist. Into his touch. The morning wind thrashes violently around us, salt and spray sticking to our skin and clothes as it whips our hair about. But I'm not afraid of him or his darkness.

"Fuck being patient, Raven. I haven't seen the sun in at least two weeks."

He's likely not speaking in metaphors. He came from his hospital in Minnesota after a month of a nightmare, the last five days of which he was stuck in the ICU, only to be discharged and then taking an overnight private jet here, and we've had no sun for more than a week, despite it being hot, muggy weather.

"And yet you got up early this morning and ran. Before the sun was set to come up, even with the forecast of clouds."

He shakes his head, not understanding.

"You had hope this morning that today would be different. 'He that can't endure the bad will not live to see the good.'"

He squints at me. "Who said that?"

"It's a Jewish proverb, so I don't know."

"Your mother was Israeli? Mossad?"

"She was." I lick my lips, a frog in my throat whenever I think of my mother. "My mother, the secret spy. I still don't know how she died. I don't even know if I'm supposed to know she was Mossad, though clearly, you do."

"But you loved her? Remember her?"

"She was my mother," I say simply, because show me a child who doesn't love their mother. "She was beautiful and strong and brave. I don't remember her much. Bits and pieces, moments in time." I remember her not being around a lot. I remember crying, begging for her to come home. Asking why she left. Then she died when I was seven on an assignment and I resented her for that. Resented her for not leaving that life for me. Wondered why I wasn't enough for her to do that. My father had already retired from MI6 by that time. Having had his life saved by Dr. Fritz and then swearing his life and allegiance to him and his family.

To me.

"Sounds like you're describing yourself, Raven," he says. "A woman who has endured the bad but still somehow sees the good. How do you do that so easily when life is so quick to turn painful and ugly and dark?"

I shrug because I just do. "I don't know. Some days I'm better at it than others." Some days I feel listless and abandoned. Not good enough. "I guess it's like that sun. It's always there even if some days are cloudy. You just have to find it. A famous Rabbi my mother loved said, 'If you don't know what you're living for, you haven't yet lived.' I live for my father and my cello and myself. For the chance to attend The London Conservatory. For one day seeing the world and playing everywhere I can. That's my dream. But life is life, Luca. You can't control it and you sure as hell can't stop it. I know what I wake up every day for. What I'm living for. What do you live for?"

I wonder if it's because he's rich and his life has always been easy until it wasn't. Until he was in the wrong place at the right time but ended up throwing his life off-kilter all the same. Does he not see the sun because he's always come to expect its rays on him?

He blinks at me rapid fire as if he's not sure what to do with that. "Medicine. And I don't have that anymore."

"Do you know that for sure?"

He looks away.

"You don't live for your family? Think of Landon. What he's endured and still fights for. Every day is a different battle, but what defines us is how we choose to fight it."

He grunts, propping his hands on his hips and swishing the sand around with his foot. Landon lost his wife a couple years back in a tragic accident. Since then, he's been raising Stella on his own while finishing his cardiology residency—no small feat. And yes, he's a billionaire and has a family who loves and supports him endlessly, but that doesn't take away a person's pain and that doesn't make everything easy street.

A wry smirk hits his lips. "You sure you're only eighteen?"

I laugh. "I've lived an unusual life. I had two parents who were both trained spies and I grew up living in a staff house owned by a bunch of billionaires."

"Thank you," he whispers, stepping in and towering over me. "That's the first thing anyone has said that's actually managed to make me think."

His nose hits the base of my neck, right over the dip before he glides up, achingly slow. I close my eyes, desperate to regain the breath it feels like he stole. I'm not strong with him. And truth, I'm not sure I want to be. I'm too new at this to pretend. Too unsure and scared and thrilled.

All I know is that he's breathing me in. And my hands are now in his hair. And it's soft and thick. And he groans when my nails rake down his scalp. And his lips and tongue, I swear, they just whispered past the underside of my jaw, stealing a taste.

My teeth bite into my bottom lip so hard I'm shocked I'm not tasting blood. Because holy freaking shit, Luca Fritz is *smelling* me. And *tasting* me. My knees just about give out on me.

"Breakfast," he declares as he pulls back and creates space between us. But his eyes. Those clear, practically iridescent green eyes, they're all over me. Waking me up. Showing me what being alive when the right man looks at you a certain way feels like.

"Breakfast," I agree, doing my best to rein in my breathing, but my heart already knows we're in trouble.

3

"When did you get those done?"

"Huh?" I spin around in the ocean, my body slowly acclimating to its frigid temperature. Today is yet another hot but cloudy day. Maybe if there was sun, the water wouldn't be so damn cold. Luca made me run again this morning and my legs have never been so sore.

"These," Luca says, turning me back around and grazing his fingers over the tattoos I have on either side of my spine.

"Oh. I got them on my eighteenth birthday. I'd wanted them for ages, but my father made me wait until I was legal." I practically roll my eyes at that, considering my father has plenty of tattoos and most of them were not done legally.

"Your back looks like a cello."

I snicker at the way he says that and then shiver against his cool, wet touch. "The parts of a cello, at least the body of it, resemble a human body in a lot of ways."

"Explain that to me."

I pivot to face him because if he keeps touching me like this, pretty soon I won't be able to talk. Ridiculously pathetic, I know, but I seriously cannot find it in me to care. "This is the body." I wave my hand over myself from my shoulders down to my hips. His eyes follow, getting stuck on my breasts in my bikini and then my tiny bottoms. "This is the waist." My hands sweep along the dip between my ribs and hip. "And these are the f-holes." I angle my body and point to my tattoo.

He blusters out a laugh. "The f-hole? You had something called an f-hole tattooed on your skin?"

I grin cheekily up at him, giving him a wink. "Two of them. And yup, I sure did. I didn't give them that name. That's just what they are."

"And do you like it when someone touches your f-holes?"

I suck in a shaky breath. "You're the first one to touch them."

Something dark and delicious passes over his features, making my heart explode in my chest with nervous anticipation. And judging by his expression, he didn't miss my meaning. His eyes are on mine before they dip, watching himself as he continues to paint me with water.

"I like them. Your tattoos, that is." His voice is tight, hoarse, the sound making my nipples harden more than the freezing water is.

"Yeah?"

"Yeah."

Piercing green eyes penetrate mine, making my stomach lurch.

"You ever think about getting one?" I ask, wading away from his touch, deeper into the water. Fighting the cold and the waves as they crash against my skin, making me rock on the balls of my feet to meet them. Anything to escape this rising tension between us. Each time we're together, it only grows. A perpetual buzz. A beat. An unspoken pulsing intensity that's building and building, flirting with the line that both excites and terrifies me.

"I've thought about it but never did it. I went with Kaplan to get a couple of his, but I could never think of anything I wanted inked on me."

"You could always get 'kiss this' tattooed on your ass."

"Only if I end up in prison."

I giggle, running my fingers through the water. "I think that might not send the message you want."

His arms wrap around me from behind, his bare chest against my back, and I force myself to stay where I am, to stare out at the expanse of ocean in front of us. And not turn around.

"You worried what'll happen to me if I drop the soap?"

"Unless that's your thing and I've been reading you wrong all this time."

His lips meet the crook between my neck and shoulder. "Definitely haven't been reading me wrong."

"THE STARS at night are big and bright." Clap. Clap. Clap. Clap. "Deep in the heart of Texas."

I laugh at Luca's off-key singing, the tall grass that lines the outskirts of the Fritz property tickling my bare arms and legs. It's been an unusually warm June for Martha's Vineyard, hot, hot days leading into hot nights.

And for the last seven days and nights, I've done nothing but spend time with Luca.

Running. Swimming in the ocean. Biking into town. Hiking to the lighthouse. Sharing fucking ice cream and eating breakfast only to linger over dinners. He reads medical journals while listening to me play. It's the strangest relationship I've ever had. Not that I have a ton to compare it to, but still. Weird.

I can't read him. I just know he likes being with me. Otherwise, he wouldn't continue to seek me out the way he has been. Touching me in innocent ways that feel not so innocent whenever he can. And then touching me in not so innocent ways that confuse me when he doesn't follow them up with more.

It has to be more than boredom. His family left the morning we went for our first run, so it's been just us. Together. A lot. But it's more than that. I know it is.

Especially when his fingers twirl strands of my hair the way they are.

"When do you leave for London, Little Bird?" he asks after falling quiet, both of us lost in the gorgeous starry night.

"Middle of August. When do you go back to Minnesota?"

He grunts. "As soon as I can."

I know that's a difficult question for him to be asked and to answer. He's worried he'll never be able to go back, and I know he's in pain some of the time. I catch him wincing on occasion, but I also know his pain runs deeper. Surgery is his life, he told me, and if his shoulder never fully heals...

"You'll like London. It's a cool city."

"I've been. Twice before with your family."

"Oh." He chuckles. "How is it that I sometimes forget who you are? I've known you your whole life and that's how this feels, like I've known you forever, and yet not. Like I'm also just meeting you." He laughs again, the sound lighter than before. "I'm likely not making any sense."

I shift in the grass, my head rolling up so I can catch part of his profile. "I know what you mean. It does feel that way. Probably because both are true. We've known each other my whole life and yet we're just now getting to know each other."

"Exactly. It's easy and comfortable and yet it's also..."He trails off and I don't press it.

Being with him already does insane, wild things to my heart. I want to freeze time. That's how perfect all of this feels. I'm like a freaking teenage Taylor Swift song. All angsty, with uncontrollable girly emotions and shit. One day I'll write a song about this and play my emotions, but today is not that day.

"Do you like Minnesota?"

"I honestly don't know. I don't see much of it. When I'm not in the hospital, I'm either sleeping, eating, or doing laundry."

"Or dating."

His hand stills in my hair. "Or that. I do that a lot there."

A beehive of ugly green monster bees swarms through me. "You must miss it."

"Not even a little," he quickly replies. "I have a reputation and I've earned it. I know I have. I'm a playboy—though I fucking hate that term—a manwhore, a slut. I liked sleeping around, but it's gotten boring. One woman bleeds into the next and they're all the same. All of them. I'll ask them what they want to do when we go out and they throw things back at me like go to a sports bar or a hockey game or an expensive restaurant where they know we'll be seen and likely photographed. Or worse, they'll say I don't care, whatever you want to do."

"I'm not following," I admit.

"These women... they say and do whatever they think will make me happy. Will make me *like* them. Or get them their Fritz fifteen minutes of fame. They laugh at my jokes whether they're funny or not and never tell me anything real. Only what they think I want to hear. I have no real conversations with them, Raven. It's a boring date with a boring woman, typically followed by boring sex."

"Have you tried a real relationship?"

"No. I mean, not since college. I had a girl in college I dated for a bit. In med school, we lost Reese, and I did whatever I had to do for Landon and Stella after that. I was always with them or in class and didn't think much about women other than the occasional, random hookup. Losing Reese was like losing a piece of all of us. Then I started my residency, and I just didn't want to get distracted or bogged down or disappoint anyone."

"But now you seem to have outgrown your bachelor, playboy life?"

"Yeah," he murmurs, his voice losing some of its strength. "I think I have. Being with you is so different. You're nothing like those women. You're real and honest and talk back to me and make me laugh and smile and think and keep me on my toes and you're fucking gorgeous, Raven. You seriously are. Until experiencing all of this, it's not something I realized I... something I realized I *want*. Something I was *missing*. Hanging out with you has been eye-opening, almost. You don't give a shit about the fact that I'm Luca Fritz or a neurosurgeon or a stupid billionaire. But I'm a mess. Lost in my head and feeling trapped in a body that might never do what I want it to do again. I need surgery, Raven. I fucking miss it so goddamn much I can hardly take a breath or get through the day."

My eyes are the size of dinner plates as I stare up at the night sky. My heart, oh Lord help me, it feels like I'm going to have a heart attack right here in the grass. Can you die from happiness? From a feeling?

I suck in a deep breath and hold it steady in my lungs.

Just do it. Just freaking do it, Raven.

On an exhale, I sit up, throwing caution to the wind. I press his bent knees down into the grass and stare down at him. I'm trembling so bad right now I'm positive he can feel the ground vibrating beneath him.

"What are you doing?" he rasps.

I shake my head, unable to answer him with words because if I speak, I'll lose my nerve. Sucking in another deep breath, I straddle his hips, sitting just above the spot I want to be sitting on most, but trying not to make this, well, about me.

He doesn't say anything, just stares up at me, one arm behind his head, his other grasping onto my thigh like he's not sure what to do with me in this new position. We're bathed in darkness. The only light shining down on us is coming from the huge full moon and the stars. It's not much, but it's certainly enough for me to see his face.

Grasping the hem of his shirt, I tug on it, making my desire clear.

Wordlessly, he lifts it up and over his head, dropping it into the grass where my body just was. I love his chest and abs. I could stare at them all day and never grow tired. So sexy and muscular without being bulky. Fucking perfect.

But that's not why I did this.

He's shaking beneath me. So unsure of my intentions and next move, but he's not stopping me. Not even a little.

Pitching forward, my fingers graze the red puckered skin of his scar on his left shoulder and his grip on my thigh tightens. This is the first time I'm touching him like this, and the sensation of touching Luca isn't lost on me. But again...

"Tell me what happened. Tell me about that night."

4

The woman sitting on my lap is a goddess. I told myself after that first night, I wouldn't seek her out. Now I can't stay away. It's been a constant battle not to touch or kiss her or steal an innocence she all but admitted she still has. She's funny and insanely smart and incredibly talented and fiery and absolutely fucking stunning.

Nothing I just told her was a line or a lie. She's the package, the one every man dreams of meeting and making their own. I cannot remember a time I have wanted—been this fucking drawn to—a woman. I spend time with her—all damn day— and then I say goodbye, but when I reach my room, I miss her. I miss her when I'm not with her. I think about her when I'm not with her. And that's not something that's ever happened to me before. Ever.

Because, like I said, she's a goddess.

She's helped me to smile again when no one else has been able to. She's helped me see things differently, gain a perspective I felt was lost on me. She's helped me to forget how my world is in limbo, possibly over... until now.

Tiny fingers run along my scar, and I hiss out a breath. Not because it hurts, but because it's her touching me there and I'm already semi-hard just from her sitting on me. Hell, just from being near her, I'm always semi-hard.

"Tell me," she persists when I don't answer her.

"Why do you want to know?"

After it happened, there were some reports in the media. 'Luca Fritz steps in and saves a woman and child, shot and injured in the process.' But what no one knows is what happened before and after. The NDAs our family attorneys made everyone who knew sign.

"Because in case you missed it, I care about you. I care about you a lot. Some might call it a girlish infatuation. Others might call it something else, but the point is, you don't talk about it, and you need to talk about it and since I care about you the way I do, you know you can trust me."

I do trust her.

It's been a week and I already feel as close to her as I do to my brothers and Rina.

I can talk to her about anything, and she does not judge me. It's the same with her. Every fucking word out of her mouth makes me like her, want her more. Can you fall for someone in just seven days? Someone so completely wrong for you?

Why does she have to feel so right?

The hand on her thigh slides upward only to glide back down, and for a moment, I revel in the feel of her soft flesh. Already knowing—especially with her like this—I'm nearing the end of my willpower.

I swallow, my throat suddenly bone-dry. "I was leaving the hospital late at night, heading to the parking garage, when I heard a noise in an alleyway that cuts between two of the buildings. There was a man yelling at a woman in Spanish, pointing a gun at her, and she was crying, begging with him, as she tucked a little girl behind her body. The girl was bleeding profusely from her arm and her forehead, crying and shaky, pale as a sheet and tacky with sweat from the blood loss, but clinging to her mother for her life."

"Then what?" Raven urges when I fall silent, picturing that moment. A moment that changed my life, but I can't find it in me to regret it. I'd do it again, especially since it led me here, to this moment with her. It's also led my mind to other things. Thoughts. Ideas. I just need to get back to Minnesota to make them a reality.

"I didn't hesitate," I tell her, lost in the memory of that night. "I didn't think twice. The little girl was obviously very hurt and desperately in need of medical attention. I was petrified the man was going to kill them both. I stepped between them, asked him in Spanish to lower the gun. Told him I'd help them. That I was a doctor, and I could help."

Raven sucks in a breath and holds it, her eyes troubled as she stares down into mine.

"The second I told him I was a doctor, the gun went off and hit me in the shoulder. He instantly realized what he'd done, freaked out about shooting a man, and ran off. I don't remember much after that. I helped the woman and child into the hospital, listened as she told me her husband was afraid they'd be deported if she got the child help, and then hours later I woke up in recovery."

"What happened to the man?"

This is the part that few seem to understand, and I refuse to comment on it publicly. "They found him, but I didn't press charges."

Raven stares straight into my eyes until some sort of understanding passes over her features. "Okay. Then what?"

"The surgery had been successful, but I was stupid, and I didn't rest or rehab it the way I should have, anxious to return to my rotation and the OR. Arrogant. I was so fucking arrogant, thinking I was invincible. I ended up getting a staph infection. A bad one. I passed out at work with a fever of a hundred and four and woke up nearly a week later with my parents and siblings by my side, learning I'd been intubated and placed in a medically induced coma. Now I'm here, lucky I'm alive but stuck on medical leave, forced to rest and rehab. I'm not allowed to return until I pass medical clearance and that includes being able to use and manipulate instruments with a steady, competent hand."

"Because you're a neurosurgeon?"

"Yes. Steady, perfect hands and accuracy are the name of my game."

"And you're worried you won't ever have that again?"

I stare up into her eyes and utter a truth I haven't even admitted to myself. "Yes. I'm worried I won't ever have that again. My hand shakes when I hold it in certain positions for too long."

"That's why you've been depressed."

It's not a question, but I answer her all the same. "That's part of the reason. Getting kicked out on medical leave, told I can't return until I'm one hundred percent when I might never be one hundred percent is another. I don't know what I'll do if I can't go back, Raven. I don't want to be a neurologist. I want to be a neurosurgeon. It's what I've spent the last four years of my residency doing."

"Are there exercises you could do to help?"

"Yes, and I've been doing them."

"Are you getting better?"

"Yes, but not as fast as I had hoped."

She smiles down at me. "Then you need to learn to be patient, Luca. You of all people understand how the human body heals and trying to speed up a process that's not meant to be sped up already cost you once."

It sounds so simple when she says that. But it's not. "What

would you do if you injured yourself and couldn't play cello anymore?"

She considers this with honest intent. "I'd be a mess. I'd mope and feel sorry for myself. But then I'd get the fuck over it and do whatever I had to do to get myself able to play again. Because playing is my life. And if at the end of it I couldn't, at least I'd know I gave it my best shot and I'd find something else musically related. Like maybe I would teach kids how to play instead of performing. Not what I'd choose for my life, but still in the game."

"You think I'm being petulant?"

She laughs lightly. "A little. I get why you're depressed, and I get why you're feeling hopeless. But what are you doing to fix it? Are you doing all you could?"

I don't know. I got here with no motivation to do anything other than feel sorry for myself. But with her... with her, I want to be better. I want to be everything she thinks I am. She stares at me with stars in her eyes and I want to be deserving of that.

She's the kid and I'm the adult and yet with every moment I spend with her, I feel less and less of our age gap. I want her. But what happens if I do get myself back on track and back to Minnesota? What happens when she goes to London in August? What happens when our dreams take us in opposite directions?

I don't want to hurt her.

I never thought about it all that much before. I always made it clear, medicine first, casual dating, no attachments. If the woman got hurt or I moved on before they wanted me to, I would remind them of that. I never made promises I didn't keep.

But with Raven, I find myself wanting to make promises I know I'll break.

How? "What are you doing to me, Little Bird?"

"Same thing you're doing to me."

Shit. We're both fucked now.

In her next breath, she pulls her shirt up over her head, tossing it near mine, and then she's on me. Her large, soft breasts covered in her bra hit my chest and before I can formulate an argument or the will to stop, my hands are in her hair and her lips are fused with mine.

It's instant. Brilliant magic. And I know in this moment, I'll never be the same again.

I'll never feel this feeling when kissing another woman again.

I can appreciate the rise and fall of her chest against mine, how she sucks in a deeper breath every time we deepen our kiss as if she never wants to come up for air again. I expected hesitance. I expected uncertainty and learning. There is none of that. This is passion unleashed. Uncaged. This is hands and tongues and lips and teeth. This is sound and breath and touch.

My tongue swirls with hers, my head angled, needing to crawl as far inside her as I can. Her taste is incredible, the way she sucks on my tongue and nibbles on my lip and pushes her lush lips bruisingly against mine... mind-blowing.

Beads of sweat are forming on my brow, my hands trembling as I do all that I can to hold this position. To keep them in her hair and away from the clasp of her bra. The button of her shorts.

As if sensing my fight, she whispers into me, "Touch me, Luca. Take me. I want it."

Fuck. Just fucking hell fuck.

"Has anyone ever touched you, Little Bird?"

"Yes." She pulls back, planting her hands into the earth on either side of my head so she can stare into my eyes, her hair a black curtain around us. "I've fooled around with guys. Just never had sex before."

"Raven..."

"I'm eighteen, Luca. And though you call me Little Bird, I'm not fragile. I'm telling you I want this and I'm telling you I want it with you. If that's too much for you, I get it, but if it's not…"

She leaves that hanging in the small space between us and there is no fucking way on this planet I am allowing another man to take what is mine. I'd kill any man who touches her. Raven. She's *my* Raven now.

"I want it to be me. Are you on anything? Because I do not have a condom with me."

"The pill."

Jesus. This is actually happening. She's eighteen. So young. *Too* young.

I can't even ask her not to fall in love with me or not to grow attached because I fucking want her to fall in love and I want her to be attached. Even if that makes me an asshole—I know it does. I want all of her for as long as I can have it.

Capturing the back of her head, I pull her back down to me, kissing her soundly, my lips rough and unyielding. I don't know how to slow down. I don't know how to be gentle. I want her too badly. Our kiss grows harder, wilder. My hand finds the clasp of her bra and I unhook it, sliding it off her shoulders and slipping it away from between our pressed bodies, all without removing my mouth from hers.

But the feel of her soft tits against me… her hard nipples I'm desperate to suck on…

With my hand on her back, I flip her over, my lips grazing down her jaw, her neck, to the top swell of her breasts.

"God, you're so beautiful," I tell her as I pull away so I can look. My hands cup the large mounds that more than fill them up, squeezing, testing their weight, watching her face as I touch her. "Good?"

"Yes. More."

"Good girl," I purr before I can stop it and then capture one of her nipples in my mouth. Her hips shoot up, seeking, grinding into my already straining cock. A moan flees her lips and shit, her breasts are so sensitive. Especially when I twist the other nipple while devouring this one. She's tearing at my back, hers arched.

Lifting them higher, I suck at the soft underside of them, unable to get enough of her smell and taste. The feel of her when none of it seems like enough. She asked for more and that's the one word on repeat in my head. *More.*

She cries out, pressing my face deeper into her chest, and I give her what she wants. I want to give her everything. All of me. No end in sight.

Teeth. Tongue. Lips. Fire. Thirst.

"Can you come like this?"

"I... I... I don't know."

My hand roams south, undoing the button and zipper on her shorts, and then my fingers are there, sliding beneath her panties and finding her absolutely soaked for me. My thumb hits her clit, rubbing it in circles as my mouth and other hand work every inch of her tits.

"Luca. Yes. Oh my God, yes!"

She grinds up into my hand, riding it as I swirl her slick clit over and over as she falls apart before my eyes. Her moans. Her face. The feel of her. All of it searing into my brain. The moment she sags into the grass beneath her, I slip off her shorts and panties, staring in wonder at the sight before me.

She is fucking perfect. Every inch of her is heaven and sin. Pure seduction. The most beautiful woman I've ever seen. Tremulous hands frantically go for my shorts, fumbling with the button, but she's not ready yet. I'm not small and she's tight as a drum. I want this to be good for her. Hell, I want this to be fan-fucking-tastic for her.

Taking her hands, I shake my head, bringing them up to her breasts so she can play with herself, and I can watch. "Touch yourself. I'm not done with this sweet pussy yet."

Actually, I'm just getting started with it.

My heart speeds up as my hand trails up the inside of her thigh. Spreading her legs wide for me, I kneel between them, rimming her hole with my middle finger while she stares at me, her hands kneading her breasts. Her hips rock against me, urging me to push inside her, but I like teasing her instead. I like watching the fire in her eyes. The desire as it takes over her.

"Fuck, that's so hot."

My angry cock is desperate for release, but for right now, I can't seem to stop touching her. Her breasts, her skin, her pussy. I want to feel and taste every inch of her.

Pulling my finger away, I suck it into my mouth and then offer it to her. She takes it eagerly in her mouth, sucking on me like it's my dick, and I groan, imagining her mouth on me. "You're going to do exactly that another time with my cock, Little Bird. And I can't wait for it."

"Mmmm," she hums around me, evil temptress that she is, and I slip my finger from her mouth and plunge it deep inside her. Slide it out and do it again. Only this time with two fingers, going in as deep as I can.

Unable to stop myself, I crouch down, flicking her clit. Her taste sweeps around my tongue and crawls inside my head. There is nothing else out here but us. The sound of the waves in the distance and the wind rustling the grass around our bodies. Crickets serenade us as the moon bathes us in her soft glow.

But all I can focus on is the woman beneath me.

I pump into her, getting her wetter, working her up higher, and just before she's about to come again, I remove my shorts, line my dick up with her entrance, and slowly slide inside of her. My lungs empty with a whoosh, feeling when I hit a spot of resistance only to keep pushing, wanting the hard part of this to be over for her.

She emits a breathy cry, her head tilted to the side, her hands fisted, one on my chest, the other tucked under her chin.

Finally, once I'm seated, I hold still—an act of fucking heroism with how good she feels—and close my eyes. A cascade of chills snakes up my spine because suddenly I'm completely overwhelmed. My heart thunders, beating off rhythm.

"God, Raven." I cup her face in my hand, gliding my thumb back and forth over her cheek. "Are you okay?" I ask softly.

Only, it's also a question for myself. Because I'm not okay. Not even a little. Being inside her is everything I never realized being inside another person could be like. Inside her, I'm home. The place I'm always meant to be, nowhere else.

I shudder, staring down at her, fucking high out of my mind in a way I've never experienced before. Her. This. Here. She's everything. I haven't even moved yet, and I already know I'll never tire of her.

"Baby, are you okay? You have no idea what being inside you right now is doing to me."

She sucks in a breath and holds it.

"Breathe, Raven. Take a breath. You're squeezing the hell out of me."

"I'm okay." She exhales heavily, her body relaxing some.

"Tell me when you're ready."

I play with her clit, rolling it between my fingers, teasing it without giving her too much pressure. I'm dying, harder than I ever remember being, and the need to move is almost over-powering.

Slowly, she rocks her hips, digging her heels into the ground and rolling back and then up. A hiss slips past my lips and I swear fucking reindeer dance behind my eyes. Nothing has ever felt this good, and I realized it's two things happening at once.

I've never had sex without a condom before.

And it's being inside her.

"I am dying right now. So good. You feel so good."

"It's so tight and I feel so full."

Jesus Christ. Is she trying to make me blow my load? Falling forward, my hand plants into the ground, my other grabbing her leg and hiking it up over my hip.

"Open those pretty eyes. I want to see them on me when I slide inside you." Her eyes blink open, locking on mine. "Good girl." Pulling almost all the way out of her, I thrust back in. Harder than before. I do this again and again, over and over, eyes glued to hers.

So trusting. So beautiful.

Yet another thing I've never done, looked at a woman like this while being inside them.

My mouth captures hers, sucking on those plump lips, needing to taste her.

"I am fucking dying right now, Raven," I pant into her. "Do you feel it? Do you feel me coming apart? Do you feel how perfect we fit together?"

Her hands grip me, one in my hair, the other on my shoulder as I pick up the pace, lifting her other leg and wrapping her fully around me.

"Luca. Oh, fuck, it's starting to feel so good."

I pull myself up higher, bringing her body with me as I begin thrusting in and out of her more steadily. Her tits jiggle and bounce, and I reach out, squeezing one, holding it as I take her. Glancing down to where we're joined, my cock glistens darkly in the moonlight, and I wonder if I'm coated in her blood. That thought turns me into a beast and I move faster, slapping into her with hard, deliberate strokes. With each thrust, she raises her hips to meet mine, her legs pulling me deeper each and every time.

There is no close enough. No deep enough.

Falling forward, my teeth graze her nipple, biting the top of her breast. She cries out, gripping the hell out of my hair. I land on her neck, sucking on her sweet, sweaty skin.

"More? Can you take more?"

"Yes. God, yes. Don't stop. I'm getting so close."

Her cries grow louder, her moans raspier. My name scratches the air as I dig in harder and harder, faster and faster, knowing I'm hitting her just right when her body starts to tremble and then convulse.

"That's it, Raven. Come all over me. You're such a good girl. Come harder, baby. I want to feel your sweet cunt gush." That's all it takes to push her completely over the edge on a scream as wave after wave rolls through her, sucking me in and refusing to let me go. Her nails rake down my back and I growl through clenched teeth, my eyes glued to her face as she comes.

No longer able to hold off, I follow her over. The way she sounds and the way she feels is like nothing else. A deep, feral howl wrenches from my lungs and I fall still, heavy on top of her, spilling everything I have inside her. Marking her. Claiming her. Fucking out of my head with her. I pant for my life as sparkles of light flash behind my eyes.

After a few beats, thoughts of what we just did swirl through me, coming in hazy bits and pieces. A contented smile crawls up my face. I roll us over, worried I'm crushing her, and she lands on top of me, my still semi-hard dick half inside of her.

She shivers and I hold her closer, rubbing my hands up and down her back and arm. "Are you cold?"

"No."

That's it. Nothing else.

"Are you okay?"

She props her head up, her hair a tangled, beautiful mess. "Luca, I'm so good right now I'm terrified."

A light laugh trickles past my lips because I know exactly what she means. I'm done for. A goner. My chest squeezes with this realization, only it doesn't scare me. Instead, I feel light. Free. Whole. I'm falling for her, and I should stop it, but it's the best feeling I've ever had and there is no way I can even attempt to try.

I cup her face in my hands, holding her eyes to mine. "Don't worry, Little Bird. I've got you and I'm not letting you go." No way I ever can now.

5

"The waiter is checking you out," Luca says with a bear of a scowl on his face.

"He is not." He absolutely is. He always does whenever we come here.

"Little Bird, he's been staring at your tits every time he talks to you. And when you got up to use the bathroom, his eyes followed your ass the whole way."

I make a show of rolling my eyes while I take a sip of my water. "You sure he's not checking you out? You're the celebrity here."

"And you're the hottest woman on the planet. So yeah, I'm pretty fucking sure."

"Hottest woman on the planet, huh?"

My heeled foot finds his leg beneath the table and slowly slides up until the toe reaches one of my favorite spots on him.

"You're trying to distract me with your feminine wiles."

I fight my grin at his grumpy face and use of the term feminine wiles. "Is it working?"

He grasps my foot under the table and slips off my heel. Deftly, he massages the arch of my foot while he presses it deeper against his hardening cock, rubbing me against him. "What does that tell you?"

"It tells me—"

"Is there anything else I can get you?" the waiter interrupts and yep, his eyes are glued to my cleavage.

Luca growls and I press my foot into him, urging him to be nice. "No, thank you. I think we're all set."

"Just the check then? No coffee or tea? Dessert perhaps?"

"She said we're all set."

Oh boy.

The waiter gives a quick nod and scurries off.

"Fuck this."

Luca stands up, tossing his napkin down on his empty plate.

"Luca. Don't."

He plants a long, lingering, toe-curling kiss on my lips. "I'll be right back."

I flip around in my seat, watching as Luca storms across the restaurant toward the waiter, who is in the back, punching things into a built-in tablet. Slipping my heel back on, I stare as Luca says something to the man that causes him to turn red and blanch and then cower back a step, nodding his head like a bobble doll.

Luca pats him on the shoulder, hands him his credit card, which the waiter runs through quickly, and then not even two minutes later, Luca returns with a look that instantly makes my panties wet. He takes my hand and helps me to stand, grazing my knuckles across his lips.

"What did you say?" I ask as we step outside, and he helps me into his family's Tesla.

He runs around the car and, after starting it up, turns to me with a cocky grin. "I told him if he ever looks at anything but your eyes again, I'd cut him up into tiny pieces and use him as chum for the sharks and other predatory fish."

"You did not."

"Of course I did. He was staring at what's mine, not to mention it was beyond rude and disrespectful to you."

He pulls away from the sidewalk, driving us back toward the Fritz estate, and I reach my hand over, resting it on his upper thigh. "Do I get to show my appreciation for your noble act?"

Luca grasps my hand and places it over his hard cock. "Unzip me and take me out." He shifts in his seat, angling toward me and giving me easier access as we drive down the dark, empty road. I make quick work of his button and zipper, eagerly doing just as he commands, and then I slide across the center console and take him right down my throat.

He hisses out a curse, one hand getting lost in my hair, the other on the wheel. I slowly slide back, my tongue gliding up the underside of his dick before swirling it around the head, only to dive back down. My hand reaches into his jeans, ignoring the teeth of the zipper, and I find his balls, massaging them as I bob and suck on his cock.

"You're going to get us into an accident."

"You focus on the road, and I'll focus on your dick."

He smells musky and masculine and tastes even better. Going down on Luca might be one of my favorite things to do with him, if only because I get to watch him come apart. In the month we've been together, I can't get enough of him. I'm stupidly, head over heels, insatiably, irrevocably in love. It's like living in a fantasy.

A bubble I never want to burst.

"Such a good girl, taking my cock like that. That's it. Swallow me down. Oh fuck, Raven, that's perfect."

I hum, getting off on how he calls me good girl, even though I know it's a little sick and a bit misogynistic. I don't care. He's not degrading me, he's worshipping me. Praising me. I let him bottom out in the back of my throat, gagging slightly. My finger presses into the space between his balls and his ass, and he jerks up, forcing himself deeper into my mouth with a loud groan.

"Shit, baby. You do that again and I'm gonna come right down your throat."

I quicken my movements, using my other hand to help jerk him into my mouth as I suck and slurp and bob up and down. His hand grips me by the roots, but no, no way. I abandon my hold on him and cover his hand with mine, urging him to fuck my mouth.

He loses it then, thrusting up and taking my mouth with abandon. It's nearly impossible to breathe when he does this, tears lining my eyes and slipping down my cheeks. I take him as best as I can, swallowing and sucking hard, hollowing my cheeks, and flattening my tongue. But when I give him a hint of my teeth, he fists my hair, rattles out a loud curse followed by a bellow, and shoots hot cum straight into my mouth.

I swallow him down, licking at anything left on him, and then sit up slowly, wiping at my swollen lips and tear-streaked cheeks. He tucks himself back in, zipping and buttoning up quickly. "Come here." He grabs me, pulling me in for a kiss while keeping his eyes open and on the road. "That was incredible. If not a little dangerous."

I laugh. "You didn't run us off the road."

"I nearly did. Twice."

"Then you better keep your eyes on the road."

Sliding up the hem of my dress, I let him see my thigh-highs, the garters holding them in place, and the black satin of my panties.

"Jesus hell. You've been wearing that all night?" He runs a hand through his hair, gripping the wheel. I start to toy with the satin covering my pussy, running my fingers up and down my wet slit. "Fuck, I can smell you. Show me your pussy, Raven."

I shake my head. "Uh-uh, hero. You're driving, remember?"

"Shit, you're a tease." In his next breath, he reaches over, grabs the crotch of my panties, and rips them from my body. I let out a surprised yelp, but all he does is push my thighs wider apart. His eyes flash back and forth between me and the road. "Keep your dress up. God, that's so sexy. You have no idea how hot you look like that. Those thigh-highs and that garter and your glistening pussy, just begging for my mouth."

He has the filthiest mouth and I'm so there for it. I'm most definitely leaking all over his parents' hundred-thousand-dollar car.

My fingers return to my pussy, and I pump my finger in and out, knowing it's driving him wild. He's already hard again, bulging through his jeans, and I lick my lips, wanting another taste of him. I'll never get enough, and I tell him that, making him groan as I moan.

He reaches over, slipping a finger inside me along with mine, fucking me to the same rhythm I'm fucking myself. It's wet and it's lewd and I'm already so close, having been halfway there from going down on him. We're getting near the estate, farther from town, and I don't want this to end. I want him to drive us around all night while we do dirty things to each other. I don't want to go home. I never want to go home unless he's there with me.

I have no home if I'm not with Luca.

He twists his hand, changing up the angle of his finger and using his thumb to rub my clit. "Oh!" I cry out, my back arching away from the seat. "Talk to me, Luca. Tell me what you're thinking."

He pumps me faster, works me harder, and I'm losing my mind, so close as warm tingles start at the base of my spine, slowly spreading upward. "When we get back to the house, I'm going to sneak into your room with you. Tie your wrists to your bed. And eat your sweet, dirty little cunt until she squirts all over my face. And then I'm going to fuck you—"

His words get cut off by my scream, my hand gripping his, pressing him deeper inside me, holding it harder against my clit as I come and come and come and holy shit, it's not stopping. It's wave upon wave of sparkling light and tingles and electricity flowing through my every cell. Luca continues to talk, but I can't make sense of his words. All I know is that I'm dying and reborn. And when it's over, I sag into the seat and laugh, a little crazy and a lot deranged.

"Delicious," he murmurs as he licks me off his fingers. "Yup, I'm definitely eating that first chance I get."

"Okay. Whatever you say."

"Good because, honey, we're home."

And we are. He somehow parked us in the garage while I was busy having the best orgasm of my life. "Thank God because that was awful. Worst orgasm of my life."

He chuckles, but it's not in humor. It's dark and dangerous. Promising I'll pay for that. The door slams behind him and in my next breath, mine is opening. I'm unbuckled and tossed over his shoulder, my limbs limp, unable to fight.

"Your shoulder!" I squeal.

"I have you on the other one and it doesn't hurt."

I giggle as he sprints us back in the direction of the staff house.

"Shhh." He smacks my ass. "You're going to get us caught." But he doesn't set me on my feet. Instead, he punches in the code for the main door and sneaks us up the stairs and down the hall. My father's light is off since he has to be up early to fly Dr. Fritz over to the hospital on Cape Cod tomorrow morning.

Luca opens my door, shuts, and locks it before walking us to my bed. Slowly, he slides me off until I'm standing before him. He stares intensely at me, all humor gone from his face. "I have to be up early. Your father is flying my father and me to the hospital."

I forgot Luca is going too. He's been going with his father three days a week to work in the simulator lab they have there. Rehabbing his shoulder has become his main focus in the last few weeks. If he's not with me, he's working his shoulder or doing mock surgeries in the lab. Even when he's with me, he's still working on his shoulder. He's not quite where he wants to be, but he's close and I'm thrilled for him and terrified for myself.

I can't let him go. I just can't.

"So this is good night then?"

Delicate fingers coast over my forehead, down my cheeks, along my jaw, through my hair and across my neck, all the while his eyes never waver from mine. "You seem disappointed by that."

I shrug, feigning indifference and not fooling him for a second.

"You don't have to pretend you're not obsessed with me. It's obvious."

"Obsessed with you?" I squawk, rolling my eyes derisively. "Please. You're the one obsessed with me. I have to try not to throw up in my mouth every time you kiss me."

He chuckles, toying with a strand of my hair, his eyes dancing about my face. "Raven Fairchild, I've fallen so in love with you."

My breath catches in my throat, my eyes instantly filling with tears. "You have?"

"More than I ever imagined was possible to love someone. In a way that makes me want to keep you, hold on to you forever."

Trembling hands press into his chest, right over his heart. "I love you too. So much, Luca. I've loved you nearly my whole life, but I'm so in love with you now."

His lips crash to mine as he lifts me back up, squeezing me into his chest, wrapping his arms impossibly tight around me. We tumble onto my bed, clothes falling away as mouths and hands and bodies seek. Love. Become one.

I move on top of him, taking him in as deep as I can while we stare into each other's eyes. His hands cup my breasts, squeezing and playing with them the way he knows I like. Sweat coats our bodies as passion spreads like wildfire between us. His fingers trace along my skin, across my ribs, over my collarbone, and between my breasts until they reach the spot where we're connected.

I'm light headed. Trembling in euphoria as we come together. I fall on top of him, breathing hard, everything inside me feeling different. Perfect. Whole. My heart gallops in my chest, matching the cadence of his.

But when the hour becomes too late—or too early as it is—and will no longer be denied, Luca and I dress quietly in the dark of my room. Me into pajamas, him into what he wore to dinner. Tiptoeing out of the house, he kisses me, holding my face in his hands.

"I love you." His forehead meets mine.

"I love you." Always. Forever.

Another kiss and then he's gone, slinking off into the shadows, heading for the main house and his bed, needing a few hours of rest before he has to get up. My hand presses to my heart and I blow out a sigh. Smiling in a way I've never smiled before, only to have it slip off my face as I turn around and find my father standing there inside, waiting for me.

I close the main door behind me and walk to him, swallowing hard at the steely glint in his eye. The man is a former assassin for the English government, and I've never been afraid of him a day in my life. But this look is enough to shake my insides.

"I'm an adult, Dad."

"Which is why I haven't said anything until now. I thought it was just fun. Nothing serious. But, Raven, what are you doing with him?"

"I love him," I tell him honestly.

My father's anguished gaze drops to the floor, his hands going to the top of his dirty-blond head. I have his eyes, but my hair is my mother's.

"Luca Fritz isn't a man to fall in love with."

I bristle at that. So hard, I have to take a step back. "He loves me too."

"Of course he loves you too," he barks, staring at me once more. "Look at you. You're young and beautiful and everything he needed to get himself back on track. But, Raven, he's going to break your heart. He's going to leave. Soon, in fact, if he can help it. I heard him discussing this with his father just the other day."

A tidal wave of devastation slams into me and I rock back on my heels. "I know." Because I do. I'm not delusional. Just in love. Tears fall helplessly down my cheeks and my father drags me into his chest, holding me, rocking me as I cry.

"My darling girl, I should have stopped this sooner. I should have known you'd give him your heart. I'm sorry. This is when I wish your mother were still alive. She would have done better."

"I don't want to stop being with him. I don't want to give up and walk away. And I don't think he wants that either. I think he wants me, Dad. I think he wants to try and make us work somehow."

He pulls back and cups my face, staring into my eyes. "Has he said that?"

"No. Not outright. But he said things that sort of indicated he wants beyond this."

My father blows out a breath, looking tired and torn and wrecked. "What about London? This is your dream. To play on stages all over the world."

"I can still do that last part and be with him."

Agony sears across his face. "Don't give up your dream for someone else, Raven. You'll always regret it."

"You did. For Mom. For me. For Dr. Fritz."

"You were my dream, darling. Your mother too. And I owed Dr. Fritz a debt greater than I could ever repay. I don't regret giving up that life for this. But you're so young. You have so much ahead of you."

"What if Luca's my dream now too? Like Mom and I were for you?"

His eyes hold mine and then he sighs, crestfallen. "Then as your father, I have to tell you to follow your heart. But also as your father, I have to tell you, if you give up on London for Luca, I think you'll be making the biggest mistake of your life."

With my lips pressed into Raven's neck, I shift her on my lap, holding her tighter against my chest while listening to her laugh at whatever nonsense Oliver is talking about. My heart has been thrashing in my chest all day. My nerves on edge. I got the green light today to go back to Minnesota in a week.

One week to figure out what we're going to do.

We haven't talked about it. About any of it. I've told her I want her forever. And I mean it. I never would have imagined such a thing being possible, but she's it for me. I don't care that she's too young. I don't care that I have three years left of my residency. I don't care about anything other than her. In two months, I've gone from needing no one to needing her.

To making declarations and saying vows.

"What's the hardest cello piece to play?" my brother Oliver asks, responding to whatever Raven had said prior to that.

"*Prokofiev's* Sinfonia Concertante, Op.125. It's very fast to play. In particular the second movement is exceedingly challenging. There are virtually no resting points throughout the entire piece. I actually played it as my audition for The Conservatory."

"Ballsy," Kaplan states, impressed. "I like it. Obviously, it worked for you since you got in and start soon."

Raven stiffens in my arms, and I pull back from her neck, wondering at that. All she does is offer a jerky nod and now my eyebrows are pinched in. What on earth does that mean?

Raven goes for my beer, and I smack her hand away. "Too young."

She gives me an elbow jab to the flank and takes a sip anyway.

"You two are disgustingly adorable," Carter declares, sliding his glass of bourbon across the table back and forth between his hands like it's a hockey puck.

"Thank you, little brother." I grin at him. "How are things going with that Alanna chick again?"

He flips me off. "When I'm as old as you are, maybe I'll be ready to settle down."

"And maybe I'll marry you now that I'm ordained," Oliver quips, finishing off his drink and signaling for another round for all of us. "I'm awesome at it."

Carter lets out a snort, emptying the rest of his glass down his throat before handing the empty to the waitress. "Round of shots?"

"No," Landon and Rina growl, while Kaplan, Oliver, and I all say yes.

"Seven shots of tequila, please," he says to the waitress, who stares into Carter's brown eyes like he's the second coming of Christ. She fumbles over her words, nearly drops her tray filled with empty glasses and then scurries away.

"Seven shots?" I question.

Kaplan rolls his eyes at me. "Like you didn't drink when you were eighteen?"

"She's too young."

Raven shifts so she's sitting sideways on my lap, giving me a glare that would make a lesser man's balls shrivel up. As it is, mine give a little scared squeak. "Last I checked, you're not my father."

"No, but I'll happily punish you later for breaking the law. A spanking will definitely be in order."

"And now I'll happily take that shot whereas before I wasn't planning on it."

"Ew!" Rina pretends to gag. "Gross. I've had to hear enough about your sex lives over the years, but I don't need the details of your kink."

"Just like how Carter and I didn't want to witness you getting picked up in a bar on New Year's by some guy you didn't even get the name of. Clearly, we don't always get what we want."

Rina gives Oliver a cheeky grin. "You saw him. Mister Sexy Voice was *so* hot."

"Mister Sexy Voice?" Raven laughs.

Rina winks. "That wasn't the only thing sexy about him. I'll tell you more about him when you're not being smothered by my brother."

"Can we not?" That's Landon, and it's the first thing he's said all night. Not atypical for my miserable twin at all, but I feel like he's quieter than usual.

A small nudge to his arm and his eyes finally drag away from the table he's been staring at up to meet mine. I give him a *what's up* look. He returns with *it's nothing.* I come back with *bullshit, dude, just tell me.* He sighs. Then I get the look. The look that says, *I didn't want to bring it up, but you're as fucked as a man can get and still be able to walk.*

Now it's my turn to frown.

I nod. I am.

What are you going to do?

I respond with, *Fuck if I know.*

But honestly, I don't see why Raven and I can't make this work. She'll be in London, and I'll be in Minnesota, and we'll just figure it out as we go. Both of us will be busy and we'll talk and see each other whenever we can. Hell, I have access to a private jet. I can fly in for occasional weekends or whatever and we'll see each other on her breaks, even if her first one isn't until Christmas.

I made her promises just last night in front of Oliver and Rina and freaking God, for that matter, and I intend to keep them.

Feeling a bit more satisfied with that, I relax, holding my woman against me.

We all do our round of shots, and the night continues. All of us having fun, especially Raven, who hasn't stopped smiling or laughing. She's adorable like this and her smile is infectious. My dark-haired beauty with the soul of an angel.

She has no idea all that she's done for me.

I got to this island in pain, depressed beyond words or actions, and she showed me the sun. Reminded me that giving up is never an option. That fighting for what you want and love is essential.

I plant a kiss on her cheek. "I'll meet you outside. I'm just going to hit the bathroom first."

"Sure." I get another kiss and a naughty wink, and then she follows alongside Rina, the two of them talking about Rina's job as an emergency room nurse in Boston and how she's anxious to switch to the ICU.

Entering the bathroom, I do my business, wash my hands, and by the time I make it outside, the parking lot is near empty and they're not standing by my car. I scan around, searching for Raven and Rina, since I drove them both, but come up short. A pang of unease hits my gut as I walk toward the side of the building. I don't like them out here alone and I'll kill my brothers for leaving them if they did.

"You're not seriously considering that, are you?" Oliver asks, his voice even, but I catch an undercurrent of something all the same.

"It's just London," Raven retorts, sounding a touch defensive. "Just a school."

"But it's not just a school. It's the best music conservatory in the world," Rina replies. "You told me when you got in that it's been your lifelong dream to go there. That less than one percent of applicants get in and you not only got in but got a full scholarship."

"I know." Now Raven sounds sad. "But dreams can change, right? I mean, there are music schools all over the world. All over the country. And honestly, do I even need to attend college to be a musician? My dream is still my dream. It just... looks different now."

What the hell is she saying? She's thinking of not going to London?

"Raven, I know you love Luca and I know he loves you, but isn't there another way? Can't you try a long-distance relationship? See how that goes?"

"I'd be in London. He'd be in Minnesota. It's a six-hour time difference and a world apart. We would never see each other, and I doubt we'd be able to talk much either with what our schedules would be like and the demands of our work."

My hands hit my hips, my breathing ragged because what she's saying is like a sucker punch straight to the gut. All hope I had been feeling plummets to the asphalt. She's right. I work eighty-plus hours a week. My hours are all over the place. And she'd be in London. A different country on a different continent.

We'd both be miserable.

"We knew the situation when this started," she continues. "Neither of us expected this. I didn't think he'd... well... I never imagined Luca would feel the same way back. That I'd fall this hard. It seems crazy, I know, but that's what love is. It's crazy. It's following your instincts and your gut." She blows out a heavy breath. "If you have any suggestions, I'm listening. Believe me, I've thought about little else for the last month."

"I... I don't know," Oliver admits. "I've never seen Luca like this before. With anyone. He's crazy about you and I want you both to be together. But... shit, Raven. I don't know."

I fall against the side of the building as I listen to her. Hear her words. My face in my hands, my chest pinching so tight it's difficult to breathe.

"He's got three years left on his residency and he has to be in Minnesota for that," Raven says. "I get that. Nothing says I can't play cello and be with him. I just can't play cello for The Conservatory and be with him. Honestly, I don't know what else to do if we want to be together and make it work. You know how long-distance relationships go. They never last."

Scrubbing my hands up and down my face, I feel sick. Dizzy.

"Raven, have you even talked with him about this?" Rina presses. "Maybe he has another idea?"

"All I've heard him say is that he doesn't want to lose me. That he wants me for forever. You were both there last night. You know what we said to each other. The promises we made. This is me doing that. Keeping those promises. It's a sacrifice. I know it is. A huge one and my heart hurts over it. But what else am I supposed to do? I love him and I want to be with him."

I should have never suggested that stupid idea. It seemed so right at the time. I looked at her and I thought, yeah, shit, she's forever. She's my one. So why not make it quasi-official? But now look what I've done. Raven is talking about giving up on London. Her fucking *dream*.

For me.

Can I let her do that? Find some crappy job with some mediocre symphony or end up giving cello lessons to kids?

Rina just said it: less than one percent get into this school and she not only got in, she got a scholarship. She's a savant. A once in a lifetime, if that, cellist.

And I'm headed back to Minnesota—my dream.

But... Raven is my dream too. Like she said.

Fuck. Just fuck.

What the hell am I going to do?

I KNOCK on his door at three a.m., having paced my room for the last two hours. I dropped off Oliver, and Rina, then walked Raven home. I didn't go inside as I always do with her. And I know she sensed something was off.

Landon opens his bedroom door, not surprised to find me on the other side. He steps back and I enter, immediately going for the couch by the window, opposite his bed. "I don't know what to do," I start without any preamble, my elbows on my parted thighs, my head in my hands.

Landon grabs his glasses from his nightstand and sits beside me, silently waiting for me to elaborate.

"She's talking about walking away from London. I heard her tell Oliver and Rina. She wants to be with me and doesn't believe that being long-distance will work."

"Do you?"

I think of this. About the hours both she and I will be trying to keep up with—me with work, her with school. I think about the men in London, at bars and in her program. I'll go out of my mind. "I don't know how to be away from her, man. I don't even know how the fuck it happened, but it's there."

"Because you like fucking her and are a caveman who doesn't want anyone else to touch what you have or because you love her?"

"Both. I don't want anyone to touch her. But I love her." I

sigh, feeling like I'm being held down by a three-hundred-pound weight. "I think I love her the way you loved Reese."

Landon stiffens beside me at the mention of his wife. His dead wife. "You think?"

"I know. She's it for me. My one."

"Reese is dead because of me."

I snarl, dropping my hands to glare at my twin. "Fuck you with that shit. She is not. It was an accident."

He shakes his head, giving me a look that demands I shut up and listen. "I got her pregnant when she was twenty. By twenty-one, she had a kid. She graduated from college, but then was home with our daughter. She never became a photojournalist. She never traveled the world taking photographs. Her life became about Stella and me since I was in med school. That was it, Luca. And that night, all she needed was a break. She kept saying 'I need to feel human. I need to feel like me. Even just for a few hours.'"

Landon swallows hard, his eyes glassing up.

"I didn't understand what she meant at the time. I love Reese with all my heart, but I didn't understand that, and it cost her her life. I was pissed she felt like she needed a break when staying home with Stella felt a hell of a lot easier than going to medical school and studying for a genetics exam. But I was wrong. She was not only losing sight of her dream, but she was also losing sight of herself beyond Stella. Beyond being a mom and a wife. Never in my life will I regret anything more than my actions that night, but my ignorance was hubris and fatal."

"By following you and your dream, she gave up part of her identity?"

He slaps my shoulder as if to say *bingo*.

I sit in stunned silence. "I can't let Raven do that. She's so fucking talented, brother, you have no idea. But what am I supposed to do? I have three years left of my residency. I can't walk away from that. I'm so close to being done and I've worked so hard to get myself back to top physical form where I can do surgery again. That's *my* dream."

"She'd never let you give up your dream."

"And I can't let her give up hers. So where does that leave us?"

"How much do you love her?"

I blink at him, scared of where this is headed. "More than anything."

"More than yourself?"

I lick my lips. "Yes."

"Enough to let her go?"

My first reaction is no. I can't do that. *I can't.* These two months with her have been the best and worst of my life. I'm twenty-nine years old. I've dated women. A lot of women. And none of them have been her. She. Is. It.

But she's only eighteen. So young, with so much ahead of her. While I've dated a lot of women, Raven hasn't dated a lot of men. Just a couple guys in high school who didn't amount to much. So where she's it for me, I might not be it for her. As much as it makes me violent to even contemplate that, I have to admit, it's a possibility.

That and she's so insanely talented.

She deserves London. She deserves to play for the world. She deserves to see and experience everything this life has to offer her.

"I have to let her go."

I fall back against the couch, covering my face with my hands, feeling so wrecked I can't even take a deep breath. It hurts too damn much.

"Not forever. Just for a while."

I bark out a sardonic laugh. "She'll never let it happen, Landon. She's stubborn. And she loves me. As much as I love her, she loves me, which is why she's planning on following me."

"You'll have to make her listen then. Somehow."

Make her listen. I nearly growl at that. I heard her tonight. My girl is determined. She had it all figured out. And if I let her do that, follow me, she'd grow to resent me over time. How could she not? We'd be doomed from the start.

Maybe we have been all along.

I think about Reese. About what Landon said about her. I remember that. All of it. We were in medical school together at Harvard. We were in school for absurdly long hours and if we weren't in school, we were studying. Reese had Stella in a morning program two days a week, but that was it. And maybe she could have put her in day care, but photojournalists don't exactly work regular hours or live regular lives and neither do medical students.

She chose Stella and my brother because she loved them and, in the process, sacrificed a big piece of herself. I won't let that happen to Raven. I love her too much to allow that.

I blow out an uneven breath. Yoda was wrong when he said to train yourself to let go of everything you fear to lose. There is nothing worse than losing someone you love. Nothing.

"I'm marrying her for real one day." Even if I have to break both our hearts now.

7

Let it never be said that alcohol isn't the universal cure for everything. At least that's what I'm counting on.

"How many of those are you going to have tonight?"

"As many as it takes," I tell Kaplan, who has been watching me like he's not sure what the hell to do with me.

"Have you tried, I don't know, growing a pair and talking to her?"

"Yes, asshole."

Twice. I tried twice. Yesterday and again today. Yesterday for over an hour, we talked. I pled my case. Tried to rationalize with her. And she didn't listen. She. Did. Not. Listen. She was all, 'I'm coming with you to Minnesota, I don't care what you say, and who needs the cello anyway.' But I could see the fucking pain in her eyes. I could feel it pouring off her. She loves me, but she doesn't want this. I know she doesn't. She just doesn't know what else to do.

So I'm solving that problem for her.

I tip the glass of brown liquid up to my mouth and swallow it all down. Then I grab the bottle the bartender graciously left for me when I tossed him two hundred dollars and pour myself another shot of Jameson.

"Do me a favor, Kap?"

"Sure, brother."

"Never fall in love. Especially with the right woman."

"No plans to."

I nod, staring down at the bar top and realizing I spilled about a shot's worth onto the wood too. Is it gross if I lick it up?

"Fuck yes, it is."

Shit. I'm musing out loud.

"Remind me why you're doing this?"

"Because my little bird needs to fly away. And I love her enough to do that for her. Even when she can't do it for herself."

I feel his hand squeeze my shoulder. "If you love something..."

"Fight like hell one day when they're ready to come back to you. I got it."

"Shit, Luca. I've never seen you like this."

I take my shot, not feeling or tasting anything at this point. "So I keep hearing. Not sure if that's a good or a bad thing."

"Do you want me to call Landon?"

"No. I haven't let him sleep for two nights. Plus, even though he's trying, I think it hurts him to talk about this."

"Between what happened to Rina, Oliver, Landon, and now your sorry ass, love can go fuck itself."

"Gently with a chainsaw. I'll drink to that."

"Me too." Kaplan holds out his glass and I pour him a shot and myself another and the two of us drink. Until the door to the bar opens and in walks the sexiest fucking woman I've ever seen. Wearing a red blouse and matching heels and tight as sin black jeans.

"I can't do it."

"You can. And she's going to be seriously hurt for a while. But don't worry, one day she'll get over it."

"That's the worst thing I've ever heard. Thanks for the pep talk."

"It's what big brothers are for."

I flip him off just as Raven reaches us, staring at the bottle, the mess of Jameson lining the counter, my empty glass, and finally me.

"Rough night?"

It's about to be.

"Do you want water or something? A soda maybe? How about a Shirley Temple? I hear it's what all the cool kids drink."

She huffs out a breath and Kaplan wordlessly gets up and leaves me to it.

"What are you doing?"

"Breaking up with you. I thought that would be obvious."

Her eyes flash, but she just shakes her head. "Nice try."

I stand slowly, partially because I'm drunk as fuck, but mostly because I'm making a show out of it. My eyes drag down to the end of the bar and my stomach churns at what's waiting for me there. It's now or never.

"Look, Raven…" I meet her eyes. "Honestly, I should have done this earlier and I'm sorry I didn't. I never wanted to hurt you. But, well, it's time we move on. Go our separate ways."

A flush races up her face and her lips part. "Luca, what are you doing?"

"I'm ending this."

She falls onto the empty barstool beside her.

"You're not serious."

"I am actually. I tried to have this talk with you yesterday and again this morning, but you weren't listening. I have to think of myself and what's best, and that means going back to Minnesota. Alone."

Her eyes cling to mine, desperate as they try to read me.

Only I'm drunk, have broken up with more women than I can count on two hands and two feet, and have prepared this speech for the last three hours. She won't find anything I don't want her to see. And right now, I want her to see indifference.

"But... these two months... the other night... the things we said."

"It's been fun. You were a great lay. But I'm over it. Not once did I ever invite you to come back to Minnesota with me."

"Actually, you did. You talked about forever. You talked about not letting me go. You talked about doing whatever we had to do!"

"I was also depressed and in a bad place. That's all behind me now. Can't we just say we had a good time together and have a clean break? Make this easy instead of fucking drama?"

She shakes her head. "You're lying. I know you're lying."

"I'm not." Hard motherfucking swallow. "Little Bird, it's over between us. Go fly away. London is where you're meant to be, and Minnesota is where I'm meant to be."

She stands up, fury shooting through her like a brush fire. "You're such a coward. Why can't you just tell me the truth?"

"Fine. You want the truth?" I lean forward, getting right up in her face. "I don't want you to come to Minnesota with me. I told you that yesterday *and* today, but you weren't listening."

"No," she clips out. "You told me you didn't want me to give up on London for Minnesota. You didn't want me to give up on my dream for you."

And stubborn woman that you are, you held firm.

I shrug. "That too. But it doesn't change the reality and the reality is that it's over."

"Why are you doing this?" She smacks a frustrated hand on the bar. "It doesn't have to be like this. You told me you love me, Luca. You told me you want forever. I chose you over the only other thing I love as much." Her chin drops and she shakes her head. "I can't believe I sound like one of those girls." Her eyes meet mine again. "Is that what I am? Is that what you've turned me into? Why did you tell me those things if you didn't mean them?"

Because I did mean them. Every fucking word, I meant. I just had no clue we'd end like this.

"What did you expect?" I shrug. "You know me. I'm Luca Fritz. Billionaire playboy. In love with a new woman every week. You said so yourself that first night."

She steels her spine, tapping her nails on the bar. "I know what you're trying to do and I'm not going to let you."

Dammit, Raven. Walk away. Give it up.

I pour myself yet another shot and wolf it down. Then I give the signal. The nail in the coffin. The kill switch.

"You don't have a choice." I clutch the end of the bar, so she doesn't see my hands shake. I'm two seconds from throwing up as I force out, "I don't love you. I don't want you. Get over it and move on. I have."

That's when a pretty blonde wearing a nothing of a black dress comes up to me, wrapping her arm around my waist, her other hand on my chest as she stares up into my eyes. "Hey, baby," she coos at me. "Sorry I'm late, but I'm ready to go now if you are."

"Luca." It's a shattered whisper, tears now tumbling from Raven's eyes, rolling down her cheeks one after the other in an endless stream.

I'll never get her back after this. Why couldn't she just listen? Why couldn't she just go to London instead? Why did she have to fight so damn hard for me when all I'm trying to do is save her?

You'll be so unhappy with me, Raven. You'll grow to hate me. Your fucking soul will die without your music and if you don't do this... if you don't follow your dream...

I meet her eyes, everything inside of me dying. Falling apart. "I'm sorry, Raven. It's just how it is. How it has to be. I didn't want it to end like this, but you just wouldn't listen." *You love me more than I deserve.* "Go to London. Travel the world. Play your music. And forget about me."

With one final look at her, I force myself to meet Joselyn's eyes. "I'm ready. Let's go."

"Hey, Luca?" A sharp crack hits my face in the form of Raven's slap. "You don't have to worry about me forgetting about you or following you anywhere. After tonight, you'll never see me again. It'll be like I never existed to you at all."

And then she's gone. Storming out of the bar and out into the street. Instinct takes over and I go to follow her, practically shoving poor Joselyn—a local waitress and casual fling of Kaplan's—who is only trying to help, to the ground.

Someone catches my arm and I spin around, ready to kill whoever is trying to stop me, only to meet Kaplan's hard green eyes. "Let. Her. Go."

That's when the dry heaves start and before I know what's happening, Kaplan has me outside the back of the bar, up against the wall so I can splatter paint it with Jameson and bile. Once everything inside me has been expelled, my head meets the rough wood siding, and I do my best to remember how to breathe.

Closing my eyes, all I can see is her. The hurt I inflicted all over her face. The pain. The goddamn heartbreak that absolutely matches my own.

"I didn't know what else to do. How else to make her go."

"I know."

"How am I ever going to get her back? Did you see the hurt in her eyes? The vitriol? How am I ever going to get her back?"

"I don't know, brother," Kaplan says. "I don't know. You'll just have to have faith that if it's meant to be, it'll be."

"And when that gets me nowhere?"

"Then you summon the devil and learn how to fight dirty because it's all you'll have left."

8

Time ticks slowly as I step out of the bar, my mind ricocheting, incredulous, my heart aching, broken. Off in the distance is a cab driving slowly down the road—likely the cab I took to get here—and with panic surging me forward, I sprint after it, kicking my heels off and not giving a shit at all.

My hand slams against the passenger door and the cab comes to a screeching halt. "I need to go back to where you picked me up," is all I manage as I get in and fall back against the plastic seat. The driver doesn't say anything as the car starts to move, and my tears fall.

Did that just happen? Did that honestly just fucking happen?

Three nights ago, we promised forever to each other. We looked into each other's eyes and swore love and loyalty and a lifetime. A shiver runs up my body and I wrap my arms around my chest, dragging my knees up, but it doesn't matter. I'm frozen through and yet boiling hot.

I knew he'd break my heart.

I mean, from the start of this, I knew he would. But then everything changed and I just...

I didn't see this coming.

He wanted me to go to London. Last night, he told me to go to London. That I had to live my dream, or I'd regret it always. I told him London would always be there. He wouldn't be. Not being with him would be a bigger regret. I can play cello anywhere. I can always figure that out. I chose him because I love him. Didn't he see that? Or was that just the start of things and he was trying to let me down gently?

God, I'm so stupid.

He was breaking up with me then and again earlier today, and I misread it all. I thought he was looking out for me. Worried about my not pursuing playing professional cello. But no. He wanted a clean slate when he went back to Minnesota. No attachments and nothing to drag him down.

Like the eighteen-year-old kid who fell in love with a notorious bachelor. A playboy. Isn't that what he said he was? That night in the grass, the night he took my virginity, he told me he dated a lot. That he liked it. Or used to? No, clearly not used to.

I trusted him. I believed the words he was telling me were true—that he felt the way I did.

And that woman. That blonde who stared up at him as if she knew exactly what his mouth tastes like. What his dick feels like inside of her. Are they together somewhere now? Is he taking her back to the estate? Fucking her in the bed I fell asleep with him in time and time again?

The cab pulls up to the front of the Fritz estate. I pay the driver and get out, running down the long driveway and around it, heading for the staff house. The door crashes against the wall, but I'm already flying up the stairs, tearing into my room, dragging my suitcase down, and filling it with everything I have here.

"What's all this?"

I turn and my father sees my face, his growing from curious to heartache and sympathy in a nanosecond. He crosses the room and envelops me in a hug, and any remaining composure I had been clinging to falls away as I absolutely lose it in my father's arms.

"He ended it then, yeah?" he asks after an eternity of holding and shushing and comforting.

"I think he had been trying to for a couple of days and I was too stupid and blind to realize it." I wipe my face and pull away from him. "Can you get me to Boston tonight?"

"Boston?"

"I want to go to London as soon as I can. Now, if possible."

"Oh, Raven—"

I shake my head, cutting him off. "I don't want the lecture and I don't want the platitudes. I just want to get out of here and away from him. I never want to see him again. Ever. He wanted me to go to London, so that's precisely what I'm doing."

"Is that what he told you? That he wants you to go to London?"

"He told me a lot of things. Tonight especially, but yes. He told me to follow my dream and go to London because he doesn't want me to come with him to Minnesota. He doesn't want me at all."

My father stares at me for a very long moment and then over my shoulder, out the window. He rubs at his mouth and finally nods as if he's come to some sort of conclusion that's eluding me.

"I'll fly you to Boston tonight, we'll stay in a hotel, and I'll change our tickets for tomorrow."

More tears spring to my eyes. "Thank you, Dad. You're the only person in this world I have. The only one I can rely on." Because everyone else abandons me. Leaves me the first chance they get. I'll never be enough to make someone stay and choose me, and that's just life.

"All right now." He kisses my forehead. "I'm going to let Dr. Fritz know I'm leaving early for London and get everything arranged. Finish packing and we'll leave in two hours."

With that, he closes the door, leaving me here in my mess of a room with my mess of a heart.

I don't love you. I don't want you. Get over it and move on. I have.

It's as if every drop of blood in my body has been replaced with poison. Shredding my veins and killing my internal organs. With each pump of my heart, that poison grows stronger, deadlier. I've read about heartbreak and seen it in movies, but it's one thing to read and see and another to *feel* it.

It's as if time has come to a standstill. As if I made him up in my head because he no longer exists in reality. We loved for such a short time, but I already know I'll never be able to fully wash him from my skin. He's etched, embedded, and that's what scares me the most about how this feels. Because I'm not fine and what if I never am again?

His smiles and laughter. His kisses and forehead presses. The way we held each other, intertwined, any distance too great. The hours of talking—the things we told each other—everything. The way he looked at me. The way he fucking *looked* at me... as if I was all he saw. All he ever wanted.

I'm so ashamed. So weak and tired and dejected.

His eyes tonight... so cruel. So casual and fucking honest.

I was the needy girl, desperate for his love. And he used that. All of it. Until he was fixed and no longer had a need for me. I'm reeling. Trapped in this avalanche, suffocating and unable to move.

I finish packing everything up and take a turn about the room, touching surfaces and smelling the pillow he slept on. It still smells like him, and a burning pang hits me straight on. It might not have been real for him, but it was for me. All of it. Every second I was with him, I loved him.

Pretending otherwise would be a lie and I will not do that.

I may be young, and I may be that girl who fell for the wrong guy, but I won't do that. I'll mourn the loss of him and then I'll move on because that's all I can do. London will help. School will help. New friends. New life.

My eyes catch on a stack of Post-it notes sitting in the corner of the tiny desk and before I can think twice about it, I scribble a message, staring at the words. At the swirls of the letters that form my heart.

Peeling it from the rest, I hold it in my hand and before I can talk myself out of it, I'm out the front door, crossing the dark grounds, the wind whipping through my hair. I punch in the code for the back door and wind my way up through the house. It's quiet and even though part of me feels at home here, I know that's a fallacy.

I no longer have a home. I'm not sure I ever did.

His door sits at the end of the hall and as I approach it, I slow my steps, doubt starting to creep in. What if he's in there with her? But I don't hear anything. It's nothing but muted silence and it's now or never. My hands press into the wood, running my fingers along the white paint and leaving the Post-it behind, stuck to his door where he won't miss it.

Even if he never sees it and it's found by someone else, at least I said it.

It's my goodbye.

Tears like raindrops fall from my face, but I do nothing to wipe them away. It feels like I'll cry forever, but I know that's not what will happen. I'll go to London, and I'll miss him. I'll suffer a thousand times over as I question every moment we spent together, but I won't die. I will come out of this smarter. A better cellist. A stronger woman.

And no matter what, I'll never allow a man to do this to me again.

PART II

FOUR YEARS LATER

9

With my back straight and my legs spread, my wrist angled just so and the fingers on my opposite hand ready to move, I suck in a shaky breath and wait for my cue. My heart pounds in my chest at least two measures faster than the music. Not an uncommon occurrence for me in this position, but tonight is different and my body is acutely aware of it.

I've been anxiously anticipating while simultaneously dreading this night for three weeks now. Since the moment I accepted this position and moved back to a city I swore I would never live in again. Life is funny that way. We swear we'll never do a lot of things again and yet, more often than not, we break those promises.

Like me with drinking tequila.

But I was pretty damn adamant about never returning to Boston with the exception of random, short, stealthy visits. Life had other ideas for me and now here I am.

A jolt of adrenaline spikes through my veins as the violin in the seat behind me hits its final note and now it's my turn. Breathing through the nausea, my eyes close, and I focus my thoughts. There is nothing else, I tell myself. No stage lights, no applause from the audience or other performers crowded in around me, listening intently to my playing. Waiting for me to fuck up.

No. There is nothing except the music.

The piano accompaniment begins and it's with that my body takes over—practically from muscle memory—hitting every note with confident precision. As with every time I play, I'm carried to a higher plane of existence. And all those nerves and their accompanying jitters transition to euphoria.

Even with the looming notes that plague the back of my mind.

Saint-Saens' "The Swan (Le Cygne)-Carnival of the Animals" is such a lovely piece and playing it for a charity event as a first chair cellist for the Boston Symphony Pops Orchestra in my home city with my father as well as Dr. and Mrs. Fritz— who are essentially my second parents—in the audience is like the brass ring of a career that by all means should just be starting considering I graduated from The Conservatory in London only four short months ago.

It's bittersweet. A lot of ups and downs, but I'm proud of where I am now.

The places I've played—concert halls I only dreamed of as a kid—over the three months prior to me moving back here.

The piece comes to a close, the final notes of the symphony resonating through the air leaving a rise of gooseflesh on my arms, and my hands rest, my head tucked into the side of my instrument. Expelling a breath, I open my eyes to the sound of thunderous applause throughout the symphony hall. I nod in gratitude when our conductor motions for me to rise and take a formal bow. Bastard knows I hate that crap, but I do it all the same, holding the neck of my cello, Azrael, in my right hand while bowing forward along with all the other soloists who join me.

Thankfully, the rest of the orchestra stands, all of us taking our curtain call with our conductor Antonio last.

A sense of elation swims through me as the curtain falls, shielding us from the exiting audience. Giddy bubbles swim up from my stomach, peeling an epic smile up my lips. I made it through. My first performance here as a soloist.

Now if only the rest of the night could go this smoothly.

I congratulate my fellow soloists, hugging and kissing the cheeks of everyone I pass, gliding across the stage and heading for the back rooms. Desperate to put Azrael away, clean up a bit, and get out of here as fast as I can.

Unable to stop the fresh wave of unease as it sours in my gut like curdling milk.

Not tonight. Please, not tonight. Not on my perfect night.

Catarina, one of our oboists, squeezes my arm, giving me a wink as she passes. I return the gesture. She and I have gotten very friendly in the weeks I've been here. "Slammed it, bitch."

"You too!"

"I'm sure your dad loved it."

I snicker under my breath. My father pretends to enjoy classical music as many proper Englishmen do, but secretly, he listens to heavy rock. Says it reminds him of his MI6 days, but no one knows about that except the Fritz family he works for. Well, and the British government. "I have no doubt he did."

"See you back there?"

"In a minute."

Another hug and a few more congratulations and I push my way through the lingerers to the back room I share with a few of the other female performers.

"Ah! The star has arrived, burning hot and stunningly gorgeous."

I roll my eyes at Catarina as I tuck my baby into her case, zipping her up.

She laughs, putting the final piece of her oboe into its case.

"Truly, though, kitten, it was beautiful. I know you were nervous about tonight, but you played it to perfection."

"Yes," Quill, an English violinist, agrees. "You were brilliant. Why were you so nervous anyway? If I had half your talent, I'd rub it in everyone's face just to watch them pee themselves with envy."

"That's some lovely imagery there."

Quill winks at Catarina, blowing her a kiss.

Catarina turns on me, pointing a finger as if she just came to realize something vital. "You know, she does have a point. Why *were* you nervous?"

I lean against the long counter, taking a towel and blotting at the sweat on my chest and the back of my neck. No one knows I occasionally get stage fright—friends or not, admitting that sort of weakness is career suicide. My fellow performers are how it all began in the first place at a time when I was already going through a rough patch. I've battled through it. Worked to move past it. And for the most part, I have. Occasionally, on days such as today, it reacquaints itself with my more fragile side.

But that's not why she's asking that question.

I open my mouth to respond when there's a knock at our door. "Yes," I call out, using the distraction for what it is. Taking the pins out of my updo, I let my heavy mane of ink-colored hair fall around me.

"I have a flower delivery for Ms. Raven Fairchild."

That. *That's* why I was nervous.

Fuck. I knew this would happen. I knew they would come. I shouldn't have come back here. I should have run for the exit the first chance I got. Now it's too late and I have an audience to boot. Dammit! Cold tentacles of dread snake around my throat, strangling me.

"I... uh." I shake my head, raising my voice so the guy can

hear me through the door. "Um. Just a moment." Crap. I need to think. No way can I escape now.

"Those are *the flowers,* aren't they?" Quill asks, her voice painted in unmistakable awe as she says *the flowers.* "I've heard about those."

I spin around in place, my incredulous eyes wide, my breath stalled. "You have?"

She nods enthusiastically with a Cheshire grin. "Oh yes. Everyone has heard about them because everyone has heard about you, love."

"The infamous hand-delivered, anonymously given flowers," Catarina exclaims, jumping in beside Quill as if she's telling her a secret, though her voice carries throughout the small room. She fans her face. "The speculations run wild."

"*I* heard they were from a real-life prince whose heart you stole only to leave him behind."

"Oh! *I* heard they were from a mysterious billionaire who fell hopelessly in love with you only to then break your heart."

I glare, mystified by this. Sort of amused but mostly horrified. Both assumptions are partially true in one aspect or another, though I have no clue how the rumors and speculation ran this rampant. Not that I know with absolute certainty it's been *him* who has been sending the flowers.

At least that's the lie I told myself every time they came.

I knew it was him.

There is no one else, and anyone else they could have potentially been from have denied it. No, the man loves messing with me. Attempting to shove and insert pieces of himself in any remaining cracks or fissures in my healed wounds he can.

"They asked you about them in that interview after the award show," Catarina continues. "You claimed you never knew who sent them to you even though they've shown up after every major opening night performance, no matter where in the world you were performing."

I'm impersonating a goldfish as I stare at the two women before me.

It was one interview. Two years ago. After I won an International Classical Music Award for one of my original pieces and an enormous bouquet showed up. But...

"Bring them in!" Quill calls out, prancing happily to the door. "We're all decent in here. Let's see what you have for our fair Fairchild."

"No!" I cry out, my body seizing as my heart rate shoots through the roof. "You don't—" Only my panicked words are cut off as Quill flings open the door and in walks a tall, broad man wearing black slacks and carrying a ginormous bouquet of exquisite purple and white orchids in a crystal vase.

Orchids this time. Always different. Always beautiful.

And instantly my greatest fears surrounding not only the flowers but with returning to Boston are mercifully squashed as the bouquet is lowered to chest height and there stands someone I've never set eyes on before. I blow out a sigh of relief.

What on earth would I have done if it had been Luca standing there? Other than smash the bouquet over his pompous head, of course.

"Are you Raven Fairchild?" he questions.

A frown glues the corners of my lips down and when I don't answer, Quill does it for me. "That's her."

I hate the flowers. I hate all they represent. I stare at them, beautiful and fragrant in his hands while a strange and unwelcome pang twists up my gut.

"These are for you."

I step back, waving my hands back and forth, refusing to accept them. He doesn't look surprised by my refusal as he sets them down on the counter.

"Who are they from?" Catarina plows past me, rushing over to the flowers and digging through them. "I don't see a card."

"I don't want them. Please take them back."

"I was told when you said that to inform you that's not an option this time." And with that, the man leaves.

"That son of a bitch," I hiss under my breath.

"Who?" Catarina questions, her gaze searching mine in the reflection in the mirror as she makes a show of inhaling the perfume of the flowers. "Who's a son of a bitch? Because these flowers..."

"They're gorgeous," Quill coos, throwing me a side-eye as she joins Catarina. "And yes, who is a son of a bitch? You obviously know who they're from or you wouldn't have tried to send them back and you wouldn't be referring to whoever he is as a son of a bitch."

I send the flowers back. Each and every time. Not tonight. Why not tonight? What game is he playing? I loved Luca Fritz in ways I shouldn't have. In ways he didn't deserve.

Only I was too young and too stupid and too besotted to see through the pink haze of the love potion he had me under. The man saved my life when I was a child and since that day I've loved him. Watched him from my looking glass otherwise known as the staff quarters in the back of the Fritz compound. Cyber stalked him when he left for college and cried into my pillow every time he was photographed with women.

Which was freaking often. The media loves their favorite notorious Boston billionaire bachelors otherwise known as the Fritz brothers.

I was the girl you never want to be, and at eighteen, I was still that girl.

Only that time, that night on the island, he saw me. He wanted me back, pursued me even, and I was helpless to resist. Giddy with dreams come true and wishes upon stars granted.

Four years later, I'm a woman and I hate the bastard for tricking me into believing it was real. "You can have them," I tell them without answering their questions, unable to be in here another second with those flowers consuming all the available oxygen. "I should be done with dinner around nine, so I'll be at your place by nine-thirty or so."

"Sure. Whatever you say." I ignore Catarina's smug smirk and bolt out of the room like my ass is on fire. I need a minute to collect myself, to right my brain, and I can't do that with those fucking flowers sitting there or Catarina's and Quill's inquisition.

My cello can stay here as we have another performance tomorrow early afternoon, and no one will touch her. I run into the dark hall, turning left at a blind sprint, only to slam straight into a hard body. I teeter back on my four-inch heels as two hands swoop out, catching me and holding on tight.

"Ah, Raven. I was just coming to find you," Antonio says, his thick Italian accent a purr. "My girl, you were exquisite." He pulls me in for a hug, kissing both my cheeks. Sweat glistens through his wild, dark hair as he runs his hand through it, brushing it back off his face. Despite his roguish good looks, the man keeps the eccentric stereotype for conductors alive. "Your best performance yet. *Magnifica, mia bella.*"

"Thank you." I give him a small curtsy. "The whole night was flawlessly and gloriously conducted. Well performed by all."

I search frantically around the dark corridor, only lit by the remnants of the stage lights as they filter through back here. It's fairly empty, most people either changing in their dressing rooms or having left.

"*Si. Grazie.* But I did not come for you to discuss the performance. I am pleased I caught you before you left. Raven?"

Antonio says my name with purpose, forcing my attention back to him and giving me the look. The one he's given me since I started here with the orchestra a few weeks ago. "Will you join me tonight at the reception?" The sparkle in his eyes and the quirk of his lips make his intentions impossible to misread.

It is never a good idea for a musician to get involved with their conductor. It's asking for trouble and Antonio is a good twenty years older than me. Not that it matters to him, though. He sees talent and beauty and cares about nothing else. I've heard the rumors about him. Knew of them before I even came on here.

"Yes," I answer, anxious to go. "Catarina, Quill, and I will be attending together after I have dinner with my father."

He takes a step toward me, his head dipping until we're practically eye to eye. "Will I be able to entice you to have a drink with me? Just me? Perhaps more after?"

A throat sharply clears behind us, but I didn't have to hear it to know he was looming there. I had already felt his presence. Smelled his cologne. Hated the way my body began buzzing with electricity that only has one source.

Antonio glances over my shoulder and immediately frowns at what he finds. A man getting closer, the soft tap of his expensive shoes an indication of that, yes, but that's not how I know he's moving in behind me. Staking a claim he has no right to.

"He is waiting on you, yes?"

For a beat, I'm tempted to scream no, take me with you, or be a total bitch and walk off with Antonio. I knew this moment was an inevitability. I knew I'd have to see him. Maybe getting it over with is just easier? I doubt it. There is nothing easy about this man or this situation and I hate him all the more for putting me in it.

Instead of fleeing the way my body is begging me to, I put on my big girl panties and with a resigned sigh say, "I'll see you later, Antonio. Thank you again for tonight. It was magical."

Antonio makes a show of kissing both my cheeks again and with a parting glance, leaves me here alone in a dark hallway with *him*.

Billionaire. Doctor. Playboy. Boston prince. Gorgeous in a way no man should ever be.

Heartbreaker extraordinaire.

Gulping down my nerves and releasing a silent breath, I slowly turn around and look up. His piercing green eyes lock on mine, and if I thought my heart was beating fast before, it has nothing on me now.

"Luca Fritz. How unlovely it is to see you again."

"Raven Fairchild. How lovely it is to see my beautiful wife again."

10

For four years I've planned this night. Four years of dreaming about when all the stars would align, and the timing would be perfect. She finished school. Spent three months traveling, playing. Now she's here, back in Boston. It was all moving along as I'd planned. I'd show up here tonight. I'd look into her eyes.

And *bam*.

That spark.

All that energy that effortlessly flows between us.

It'd still be there. Stronger and brighter than ever. And she'd forget or forgive me instantly for all the horrible things I said to her that night four years ago.

But the "I want to cut your balls off, drop them in a vat of hot oil, and then feed them to you" look in her eyes tells me I'm not going to be granted my fairy-tale wish. That all my plans are about to go to hell and anything I say will fall on deaf ears.

Here's the thing about that, though. I don't care. I mean, I care. But I also don't *care*. Because in the four years since I've been within touching distance of this woman, I've not grown any less obsessed. I went from being a remorseless playboy bachelor to falling in love to a sorry sack of shit to blindly optimistic and hopeful.

Then she says this...

"You miserable bastard. What the hell are you doing here? You have some fucking nerve showing up and interrupting my night."

"You look beautiful, Raven. More beautiful than my memories do justice."

"And you look like shit. How about you crawl back into the hole"—she snorts, rolling her eyes at her miserable pun—"you likely just left. I'm sure she'll welcome you back."

I ignore all that. "I was hoping I could take you somewhere and we could talk."

She laughs sardonically. "Talk? Are you high? I have absolutely nothing to say to you that I didn't say four years ago when I walked out of that bar. Now go. Leave me alone. I have places to be."

"Like with your conductor?"

She grins evilly, shrugging.

"He's too old for you." I snarl, my eyes casting over her shoulder in the direction of where her fucktwat, handsy, has a reputation worse than mine conductor just was.

She snorts out a bitter guffaw, planting her hands on her waist. "That's sort of a pot-kettle thing, wouldn't you say? And I'm not your wife, dick. I never was."

Ah, I was wondering when she'd circle back to that. Maybe that wasn't the best way to start things off? I'm already screwing this up and I just got here.

I walked in a nervous wreck while I forced some confidence into my veins and mind. This is my second chance. My shot. I had to keep reminding myself of that. That I'm not a quitter. I'm a fighter—thanks to her in large part. I expected she'd still be mad. But I also assumed she'd have figured it all out by this point. She's too smart not to.

But seeing her like this...

"I see time and distance haven't softened you the way I'd hoped. I seem to remember a ceremony. Vows exchanged. Kisses sealing the deal."

"None of it was real and you know it."

I get why she's saying that. Because no, it wasn't real. I mean, Oliver officiated over our mock wedding, but it was more of a thing than anything else. Oliver had just been ordained online to do another friend's wedding, and Raven and I had no wedding license.

So... not real.

That doesn't mean I didn't mean what I said to her that night. All of it. I did. Every word. It's how we got to this mess of a place. I loved her, so I had to save her. Even from herself.

But all she remembers, *all she knows*, is that a few days later I shredded her heart into pulp.

Intentionally. Cruelly. Unrepentantly.

As is never the case with me, suddenly I am at a loss for words.

Our eyes meet and neither of us looks away. Instead, I stare. *We* stare. Because yeah, she's most definitely staring.

Directly. Unabashedly. Obsessively.

It's not all in anger. I'm the spark to her blowtorch. She might be burning hot, wanting to melt the skin from my face, but dammit if the way she's looking at me doesn't also make my dick harden in my slacks. The effect of her eyes on me is no less potent than it was four years ago. If anything, my reaction is stronger for having been denied it for so long.

"Raven." I whisper her name, a low, gentle hum, my heart a chaotic wreck, making my palms sweat. "God, just being this close to you again. Just seeing you. I've dreamed of little else for four years. Please, can we talk?" I swallow thickly, my throat bone dry, my insides tumbling with desire. "I have so much to say. So much to tell you."

She's so fucking beautiful, I can hardly stand to be this close and not touch her.

She shakes her head. "I could have gone forever without seeing you again," she bites out acerbically, bitterness clinging to every syllable.

"And I couldn't go another second without seeing you again," I throw back at her, taking in every line of her face, the glimmering aquamarine of her eyes. "I still have it, you know. Your note. It's in my wallet where it's been since you left it for me."

"You do? Can I see it?" She holds her palm out and for a second, I flinch in the direction of my wallet before I think better of it.

"You'll rip it up."

"Sure as Santa and reindeer at Christmas, I will. You shouldn't hold on to it anyway. That was written hastily and placed on your door impulsively. It's certainly no longer true."

"Liar, liar pants on fire. Because if that were the case, my little bird, then why are you still so angry?"

Her fists ball up, fury slicing through her features with the heat of a thousand suns. Somehow, I'm standing before her. Close. Right here. I nearly groan. She smells like all my greatest memories and deepest heartache. Like sweat and heat and lust and madness and fucking sex. Like my Raven.

How can I not draw closer? How could I not come tonight?

Does she know about all the nights I've come before this one, traveled all over the world, sat in the shadows, and kept myself away so she'd have it all?

Which she does. The woman has taken the cello and made it her bitch. Won awards. Earned accolades. Has rock stars banging on her door, though I'm not supposed to know about that. She's been offered positions by every major symphony from every corner of the world.

And yet, she chose this one. This. One. Here in Boston. The city where she knew, *she fucking knew*, I was living in.

Her fist lands in the center of my chest and for a second, I revel in that. She's touching me. That is until she pushes me back with all her might as I press into her, forcing her fist deeper against me.

The heat of my body seeps into her knuckles and I watch as she shudders at the feel of me beneath her touch. Even through the layers of my suit. That fist pounds again, harder this time, wanting to break me apart. But then stops, her gaze shifting to my left shoulder, wondering about it. Knowing the scar is now likely fully healed, a scar she spent hours tracing with delicate fingers. With her tongue.

She fixed me. Made me whole. Gave me purpose and reason, and I broke her heart in the end. I know I did. I know I have miles and years and hurdles of heartbreak to make up for.

"Why are you here? Why are you doing this to me?" Her voice cracks. "Why tonight? Why tonight of all nights?"

"Because it had to be tonight," I tell her. "It had to be here. I tried for three weeks to find you at the compound, but you were never home or if you were, you did a brilliant job of hiding from me." I push out a breath, my eyes locking with hers once more, my expression one of pure awe. "I'm so fucking proud of you, Raven. Everything you've ever dreamed of for yourself, you've accomplished and more."

Tears line her eyes that she refuses to let fall. I hate that she's still so sad. That the pain I caused her still has this effect on her. That me just standing here cuts through all her layers and walls and fortresses and castles and villages and towns and cities she's erected. She built a world of resistance around her heart with the singular purpose of keeping me out.

I know it. I can see it all over her. But the fact that I can still sneak through the back door—and no, that's not a dirty metaphor, at least not yet—and disarm her completely is why I'll never give up.

My hand comes up along her face, brushing her long hair back and out of the way as my fingers dive into it, cupping her jaw.

Her skin.

Fuck, her skin sets mine on fire. So soft and silky and electric. My breath hitches, rattling in my chest as her eyes darken. My body inches in. My head dips. Those now half-mast eyes of hers cling to my lips. Beneath her fist, my heart pounds, and I place my hand over her heart, smirking when I feel how hers perfectly matches mine.

Someone walks past us, their gaze curious, and I grab her arm with my other hand, dragging her deeper into the shadows of the hall behind the side stage curtains. It's darker back here. More intimate and it drives me against her, holding her tight.

"Don't touch me," she seethes, shaking my touch from her skin. "I hate you."

My hand falls, my expression hardening. "No. You just hate what I did to you."

"No. I hate *how* you did it. I knew Luca Fritz was going to break my heart from the start. I knew the power you had over me. That's not what has me bleeding vitriol now and we both know it. I hate that I gave you so much of myself when I should have known better. I hate that I believed you when you swore love and devotion and forever. If you had just stuck to your every woman go-to plan of treating me like a fling from the start, I would have been better off."

"You never got it? All this time, you never understood what I was doing?"

"I did understand! I just didn't care," she yells. "You were a liar and a user and a piece of shit who didn't care who he hurt or how he did it."

I grunt, running a hand through my hair. "Always so honest.

So fucking brave and resilient. You've got it all wrong, haven't you?"

"Not anymore. Especially where you're concerned. I don't want the flowers. I don't know why you continue to do that when I always send them back."

I get right up in her face, my anger getting the best of me as I snarl against her jaw, ready to bite her. Mark her. Fucking claim her, bullshit be damned. "Didn't my man tell you? There is no more sending them back. I've been patient, but my patience is done."

"That's not your call to make." She shoves me back. But her eyes are hooded. Dark. Turning my already hard dick to stone. "It's mine, asshole. I left you and that island four years ago. I was done with you then and there, Luca, the note notwithstanding. I believe I told you that in the bar."

I smile at the way she says my name, a smirk I'm unable to control on my lips that pulls at the most venomous parts of her. It antagonizes and I don't care. I want it. Harder. Rougher. I edge in closer, my body nearly pressed to hers, my hand back on her jaw, forcing her gaze right into mine. My nose glides along hers, across her cheek, and into her neck where I take a deep inhale.

Goddamn intoxicating.

My eyes close, but it's her shiver that tells me she's still an unwilling slave to my touch.

My hot breath fans her skin as I whisper into her ear, "That's where you're wrong, Little Bird. No more flying away from me. I let you go and had to watch as you spread your wings, but now you've flown home. Back to me."

She pushes me back for what feels like the thousandth time, and I growl, more than frustrated.

"Dammit, Raven. I know you're mad. I know you hate me. I know you have a good reason to. But I don't care. I never cared about that because I always knew we'd get back here. Please, you have to listen to me. It's been four years of living without you. Living with the knowledge that the best and worst thing I ever did is what I did to you."

"Fuck you, Luca. I didn't come home for you. I came home for me. I came home for your mom. You are not part of my world or my equation any longer. And you never will be again."

Shouldering past me, she takes off. Running at full speed for the exit.

Dammit. How is it possible I never stop screwing up with her?

11

I bulldoze through the back door and continue without slowing, my heels clicking on the damp city sidewalks. Cold rain pelts at my face, wetting my hair and dress. I shiver, having forgotten my coat in my haste, but it's too late now. I can't go back in there. Goddamn him. Did he have to do this?

How dare he? Just how *dare* he?

Sin in a bespoke suit. Seduction in a panty-melting smile. Stupidity for every woman who falls for it. Argh! My mind frazzles, shooting in a million directions a million miles a minute. Fire burns my chest. Venom seeps through my pores. Pain prickles in the cracks of my barely reglued heart. Searing, poisonous hate flows like a current through my veins.

I didn't want to be in there with him and yet my pain and indignation forced me to stand my ground. I won't be weak with him again. But his words... I just had to get away.

When Luca broke my heart, I did what any heartsick girl who fell in love with the wrong man would do. A man too old for her. Too out of her league. A man she had no business loving in the first place but had all her life. I told him I'd always love him on a Post-it note and left it for him on his bedroom door. I wanted him to know what he had done. What he was giving up—real, honest, pure love.

Then I left that island, left the state, left the country, and never looked back.

Then the flowers started.

Maybe it's the lack of closure that's causing this reaction? The way we ended was so brutal. *Why do you keep trying to hurt me when I've already been hurt enough by you?*

"Miss Raven?"

I startle, nearly tripping over my own feet as I come to an abrupt halt, brushing the wet strands of my hair sticking to my face back. "Jerimiah?" My hand goes to my chest, over my pounding heart. "You startled me. I'm sorry. I didn't see you there."

"I heard you playing tonight. It was beautiful."

A small hint of a smile presses against my lips. "Thank you. I should have known you'd be listening."

"Wouldn't have missed it. Mister Antonio left me a ticket, but I just couldn't."

I nod in understanding, taking in his dirty, dark skin and sunken eyes, his ratty clothes and hunched stance and as always with him, my heart breaks.

"Can I get you anything? Help you get somewhere dry?"

"No. I'm—"

"Raven?" Luca's voice booms through the dark night, the tap of his shoes loud and urgent until he's pushing me back a step, placing himself protectively in front of me. One hand holds his umbrella up over my head, his other angled out in front of him.

His eyes are all over Jerimiah even as he talks to me. "What's going on? Are you okay?"

"I'm fine."

"Who are you talking to?" His hand reaches out, grasping my bicep and pushing me back behind him as I try to move to the side of him. He shakes his head, telling me no. "Is he bothering you?"

Jesus, Luca. Always so fucking overprotective. Superman has nothing on Luca Fritz. It's how we inadvertently got here in the first place. Luca's penchant for heroism has landed him in the wrong place at the wrong time in the past, but I know he still can't stop himself from stepping in. It's nearly tempting to mess with him, but after all he's been through, I would never do that to him. Or to Jerimiah for that matter.

"He's not, Luca. Even if he were, do you believe I couldn't stop him on my own?"

Luca lets out an uncomfortable grunt. My mother was Mossad. My father is a former MI6. I was a little girl when my mother died, but my father trained me and trained me well.

Luca knows this. He just doesn't like it.

I push his hand off and step beside him, nudging him back a bit so he doesn't spook Jerimiah further.

I lower my voice, speaking evenly, "This is my friend, Jerimiah. He's a cellist. A brilliant one. He lives in this alley behind the symphony and watches out for us fellow musicians."

Jerimiah ducks his head, creeping back ever so slightly into the shadows of his alley. He doesn't like attention and he certainly doesn't like attention from men like Luca. Men who are tall and broad and ready to attack.

Luca's head whips in my direction and when he sees I'm telling the truth, he softens his stance and his voice, turning back to Jerimiah. "Well, in that case, it's a pleasure to meet you, Jerimiah." Luca offers Jerimiah his umbrella. Jerimiah glances at me, his gaze unsure, but I give him a warm smile and nod my head.

Jerimiah slowly takes the umbrella, holding it half over his head, almost as if he's not quite sure what to do with the gift.

"It's yours. I don't want it back," Luca assures him before

shrugging off his suit jacket and holding it over my head with one hand to keep me dry.

Only the wanker doesn't realize that by doing that he's also swallowing me up in his body heat and heavenly scent. It's making me postal and if Jerimiah wasn't standing here, skittish as a cat in a roomfull of rocking chairs, I'd dick punch Luca for being so thoughtless and chivalrous at the same time.

"Thank you, sir. That's mighty kind of you."

"Here. This is also for you." Luca hands me his jacket, making sure I'm holding it over my head and then pulls out his wallet, handing Jerimiah what looks to be a few hundred-dollar bills. "Please get yourself something to eat and somewhere dry. Anyone who is good to Raven, I want to make sure is taken care of."

I roll my eyes at that. "That extends to yourself?" I hiss under my breath.

Whatever. I'm done here.

I toss Luca's coat back at him, forcing him to catch it. The man is absolutely soaked, but so am I, so who gives a shit at this point?

"Night, Jerimiah. I'll see you tomorrow morning."

I stalk off, headed for... crap. I didn't drive my dad's car tonight. I took the T. Dammit! I ran in the completely wrong direction from where I need to go because freaking Luca Fritz felt the need to be the ghost of lovers past and ruin my night.

I could weave around and end up by Northeastern or back-track by Symphony Hall, but—

"Raven, stop!"

I pivot around and cross the empty street, heading up back toward Symphony Hall and the nearby T stop, but he's chasing after me, one of his strides equaling two of mine.

"Fuck off, Luca."

"Dammit, you're so stubborn. Stop running from me and let me drive you. You're soaking wet and likely late for dinner."

I am late for dinner and no doubt look like a drowned rat. But luckily, I can blame it on the T and not the good doctor who felt the need to stalk me into the street because I sure as hell don't want to have *that* conversation with my father, Dr. Fritz, or Octavia.

He catches up to me quickly, despite my quickening my pace to a near sprint. His hand latches onto my arm, and he spins me in place to face him, my momentum carrying me a bit too fast, and I slam into his soaked chest.

Righting my body, I thrust myself away from him, but he's not letting me go. Not this time.

His coat flies back over my head, shielding me from the cold, pelting rain, ruining what is likely a ten-thousand-dollar suit and not caring a bit.

He stares down at me, his eyes pleading. "Let me drive you. Please. I won't talk if you don't want me to, but it's dark and pouring, and I don't want you on the T and then walking to Mistral."

I smirk. "How did you know that's where we're eating tonight?"

"I bribed my father with news on Landon's girl."

"Landon has a girl?"

A smile blooms across my face and he matches it. Landon experienced heartbreak that makes mine look like a child's birthday party. The idea of Landon in love is something else. For a quick beat, I forget to hate Luca as I practically squeal with delight.

"He does," Luca says. "A total spitfire who doesn't take his crap. I guess that's the one thing he and I have in common— difficult women who love putting us through our paces."

And just like that... bubble burst.

I shake my head. I don't understand him. Why he sent the flowers all these years. Why he showed up to random performances—I know he did even if we didn't see each other or speak. Why he's here now, chasing after me and talking like a man in need of a second chance.

"I don't need a ride. I'll take an Uber."

"Without your purse or phone?"

Right. Without my purse because clearly my jacket isn't the only thing I forgot tonight.

I inwardly sag. Cold and wet and pissed and epically annoyed. "Your fault. You sent the damn flowers, and it threw me off."

He licks his lips, shifting into me, water dripping off his hair and clinging to his eyelashes. God, does he have to look like this? So freaking gorgeous? He makes me feel so small when he stands close like this. The man is well over six feet and built of solid muscle, and though I'm not pint sized, he towers. I always loved that about him. How safe and worshipped his size made me feel.

His gaze grows more insistent, telling me he's not letting go, and now I outwardly sigh. Out here without a phone or a purse, I'm up shit creek without a paddle.

"Please, Raven. I'm begging now."

"I'll let you drive me, but you need to keep your mouth shut. As far as I'm concerned, you're my Uber driver and I do not know you. We have no past, but more importantly, we have no present or future beyond this ride."

Without a word, he ushers me along, still holding his coat over my head though at this point the gesture is futile. I'm just glad I don't have Azrael with me, even if she's in her hard case. The idea of getting her wet makes me shiver.

"Cold?"

"Aren't you?"

"Come on. My car is just up here." We pick up the pace, jogging across the street against the light, heading straight into a parking lot. Luca digs into his pants pocket and hits a button.

A crazy SUV like I've never seen before lights up.

"What the hell is that?" I ask as he opens the door for me, making sure I'm seated before shutting it behind me and running around to the other side to get in. The inside is all smooth, sleek, sporty, and smells of leather and him.

"It's my new Aston Martin DBX," he answers, starting it up. "I had to preorder it over a year ago and I finally got it about two months ago."

"*Diary of a Rich Kid.*"

He chuckles, the sound warm across my skin. "Maybe, but you're the first girl I've had in here. What do you think?"

"I think that you're wasting it on the wrong girl. I'm far from impressed."

"That tells me I'm wasting it on the right girl. The ones who swoon over a car are the ones to stay away from. Come on, Little Bird. I know you like fast, hot, sexy rides. Tell me what you think."

He turns up the heat, pointing the vents straight at me. A welcome blast of warm air hits me and I hold out my hands, trying to capture more of it. He hits another button, and my ass starts to warm up too. Still, I don't think I've been this wet, cold, and miserable in a long time.

"It's..." The coolest, sexiest car I've ever been in. "Something," I go with instead.

He smirks, catching my eye as he runs his thumb across his bottom lip before licking it. Jerk. He knows how sexy I find his mouth. "It most definitely is something."

"We're getting all this expensive leather wet. Aren't you worried we'll ruin your precious new car?"

"I'd ruin every inch of this car if it meant I had you wet."

I grunt, folding my arms. "I said no talking. And definitely no innuendo. Especially in that low, seductive voice you like to use. And no calling me Little Bird. That's off-limits."

"You'll always be my little bird, so I will have to respectfully ignore your demand. And my voice is my voice and if it seduces you, again I'll have to respectfully decline stopping. But you started talking to me first, so it's too late now. Besides, you're my captive unless you plan to jump out of a moving car onto the street."

I purse my lips, twisting to glance out the window, and he laughs.

"I'm contemplating it."

"I know. But do me a favor and stick it out. I'd hate to have to jump out of the car after you and save your life tonight."

His hand meets my thigh and I pinch the skin over his knuckle as hard as I can until he jerks his hand away, shaking it out and returning it to the wheel. "Devious woman, that hurt."

"Then you shouldn't have touched. Be thankful I didn't punch your dick. Lucky for you, you're driving."

"But it would mean you'd be touching my dick."

"Christ, Luca. Just. Stop. Talking!"

Mercifully, he falls quiet for a few moments as we stop at the light on Huntington between the Prudential and Copley. My face goes back to the window, watching as people rush in and out of the mall, trying to avoid the rain.

"If I could turn back time—"

"Who are you? Cher?" I interrupt, my head whipping back around to glare at him. "I don't care, and I don't want to hear it."

"Fine. No Cher. How about this then? I'm sorry, Raven."

I shake my head, twisting and staring hard out the passenger window like it will save me from the man beside me. "I don't care."

"Yes, you do. You care a lot and I know that apology is long overdue."

It is. Long freaking overdue and so useless it's almost laughable. What good does I'm sorry do for me now? But the legit question is, why *do* I still care?

Why can't there be an off button or a fuck-you switch when you need to cut someone permanently out of your head and heart? Maybe we hold on to pain like this as a form of learning from our past mistakes, but in truth, there should be a statute of limitations on that sort of punishment. I paid the fine and served the time and now I deserve to be done with it.

I've learned the hard way that I can be both strong and vulnerable. That it's okay to be both. But right now, I need to be the former and not the latter.

"What are you sorry for?" I ask because I have to know. I need to hear him say the words or I'll never be free of him. I knot my fingers together on my lap, squeezing them as hard as I can to stop their trembling. Same thing I'm doing by clamping my teeth down on my bottom lip.

The car starts to move again, heading deeper into downtown Boston and taking me toward the South End. "For ending it the way I did. For taking the cowardly way out when I should have manned up and talked to you more about it. I tried, Raven. I swear to Christ I tried, but you wouldn't listen. But maybe I didn't do enough."

Manned up. Meaning he's not sorry he ended it. Just sorry for the way he did it.

I blow out a silent breath, my chest clenching so tight, I have to press a palm to it to alleviate the pressure. It hurts. Everything inside does and at this point, it shouldn't. Four years. I should be long since over it by now.

My mind is appalled I'm reacting this way while my heart is flipping it off, demanding it let us grieve.

But I did grieve.

I mourned and ached and rioted longer than I should have. Until I told myself I was done with it. With him. That I *had* to move on. Then the bastard shows up tonight and it's like starting from day one all over again.

Yet, hearing him admit this... it's the slap to the face I needed. For too long I had been ridiculously clinging to nonsense. The flowers. The randomly showing up all over the world at my performances. I couldn't help my toxic thoughts. The ones that hoped maybe he regretted ending it. Maybe he missed me and ached for me the way I missed and ached for him.

But no. That was his guilt for hurting me and nothing else.

So dumb. So young. So naive.

"Thank you for the apology," I tell him once I'm able to speak without my voice betraying me.

"But you don't forgive me," he muses, a slight quirk to his lips.

"Nope. Not even a bit. But you said it and it's done, and I heard you. Now you can stop with the flowers and the randomly showing up."

The car slows as we approach the restaurant. "That's not why I was doing those things. And not sorry to tell you, but I don't plan to stop."

I growl. "I have no idea what I ever saw in you. You're aggravating as hell."

He chuckles, the sound unfortunately dragging a small, reluctant smile to my lips.

"Wanna have hate sex with me then? Work out some of this aggravation you have? The back seat may appear small for a man my size, but I have no doubt we can make it work. Or... you know... go on a real date with me? The kind where I take you out and show you off and hold your hand and stare into your eyes and beg you to let me have a second date."

"The kind you have with your other girls?"

"Raven, they're not my girls. None of them are because none of them are you. Most of the ones you hear about online are bullshit and I never make it past their front door. I go home with them to get them there safely, but I never ever seal the deal."

"Uh-huh."

He audibly sighs, his hand back on my thigh forcing my

gaze over to his as he stares intently into my eyes. "I tried. I tried like hell for four years to let you go. Nothing worked. Nothing was you. You showed me sunshine when all I could see was the clouds."

"The sun was always there, Luca. It was just hidden from you behind those clouds."

"No, Raven. It wasn't always there. I only saw it after I saw you."

12

I dropped Raven off at the restaurant, watching her walk away without even looking back. Her makeup was running down her face and her hair was soaked; her black dress clinging to her body. Even in that state, she's the most beautiful thing I have ever seen.

Still.

The fire in her heart isn't out. That's something. How does she not see that nobody feels the way I do about her? She was the one who saved me. Gave my life purpose. Redirected my darkness. In ways she doesn't even know about. In ways I haven't been able to share with her yet. The plans I have...

She has no idea how we got here, and clearly, I'm doing a piss-poor job of explaining it the right way. She says stuff and I react. That's how I've always been, especially with her, but I need to somehow find a way to control that.

I don't want to rehash our past. I don't want a do-over. I want a fresh start.

Everything between us was four years ago, and we were different people living different lives who came together at the wrong time.

The only thing that hasn't changed is the way I feel about her.

My car hits I-95 North and I take off, needing to clear my head with a fast ride, not even giving a shit that I'm still soaked as I weave in and out of cars. I could go out and see Landon. I could go and find my other brothers, Oliver, Carter, or even Kaplan since Kap is the only single bastard left of us. Not even our baby sister Rina is single anymore and I would have sworn to Jesus she was in it to win the single life.

But that hasn't been me despite what the tabloids still love to print.

I worked my ass off in college and medical school and then in my residency because I had a goal. I hadn't been jilted in love or sworn off relationships. I just didn't have time and screwing around without strings fit my lifestyle better.

Until one night.

One night when my life was falling apart around me, and I saw *her*.

After that, there was no going back and there isn't now. I have to remind myself of that. I ruined her. In the worst possible way. I did that, knowing the potential outcome.

I let my bird fly.

Now it's time to catch her again.

My car purrs, racing along highways and between cars until I grow bored and end up somehow at Rina's. A spot outside her door in Beacon Hill feels like an invitation and I park only to knock on her door seconds later.

Her boyfriend, Brecken, answers, his eyes all over me before he steps back and waves me in. He gets it. He met Rina in a bar, and they had a night. Then four years later, they met again, and he had to fight heaven and hell to win my sister, who stopped believing in love when love showed her its violent, ugly side. Over a year together now and here they are.

"They're early! I haven't finished getting everything ready

yet." Rina comes flying down the stairs, her blond hair dancing behind her. She stops short when she spots me, surprise flittering across her features. "Hey," she says, her gaze catching on Brecken before bouncing back to me. She takes me in for a minute and then without me even having to say a word, she finds my arm and drags me into a hug. "Ewwww, you're soaking wet. Gross."

"Sorry. I ended up fighting with a raven-haired beauty in the rain."

"We're going tomorrow," Brecken announces once Rina lets me go. He ushers me into the kitchen. "For the Sunday Matinee. How was the show?"

"She's brilliant."

"And the rest of the performers?"

"Didn't hear them."

Rina grins but hides it in her wineglass. "Uh-huh. And what brings you here now?"

"A change of clothes, naturally."

Brecken groans, his head falling back. "Fine, I'll go grab you something dry to wear. But it won't be my best digs."

Brecken runs off, taking the stairs two at a time and I turn back to Rina, who is studying me carefully. "What? Don't look at me like that. I like her, okay?"

She snorts. "Like her? Yeah. You like her all right. But you need to stop *stalking* her."

I tilt my head. "Different and you know it."

Rina takes a sip of her wine, holding her glass up in the air as she considers this. "Only because you're my brother do I know it."

"Really? That's the *only* reason you know I'd never physically hurt her?"

She stares into her glass. Blows out a breath. "No. I know you're not that guy. Sorry. She's my friend and I keep her secrets close, but it's no secret she was hoping to avoid this with you."

"Sucks to be her then. She should just give in now and save both of us the fighting and drama."

"Here. Go change." Brecken tosses me some clothes and I head into the powder room, grateful to be getting out of my suit that's not only ruined but has been sticking to my ass for the last couple hours. I put on the pair of jeans and the dark-green Henley he gave me, grateful that Breck is about the same size as me.

When I exit, I find them holding each other, Rina smiling up at him as they stare deeply into each other's eyes. A spasm twists up my chest. Both the good and the bad kind. "Can I be best man at your wedding?"

Brecken exhales, stepping back and dropping his elbows on the stone counter. "Um. No. That would be Wes and that's nonnegotiable even if I am marrying into a family of brothers."

"We're not getting married. We haven't even been living together a year."

"I'm giving you a month, Rina. Then it's Vegas or here or anywhere, but my ring will be on your finger." He twists back to me. "So yeah, you can't be best man, but you can be a groomsman and shit. I'll need someone to write the prescription for the sedatives I'll be forced to give her."

"You're not drugging me, asshole."

"Fuck," he hisses, the color draining from his face.

Running his hand through his hair, he grabs her, dragging her into his chest, holding her as tight as he can. Rina was drugged once. By an ex who did unspeakable things to her after he kidnapped her.

"You know that's not what I meant," he whispers into her, his lips planted in her hair. "I just want to marry you and you won't marry me unless I take drastic measures. That's all."

She growls but kisses his chest before going back to her wine.

"He's right," I tell her. "You know we would have killed him six ways to Sunday by now if we thought he wasn't perfect for you. You should just pussy up and marry him."

"Pussy up?" she chokes on her sip of wine, her eyebrows at her hairline.

"Vagina up? Pull up your big girl panties? I don't know how it works for women and telling you to grow some balls doesn't quite fit. However, talking about that part of your anatomy is making me nauseous. But truly, marry the guy already. Put him and the rest of us—who have to continually hear about him wanting to marry you—out of our misery."

This time I get a huff and an eye roll from her.

"Enough. I'm waiting on the girls to come over and if I don't drink this glass now before the pregnant trio otherwise known as Halle, Grace, and Aria get here, they'll take the bottle from me and club me to death with it since they can't have any. Margot and Amelia are my only saving grace with this, and Amelia made the awful suggestion of us not drinking since the others can't. Incidentally, I had also invited Elle, but she and Landon have both Stella and Layla tonight, and Raven, but she said she had other plans." A pointed eyebrow flies my way.

"I heard Raven talking to her dicklicker, the way too touchy-feely conductor about some sort of reception tonight. Twat's lucky I didn't break his hands. It'd be sad to see his career end that way."

"No kidding. But for real, you men need to leave. The pregnancy invasion will be here any minute and I need to get my drink on first." She polishes off her glass and pours herself another.

Grace is pregnant with my middle brother Carter's kid. They work together as OB-GYNs and she's also best friends with my baby brother Oliver, who is fake engaged to Amelia, though he's itching to make it the real deal. Layla is Amelia's little sister, and she lives with Amelia and Oliver. Trying to keep it all straight is a fucking migraine if ever there was one.

Halle, Aria, and Margot are Rina's friends, but have now been taken into the family fold since Margot works with Grace, and all the women are great friends. Evidently, they're trying to indoctrinate Raven now that she's back in town.

I flip my baby sister off before standing up, rounding the island, and kissing her head. Then I turn to her man. "You interested in getting a drink? I don't want to go home yet."

"I was planning to anyway. Carter, Oliver, Drew, Jonah, and Wes are meeting me at the bar around the corner." Drew, Jonah, and Wes are the husbands and fiancés of Margot, Halle, and Aria respectively.

"What? And I wasn't invited or is this like some sort of significant other bondingfest? Landon, I already knew, was home with the tweens and his ladylove. But where's baby face killer tonight?"

"You were going to the symphony tonight as I recall," Brecken states. "And no, to answer your question, toddler-faced Kaplan isn't coming."

"He doesn't look that young."

Brecken and I stare incredulously at Rina.

"Baby, he does," Brecken counters as he grabs his coat from the closet by the front door, throwing it on. Mine is so wet, I don't think it'll ever dry. "You'd think if your face looked like you were twenty-five instead of thirty-five, you'd grow a beard or something."

"And hide that chiseled-from-stone jawline? Pfft. Have you met, Kap? But still, I'm hurt. The symphony ended like two hours ago. Now you're going out with my brothers and friends?"

"Don't be such a little bitch. You're here now, so balance in the force is restored."

I smack my soon-to-be brother-in-law on the back. "You're misquoting. The line is, 'You were supposed to bring balance to the force, not leave it in darkness!' And it doesn't quite work in this scenario, but I appreciate the effort. Let's go."

Just then the front door flies open. "I'm here!" Margot cries out, her dark-brown curls flying everywhere. "Pour me all the wine. The others are on their way and I'm going to need alcohol if I'm to make it through a night with three pregnant women talking baby showers and deliveries." She frowns when she spots Brecken and me. "Wait, I thought this was a dickless night. How am I supposed to complain about Drew pushing me down the aisle if men are here?"

"These two clowns were just leaving," Rina exclaims. "Here. I already poured you a glass and the food is on its way. Help me set out the candy I bought because Carter is all over Grace every time she tries to sneak anything. Have fun, you two." She gives Brecken a long kiss before she shoves him in the direction of the door. I offer Margot a wave and kiss my sister on the forehead, then Brecken and I leave, heading out into the dark, wet night. Thankfully, the rain stopped about an hour ago.

"Did you ever think this would be us?" Brecken muses as we turn up Congress Street. "Totally crazy in love with our women and still having to chase after them?"

I think about that for a second. "Honestly, no. At least you have Rina. My reunion with Raven tonight did not go according to plan."

Just then a hand hits my back and I startle for a second until I realize it's Carter and Oliver. "What did you think would happen?" Carter asks, his arm slung over my shoulder. "That she'd see you again and immediately forget the last four years while simultaneously falling into your arms and onto your dick?"

I shrug him off as we enter the dimly lit bar that's shockingly mostly empty. This place with its amazing food, Boston chic ambience, and good music is always packed no matter what night of the week we're here. And tonight's Saturday.

We greet Jonah, Wes, and Drew, who are already here, and take seats at the bar.

"Kind of, yeah," I answer Carter. "I knew she was hurt, and I knew she liked to pretend I didn't exist, but I just never..." I never thought she actually *hated* me the way she claims.

"You hurt her."

"Thanks for the reminder, Oli. The ability to speak does not make you intelligent."

"Stop quoting Star Wars like a loser and let me talk."

"Brecken started it," I throw back at him.

"And now you're back to being petulant," Brecken drawls.

"Whatever," Oliver growls, slapping his hand on the bar in frustration. "What I meant was you hurt her. But it's more than that. She was in love with you. Ready to flip her entire world upside down for you. You became her dream and then you broke that—"

"For her own good," I snap, interrupting him.

Oliver smirks at me, shaking his head as he holds up a consolatory hand. "I know that. But does she?"

How can she not is my automatic response, but I'm thinking I'm wrong about that. Tonight she did not behave or react in a way that suggests she does know. Maybe I was too presumptuous in assuming she'd eventually see through what I did that night. I thought she knew me and that once she got over the initial sting, she'd read it for what it was.

Oliver's right, though. Raven was ready to flip her world upside down for me. She was ready to give up on London and The Conservatory to move to Minnesota with me while I finished out my neurosurgery residency. I couldn't let her do that. I couldn't. She was eighteen and so talented and I wasn't going to let her ruin her life before eventually growing to resent me.

But she wouldn't listen. She just wouldn't fucking listen, so I had to take extreme measures to get her to. And this is how it turned out. With her hating me and wanting nothing to do with me when all I want is her. I knew that night I'd have to fight heaven and hell to win her back so, bring on the chips and popcorn and settle in. The show's about to begin.

"I did that with Aria," Wes comments, snapping me out of my thoughts. He squeezes the back of his neck. "I was crazy for her when we were in high school, but then I left, and my life fell apart and I didn't... I didn't come back for her when I should have. I did everything wrong."

"So how did you win her back?" I press when he lets that sentence hang to check his pager, ever the trauma surgeon.

He shrugs, giving me a "duh" look. "I fought for her, man. I was persistent and honest, and I talked more than I think I've ever talked in my life until I made her not just listen but hear me."

Huh. Yeah, I think I need to work on that.

The bartender comes over and we place our drink orders. "Why is the place so empty tonight?" Drew asks as we glance around.

"See them?" The bartender points to the back of the room where there's a partially sectioned-off private space. "Private event and they rented out the whole place. Have a bar and food set up back there too."

"Oh," Jonah remarks with a chuckle. "Does that mean we're not supposed to be here?"

"Brecken and his guests are always welcome."

The bartender fist pumps Brecken and then goes about making our drinks.

"He's the owner," Brecken informs us when all our curious gazes fall on him. "He was having a little bit of financial trouble and I helped him get his investments in order and his business back on track."

Brecken is an investment banker. A brilliant one at that and has taken over a lot of my investments as well as my brothers'. Jonah, too, is a billionaire doctor and judging by the nod he's giving Brecken, he's doing the same.

We start talking Bruins hockey—Brecken is a psycho fan with season tickets—and Patriots football because we're fucking New England sports fans and that's what we do, when something catches my eye. Or more like someone. That Antonio guy. I'd swear it's him talking to a couple of other men in the back.

My bourbon is set down in front of me and I take a sip, still staring at him. I only saw him in the dark when he was talking to Raven and didn't pay much attention to him when he was on stage. But...

"Hey." I stop the bartender before he can go back there. "What's the private party?"

"Musicians from the Boston Symphony. They had a special charity performance tonight or something and they're glad-handing some big donors."

A smirk springs to my lips for all of two seconds. Then it dies in place as I catch sight of Raven talking to Antonio, him standing close. Too close. And unfortunately, Raven has changed her outfit since I saw her only a few short hours ago. Now she's wearing a sparkly silver cocktail dress that is impossibly short and tight. Not to mention a solid two sizes too small, especially across her tits that are practically spilling out of the deep V-neck.

And this dickhead isn't missing that for a second.

Her hair and makeup are fixed too, eyes smoky and rimmed in kohl. I wonder if she ran all the way back out to the compound to change or if she went to a friend's place to clean up. As with every time I see her, my heart starts to pound and my stomach clenches. But this is more than just the visual of her. It's this motherfucker ogling my girl when she looks like a fucking goddess and is dressed like a stripper.

My hand tightens around my glass as I bring it up to my lips, downing the rest of my drink in one swallow.

"What's wrong?" Carter asks. "What are you staring at? Wait," he says, squinting. "Is that... oh fuck, it is."

"Seems fate believes I deserve a second chance tonight after all." I set my glass down and swivel in my chair.

"Who's the twatwaffle she's talking to?" Brecken demands.

"Her conductor."

"He's gotta be in his forties," Oliver jumps in.

"Easily," Carter agrees. "And is all over her. So how are we playing this? Distraction, subterfuge, or gangbusters?"

"We're all doctors here except Breck," Drew deadpans. "Easy enough to kill a guy. What we're really lacking is a lawyer in our crew."

"Yeah. Where's Josh when you need him?" Wes laughs. "Is he with the women tonight?"

Josh is Aria's gay best friend and a lawyer, so there you go. Problem solved.

"Looks like killing him won't be an issue then," I grit out sardonically.

Raven laughs at something he says, and he touches her back, drawing her closer, and I see fucking red everywhere. It's like the room has been doused in blood, so potent I can taste it on my tongue. Heat crawls up my spine and no. No motherfucking way am I letting this go down. Not this guy. Not any guy.

No one will have Raven other than me.

And I'm about to make damn sure of it.

13

Antonio's breath smells like he swallowed a dumpster for dinner only to chase it down with a vat of stale beer. It's all I can do to keep smiling and not throw up all over his stupidly expensive Italian leather shoes. It's a good thing I've been pounding tequila like she's my best friend and totally gets me.

After the night I've already had, I think she damn well does!

First, there was the Luca incident. That alone is like a tsunami of feels that would lead anyone to hitting the bottle. Then I got to the restaurant, went to the bathroom, and turned on the hand dryer in there, pulling my dress right up against it since I was soaked.

Did you know that polyester is fucking flammable?

Yeah, my dress actually started smoking and had a few sparks that burned holes into it. I managed to wash my face, finger brush my hair, and make it out of the bathroom to have dinner with my dad, Dr., and Mrs. Fritz, all the while ignoring their questioning, troubled glances.

And just when I was finally drying my drowned rat body

out, my Uber pulled up, hitting a massive puddle, and dousing me in muddy, disgusting, street rainwater. I found myself at Catarina's and threw myself on her mercy. That's how I ended up walking into this bar looking like a version between a Vegas showgirl and a call girl. And before you go asking, yes, there is a difference between the two. I'm freaking glitz and glam and over-the-top sex.

Hence the tequila.

And me trying to ignore Antonio's slightly too friendly hands. And that breath!

"That's when I told the Queen that she may run England, but I run how the symphony is conducted."

I laugh, only because not only is he lying through his overly whitened teeth—he's never met or had a conversation with the Queen before—but how is he not aware that the Queen of England doesn't actually run the country?

"Right." I need another drink.

"Would you like to go somewhere else? You look a little bored with the crowd."

No. Just bored with you. "I'm not ready to leave yet. I think I'll go grab another quick drink and use the ladies' room."

"Oh. Would you like me to join you?"

That's where I pause, staring up into his mocha Frappuccino eyes. I nearly ask him which one he's referring to, the drink or the bathroom, but decide a resolute, "No, thanks," is easier to manage.

His hand has been hovering on the spot above my ass all night and no matter how much wiggling or attempting to go off and find other people to talk to, I haven't been successful in shaking him. He's followed me all three times I've done that. It's creepy and annoying and if it were any other guy, he'd be nursing sore junk and possibly a broken nose by this point.

But I can't exactly tell Antonio to fuck off. A pity, but

welcome to being a woman, right? We get harassed and since I don't want to lose my brand-new job or make a huge stink that will end up with me getting fired—the board loves him and calls him Maestro—I've been pounding shots and grimace-smiling through it.

"Are you sure, mia bella? I am happy to keep you company."

"When she's peeing?" Quill smarts and thank God... Quill. "I don't think so, Antonio. Let the girl go use the ladies' room in peace."

"Besides," Catarina chimes in, coming in on my other side. "Viktor Popov just arrived and is looking for you."

I have no idea who Viktor Popov is, but whoever he is, Antonio's entire put out disposition drastically changes as does his posture. He rights his spine and immediately tells me, "I'll find you after, Raven," before scurrying off.

I sag, my relief a pulse through my body. "Thank you. Thank you both. Wet cat food mixed with dog shit is more palatable than his breath."

Quill snorts. "He smokes like a chimney and alternates between espresso and sweet wine. Bad breath is inevitable with that."

"Bad breath is putting a kind spin on what he had going on."

"Better you than me. But I'd run while you can. He has a thing for hot, fresh meat and you fit into both categories."

"So I've gathered. One more shot. One pee break. Then I'm taking an Uber home and sleeping until I can't anymore."

"Alone?" Quill jabs, though the sparkle in her eyes tells me she's clearly fishing. Someone obviously hasn't let the flower incident go.

"Alone. But that was a nice try." I'm not looking for strings or insanity or mess. Having experienced enough of the latter and knowing Antonio is all three, I'm all set.

"But you haven't seen the *insanely* hot crew of men at the bar," she emphasizes. "Come on. Let's go hit on them and see if we can get you laid tonight."

My eyebrows scrunch, already doubting her. "I thought we rented out the place." I glance over her shoulder but only see the back of their heads. Truth, I don't even know why I'm bothering to look. I'm not interested in a hookup, even if that might just be the ticket to a little mental sanity. Men who are looking to play with my heart and toy with my emotions? Not so much.

Ugh! I try. I try so hard not to put Luca's face or his words into everything with every other guy, but they always seem to find their way there. I never should have come back.

"Go out there and have your shot. I mean it. You'll thank us later. If we weren't with a woman and a man already, you'd have wingwomen." Catarina winks at me and I nearly roll my eyes, but still manage to smile gratefully.

These two have had my back since my first day here.

I wasn't able to think about another guy for a solid two years after I left Martha's Vineyard. I threw myself into my music. Into all the music I could learn. And then once the stage fright started and it became more than I was able to handle, I decided to turn the psych classes I'd taken at a local university into a second degree.

It wasn't until I hooked up with my professor in one of those psych classes that things started turning around for me. I turned my heartache—the crippling betrayal that had been sitting in my gut like a poisonous weight—into hatred and bitterness. He was also the least available man on the planet— married into a polyamorous relationship.

He wanted sex and I wanted to forget. Worked perfectly while it lasted.

After him, I had a few one-night stands, seeking more fun and escape.

But it was never all that it was cracked up to be. None of it was. How do you go from having amazing, mind-blowing, dirty sex with a man you love and trust to random, awkward, and kinda boring sex with a stranger?

I didn't date anyone. Not seriously anyway. Luca Fritz had ruined me in so many ways.

For all four years, I was in London and then again on the plane ride home, I swore to myself I was done with him. That my life should be about pleasure. Fun. Experience. Not the man who gave me all those things only to rip them away from me.

That was my promise, especially when Luca's face is splashed all over every tabloid in the world—even in England —with a different woman on his arm each and every time.

Bastard had no trouble moving on despite the bullshit he tried to spin with me tonight.

I kiss Quill's cheek and then Catarina's. "I'm going to have this dress cleaned and then return it to you."

Catarina frowns. "I told you to keep it. Molly hates it when I wear stuff like this now."

I shake my head. "This dress is so not me. But thank you for letting me borrow it. And for grabbing my purse and coat from the back room for me. I'll see you tomorrow morning for the show." We have a Sunday matinee that I'm seriously not looking forward to. But one more shot will put me snuggly to sleep once I get my ass all the way back out to the compound.

I need to move. I need to move closer to the city. I don't have a car and I can't exactly afford one either. As much as I thrive on being close to my father and Octavia, I can still go see them often, even if I'm living in the city.

On higher than high sparkly heels, I sneak out of the back room and out to the main bar. I head quickly for the bathroom, do my thing, and then as I'm leaving, order my Uber to take me home—for almost forty dollars, I might add. Yeah, I definitely need a place in the city. Not even two steps out of the bathroom and I'm shoved back inside it with enough force to rip a startled gasp from my lungs and cause my heart to explode in my chest. The door slams shut, locking with a resounding click before I can even comprehend how it happened.

"What the—" I stagger back another step. Locking onto a pair of fathomless green eyes. "Are you following me?"

Luca gives an impatient grunt. "You're around the corner from Rina's. This is our usual bar."

Of course it is. Why would I be in any other bar in this city? The universe is a total bitch like that and clearly has it out for me. I swear off one man for the rest of my life and he's thrown in my path twice in one night.

"We need to talk," he says urgently. "Can we go somewhere and do that? I have things I need to tell you."

"I don't want to talk anymore and I'm not in the mood to fight either. Just go and leave me alone. I need to get back out there."

I shift and Luca follows my movements, his expression telling me I'm not getting away that easily now that he's got me where he wants me. He takes a hard step forward, his eyes loaded with darkness. With desire. With rage. That last one seems to creep back up, eclipsing the other two, almost as an afterthought and a remembrance of why he stalked me in here in the first place.

"You feel this too. I know you do. You can't hide from that. What the hell were you doing letting that man touch you?"

"Watching me, were you?" I taunt, tilting my head and smirking because no one ever said I don't know how to be a bitch when provoked.

"Answer me, Raven."

I stomp my foot down, the heel hitting the floor hard,

vibrating through me. I'm so done with this. With him. "Why should I? I owe you no explanations."

"The fuck you don't! You're mine." His fist slams into the tile wall and I jolt back.

"I am not yours," I seethe, choking on my breath. "And we're not doing this again. You're wrong, Luca. I feel nothing for you."

He smirks arrogantly, advancing a step. "That's why your tits are practically spilling out of your dress with every uneven breath you're taking, right? So unaffected," he mocks. "I bet if I wrapped my hand around your neck, I'd feel your pulse racing against me. What does the sight of me do to you, Little Bird?"

"Other than make me homicidal?" I'm light headed as I suck in ragged breaths. Hating how out of sync my limbs feel. I don't like the way my body innately responds to him. "I mean it. I'm done arguing with you. I just want to go home."

"This isn't an argument, honey. This is foreplay."

"Shut up and go, Luca."

He ignores me. "You looked bored and miserable with him. Yet, the second you see me, your face is flushed and your body reeks of desire." Another step and I barrel back into the wall of the small bathroom, watching like a doe in headlights as this predator advances on me. "Show them to me."

"W-what?"

"Your panties. Show me your panties, Little Bird. Take them off and if they're not wet, I'll leave you alone."

Goddamn him.

I shoot off the wall, trying to race around him. Only this time he's onto me. He catches my hand, simultaneously stopping my exit while dragging my palm to his mouth and kissing it before sucking a finger into his mouth. I stifle my whimper and what am I doing? I'm letting him touch me? Caress me with his tongue and lips and eyes? No!

"Show. Me. Your. Panties." Each word is staccato, wrapped around a lick or a kiss.

He thinks he's winning. And I can't let that happen. I may be affected, but he's the desperate one. The one chasing. "You want my panties? You can have them. Doesn't mean you're getting what's beneath them and it doesn't mean you're the cause of anything you think you find. You were four years ago. Barely memorable by this point. You're the only one holding on here, *honey*."

Yanking my hand from his, I do a cute little shimmy, dragging the tiny scrap of a dress up even higher. Right to the point where my pussy is barely covered. His green eyes are the deepest of jade and darkest of midnight as I reach up beneath the dress and slip my panties down my hips and legs.

I step out of one leg, practically sweating as he licks his lips and inhales deeply, and when the silk snags on my other ankle, I kick them up to him, forcing him to catch them as I saunter past him, out the bathroom door and back toward the bar.

"Suck on those, asshole. It's the closest you'll get to my clit."

My glimmer of satisfaction quickly dies when I check my phone and discover my Uber is more than five minutes out. So much for my grand escape. I could go back to my friends, to the party in the back room, but that feels more like defeat and five minutes is enough time to enhance my buzz and drink away this night.

That is until I come to a screeching halt, too many sets of eyes trained right on me, and I know what I must look like. Luca's brothers, except for Kaplan and Landon, and his friends are all sitting at the far end of the bar. All staring at me. In my hooker dress I'm now rocking without panties. Embarrassment floods my face and I offer a stupid wave.

It's not the first time I've seen his brothers since I've been home these few weeks and even before that when I'd come home to visit. It was only Luca I've been avoiding. But right now, this feels like a walk of shame, and I don't want an audience for that.

Carter goes to stand and my hand flies up, stopping him in his tracks. "Not tonight, okay? Just stay where you are." If they hug me, I'll crumble. I'm barely hanging on as it is. "Your brother's an asshole I never wanted to see again." They're all smiling at me, amused, and I don't even know who I am or what I'm saying anymore. I just want to go home and go to bed and forget this night.

"We know, Raven," Oliver calls out, waving back at me. "Good to see you again, though. Amelia was sad you couldn't make it to Rina's tonight."

Sigh. I wish I had. Then I wouldn't have seen Luca again. Then I'd still be wearing underwear.

"You're still on for whatever you have planned with Rina, right?" That's Brecken. And now I feel even more miserable than I did two seconds ago.

"Grace misses you. Said she was going to call you this week. Hasn't stopped talking about it." That's Carter.

"Yep. Can't wait to see them either." Kill me now. I throw the guys another wave and turn slightly so I'm not facing them anymore. The bartender approaches me and thank the Lord for people who serve alcohol. "Two shots of Patron, charged to the man exiting the ladies' room," I tell him, but the words don't get far. I mean, he hears them, but they don't linger in the air, and I don't have time to watch him pour me two shots because a dark shadow looms heavily in my periphery just as the words escape.

And much like earlier tonight, I don't have to look.

I *smell* him.

I *feel* him.

"You got what you wanted. My panties. Now shoo, fly. Shoo." I swat him away as I would a bug.

"These are just a tasty appetizer." His fist clutching my black panties lands down on the bar between us, his fingers rhythmically running along the material before he tucks them into his pocket. "An amuse-bouche. I happen to know the main course is the only thing that can satisfy me." It's in this moment the bartender looks up, straight at Luca, clearly having over-heard him. "I'll have three fingers of whatever I've been drink-ing. She'll have the same. The three fingers that is, but that's for me to handle. Not you."

I groan, shaking my head at the bartender, who looks as though he doesn't know what to do. All I want is to collapse against the bar. And order both of those two shots to be doubles instead of singles. And crawl under the covers of my bed and never come out again.

"Did you really just say that? God, you're such a—"

"Dick?" Luca smirks, cocking an eyebrow, his voice light, playful. "Read your mind on that one, right? We can use that too if you prefer."

An unrestrained laugh bursts from my lungs and Luca grins at me as if that was his master plan all along. To get me to relax. To get me to laugh and smile with him. And his smile. That twinkle in his eyes. The way it makes my insides feel.

It disarms me in ways I don't want to be disarmed with him. Not anymore. Not again.

"Asshole is what I was going for since I'm thinking that's my new favorite pet name for you." But I'm still laughing. It's all I've got left. Because at this point, I'm just drained. He's turning me into that crazy girl again. The one who somehow remem-bers the man I spent two inseparable months with.

"Glad I can still make you smile. I wasn't sure I'd ever get the chance to see that pretty thing on your face again."

My smile instantly slips, his quickly following.

"Are you going back to him?" He juts his chin toward the back room where I was earlier.

I don't look even though I'm mildly curious if Antonio is somehow there, watching this unfold. I doubt he cares. He's an "if I can't fuck her, I'll fuck someone else" type of guy. The bartender blinks warily at me as he pours my chilled—I should have mentioned I don't like them chilled—shots of tequila into two small glasses.

"Is that why you ordered two?"

I sigh. Then I lift one of those glasses and down the clear liquid like a champion alcoholic. No lime or salt because who has time for that?

I meet Luca's gaze. "Nope. They're both for me. You can keep your three fingers to yourself. I'm not interested." Then I grasp my other glass and drink that one down too, trying not to grimace at the harsh alcohol as it slides down my throat. I set it down and wipe my mouth with the back of my hand. "Thanks for the drinks and the panty raid. I'm off to bed now."

Luca is unfazed and just how disappointing is that? "We need to talk, Raven."

"We're done talking. There is nothing left to say."

"There's everything to say." He snarls. "Let me give you a ride. That way I can make sure you get home safe."

I turn into him, staring up into his eyes that try their best to breach all my defenses. I grin evilly. "If I wanted a ride, I'd fuck Antonio or one of the bartenders or waiters here. I'm more than capable of getting myself home and off without any assistance. Not the first time I've left you in a bar and taken another ride home."

His expression turns murderous, his fist balling up as it lands on the bar between us. But it doesn't stay there long. In one swift motion, it lands on my lower back, his other hand in my hair as he drags me impossibly close, his face right in mine. And let me tell you, his breath? Yeah, nothing like Antonio's. Luca is nothing if not sweet and enticing. Alpha and sexy.

He lets you fall for the ruse. Gives you the illusion of being captivated.

Only to rip the rug right out from beneath your feet.

He opens his mouth to say something that will likely rip me

apart further when my phone pings on the bar beside me. "That's my guy." I reach up and kiss the corner of his mouth. "Hope to see you never ever again, Luca Fritz."

I grab my phone and get the hell out of here. Slipping into the back seat of the car and trying to catch my breath. My body shaking. Dammit! The man has my panties. And I let him keep them.

14

All day I've been out of sorts. Lost in thoughts of last night. Wishing I had done just about a million things differently for about the millionth time in the last four years. But her panties stay in my pocket, even now. And yeah, I'm sick enough that I jerked off with them over my face last night and again this morning. I even licked them a time or twenty too.

Because no amount of jerking off will sate this hunger.

Will quiet this beating rage.

I want to talk, tell her absolutely everything, and yet every time I'm near her, my baser instincts kick in and I'm reduced to a horny teenager who can't control the blood flow to his dick. I've always been like that with her. A man incapable of learning limits or restraint.

It's how I know she's the one.

Because I want to fuck her from dusk till dawn and then spend the day in bed with her talking, only to repeat it all over again.

"Are you secretly a sea monster?" Layla calls out to me as

I'm walking past the library at my parents' compound, pulling me out of my thoughts.

An amused smile quirks up my lips as I peek my head into the room, finding her and my niece Stella sprawled out on the floor, about a dozen books between them.

"Is this a legit question?"

Her feet scissor back and forth in the air. "The guy I quasi like in a totally casual way, so if you mention it to Oliver or Amelia, I'll cut you up into such tiny pieces they'll never be able to find you texted me last night that there is a movie called Luca. It's about a sea monster who lives in Italy. I happen to know you own a home on the Italian coast."

"Oliver owns half of it too."

The blond wisp who is getting bigger by the day, waves me away. "He doesn't have the right name and I've seen him swim in our pool. Not a sea monster."

I step into the room, resting my shoulder against the door-frame and folding my arms across my chest. "If I'm a sea monster, does that make Landon one, too, since he's my twin?"

Layla glances over her shoulder at her BFF Stella. "Is your father a sea monster?"

Stella rolls her eyes. "Are we actually doing this as a serious conversation?"

Layla thinks on this for about ten seconds and then completely switches gears the way teenagers are apt to do. She rolls onto her back and butterflies her arms behind her head, staring up at the ceiling. "Whatever. When I grow up, I want to be Raven Fairchild. I mean, how cool is her name? She's named after her hair color *and* a bird? And for real, she's totally awesome at cello. I mean, if I can be half as bomb at surgery as she is at cello, I'm like set for life."

My pulse quickens. "How do you know Raven?"

"She was here earlier, hanging out with Aunt Rina, Amelia, and Grandma," Stella replies.

"Yeah. What she said. Octavia had her play for us too. I'm obsessed."

That makes two of us, kid.

"Totally," Stella agrees as she thumbs through pages of what is likely a first edition book without reading it. "She used to play for me when she'd babysit for me. Dad told me once that a particular lullaby she'd play me was one of the only things that would put me to sleep."

"Maybe I should have her make me a playlist. I can't fall asleep to save my life. How come she's so close with your aunt and grandma if she works for your family?"

"She's sorta my... cousin by extension, I guess? Like you." Stella shrugs, then tilts her head at Layla. "You're living with my uncle Oliver because your sister is fake engaged to him, but now it's kind of real since they're in love, so that makes you like my cousin, right? Raven is sort of the same since her dad works for my grandparents and is like a brother to my grandpa. She used to babysit me a lot when I was little before she left for college or whatever you call music conservatories. Anyway, I have a lot of extended family who isn't actually my family at all."

"Your life is complicated. Being Stella Fritz is no joke. How cool would it be if I was an awesome surgeon one day like your grandpa and we're cousins? For real cousins."

"You know, Layla, I'm a pretty awesome surgeon too. I operate on brains, on both adults and children. It doesn't get much cooler than that."

Layla snorts. "But your name is *Luca*." She scrunches her nose. "How uncool of a name is that? And Raven is like so pretty. I think I want to be her or Grace when I grow up since Grace is an OB-GYN and a surgeon. Maybe Amelia too because she's pretty awesomesauce. Even if she is my sister." She points at me. "But if you tell her I said that, again with the cutting you up into tiny pieces."

I can't help my smile as I watch and listen to these two. Rina was never like this when she was a teenager. Then again, she had five older brothers to try and keep up with. She didn't have a Layla the way Stella does.

"I want to be a chef and run my own restaurant, serving food I grow, so I'm not sure I want to be anyone but myself."

"Well said, Stella Bella."

"That's such a grown-up response." Stella rolls her eyes at me. "I already know it's awesome to love who I am, Uncle Luca."

All I can do is shake my head, folding my arms over my chest, but then I pause. "Wait. Why is my name uncool?"

"Hello, ten minutes ago." Layla scoffs, picking up one of the books and swirling her finger along the filigree etched into the leather binding. "And it's because no one is named *Luca*."

"You just told me there is a movie with a character named Luca."

"He's Italian."

I'm at a loss.

"If you weren't hot and a Fritz, no one would think you're cool."

"Ouch." I clutch my chest. "You wound me. I'm insanely cool."

Layla starts cracking up, giving me a look that says gotcha, and I think the kid was messing with me. This entire time. Devious little thing that she is, I should have known better.

"Ewww!" Stella makes a gagging sound as she pretends to throw up all over thousands of dollars' worth of rare books. "You think my uncle Luca is hot? Gross! That's like saying you think my dad is hot."

"Your dad *is* hot."

Stella shrieks, covering her ears and flailing on the floor as Layla laughs manically.

Before this can get out of hand, I interrupt. "Where are your people?"

"In the solarium, I think," Stella informs me, still pretending to throw up in disgust. "That's where they were when Raven played for us, and Grandma mentioned something about cocktails out there."

My insides jump. "Is Raven still here?"

"She went back to the staff house right before you got here."

But she is here. On the property. And it's... I check my watch and grin. "It's only a little after five."

"So?" Layla questions with the snarky tone of a teenager.

Right. Stella and Layla don't care that it's only a little after five. But I do because we won't be eating until at least six. "I'll see you ladies at dinner."

With purpose in my stride, I sneak through the main house, avoiding the solarium and the sound of voices I hear coming from that part of the house.

"Why do you look like a cat burglar sneaking through the house?"

"Shit!" I jump ten feet in the air, knocking into a sculpture of a naked woman that I quickly fumble with—and catch, thank God!—because if this crashes to the floor, two things will happen. One, my mother will freaking kill me. Two, I'll miss my chance to sneak out and see Raven before dinner. "Goddamn it." I set the sculpture back in its place, by her tits might I add, and then glare at the smirking blonde before me. "Gracie Lou Freebush, you scared the Jesus out of me."

Grace, my brother Oliver's lifelong best friend and now... well, I guess Carter's baby mama, only grins wider, holding what is likely a ginger ale in her hand. "I can see that. And I can't decide if I should stop you or not. Raven is a friend, you know."

"You didn't see me. How about that?"

"Hmmm... what do I get out of it?"

"I'll stop calling you Gracie Lou Freebush?"

"You won't."

She's right. I won't. "I won't offer to birth your child the way everyone else is."

"Like I'd let you anyway."

"I'll send you a secret supply of gummy worms without telling Carter."

A sparkle hits her blue eyes. The woman loves anything gummy, and being pregnant, Carter is having her cut out junk. "Now you're talking. Fine. Go and win her back. I can see you're a man on a mission. But be good to her, Luca."

"I plan to be very good to her." I bounce my eyebrows suggestively.

"Stop being the playboy." She points a stern, motherly finger at me. "This is my only warning. As a woman who has been jilted in love, don't do this with her unless you mean it."

I walk over to my adorable one-day-to-be sister-in-law and kiss her cheek. "Promise. My playboy days are long over despite what the media says about me."

"I know that and you're lucky I do. I know that. I never saw you and I'll distract the masses with disgusting pregnancy stuff. Good luck. I'm betting she kicks you in the nuts and sends you packing." Grace starts laughing at her own horrible musings as she walks back in the direction of the solarium at the back of the house.

What happened between Raven and me is not a secret. My entire family knows as well as her dad because I told him. He flew me back to Minnesota after he returned from dropping Raven off in London, and he and I talked the entire flight. Oddly, he didn't blame me the way everyone else did and I think it's likely because either he never wanted his daughter to end up with me or he understood and appreciated what I was up to when I ended it with her. He never would say.

He didn't kill me, so I took that as a win.

Raven left the main house, likely because she knew I was coming for family dinner the way we try to do every Sunday night. Especially since my mom was diagnosed with recurrent breast cancer and has been undergoing treatment.

And if I were a better man, I'd respect the fact that she doesn't want to see me and leave her alone. But I think at this point, it's pretty damn obvious I'm not a better man. She thinks she hates me. And maybe part of her does for what I did to her.

I deserve it.

I was an asshole. Worse than that. I watched her heart break before my eyes, and I kept going. In fact, I dug the knife in deeper. I didn't have a choice. But other than hurting her and going four years without her, I don't regret what I did.

She was so young and so in love and terminally blind to the reality of us.

I was not going to ruin her life. I was not going to kill her dream.

Even if it meant I had to kill us.

But it was temporary. In my mind, in my heart, I knew she was it for me and I knew I'd find my way back to her. When the time was right.

In all the years I lived in my parents' home, I've only been in the staff house one other time. And both times revolve around Raven.

It's quiet and dark as I enter the large home. Sophia, our head chef, is preparing Sunday dinner for my entire family and her husband, Carlos, is likely in the stables looking after my mother's fleet of horses. We have a driver, Travis, who is singing horribly off-key to some country song—no doubt driving Raven mad. Our head groundskeeper and last, Morgan Fairchild, Raven's father, lives here, as do a floating pool of security and gardeners, depending on need.

Taking the stairs two at a time, I slink past door after door, all the way down to the end. The building is a series of apartments and single rooms and I already know Raven is occupying one of the single rooms because Morgan is now in one of the one-bedroom apartments. But Morgan has never been one to stay still or stay quiet. I'm counting on him not being in the house since there is no light from beneath his door and I don't hear him moving in what I know to be his place.

Thank goodness for that since Raven's room is directly across the hall. She was eight or so when I carried her up here, soaking wet, shivering, and scared out of both our minds. She'd nearly drowned in our pool, and I found her just in time.

I saved her life that day and years later, I stole her innocence like an unrepentant thief. Now I'm here to win back her heart because it's only ever been her.

When I near her door, I pad silently, creeping along until I touch the plank of wood that separates us. A sliver of light shines from the gap between the door and the floor, and I know she's in there.

"Are you trying to hide from me?"

Something hard hits the floor from within and then the air falls still once more.

"Is that why you fled back here instead of staying? Did you think you were safe from me, Little Bird? That I wouldn't come for you?"

I test the door and to my surprise, it's unlocked. A fatal mistake or calculatingly intentional, I don't care. She's standing against the window facing me, her hair wet from a recent shower and tangled on top of her head in a messy bun. She's barely wearing anything. So similar to how I found her in the garage that night. It won't take much for me to bare her fully to me.

Entering her room, I kick the door shut behind me, lock it, and plant my feet.

"You have no business being back here. Get out."

She's breathing heavily, angry as a bull at a rodeo, and I like this Raven. The one who knows exactly how to handle me and isn't afraid to do so. Her eyes breathe fire and mine do the same, ready to tear this room and this woman apart. I was a wounded predator when I crashed at her feet, and she was the innocent blackbird who had never been touched. But now we're playing on an even field.

I'm no longer wounded and she's no longer innocent.

"What if I don't?" I take a step. Then another. Closer in this small room that doesn't have much to it. A tiny bed with a dark purple comforter, a small white dresser, a large mirror on the wall, and a couple posters of dudes with cellos who I don't recognize. "Are you going to make me?"

"You think I won't?"

"No. I think you want me to touch you. Desperately."

Her body flushes against the pale linen she's hardly wearing, and my cock thickens in my jeans. Her fists ball up at her sides and I know she's trying to fight this. Trying to fight it and failing, judging by how blown out her pupils are. I came out here to talk, but with her dressed like this, with this crackling energy swirling like gasoline waiting on the flick of the match, there is no way that's happening now.

I haven't been with anyone in four years. Her. It's only been her and I'm dying.

"The last thing I want is you to touch me. It's over between us. Now get out!"

"Oh no, Little Bird. We're just getting started."

Retreating another step back, she presses into the window behind her, her chin defiantly raised, eyes narrowing into hateful slits, but it's too late. I'm right here. Right in front of her, so close I can smell her skin and feel her heat.

"You're such an arrogant bastard. Thinking every woman who looks at you wants you."

"And yet I only care about one."

"Liar. This is all about you wanting what you can no longer have."

My hand hits the bare skin of her hip and a jolt of wild, unbridled longing shoots through me. This girl. I'm starving for her. The primal need to erase every trace of any other man who came before this moment consumes me.

I tighten my grip. "You, Raven Fairchild, are all I've wanted for four years."

She laughs bitterly. "You're photographed with women practically every night. Luca Abbot-Fritz, billionaire playboy."

"That's the media. Not reality. I haven't been with anywhere close to the number of women they claim. Now, are you going to be a good girl and let me touch you? Let me drop to my knees and eat your sweet pussy? Fuck you so hard and so good you feel my cock throbbing inside you for days after?"

Please, dear God, say yes. For four years I've been a hungry, unsated beast.

Her "half-mast, hotter than the blazes of hell, I want to kill you and fuck you" expression is only egging me on. Angry Raven is insanely hot.

Splaying my fingers across her hip, I drag my hand down along the outside of her thigh and with my eyes still locked on hers, I move lower, inward. She's had plenty of time to push me off and I see the internal war she's waging splashed across her face. She wants to push me away, but she wants my touch more.

Sliding beneath the short hem of her shorts, I find the lacy edge of her panties and groan. "Fuck. You're wet." So wet, my dick pulses and I groan again as I pull them to the side and touch her bare, soft lips.

Long fingers cinch the tiny crotch of her panties, balling it up in my fist, and in one sharp motion, I rip them. The fabric tears away and she gasps, rattling the windowpane as she falls against it. The panties find their way to my pocket—apparently, I'm starting a collection—and then my hand is back, up her inner thigh, running my finger through her drenched seam to her opening.

I slide one finger inside her, stepping in close so I can press my hard cock into her, and dip down, staring straight into her eyes. I pump my finger in and out so slowly, it's little more than a tease. She whimpers, sinking her teeth into her bottom lip to try and stop her reaction to me.

But it's no use.

Shaking, fury dancing harshly in her expression, but still, she's not fighting me and she's not telling me to stop.

I lick along her jaw, up to her lips where I place a kiss, and whisper against her, "Tell me you want it and I'll make you come so hard, you'll see stars."

Her hand dives into the back of my hair, gripping me roughly by the roots. "You better be as good at this as I remember, asshole." Then she crashes her lips to mine, and I absolutely die, having reached heaven. Her lips are as perfect as I remember them being. Cupid's bows that were made for mine slide roughly against me before she dives her tongue into my mouth.

I bite her lower lip, letting her know she's not going to be the one controlling this. That's all me, sweetheart, and that's not changing despite the years of groveling I'll have to do to win her back. Our tongues thrash violently, her hands ripping at my shirt, balling it up in her small fists as I press her back against the glass.

She shivers and I pull out of her, painting her lips with her arousal that she greedily licks up. Such a good girl. I reward her for that by finding her large breasts under her tiny shirt—no bra—and squeezing them hard.

"Fuck," she hisses as my thumbs coast back and forth over her nipples, rolling them, my eyes fixed on her as I do. She thrusts into my palms, wanting more, needing it harder because her breasts, especially the undersides and her nipples, are sensitive as fuck.

My lips find hers again, tasting her sweet pussy on her, and I grind against her hip, driving my cock into her. Showing her exactly what she does to me. The sort of power she wields over me.

Only her. Forever her.

Her hands cover mine over her breasts, demanding I give her more, and I growl, tightening my fingers on her nipples, aching to see them. So I do. I drop down to my knees, slide her top up, and bite the underside of her breast. Hoping I mark it, so she remembers who these belong to. My large hands squeeze and lift, pressing her tits together, and I lick the seam of her cleavage. I've missed these so much.

These perfect fucking tits.

I suck one nipple into my mouth. Then the other. Loving how rosy and hard they are.

"Raven. My sweet, delicious Little Bird." My hands drift, lowering her shorts to the floor, and I take a deep inhale, still nipping and sucking on her gorgeous tits. She emits a loud moan as I slip a finger back in. "No one else has touched you like this. Made you feel this good. Known exactly what you need and how to give it to you."

"Stop talking, Luca."

I grin into her, and she shoves me down farther, right into her dripping pussy. Throwing her leg up and over my shoulder, I angle her back and lick her seam, tasting her arousal. Reacquainting myself with her body. My tongue plunges up, diving in as deep as I can go.

"No one will ever taste you here again. This pussy is *mine*."

"Not even close."

"Here. I'll prove it." Sucking mercilessly on her clit, I look up, wanting her eyes. She rocks into me, her thigh locking around my head as I hit her just right. I flick her clit harder, thrusting two fingers inside her. Her back arches as she lets out a shuddered moan, her hand tearing at my hair. But dammit, I need to see her as I pleasure her. "Look at me, Raven."

"No."

Goddamn her.

"I said *look* at me."

She shakes her head, pinching her eyes closed, and I remove my fingers and lips. Her hand rips violently at my hair, trying to force me back into her, but I resist, watching as she breathes harshly. Until finally, in an act of pure frustration and need, her eyes spring open and she drops her chin, her expression thunderous. So beautiful, my breath quakes in my chest.

"You're such an asshole. Stop staring at me like that and just eat me out. And for Christ's sake, stop with all the demands and talking."

"Beg me to make you come."

She pushes me back into her. "Make me come or I'll never let you touch me again."

Fuck, I love this woman. God, how I've missed her.

"Say please."

"Now."

I pull back and blow cool air on her wet heat, causing her back to arch and her eyes to flutter closed once more.

"Say it."

"Please. Now."

Close enough.

Pushing two fingers back into her, I start to fuck her with them. Not stopping. Not slowing down. I crook them at the perfect angle and hit her spot with each thrust. All the while my lips and tongue feast on her. Licking at her wetness, playing with her clit, teasing and flicking and sucking with the right amount of pressure. Getting her close and then backing her down again. Watching as she moans and whimpers and writhes against me. Against the glass. Her hands in my hair.

"Filthy girl, you love it when I tease you."

"Shut. Up!"

"Shhh…" I vibrate into her. "You're going to get us caught and then neither one of us will come."

"Oh God, yes. Don't stop."

I pump harder, my hand soaked in her, her taste edging me closer, my cock leaking in my jeans, needing to be inside her. With my eyes on her face, I suck her clit into my mouth one last time, massaging her inside spot, and she detonates against me with a garbled scream she's desperately trying to stifle. Her pussy gushes all over me and I lick it up, getting every last drop I can before sucking her off my fingers.

She sags against the glass, panting heavily, smiling softly. I fall back on my haunches, feeling smug and satisfied even if I didn't get off yet myself.

"That was exactly what I needed."

I start to stand. "Happy I could—the fuck?!"

Before I know what the hell is happening, she kicks my feet out from beneath me, tightens her hold in my hair, and drags me toward her door. It's all I can do to try and get up, so she doesn't rip out my hair, my feet scrambling beneath me. My scalp is screaming as I try in vain to free my hair from her ninja grip.

"What the hell are you doing?"

"Shhhh…" she mocks. "You're going to get us caught. Though I already came." She throws me a wink just as she tosses my ass out into the dark hall. Freakishly strong woman, I forgot all that she's physically capable of. "Thanks for the orgasm, Luca. And for the closure I never got four years ago. Have a great rest of your life. Enjoy your blue balls."

And then the wicked siren of a woman slams the door in

my face. Locking it behind her. How in the hell did that just happen? And why am I smiling? My little bird just kicked my ass and despite what she says, I already know I'll be coming back for more.

15

What the hell did I just allow to happen? Staring at the locked door, I listen for Luca, hoping he'll just go. Slink away, never to return. Men like Luca are all arrogance. All obnoxiously sexy ego.

I have to imagine getting tossed out on his ass is a new one for him and that has me biting back a smile. Even if my insides are tumbling around like a dryer.

Some movement on the other side and then a thud on my door. His fist? His forehead? I have no clue. But my heart—the horrid traitor—leaps in my chest. Despite all that, I truly, genuinely hate the man. How it's possible to want someone and hate them at the same time is beyond me, but there you have it.

He doesn't say anything as his footsteps echo in the hall and my absurd disappointment has me staggering into the door. My forehead and palms slump against it as my eyes shut. God, my heart hurts so much right now. The bastard stole my panties and I let him. Again.

Dammit, how do I still not have any self-control with him? I need to make it so I never see him again.

"I seriously need to move out."

"You're planning to move out? To where?"

I yelp, startling back a step. "I heard you walk away."

"I did and then I came back. I was debating attempting to talk to you through the door. You know, since you can't kick my ass through wood."

"Go away," I practically beg. "Please, Luca. If you ever cared for me as you claim you did, just leave me alone."

His voice softens. "I can't, baby. I have so much to explain to you."

I shake my head. "I don't want to hear it." And truly, I don't. Maybe that's childish of me, but I like to think of it more as self-preservation. I can't do this with him. I can't go through it again. I barely survived round one and already round two is throwing me into a tailspin. I'm anxious and edgy and not myself. I'm having trouble sleeping. I freaking tossed and turned all night, thoughts of him consuming and borderline obsessive.

I don't want to be that Raven again.

The one he made love him, only to ruin and leave.

"Raven—"

"I mean it, Luca. I have nothing to say to you. I don't know what you're trying to do with me, and I don't care. I want no part of it. No part of you."

I hear him suck in a rush of air and I know that hurt him. I can practically feel his torment seep through the door, and it stabs at me. I'm not trying to hurt him. Not really anyway. This isn't out of spite. I'm not after a sick form of vengeance.

I just need him to stop.

He clears his throat. "I own a building in Boston. Actually, I own a couple, but this one was an old hotel that I had reno-vated into apartments. It's nice. Very nice and as fate would have it, I was notified the other day that a tenant moved out."

"I can't afford nice and most definitely not very nice. And likely not in Boston either."

"You can. It's small. A one-bedroom with no view."

I shake my head, falling back against the door and pounding my fist against the wood. "I still can't—"

"You can, Raven. Whatever your budget is, you can afford this place. It's furnished too. Did I mention that? It's furnished, so you won't have to buy furniture. Oh, and it includes utilities."

Luca. Dammit. "How do you know all this? Don't you have a management company or something running this for you?" For every apartment I've looked at, those are the people I've dealt with. Rarely the owner. And this is Luca Abbot-Fritz we're talking about. He probably has a management company for his management company.

A warm chuckle vibrates the door and I know he's right there on the other side. Pressed against the wood, the same as I am. "Yes. I do. But I know about this because the manager of the building told me we should have pictures taken of the unit so we can rent it out. But now I don't have to do that since you're moving in."

"Where is it?"

"Close to the green line, so you can hop right on the T to get to Symphony Hall. It's also only a ten-dollar Uber from there."

I should say no. I *need* to say no. This is Luca we're talking about and living in his building isn't smart for me. But I also know it's my best option if I do want to move out. I've been casually looking online and unless I want roommates or to live in a crappier than crap neighborhood and apartment, I can't afford anything my father won't pitch a fit about.

My eyes clench as I begrudgingly mumble, "When can I see it?"

I can practically hear the smile in his voice as he says, "How about later in the week? Uh. Thursday or Friday? That should give us enough time to have it cleaned and ready for viewing."

"Thursday. This Friday I have rehearsals all day."

"Thursday at five-thirty. I'll text you the address."

"You don't have my number."

He laughs. "You have very little faith in my stalking abilities."

I ignore that. "I want to meet with the management company. Not you. Have *them* text me the address."

"Sure. Whatever you say."

Now I'm smiling, my palms flat on the door. "You can go now."

"Good night, my beautiful Little Bird."

I don't respond, but I don't have to. I can hear him walking away and I blow out a sigh. Of relief or something else, I'm not analyzing it. Pushing off the door, I pick up my shorts from the floor, but instead of putting on new panties, I slip them back on, going commando only to catch my reflection in the glass of the window.

Swollen lips. Hair in total disarray. Skin flushed. I lift my tank top and discover two hickeys, one on the bottom side of each breast. Hickeys? That son of a bitch knew what he was doing marking me up.

Lowering my shirt, I slink back across my room and fall onto my bed. I had a plan when I took the position with the symphony. Maybe a mindset is a better way to think of it.

I wasn't going to let him in. Let him play me or with me.

I wasn't going to be hurt or relive past memories or even demand an explanation.

But in the few encounters I've already had with him, I've done both. I let him play with me and I relived our past. Well, some of it.

I have to remind myself that this is Luca Fritz and he's not a normal man. He has no clue what no sounds like. He's been indulged his entire life and I'll be damned if I give him what he wants now. I'm not his toy. I am not his plaything. Not anymore and never again. The man does this. Goes through women. Dates them for a week or two or three and once they fall in love, he's gone, onto the next.

I gave him my heart and he used it like a soccer ball.

Toying with it before kicking it away.

With any luck, after tonight I won't have to see him again. Even if I move into that building he owns, it's not like I'll see him there. I can visit Octavia when he's not around. I mean, the man is a neurosurgeon. He works crazy long hours, and other than Sundays, he doesn't come here often. So… easy to work around.

That orgasm was my closure and I refuse to feel cheap or guilty about taking what I wanted. I'm a strong, independent woman. A world-renowned cellist. I decide my path—no one else.

Puffing out a breath, I remove the elastic from my damp hair and run my fingers through the strands, trying to work out the knots, when there's a knock on my door. I bolt upright, my hair flying every which way as I glare at the hunk of wood.

"Go away, Luca. You'll have to play with your own dick if you want to get off tonight. Or better yet, go find someone else who will do it for you."

"Is that why you flashed your boobs out the window?"

My eyes turn into giant saucers at the voice. A voice that does not belong to Luca.

Crap.

Stumbling out of bed, I fling the door open and turn a thousand shades of red. "You saw my boobs?" Oops. Well, that's… awkward. And slightly embarrassing.

"Well, you were holding your shirt up with the blinds open," Kaplan explains with a small, impish grin. "If it helps, it took me a second to realize what I was seeing and once I did, I threw up in my mouth and looked away. I'm now officially scarred for life."

I snort out a self-deprecating laugh, rolling my eyes at both of us. Stepping back, I wave him in, watching as the tall, hulking man enters my room, taking it in the way Luca did, only completely different from how Luca did.

"That's a lie. I have fantastic tits."

He turns and grins. "You do, but they belong to my brother, and judging by the look of you and your lovely greeting to me, he had a taste of them just before I arrived. That and you're practically a teenager."

I glare at him, cocking an unamused eyebrow for both the teenager comment and for saying I belong to his brother. He laughs but groans, taking in my outfit, and then proceeds to shut his eyes tightly.

"You have to change. Now." He waves a blind hand in the direction of my dresser and closet. "You're nearly naked. I'll turn around."

He does just that and I head for my dresser, removing my pajamas and throwing on a bra, panties, a thermal black shirt, and the first pair of jeans my hands touch.

"I'm decent," I tell him as I run a brush through my hair. "Happy now?"

He gives me a quick once-over. "Much better. Now I can think without feeling like a pervert."

"You are a pervert."

"Not with you, I'm not." He gives me a wounded frown. "Retract your claws, kitten, I come in peace."

I set the brush down and cross the room, leaning my head on his arm since he's so damn tall I can't quite reach his shoulder. "I know and thank you. For everything. I still can't believe you're doing all this for me."

His hand meets the back of his head, making his inked biceps pop, straining against his shirt as a crooked smile curls up his handsomely boyish face. If he were any other man...

"What are big brothers for?"

"You're not my big brother."

"No. But I'm the closest thing to it and I take my role as protector seriously."

He does, which is something I still don't quite understand. Kaplan's never supplied a real explanation for all he does for me, but I'm grateful for it all the same. Four years ago, when Luca hurt me, Kaplan stepped in. But not in the way you'd think a man would. He called me relentlessly until I answered and then he listened for over an hour as I yelled and cried and cursed his ear off.

Then he called me the next day and the next and since then. He's become exactly as he said, a big brother type. A protector. A sounding board and a friend, I guess, though he's thirteen years older than me.

"I tried calling you earlier, but you didn't pick up. Did you get my email?"

"Sorry, I didn't have my phone with me when I went in to see your mom. And yes, I did get it. Thank you. I already replied and have an interview set up for next Wednesday morning."

"Perfect. Maybe we can have lunch after so I can hear how it all went. What about the other thing?"

"The person I spoke with told me it would likely be between Thanksgiving and Christmas sometime. I told her I could make anything work. I nearly peed my pants when she told me who she was."

Kaplan chuckles, playing with the chain of a necklace that's sitting on top of my dresser. "I told you she was going to call."

I sit back down on the edge of my bed, crossing my legs at the knee and leaning back on my hands. "It's one thing to know. It's another to experience. I'm nervous about that. The thing at the hospital I can handle, but this…"

"Relax. They'll love you. You have no reason to be nervous about anything." He crosses the room and drops a kiss on the top of my head. "I'm out of here. Time for dinner with the family. Wanna come?" He bounces his eyebrows up and down at me. Octavia and Dr. Fritz extended the same invitation to me, and I declined. Mainly because I didn't want to see Luca, but now I saw Luca and left him with an epic case of blue balls. I'd be lying if I said it didn't feel good.

I should say no.

I shouldn't agree to spend an evening sitting across a large table from him. Even if the idea of getting under his skin a bit is a temptation almost too good to deny.

It's playing with fire. A fire I shouldn't tempt or coax. A fire that—

"Come on." He grabs my arm, hauling me up and off the bed, dragging me toward the door. "It's one dinner. You'll sit beside me and ignore him. It'll drive him wild."

I laugh, trying to jerk out of his grip. "I'm not wearing shoes! Besides, I don't want to see him, Kaplan."

"Again, you mean. You don't want to see him *again*."

"Shut it." I shove him off me. "I'm not going. I need to take care of myself and seeing him is bad for my health."

"Fine. I get it. But I still say you should hear him out. He has a lot to tell you, Raven."

I flip him off and he holds up his hands in surrender.

"I'll let it go for now. Text me after your meeting is done next Wednesday and we'll try for lunch."

Kaplan leaves and I go back to my bed, falling on it once more with a defeated sag and an exhausted sigh. I could go to Kaplan for a place to live, but he's already done so much for me. Too much for me. I can't tack on yet another thing. I want to be independent. As much as I can be and well, Luca owes me.

Men.

Just freaking men.

Or more likely freaking Fritz men.

So far nothing is going according to plan with that. I need to get myself back on track. Before it's too late.

16

All day long, I've second-guessed this. From the moment I opened my eyes after a restless night of sleep and all through rehearsal this morning. I can't decide if I'm making a huge mistake or not. I haven't heard a peep from Luca since Sunday, so here's hoping he's gotten whatever lingering lust was stuck there out of his system, and he's moved on.

But that's not what has me standing in front of the address the management person gave me, staring up at a large, stunning building on the edge of the park, laughing like a lunatic. Of course he owns this building. I should have known it when he said it was an old hotel. Not just any hotel. It was Boston's premier luxury hotel and now it's apartments overlooking the Boston Public Garden and The Common.

Before I can talk myself out of this, I approach the double doors that are instantly opened by a uniformed doorman. "Good evening," he greets me. "Are you here visiting someone?"

"No. I'm here to meet with Simon Pastor. I have an appointment to see one of the apartments."

A smile lights up his face. "You must be Miss Fairchild. Yes, we're expecting you. I'm Ross, one of the evening doormen. Please, follow me."

Oh hell. I do not belong in a place like this. I'm wearing leather pants, purple Doc Martens combat boots, and a black one-shoulder sweater. The perfectly coiffed, gorgeous woman walking past me through the opulent marble lobby is wearing designers. She throws me a curious look and I straighten my spine, giving her a smile back.

Then I do a double take. She looks strangely familiar to me, though I can't place where from.

"This is the main lobby," the doorman explains, calling my attention back to the space around me. "There is a concierge here during the day and on-call overnight. A doorman like myself is always here twenty-four-seven. The gym and spa are through there." He points to a closed door in the far corner where the woman just entered. "We have two trainers on staff, as well as a masseuse, and per the request of some of the residents, we're bringing on a part-time aesthetic nurse practitioner who will work out of the spa."

"I'm sorry. A what?"

Ross throws me a smirk. "A licensed healthcare provider who can perform facial injections and treatments."

"Oh."

He chuckles at my expression. "I'm guessing that's not something you're into? You certainly look young, though."

"That's because I am, Ross. I'm only twenty-two." We step onto the elevator, and he punches in a code. "And currently wondering what the hell I'm doing here."

"That I can't answer for you, but I will say, you're not our youngest resident, if that makes you feel better. Every floor has its own code, so you can give it to anyone who is visiting you. That way we don't have people wandering up to different floors. Many of the residents like and value their privacy."

"Right."

"Dr. Fritz spoke very highly of you when he called to inform us you'd be coming to look at 6-8-5."

I can only nod at that. But something isn't quite adding up for me. The way he's been talking about the residents and the building and the amenities. "Ross, this place isn't your typical apartment building. Do the people here own or rent?"

He clears his throat and shifts his weight, his gaze now locked on the numbers at the top of the elevator as we ascend. For a moment, it seems as though he's not going to answer me, but then just as the car starts to slow, he clears his throat again and says, "They own, ma'am."

"Thought so."

Dammit, Luca. What are you doing?

"I should go," I tell him just as the doors part and he waves for me to exit ahead of him.

"Dr. Fritz was adamant that you should see the unit even if you discovered this detail first."

"Of course he was." I fold my arms over my chest, shaking my head, my face dropping toward the gray carpet. I feel foolish. How could I not have thought this was how it would be? What was I thinking not looking into this sooner? Then again, I was only texted the address this afternoon and I have to imagine that was very intentional.

Ross places his hand on my shoulder, attempting to catch my eye. "Mr. Pierce is already in the unit. He's been there helping to get it set up all day. Just go see it. No harm in that, right?"

"Setting it up?"

His expression turns sheepish, clearly dropping more secrets than he was supposed to. Fantastic.

"All right. Let's get this over with." No way in hell I'm taking this "apartment", but I don't want to get Ross in trouble either. Sucking in a deep breath, I step out into the brightly lit hallway and follow Ross down all the way to the end of the floor.

A door opens and two burly men, drenched in sweat, exit, heading past us for the elevator. That's when I see the placard on the open door: 685. Ross presses the doorbell and immediately an older man with silver hair and dark eyes is there.

"Mr. Pierce, this is Miss Raven Fairchild."

"Oh, perfect timing." He extends his hand to me, smiling and seeming a bit relieved if I'm reading him correctly. "It's nice to meet you in person, Miss Fairchild. Please come in and have a look around."

"It was a pleasure meeting you, Miss Fairchild." Ross tips his head and leaves, shutting the door behind him before I can even respond. Or correct them for calling me Miss Fairchild. I'm too busy staring around the apartment. Or condo. Or whatever this place is.

Cool twilight filters through the two floor-to-ceiling windows that comprise the majority of one wall in the main room. It's open concept, with a kitchen off to the left divided from the eating area and family room by a large rectangular island of smooth white and gray stone. The appliances are stainless steel and top of the line, complete with a wine refrigerator and six-burner gas range above an oven and a half.

Luca wasn't lying when he said it was fully furnished, but it was clearly just done so now. It smells of brand-new leather and fabric, the upholstery stiff and not broken in. My fingers glide along the soft white linen of the sofa adorned with deep purple and black plush throw pillows. There's a fuzzy one sitting on the dark leather chair that looks like it's the most comfortable thing in the world and could swallow me whole. The coffee table is rustic, the accessories cool and modern without being cold or uninviting. The artwork is stunning, all black and white framed photographs of instruments and London architecture. There's even a large, mounted television.

The bastard decorated this place for me. Bought all of this for me.

A rush of something warm and unexpected crashes over me like a tidal wave.

"As you can see, everything is top of the line. There's a large closet in the front hall, as well as another that acts as a pantry," Mr. Pierce says and I nearly jump out of my boots, having almost forgotten he was here. "The bedroom and bathroom are this way."

In a daze, I follow him as he crosses the family room directly into the bathroom that has a marble double vanity, a large glass shower, and a bathtub I could easily go swimming in. He opens another door and now we're in the bedroom. It's not huge, but it's plenty large enough with a low-profile king-sized bed, a dark wood dresser with a mirror over it, and two nightstands.

The place looks like a Restoration Hardware showroom.

He shows me the walk-in closet, and I snicker under my breath at what I find in there.

A La Perla bag sitting on one of the empty shelves. Luca's replacing the panties he stole from me, even though mine were far from La Perla. It's a big bag and I'd bet there are more than just a couple of pairs of panties in there. I don't dare touch it, certainly not in front of Mr. Pierce.

"What do you think?"

What do I think? I honestly don't know what to think. What am I supposed to say or do with this? I'm overwhelmed. Stupidly emotional by this ridiculous gesture that is so insanely over-the-top, there is no bottom to it.

"It's beautiful," I go with that because it is. It's the perfect apartment. Every inch of it. And I have no doubt it likely sells for at least a million dollars despite it being on the smaller side.

We head back into the family room through a different door than we entered, and I gasp when I find Luca leaning against the open front door, watching me with an expression I can't read.

"Good evening, Dr. Fritz." Mr. Pierce quickly crosses the room and shakes Luca's hand. "I just finished showing her the unit."

Luca's eyes never waver from mine. "Thank you. I'll take over from here."

"Of course, sir. Have a good evening, ma'am."

Ma'am. Sir. Luca has to be at least half this guy's age. The door closes behind him with a soft click and now it's just the two of us, standing here, staring at each other in some twisted game of truth or dare. Me silently asking him what the hell he's doing. Him silently daring me to come at him.

"You're such an asshole," I start.

He smirks, rubbing a finger along his bottom lip. "Save it for someone who cares. You've called me asshole so many times this week, I half think it's a term of endearment."

"You bought me panties."

"And other things. Did you look in the bag?"

"Absolutely. Right in front of Mr. Pierce, who insisted I call him Daddy when I tried on each and every item for him."

His gaze darkens. "Christ, your mouth. It's a shame I can't tape it shut and fuck it at the same time. I'd watch what you say unless you want me to cut him up with my collection of scalpels and bone saws. What's in that bag is for my eyes and my eyes only."

"Agreed since I'll never open the bag."

He sighs. Fierce. Frustrated. Fucking delicious. His inability to remove his eyes from me coupled with the intensity radiating off him is enough to make me weak in the knees.

"What do you think of the place?"

"What do I think of the place?" I laugh the words. "I think you're fucking insane. Who does this, Luca?" My hands pan around the room. "Who lies to someone and tells them they have an apartment to rent in a building full of condos? Who has that apartment methodically furnished for their prospective tenant within days?"

"How do you know it wasn't already like this?"

"Not only did I see the movers leave, you picked purple and black pillows, knowing they're my favorite colors. There are pictures of cellos and pianos and fucking London on the walls." I pick up one of the purple throw pillows and hurl it at him. He catches it, tossing it back at me, hitting me square in the chest, and I let it fall to the floor. "Why did you do this?"

He swallows the distance between us by half. "Because I wasn't going to let you rent some eight-story walkup studio with cockroaches and brown water. Because I wasn't going to let you move to some shitty neighborhood where you'd have to take two buses and the fucking T to get to work."

"You have no idea where I was looking."

Another step and now he's right in front of me, hovering over me, tall and wickedly handsome. Angry as a god. "I know your budget and what apartments in the greater Boston area go for. I know you want to move out and when you get an idea in your head, very little holds you back from accomplishing it no matter the cost. I also spoke to your father about it, and he told me where you had been looking."

"You spoke to my father about this?"

He ignores that. "Take this place, Raven. It's in a nice building in a safe neighborhood that's not too far from work and you can afford it."

"I can't afford it. I can't even afford the pillow I threw at you."

"You can because it's already yours. All of it. Every stitch of furniture is yours. Every glass and plate and pot and pan in the cabinets too. Everything in here is yours, so whether you live here or somewhere else, this stuff is coming with you."

I stagger back a step, falling against the console table

behind the couch and causing a piece of decorative glass to sway. "Why? Why are you doing this?"

His hand dives into my hair, finding the back of my head and tilting my face up to meet his eyes. "Do you want my real answer? The reason why I've sent you flowers for four years and traveled all over the world to watch you perform and stalked your social media and stole your panties and got on my knees to touch and taste you? Do you want it? I'll tell you everything. It's killing me not to. I'm just not sure you're ready to hear it yet without thinking it's bullshit."

I shake my head, pushing him off me and heading for the window, staring out at the dark Boston sky, at the street below. No view of the park and thank God for that.

He's right. I'm not ready to hear whatever he has to say. And yes, I'd likely think whatever he was telling me was bullshit. A way to get laid or for me to forgive him so he's the good guy once again instead of the villain. The man who said one thing and did another. I don't trust him. Not with my head and not with my heart and not with my common sense.

"For four years I've fought to feel like myself again," I tell him. "I went to London instead of Minnesota. I studied and played music all over the world. Just as I said I'd always wanted. But that didn't stop me from searching out into those dark audiences, wondering if you were there somewhere. If that would be the night you'd deliver those fucking flowers to me in person. If somehow, you'd get on your knees to tell me you didn't mean it. That it was all a mistake. That you really did love me. That you really did want me. I hated myself and I hated you for those thoughts. For making me feel that I wasn't good enough to make you stay. To make you love me the way I loved you. And you sending those flowers and flying all over the world only made that so much worse."

I spin around, my fists balling up as I stare into his turbulent green eyes.

"I got my dream and I lost you. Fine. I knew it would happen with you. I was heartbroken, but I would have survived. I would have moved on. It wasn't the first time someone didn't choose me or love me enough to stay. But you didn't let go. You kept holding on just enough to drive me insane. To mess with my head and my heart that was desperate to forget you and move on. And so my dream didn't quite feel complete for far too long. I resented it. Resented my talent and with that, resented you even more. You didn't just break my heart, Luca. You found its most vulnerable, soft parts and beat them to death, and then you did it over and over again."

He swallows hard, his voice hoarse. "Raven—"

I shake my head, cutting him off. "I'm happy I'm home. I missed my dad, and I missed your parents. Your siblings too. But I made myself stop missing you a long time ago. I forced myself to stop looking into the audience for you and I returned every damn flower you ever sent me. This past week has been a case of old habits die hard, but I wasn't lying when I thanked you the other night for giving me closure and I meant it when I said we're over. That's why I can't accept this place. It's tied to you."

Luca blows out a heavy breath as if he'd been holding it in this entire time. He runs a tremulous hand over his face and through his hair, stumbling back a step and spinning around in a circle as if he doesn't know what to do with himself now. I don't either. I just said words I never imagined I'd say. Words that terrify me with their finality, shaking me to my very core.

He stands immobile, his fractured gaze trained on me as he works through whatever it is he's working through in his head, and finally his hands meet his hips, resigned. "I fucked up so many things with you. Things I never even fathomed I was fucking up, I was. I'm sorry, Raven. I'm so terribly sorry. For all of it. I thought..." His voice catches before he clears his throat. "If you take this place, you are not tied to me in any way. It's yours. One hundred percent, it's yours with no strings. If you live here for six months to save up and then move somewhere else, that's your choice. But please, don't live somewhere awful when you can live here. You'll go through the management company, and I'll never step foot in this apartment again unless you ask me to."

"I never will."

He gives me the saddest smile. One that cracks and chips at my frozen heart. "A boy dreams so a man will always have hope." With one last look, he turns for the door, pausing only when his hand hits the knob, his back to me. "Everything I did was because I love you. Was because I had to. For both of us."

With that, he opens the door and the second he shuts it behind him, I fall to the floor, holding my breath as the tears I had been fighting are no longer able to be held back. I crawl across the floor, grabbing the pillow we had thrown at each other, and drag it to my chest, burying my face in it as I wail and sob out my grief. Wishing for the millionth time in the last four years that love and pain came with an expiration date.

Because then I wouldn't have to try so hard to live without him.

17

______

The door swings open and immediately I barge in, storming past a bemused Carter as I search around, seeking the main reason I'm here.

"Nice to see you too. What the hell are you doing here?"

"Looking for Gracie Lou Freebush."

"She's in the bath. What do you need?"

I don't answer as I barrel down the hall in the direction of the master bathroom.

"Hey, dickwad. I said she's in the bath. What do you think you're doing?" Carter runs after me, but I'm faster. A man on a mission who will not be deterred.

"Grace, cover up, honey. I'm coming in."

"What?" I hear her sputter, followed by the sound of water splashing about just as I enter the room. Carter hip checks me out of the way, rushing over to the tub Grace is relaxing in and readjusting her bubbles or some shit.

I fall onto a stool in the corner of the bathroom, as far away from the tub as I can, staring down at the floor. "I'm not here to look at your woman's tits," I growl at my brother before softening my voice. "No offense, Grace. I'm sure they're lovely, but I'm truly not interested."

Grace sits up a little more, a smirk on her lips. "I appreciate that, but why are you here?"

My elbows drop to my parted thighs, my head in my hands. "I need girl talk."

"Ah. Um. Okaaay. Well, I can get out of the tub."

"I don't want to ruin your bath. You can stay in there and I promise I won't look."

"Damn fucking straight, you won't look."

"Slow your alpha, little brother. I just said I'm not interested and I'm not going to look."

"Carter?" Rina's voice rings out through the apartment.

"In the master bathroom," I yell back, and Carter's brown eyes go comically wide. As do Grace's.

"Why is Rina here?" Carter grunts.

"I told you. Girl talk. Go grab us some candy or popcorn or whatever girls eat when they're doing this. Oh, ice cream, right? You ladies eat ice cream?"

Rina comes to a skidding halt when she enters the bathroom. "Ummm... yeah, you told me this was an emergency."

"It is. Clearly." I wave my hand around the room.

"This isn't really my kink."

I roll my eyes, glancing up at my baby sister. "I'd sure as hell hope not since you're related to nearly everyone in here."

"Grace?! What's the emergency?" Oliver also comes storming in here, only to freeze midstep when he discovers Grace in the bath. He spins around, covering his eyes. "What the fuck, Luca? You called Amelia and told her there was an emergency and she had to get to Grace's immediately. So we fucking came."

"Can everyone get out!" Carter snaps, his voice pure agitation. "My pregnant woman is in the bath."

"We can see that, Carter, but what's with the fucking emergency?"

"Okay. Everyone out," Grace demands. "I'm getting out of the tub and unless you want to see me naked, I suggest you all go wait for me in the great room. Oliver, go make yourself useful and get my food arsenal. We're talking everything. Popcorn, ice cream—that's for Luca—Oreos with crunchy peanut butter, fluff, and gummy worms. I've hidden those in the cabinet above the stove where I keep my prenatal vitamins so Carter wouldn't find them and throw them out."

"So wait." Oliver is still facing away from the bathroom, looking impossibly confused. "You're okay? You're fine?"

"Clearly," Amelia deadpans. "And I think I know what this is all about. Come on." She gives his arm a tug. "Let's go get supplies. I think we're going to need them."

"I'll help," I offer.

"I'm getting wine," Rina announces. "Sorry, Grace, but that's how I roll with girl talk. It's either that or shots and I have a shift tomorrow."

Grace waves her away and then makes a motion to shoo everyone else out. I follow after Rina as Carter helps Grace out of the tub and by the time we reach the living room, Landon and his girlfriend, Elle, are standing there, as perplexed as everyone else.

"I didn't invite you, boogers. Just your women. I've already whined and complained to you assholes enough and look at where I am now."

"Who pissed in your Cheerios?" Landon shoots back.

"I did, brother." I slap my twin's shoulder, my forehead falling onto it. "I pissed in my own damn Cheerios. At night, which isn't even breakfast time. And now I need all the female help I can garner. It's why I sent for the best. I didn't want to put you out with this again."

"Aww, I'm flattered you included me." Elle comes up and

pats my cheek, her hazel eyes sparkling. "This will be fun. I've never done girl talk with a guy before. We should start a club. Help teach men to become better men and learn to speak and understand women. They'll award us The Nobel Peace Prize."

Elle's a firecracker. A woman who managed to make my grumpy, miserable twin fall head over heels. She's perfect for the job. And Amelia, who didn't trust a whole lot and had it rough, is now endlessly in love with Oliver. The fake engagement ring—which is actually a family heirloom diamond—is still on her finger as a placeholder. Rina, who lived through a nightmare no woman ever should, is now very happy and in love with Brecken. And Grace's fiancé cheated on her and now she's happy and pregnant and living with Carter.

I need these women. They hold the key. The secret men know nothing about. We stumble and fumble and fuck shit up constantly. But with their help... maybe, just maybe I can win my woman back.

Raven's words broke my heart tonight.

I knew I hurt her in Martha's Vineyard. I knew I broke her heart. Hell, that was my intention. As much as it destroyed me to do that, I had no choice.

But I didn't know what my sending the flowers and flying in to see her perform was doing to her. Hell, I didn't even know she knew I did that. It wasn't that often. And I never went backstage to see her. I never spoke to her. I knew that would be too hard. For both of us, because it fucking would have been.

Sitting in those seats and watching her from afar was torture enough, but I told myself I was doing it for her. That I was saving her from more heartache when in reality, I was doing the opposite. She knew I was there. I don't know how, but she did.

"Okay," Oliver says, handing me a glass of bourbon because my brothers are good people and they're not leaving even though I'm snarly with them. "Sit. Tell us what's going on because I'll be honest, you gave me a heart attack. I thought something was up with Grace."

I give his shoulder a squeeze before I find a chair and drop into it. "I'm sorry about that. It's why I called Amelia and not you."

"Well, I was there when you were talking to her, so now you're stuck with me."

"And me." Landon takes the chair beside mine, grabbing Elle's tiny hips and pulling her onto his lap.

"Popcorn's ready." Rina shoves a huge bowl at me that I reflexively accept, popping a piece into my mouth before setting it down on the coffee table in favor of my drink. "Ice cream is a no-go because they only have fudge pops in their freezer." She crinkles her nose in disdain as she drops the bag of Oreos on the table. "Who eats fudge pops who isn't five?"

"I kinda ditto that sentiment," Amelia asserts, adding to the growing pile of junk food that's now sprawled out across the coffee table. "How do you not have at least a pint of Ben & Jerry's in your freezer?"

"Because I'm trying not to eat junk food," Grace declares, entering the room wearing her pajamas and heading straight for the buffet of sugar and carbs with a light in her eyes that resembles love and addiction. I know it well. "Carter won't let me buy half this stuff. It's why I have to hide it, but you can't hide stuff well in the freezer."

"I can't believe I didn't know you were hiding all this crap here."

Grace sits on the floor, scooting up until she's face height with it. Then she goes straight for the bag of gummy worms, rips it open, shoves one in her mouth, and gives Carter an unrepentant shrug and a deal with it grin.

"All right, now that you've turned my place into a food orgy, tell us what's going on."

Carter accepts a glass from Oliver, who has taken a bottle to the table and everyone's eyes fall on me, food and booze momentarily forgotten in their hands. Well, except for Grace, who seems to be multitasking.

I launch into an account of everything that happened this evening with my Little Bird and when I'm finished, no one says anything for the longest time. Rina gulps down her wine, pouring herself another glass. Elle holds out hers and Rina tops it off. Amelia and Oliver stare into each other's eyes, having some sort of silent conversation. Grace is lathering up an Oreo with crunchy peanut butter and fluff. Landon is staring at me the way Landon always does, trying to read more out of me than he thinks I'm sharing. Carter is glaring down into his glass like the thing will have all the answers I need.

"This isn't how I envisioned girl talk going," I admit, finishing off my own glass and letting Oliver pour me another two fingers. Seems I'm going to need it.

"She thinks you abandoned her because she wasn't enough?" Amelia picks up an Oreo, splitting it open and licking the cream. "Wow. That's just... I know what that feels like. I kinda want to go find her and do girl talk with her instead of you."

"Same," Grace garbles around whatever is in her mouth. "I had no clue she felt that way. She never mentioned anything to me about that. Did she with you, Rina?"

Rina shakes her head, tilting her glass back and forth while watching the burgundy-colored liquid move about her glass. "No. I knew she felt that way about her mom. She had mentioned to me once shortly after she died that she didn't understand why she wasn't enough to make her stay. That if she had been, maybe her mom would have still been alive."

"Motherfucker." I shoot out of my chair and pace around the room. Staring out the huge windows into the glowing Boston skyline and then back, practically collapsing onto my seat. My limbs restless, my muscles jittery. "That's not why I let her go. She's more than enough. She's everything. I did what I did for her…" I swallow hard. "She thinks I abandoned her and then played with her. No wonder she hates me so much."

"You're gonna have to fight. And even then, she's not going to give in," Rina declares, breaking what feels like a tense silence after my confession.

"Tell me how to do that because obviously everything I've done so far is wrong."

She exchanges glances with every other woman here and then shrugs.

"But you're here," I protest. "You're women. This is what you do. You problem solve and figure shit out and understand the delicately fine art of balancing feelings and emotions." Nothing. Frustrated, I fall back in my chair. "Come on. I'm desperate. I broke her heart. I know this. But… it's all that other stuff. Rina Bina, Gracie Lou Freebush, you've both known Raven all her life. Rina, you're closest to her. There has to be something I can do to fix this. To let her know I'm genuine with this. That I didn't understand all the ways I was hurting her."

"Patience," Elle suggests, tucking some of her long blond hair back behind her ears. "You're gonna have to be patient, Luca. She's been through a lot. And let me tell you, as someone who has been through a lot, it leaves scars. You can't charm her the way you charm everyone and everything else. She knows you too well and doesn't want that from you. You're going to have to show and not tell. She deserves that from you and more."

"Exactly." Grace points at Elle while vigorously nodding. "Figure out what she wants from you first—"

"Nothing. She wants nothing from me."

"Right now, she doesn't," Rina maintains, angling her wineglass at me while she makes her point. "She's mad. But more than that, she's scared. She fell for you, Luca, and you broke her heart. She doesn't want to try again, knowing you could potentially hurt her worse this time. Understandable, especially after everything she's already been through."

"Yes," Amelia jumps in, sitting up a little straighter, and now we're starting to get somewhere. "She's scared. I get her hurt, Luca. More than just what happened that night on the Vineyard. I mean, that was pretty terrible. You had a pretend wedding where you told her you loved her and wanted her forever and then broke up with her a few nights later."

"Thanks, Amelia," I grouse, squeezing the back of my neck. "I clearly needed that reminder."

She sighs, picking up the bowl of popcorn and setting it on her lap. "Sorry, and I know why you did it. But overcoming a fear like that takes time. Believe me, it does. Trust must be earned. And right now, she doesn't trust you or your motives."

"Yes. Does she even know your motives?" Grace questions. "Have you told her? Does she know you haven't even touched anyone else in four years?"

I blink at that, watching the lines of bourbon run down the edge of the glass. "No. I tried to tell her, but any time I started to or told her we needed to talk, she shut me down. I could tell she wasn't ready. That or she truly doesn't want to hear it. Maybe she doesn't care about my excuses or reasons because she dealt with the aftermath of my actions regardless. My plan was to insert myself back into her life slowly, but I should have known better. Raven and I never did slow, and we never did anything the smart or conventional way. This past week proves that."

"Then that's how you need to play this," Rina announces. "The unconventional way. You can't change the past and you can't take away the pain she's been feeling. What's done is done, and now all you can do is work with what you've got."

"Which is nothing," Landon states, and I point a finger at him while looking at my sister, because bingo. I got nothing.

"No," Grace challenges. "You have plenty. She might say she

doesn't want anything to do with you, but she still let you give her a ride to dinner after her performance. She let you in her bedroom. She went and looked at the apartment in *your* building. She may say she doesn't want anything from you, but she's behaving otherwise."

"True," Elle agrees. "I think she's conflicted more than anything else and conflicted is not nothing. It's a starting point."

"A starting point." I test the words on my tongue. "Not much of one, but I guess it's something?"

"Remember, from there you only have one place to go," Carter offers.

"Where's that? To the curb?"

Carter snickers, his hand absently running over Grace's belly. "She already kicked your ass there today. I'm talking about up."

I polish off my drink, setting my glass down on the table and wiping my mouth with the back of my hand as I think. "I have no idea what to do."

"Do you love her?"

I laugh at Oliver, giving him an "I wouldn't be here like a sorry sap of pathetic man if I didn't" look.

"Then be patient, like Elle said. Give her time to adjust to this new life. To the notion that you're going to be a part of it since she's basically already part of our family. Keep showing up. Let her know you're not going anywhere. Keep your dick in your pants. Prove to her you want her for more than just sex. That you're the man she's meant for. Do whatever you can to earn her trust back. Eventually, she'll realize you're not going to hurt her, and she'll give you a second chance."

"Agreed," Landon says, shifting Elle so she's closer to his chest on his lap.

"Definitely," Grace states, a gummy worm hanging out of her mouth. "What Oliver said."

Everyone nods in agreement.

"Dick in my pants and be patient. Show her I'm not going anywhere and earn her trust. Right. Got it."

Only the patience and the dick in my pants part is not something I've ever been able to do with Raven. We're seductive fire and reckless passion. We're temptation wrapped in weakness. She's the pretty lie I told myself I'd win back and I'm the dirty secret she wishes she could forget. But from the moment I saw her that night four years ago, I knew I'd never be the same again. That one moment forever altered me, changed my genetic makeup.

There is no going back now.

Raven Fairchild is my endgame.

But patience? Dick in my pants? How the hell am I going to do that when every time I go near her, we ignite?

"Woo-hoo, yeah! Go!" Landon's perky, adorable blond thing yells, clapping her hands excitedly and bouncing up and down in her seat. "First down! Nice run!"

"Elle, you know I'm really starting to love you and all, but if you continue to root for the Dolphins over the Pats, we can't be friends," Amelia, Oliver's fiancée, fake fiancée, girlfriend, I don't know how to classify her, says.

Elle spins around, frowning at the petite redhead on my right. "But I cheered at the University of Miami and then I lived in Miami for years while I was married to David. I even know a few of those players down there."

"Yes, but you do realize you live in New England now and we're all big sports fans up here, right? Everyone in this booth is ready to throw down. You could start a riot." Amelia's hand pans around the room and sure enough, Rina, Brecken, Oliver, Kaplan, Carter, Luca, Dr. Fritz, my father, and even Landon and Layla are giving her the stink eye.

Elle doesn't appear the least bit concerned. "Whatever.

Grow up!" she snaps at everyone. "I'm not going to love your beloved Pats." She gets a few snarls and sighs and then she shakes her head in dismay. "Y'all don't scare me. I'm scrappy like a squirrel, and you do not want to mess with Texas."

I laugh lightly, as does Octavia. We throw each other a side-eye and a grin. I think I like Elle. I think I like Elle a lot.

Elle tosses her hands up when Amelia gives her a "Uou wanna try it, sweetheart? I'm a redhead from the mean streets of Boston" expression.

"Fine." Elle holds up a consolatory hand. "I'll cool it, but only a little and only because I know y'all are such big sports fans and I respect that about you."

"Deal." Amelia gives her a satisfied nod. "It'd be worse if we were at the Red Sox. Layla teases me about my obsession with them, but she's just as big into sports as I am, especially now that we live with Oliver."

"I guess it's lucky for me Stella hates sports and doesn't care who I root for. She still loves me anyway. Don't you, Stella?" Elle raises her voice at the end, catching Stella's attention. Stella glances up from her book to give a thumbs-up before quickly returning to it.

I snicker. "I'm with Stella on this. I'm not a huge fan of sports either," I admit. "I mean, I'll watch a game if it's on, but I don't seek it out."

Both Elle and Amelia stare at me like I just grew horns and a beak before their eyes.

"Then how come you're here tonight?" Elle queries, truly perplexed. She's a sunshine of a little Texas girl and I have no idea how she and Landon—who is eternally a broody bastard and rightfully so after all he's been through—work together so well, but clearly they do because the man stares at her like she's the moon and the stars in his night sky.

"She got roped into being here, same as I did," Grace states, placing her hand over Octavia's, who sits between us.

Octavia gives a remorseless shrug. "If I'm forced to be here, all of you have to be as well. I promised Dr. Fritz one football game a year and I wasn't coming without a buffer. Besides, nothing's better than my whole family being together." She gives my hand a squeeze and I drop my head onto her shoulder, the end of her blond wig tickling my forehead. It's real hair, which is kinda cool and kinda creepy, but I know it makes her feel better having it on.

The woman is the essence of regal beauty with a heart and soul to match.

Octavia is the only mother-like figure I had growing up since mine died when I was so young and wasn't around much before that. Octavia's recurrent breast cancer is the main reason I'm back in Boston. I wanted to be with her. Near her. It's similar for Grace, though her parents cast her aside because of her epilepsy, and with the way Octavia loves and embraces us as her own, we'd do just about anything for her. Including coming to a Sunday night football game after I played a concert this afternoon and am getting set to move tomorrow.

Something I haven't mentioned to anyone yet other than to my father this morning. He scowled at me. I'm not sure the man knows how to parent me now that I'm an adult and ends up keeping his mouth shut when keeping his mouth shut is certainly not what he wants to do.

I also haven't said anything to Luca, though I'm positive he knows since I talked with the management company on Friday.

I haven't seen him or heard from him since I lost it on him the other day in the apartment and honestly, I'm grateful for the reprieve. Doesn't mean my body isn't acutely aware of him being in such close proximity. He's been good at keeping his distance, and I've been good at avoiding looking at him.

So I have no idea if he's staring at me the way I think he is. If the hairs on the back of my neck that are standing up, the whole-body chills and shudders, or the perpetual flutter in my lower belly are from him or I have a fever and am coming down with a stomach bug instead.

Except I know it's unfortunately not the flu causing these symptoms. I can *feel* him.

"How was your performance this morning?" Octavia questions as she picks at something on her plate with her fork. She isn't eating much tonight and that frightens me.

"It was wonderful. The last charity concert before we start practicing for the Holiday Pops shows. I'm excited about that. I know they're big here and holiday music is just fun to play."

"Will you have another solo?"

My smile slips. "It's hard to know until Antonio—he's the conductor—makes the assignments, but I might. I hope I do." And I don't because solos give me cold sweats and panic attacks, but hey, that's my own thing to battle through. The fact that my stage fright decided to pick now to rear its ugly head back up is yet another log on my fire of madness.

"I have no doubt Antonio will give you a solo," Rina muses with an impish lilt to her voice. "In fact, I think he'd like you to give him a solo any chance he can get."

My eyes fly out of my head, and I glare at Rina with a zip-it look. She knows about Antonio's flirting and quasi-pursuit of me. But dammit, not in front of Octavia.

She grins like the cat who ate the canary at my expression. "What? You know it's true. And don't give me that stunned, deer in headlights thing because every man who blinks at you is hot for you. This should not come as a shock."

Grace laughs, rocking into Rina while staring at me. "She has a point. Seriously. Do you remember when you flew home for your birthday a couple of years ago and the three of us went out? Every guy in every bar and club we went to was all over you."

"Was not."

"Was too," they both say in unison, making everyone, including Octavia, crack up.

I sigh, sagging back in my seat, my face feeling like a fireball. "I was twenty then."

"And being twenty-two now somehow changes the 'men being all over you' thing? Because, as far as I can tell, it doesn't."

"Are we going there, Rina?" I challenge, a sly smirk quirking up my lips. "Your mom is right next to me. I can start in on some stories."

"Oh, sweetness, I've already heard most of them. A mother's ears unfortunately pick up everything. Especially with children like mine who end up as front-page news. Besides, I like hearing you've lived a little after... well, after things not always being so happy for you in that department." She glances over her shoulder in the direction of who I can only presume is her son and I won't do it. I won't look. I don't know if he's across the room or listening or what and I do not care.

"I want to hear more about Antonio. More about his penchant for solo time with the female musicians in his orchestra."

"Oh my God," I cry out, snapping up in my chair and narrowing my eyes at Grace this time. "The two of you are so grounded from my gossip. I should have never told you what Catarina told me." I point at her and Rina, who are finding far too much enjoyment in my discomfort. They even high-five.

"No, we're not," Grace remarks with assurance. "You love us too much to deny us."

Ugh.

"Antonio is pretty sexy if you're into that older, eccentric thing," Rina states airily. "And clearly he has a thing for his newest star. But honestly, I'm not sure I'd go there. I'd hate for his body to be found dead in the Charles River." Rina bounces her head, again in what is likely Luca's direction and all I can do is shake my head.

Ambushed. I'm freaking ambushed.

There is no winning this and I don't think I've ever been so embarrassed in my life. I realize Octavia isn't my mother, but… she's still freaking Octavia Abbot-Fritz. Sitting here at a football game and talking boys and flings and… yup, flaming face. All over me.

"I work for him and he's about twenty years older than me."

"That's quite the age difference," Octavia notes, giving me a wink as if to say she doesn't mind the girl talk one bit. Her green eyes are flatter, most of their typical sparkle dulled a bit and I wonder if she's not feeling well and is trying to hide it from us.

"My ex-husband was eleven years older than me," Elle offers. "Sometimes age is just a number."

And just like that, everyone falls into a slightly awkward silence because though Elle might not be aware of this because she's new to the Fritz crew, Luca is almost exactly eleven years older than me. I can feel a few sets of eyes boring into the side of my face as I struggle not to react.

"Oh my gosh, look." Amelia points out the large panel of glass in front of us, straight at the huge screen over the end zone. "He's proposing to her. I can never decide if that's cool or cliché." She smirks at me, and I throw her a grateful smile in return for taking me out of the hot seat.

"Both," Rina claims. "It's both. It's a great story and fun if you're both huge sports fans, but it's also a total cliché. I bet they're doing this just to go viral on TikTok."

"Agreed," Elle, Amelia, and I all say together, causing another round of high-fives and giggles, this time between the three of us.

"Brecken is a huge Bruin's fan. You could get married at the Garden during one of the games."

Rina gives Grace a glare that could skin a cat alive. It

promises murder and mayhem if she continues with that sentiment. Especially in front of—

"No one is getting married at a sporting event." Octavia raises a pointed eyebrow at all the women surrounding me as she shifts in her seat, crossing her legs at the knee and placing her hands gently on her lap. "But I wouldn't mind planning a few weddings. Making a certain engagement ring that belonged to my grandmother official." An eyebrow for Amelia. "Making something official before my grandson is born." That one is for Grace, who just laughs lightly. "And helping to put a certain man who is anxious to tie the knot out of his misery." That last look is for Rina, who just rolls her eyes because Octavia is her mother, and she can do that.

None of the rest of us dare attempt it—she's too sweet.

"Wow. This is a dangerous discussion if ever there was one," Elle states, rising out of her seat. "I'm going to get another glass of wine. Anyone want one? All of you? Fabulous, I'll bring back a tray."

"I'll help." I stand up, stretching out my aching back—playing cello for several hours a day is no joke on your spine and back muscles. "I have to use the restroom anyway."

The second we're out of earshot of the other women, Elle sags in relief. "Woo. I love Landon and I love this family, but they are intense."

"No joke. Try growing up with them."

"Lord baby Jesus in the manger, no, thanks. My family was absolutely no picnic, but I swear, if Octavia starts in on me next with this whole marriage stuff, I'll break out into hives."

"I don't blame you. At least I'm exempt from that."

I get a snort and a total "who the hell are you kidding" face. "I wouldn't be so sure on that particular conversation. From the moment I met the real Luca, he's told me time and time again that his heart already belongs to someone. Rumor has it, that someone is you."

"The real Luca?"

She breaks out into a laugh. "Yes. I originally met Landon at a bar in Boston on my first night in town, but he was introduced to me as Luca. I slept with him, thinking the damn man's name was Luca, only to meet him as Landon the next night when I opened my front door and discovered we were neighbors. Evidently, Landon, on the occasions he'd go out prowling for a woman, would do so as Luca so that if he was photographed, it would be as Luca and not as himself."

I shake my head, trying to understand what she's saying. "Landon would go out and meet women claiming he was Luca?"

"Yup. That way Stella wouldn't see her dad with a strange woman online."

I blink at her. "So... some of those photos of Luca with women..."

"Might have been Landon, yes. From what I understand, Luca never ever takes anyone to his bed." She gives me a wink and then saunters off toward the bar, leaving me to grapple with that not so insignificant piece of information.

Not that it matters, right? It doesn't. Luca and I are over and have been for four years. Me returning home and him saying a couple things and me learning this changes nothing.

I shouldn't have come tonight. Everyone—myself included —is so hyperaware of the elephant in the room. Always on eggshells. This is why I avoided him for four years. I love his family with my whole heart, but being near him makes me feel like I drank twenty shots of espresso and chased them down with amphetamines.

The bathroom is located near the entrance of the luxury suite and once I've done my business and exit, the thought of going back in there and sitting through another two hours of the game and then traffic to get home doesn't appeal. We took five SUVs here, coming as a group along with a couple security guys. I could ask my father to drive me home in one of those cars, but I know he's enjoying the game and I don't want to pull him away from that.

Staring at the room, at everyone enjoying themselves and realizing I won't be missed for a little bit, I exit the box, stepping out onto the long, wide, empty corridor that overlooks the busy club lounge below.

Luca is in that suite, but him being here isn't the reason Thursday night in the apartment with him has been recycling itself through my thoughts.

Everything I did was because I love you. Was because I had to. For both of us.

His cryptic words make me feel like a game he never stopped playing. A game he wants to win at all costs regardless of the potential outcome to the other player.

Why am I not rid of him?

I told myself I was. It took me two years to shake his ghosts and then, I only went with easy, emotionless fun. But even that fun was tainted. I had sex with someone else, but I never opened my eyes. I never enjoyed kissing. It was shallow and empty and more often than not, I preferred my vibrator and porn to the actual thing.

I've wondered if he ruined me. Honest to God ruined me for a life of happiness beyond him. I never trust anyone enough to date them. Always afraid that if I fell for someone else, it would end the same way.

Antonio is supposed to be a god in the sack and no, he wouldn't linger with me long. He has no interest beyond the physical. But he's not what my body craves and that makes me hate—

"Figured I'd find you out here."

—*him* even more.

"Does my father know you followed me out here?"

"I'm sure he does since the man was an actual spy, but I

didn't exactly ask for permission. He would have said no, and I wouldn't have listened, and I don't relish the idea of your father kicking my ass in front of my brothers."

"Go back inside, Luca. You're missing the game."

I feel him move in behind me. Not touching, but close as his body heat curls a warm path around me, the scent of his cologne finding my weakest spots. My eyes snap shut, and my teeth sink into my bottom lip, my hands gripping the railing like a vise.

Don't move. Don't turn around. Don't look at him. Don't give in.

"I have a seven a.m. surgery tomorrow." Another step and now I feel his breath falling on me. "I'm only here tonight because I knew you were going to be. Well, and my mother asked all of us to come if we could. Are you ready to go? I can drive you home."

"No, thanks."

Undeterred, his finger finds the hem of my slightly cropped sweater, playing with the wool. My teeth sink deeper into my lip.

"I'm glad you're moving into the apartment. Thank you for that."

"I'm not doing it for you."

"I know you're not." His hand glides up my back, a whisper as it hovers over my sweater until it finds my hair, dragging along it as gentle as a breeze that feels more like sharp, electric pulses. "You look beautiful tonight. So beautiful I haven't been able to take my eyes off you."

"Please stop." Only my voice isn't my own. It's breathless and needy.

His lips ghost my ear as he murmurs, "Why? Because you like my hands on you too much?"

Yes.

"Because I don't want you to touch me."

"If you let me drive you home, we'll just talk. I won't touch you. Even though you want me to."

I spin around, a feral, scrappy cat ready to dig my claws in when—

"Hi, Luca," a woman walking by in a tight, black serving uniform purrs with a smile that tells me she's fucked him six ways to Sunday. Which, ironically, is what today is so...

His head snaps in her direction. "Um. Hi, Justine."

He knows her name. Awesome.

She bats her eyelashes but keeps walking, entering another luxury suite and leaving me alone on the vacant balcony with him, only the sound of the crowd below as a buffer.

He turns back to me. "She's worked in our booth before."

"Uh-huh. Are her tits real or fake?"

He shakes his head, crowding me back against the railing, his eyes swirling a cautious path all over me. "I wouldn't know."

I bluster out a breath, reaching behind me and gripping the railing. Why do I even care? "I don't care, Doctor Playboy. Go fuck her or another woman or just go back inside and leave me the hell alone."

Fury and resentment flare in his eyes. "You have it all wrong with that."

"Do I?" I challenge, hating how I want him to tell me that what Elle said was true. All of it.

Body leaning in, his hard cock presses into my lower belly as if to say, *feel this, no one else does this to me but you*. His hands meet the railing on either side of me, caging me in as he dips right in front of my face.

"Yes. You're the last person I fucked. Can you say the same?" His eyes cut a path back and forth between mine. "Did you know sound carries all around that booth?"

"Again, I don't care."

"Yes, you do. You might hate it, but you care a lot, Little Bird.

It's all over your pretty face. Are you fucking that guy? Your conductor?"

Jesus. Is he for real?

"Yes," I lie.

He grits his teeth, clenching his jaw so tight, I hear it creak. His eyes pierce into mine. "How many blue pills does he require to get it up?"

"With me?" I smirk tauntingly. "None. I'm a magic bullet of sexual dynamo. Now go back inside."

"I should. I'm not supposed to be out here. I'm supposed to be trying for patience and keeping my dick in my pants with you."

Anger claws up my body, heating my blood, an angry torrent as I push him back, forcing him to take a step away, and I storm down the corridor. "Then why are you out here? Why won't you leave me alone?"

I suck in a ragged breath, so tired of being angry and hurt, it's just fucking annoying at this point. I can think about unicorns and kittens and goddamn rainbows till I'm blue in the face, but that doesn't take away the urge I have to kiss this man senseless, kick him in the nuts, and then toss his ass over this balcony. I think I've officially hit the unhinged stage of this gig and I want no part of it.

His hand somehow dives into my hair, and I have no clue how he got this close to me again. I think it was while I was planning his public death.

He spins me around, dragging me to him, so close, my eyes have no choice but to see his. "Because I can't stop thinking about you. Because hearing Rina and Grace talk about your womanizing conductor who is making a play for you when you're only meant for me has turned me into a living, breathing, green-eyed monster. Just the thought of it, of him touching you, tasting you, moving inside of you has me so insane I can't think straight. You make it impossible for me to think straight.

I'm so panicked and jealous right now, I'm two seconds away from going all Anakin Skywalker and killing everyone. You are mine and yet you're not and it's absolutely killing me."

I shove him off, glaring at him with every muscle in my face.

"I am not yours. For the last four years, you haven't existed to me. My dad doesn't talk about you with me. Your family doesn't talk about you with me. I was in London, on a whole other continent and yet you still tried to worm your way in. Newsflash, asshole, you should continue to screw your way through Boston because you won't screw your way through me."

"That's where you're wrong." In the next second, his hand is on my arm and he's dragging me over to the elevator on my right, slamming me against the cold metal doors. Getting right up in my face, he growls, "You might say that, but your body tells me something else. You fucking want me, Raven Fairchild. As much as I want you. I make you crazy the same as you do for me. We're it for each other. Soul mates. Star-crossed lovers. You're just scared. But newsflash," he says, throwing my word back at me, "so am I. I need you so much I'm utterly deranged with the idea that because I hurt you the way I did you'll never give me another chance."

His hands hit the metal on either side of my head, his body pressing into me without touching. The heat of him, a blazing inferno that caresses against me, is extraordinary. It's acting like a defibrillator on my heart, jolting me with electricity as if to remind me I'm only alive when I'm with him. He looms over me, that electrical undercurrent crackling between us.

He's still not touching me, tiny millimeters separating us from catastrophe. My insides are rioting. Begging for more. Begging for him to stop.

"If you believe that, then why are you out here?"

His nose meets mine, followed by his forehead, our eyes locked, but that's it. He doesn't try for anything else. "I already told you. I can't stay away. I might not have existed to you, but you're the only one who's existed to me."

"Stop. Just shut up. I can't take this anymore."

"Hear me out."

"No."

"I've lived and breathed and died on your every move for four years. Tell me how to stop *wanting* you so much. Tell me how to go back inside and leave you alone when I'm ready to tear the world apart to make you mine again. I can't do it, Raven. I don't know how. I listened and I tried all weekend, but the second I see you, I fail. Over and over again, I fail." His thumb drags along my jaw, across my lips, down my throat, his hot breath panting against my cheek. "I can't breathe without you, baby. You're my oxygen and I'm suffocating."

My breath hitches, my throat closing up on me as my heart explodes in my chest. He's raw. Primal. And it scares me. How quickly my body alters to give itself over to him. How stuck on him it's always been. With every encounter, part of me slips. My walls crumble and I won't... I *won't* do it.

My hands plant into his chest and I pry him back. "Try getting your heart broken. Does the trick every time."

He blinks at me, righting his body, all the color draining from his face. He opens his mouth to say something, when Grace and Carter exit the suite. My eyes lock with Grace's, who frowns instantly.

"Luca, Landon is looking for you, brother," Carter clips out, his tone almost reprimanding.

Luca's gaze grabs mine, a visual growl, he's ready to pounce again, only to stop himself. Unhinged, it's as if he doesn't know what to do with himself. He grunts something I can't make out under his breath, and without another word, he spins around and storms back to the booth.

I swallow hard, my hand on my chest, trying to slow my thundering heart. Fuck, that man is so intense, my fingernails are vibrating, and my stupid panties are soaked. Traitorous vagina. How long will this continue before my hair starts falling out in clumps and I have a nervous breakdown?

"Do you need a ride home?" Grace asks gently. "We have early cases tomorrow and are heading out."

"That would be great, thanks."

I'd take a ride home with Hannibal Lecter if it got me out of here right now.

19

"Raven. Wow." The woman gives me a big once-over. "Is that a stage name?"

I get asked this question a lot. Raven—it's an unusual name. Not to mention my hair is ink-black—the reason my parents named me Raven in the first place. But this woman is not asking me in a kind or genuine or even curious way. And when she sneers the words "stage name," I think she's actually asking if I'm a stripper instead of the cellist I claim to be.

"Nope. It's real. Came out with a splash of black hair and my name is the result."

"Oh. It's... cute." Her nose scrunches and yeah, she doesn't think it's cute at all. This interview isn't starting on the foot I had hoped it would.

"Thank you." Yep, I don't mean that either and I'm pretty sure she can tell.

"So, talk to me about your experience with music therapy."

Right. The whole reason I'm here.

Only, I didn't expect to see this woman and she certainly wasn't expecting to see me.

You know, since we now live in the same building.

I knew she looked familiar when I passed her in the lobby the first time I was there, and I wasn't wrong. Even though I had never seen her in person before until that moment. No, I'd seen her in pictures with none other than Luca Fritz—the real Luca. Smiling on his arm as she stared adoringly up at him, splashed across the cover of *Boston Landing* the day I landed at Logan airport, returning from London.

It was quite the homecoming.

I can't help but wonder how many times she slept with him. If he stared into her eyes while he was inside of her the way he used to with me. If he made her come with his mouth or just his fingers and dick. If he told her she was beautiful.

Ugh. Liar. Bastard. Heartbreaking fucktwat.

Shaking off all thoughts of Luca, I sit up a bit straighter, folding my hands in my lap and plastering on my sweet smile. "Well, I have a bachelor's in string instruments from The Conservatory in London and a secondary degree from King's College London in psychology."

"Hmmm... how did you manage that at such a young age?"

"In England, a bachelor's degree is typically three years instead of four, so I doubled up a lot for two of those years."

"Right. And you've done music therapy before?"

"I didn't realize the position Kaplan spoke with me about was for an actual music therapist. He explained I would come in three days a week, go to different floors, and play music with some of the kids."

"That's what we call music therapy here. Just because Kaplan Fritz believes you're right for the job, doesn't mean I don't have to do mine."

Oh boy. This woman seriously doesn't like me.

A point she goes on to prove when she asks, "What's your relationship with the Fritz family again?"

None of your damn business. "My father is their house manager and chief of security."

That has her appraising me with new eyes. The kind that suggests I'm no longer a threat to her in any way. The fact that she thought I was in the first place has me inwardly grinning, though. Women have always chased the Fritz men. They're billionaires and they're gorgeous.

But this woman didn't like me on sight.

Probably because the news that Luca Fritz put his whatever they choose to call me into an apartment where I pay pennies on the dollar rent in a building full of multimillion-dollar condos spread like wildfire. I heard a few women gossiping about it in the gym the other morning.

They didn't even bother to stop gossiping when they saw me.

After Luca walked out last week, I sat in that apartment crying my eyes out for who knows how long. But when I finally managed to pry myself off the floor and wash my face, I decided to go through things a bit. I sat on the sofa and watched TV. I opened the cabinets in the kitchen and bathroom. They were fully stocked.

The man even had them put a supply of toilet paper there for me.

And I decided I was being crazy by not taking it.

I'm paying a thousand dollars a month for an apartment I'd never be able to afford in ten lifetimes. Whether I stay there for a few months or even years, it's too good of a gift to pass up. And true to his word, I haven't had to see or deal with Luca. At least where the apartment is concerned—Sunday night at the game notwithstanding. It's been all the management company who was only too happy to give me the keys and have me sign a month-to-month lease.

My father, who helped me move, seemed even less enthusiastic about it after he saw the place, but that's another story. I know he spoke with Luca about it. He didn't deny it either. Just said that men talk, and Luca wanted to make sure I was living somewhere safe. Whatever.

"Have I used music to help children who had underlying mental health issues? Yes. One of my rotations was in an adolescent psych ward in London. Not a happy place to be, but the kids all seemed to respond well to music and were able to express themselves through it. That's what music is, Miss Barnes. Music is expression. It speaks to the soul and evokes emotion. All emotions. And yes, I do believe in music's ability to heal. I've experienced that myself firsthand. But the bottom line is, I'm twenty-two. I just graduated and moved back to Boston. So no, I don't have all the experience you seem to be looking for. But I am young, which makes me relatable. And I am talented and passionate about what I do. And I do believe I can help kids who are going through what is likely the hardest time of their lives find a little joy or peace or acceptance or be able to communicate in ways they otherwise might not be able to."

Pricilla Barnes scrutinizes me with an unreadable expression, her red talons that match her lips tapping gently on her desk. Finally, she releases a breath and leans back in her chair. "All right, Miss Fairchild. Kaplan seems to believe in you, so I'll give you a shot. Come with me. I'll show you the floors you'll be working on."

Stunned, I get up and follow her as she leads me to three different floors in the hospital. I'm not sure what I was expecting. Boston Children's Hospital has been voted best in the world too many times for them to count. They are the premier children's hospital and it's a job they clearly take to heart. Kids and families from all over the world travel here with their sick kids for treatment.

But these kids...

Walking through some of the floors and smiling at some of

the faces, all while watching the exhausted and terrified parents and not crying is an act of sheer will. I'm on a cardiac floor, an oncology floor, and a neuro floor. On each floor is an activity room where I'll set up instruments and hang out with the kids for an hour and a half, talking and playing music.

Music is my life's blood, but this is bringing it to the next level, and I tell Kaplan that as I sit with him in the sandwich shop inside the lobby of the hospital, having a quick bite in between his patients.

"See," he says around a mouthful of turkey sandwich. "I knew you'd be perfect for it."

"I'm nervous as hell but excited too. I had thought about teaching music to make some extra money, but this is so much better. Thank you again. I still can't believe you put yourself on the line like that for me."

Kaplan laughs, wiping his mouth with his napkin. "Babe, there is no me putting myself on the line. I knew the hospital was looking for someone to come in and do something like this and I mentioned your name to Pricilla, who has been after my junk and every other Fritz's junk for years now. She was only too excited about hiring you until you moved into Luca's building."

And just like that, my enthusiastic smile is gone.

"Aw, come on. You look like you just got splatter pooped on."

"*Splatter pooped?*"

"Welcome to peds. Happened to me this morning, in fact. Newborn babies' bowels are unpredictable. They like to fire without waiting for the official order. Anyway, Luca hasn't fucked her, if that's what you were worried about."

"I wasn't," I lie, and he grins, taking a sip of soda while reading me perfectly.

"Uh-huh. Sure. You obviously saw them in that magazine, but

his face or mine or even Carter's and Oliver's faces have been all over that magazine and ninety-eight percent of the time, it's total bullshit. They were talking at a charity event and the camera captured it and called it something else. I know everyone believes Luca to be a playboy, but he's not. Not anymore. Not in the last four years anyway. Did you know what always happens is women come on to him, he makes a valiant effort to reciprocate, fails, and then drops them off at home with barely a peck on the cheek?"

"As a brilliant friend of mine once said, uh-huh. Sure."

Kaplan rolls his green eyes at me, and I hate how similar all the Fritz boys look. Well, except for Carter, who looks just like Dr. Fritz senior with his dark eyes. But all the rest have this incredible variation of green eyes and it's annoying. Especially when you're trying to forget one set in particular and the way they look at you.

"All I'm saying is you can't believe everything you read or see in magazines or on the internet. If you did, then you'd think I'm nothing more than a coldhearted rake who has sworn off love and dodges every woman's attempt at locking me down and forcing me down the aisle."

"You are all of those things. Doctor Untouchable. Boston's man of mystery." I take a spoonful of my soup, chewing on a noodle and winking at him when he pouts.

He angles his head, cocking an eyebrow. "But no one knows why. Do they?"

"I don't know why either."

"See what I mean?"

I laugh, shaking my head. "Not really."

"Did it ever occur to you that Luca broke your heart for a reason?"

I groan, my head falling back. Tossing my napkin at him, I say, "Not this again."

"I was there that night. Don't forget that. I know the truth even if you don't want to acknowledge there might be more to this than you know or care to accept."

"He did it partially for me, Kaplan. I know. I may not have realized it that night and it might have taken me a very long time to work that through, but I know that's why he did it. He wanted me to go to school and play so I didn't give up on my dream, which worked out nicely since he didn't want to be tethered down with an eighteen-year-old kid while he worked on his."

"All true except the tethered down part. He would have done that in a heartbeat. He did marry you, after all."

I roll my eyes in disdain. "Whatever. It doesn't change anything for me because he still did it in such a way that left me devastated for two years. He was a cruel, uncaring, miserable prick that night. He said things that can never be taken back. Two years I sat heartbroken and inconsolable. Untrusting and man-hating. For the last two years, I've done everything I could to force him from my thoughts and my heart. But the bastard kept popping up. Kept sticking his head out of the sand. Digging that knife in deeper and deeper. And for what? To remind me he was there when I couldn't have him? To keep stringing me along while he was off pegging every woman he could get his hands on? Fuck that. Fuck. That."

Kaplan is for once stunned speechless.

Finally, he blinks and clears away his expression. "So you think you know it all, which you obviously don't, but that's why you won't let him talk and explain himself?"

"Why would I let him when I have you?" I tease.

He gives me a dark look. "Don't tempt the lion when the lion can't indulge in the meat. You should talk to him."

"There's no point. Nothing he tells me will change the reality I went through. I can't do it again with him. I can't go through that again. I don't trust him. Not even a little. Eventually, he'll grow bored with whatever game he's playing with me and that will be that. He'll move on and leave again."

"Well, fuck me sideways. I'm at a loss."

"A first for you, no doubt."

"Do you want me to buy you a cookie?"

I grin, sinking my teeth into my lip. "I'm not a child anymore, Kap. You don't have to comfort me with cookies and milk."

Kaplan stares out the glass wall onto the main floor of the hospital, his eyes dancing about until they catch on something. He smirks before turning back to me. "He'd kill me if he knew what I was doing with you."

That perks my interest, my eyebrows at my hairline. "And what are you doing with me?"

"Truth? Trying to help the woman I had hoped would one day be my sister-in-law. But I doubt he'd see it that way."

Oh. Now I'm the one impersonating a goldfish. "Are you breaking up with me?"

He laughs, getting up out of his seat and clearing our trash away. His hand extends for mine and I take it, allowing him to help me up. He tosses his big arm over my shoulders, and we walk back out into the lobby, which is noisy beyond belief with the interactive art installation they have here and the kids coming and going.

He spins me around in his arms and cups my jaw in his hands. "No. I'm not breaking up with you. But I'm not giving up on you either, if you get my meaning."

I give him a squeeze because I get it and I love him for it even if it's a lost cause. "Thank you again for getting me the job. And for being there when I needed someone and had no one."

His lips plant a kiss the top of my head. "Anything for you, lil' sis."

I pinch his side and he jumps back. "You know you look younger than me, right?"

He groans, rubbing at his smooth jaw that's sharp enough to cut glass. The man really is something else. "Aw, come on. Don't start that shit. I do not. I look my age."

"Yeah, if your age was twenty-two." I blow him a kiss. "I'll see you around, big bro."

Wrapping my coat tighter around my body, I exit the hospital, needing to get my butt over to Symphony Hall for rehearsal. Between this gig, my orchestra job, and the ridiculous thing I have coming up in the next couple of weeks, I should be set for money for a—

Before I know what's happening, someone is grabbing my arm, dragging me into an alleyway, spinning me around, and slamming me into the bricks. My knee comes up to strike on instinct, but I miss my target. A scream flees my lungs, only to be stifled by a pair of lips covering mine.

"What are you doing in my hospital with my brother?" Luca snarls at me.

I push him off me. "Your hospital? I thought you work at Brigham and Women's."

He crowds me, his hard cock pressing into my lower belly and making me ache. "I do. But I also work here two days a week. Now answer me."

I shake my head, pissed off. I didn't know Luca worked at Children's. Kaplan certainly never mentioned it to me, the devious wanker. And since no one else speaks to me about him, Brigham was all I had heard.

"You wanna know so bad, go ask him yourself. I have to get to work."

I nudge him back again, scooting around him to get out of this alley, away from him, when he catches my arm and yanks me back. Straight into his hard chest.

"Oh no, Little Bird. You're not going anywhere just yet."

20

My stomach grumbles as I step off the elevator, garnering me two looks and a giggle from a little girl. I throw her a wink and then head for the sandwich shop off the lobby of the hospital. I missed breakfast this morning, having run out of time after my run, and now I'm paying the price for it. All around me, kids and their parents are coming and going. Some looking miserable or anxious or scared, others laughing and smiling. The large ball sculpture pings and dings and moves and I can't help but smile as I catch a few of the kids marveling at it.

It is pretty awesome.

When I originally set out to be a neurosurgeon, pediatrics wasn't high on my list of subspecialties. But then I got shot by a father who was scared of his family being deported when I tried to help a mother who would do anything for her child. Needless to say, my perspective on a lot of things changed and my life hasn't been the same since.

Once I went back alone to Minnesota, without Raven or my heart with me, I threw myself into medicine. More than I ever had. I convinced a pediatric neurosurgeon to let me pick up hours with her and by the time my residency was up, I had specialized in both pediatric—ages twelve to sixteen—and adult neurosurgery.

Because my goal, my vision goes far beyond this.

Yet another embarrassingly loud grumble, and I practically groan out an orgasm when I spot the café and realize there's no line. Only I'm immediately stopped in my tracks by my boss, Dr. Alvin Grosspotter, who the majority of my patients either call Dr. Harry Potter because of his English accent or Dr. Grosspooper. It's usually the second one and I'd be lying if I said the residents here didn't refer to him as that too.

"Luca. Brilliant. I've been searching for you all morning."

He also has one of those posh accents that almost seems overly exaggerated since I've traveled to England several times and know several English people—including Raven's father—and none of them speak the way this guy does.

"Yeah, Alvin, just heading to grab a quick bite between surgeries."

"And I won't keep you, but I wanted to mention... you applied for the Treesprite Grant, yes?"

I shift my stance, glancing longingly over his shoulder back at the café. Dammit, a line is forming by the second. I turn back to him. "Yes. As did every neurosurgeon in the world, right? Why?"

"Because I received an email this morning from them, informing me you've been placed into the top twenty of potential candidates."

My eyes shoot out of my head cartoon style as my heart picks up an extra beat. "I'm sorry. Did you just say I made it to the *top twenty*?"

He chuckles, giving me a knowing grin. "I did indeed."

I stare blankly at him for a moment as I run this through my head. Because that goal, that vision I was just speaking to... yeah. The Treesprite Grant has one winner every two years.

One year is spent somewhere in either Middle or South America. The other somewhere in Africa. The location changes with each new grant term and this time it's a remote village in Brazil and one in Ghana. The point is to go out into the communities and provide free healthcare to people who otherwise wouldn't have it. Neuro healthcare at that. They also help local clinics and hospitals to improve care and teaching. It's highly competitive. Highly coveted. And legit, one person every two years gets it out of every single neurosurgeon and neurologist in the *world* who applies, and let me tell you, *everyone* applies.

It's the equivalent of winning the lottery on a global scale. You buy a ticket, knowing you likely won't win. But I started applying when I was still a resident, knowing they wouldn't pick me, but wanting the board to know how serious I am about this. It's no joke to me. Not some ego-trip, tossing my hat in the ring type of deal.

I was shot because that family was afraid of accessing healthcare. It shouldn't be like that. For anyone. And if I can help deliver and educate and enhance healthcare for those who need it most...

Which gives me a second round of pause.

"Are you telling me I have a one in twenty shot of getting this?"

"Yes. And think of the publicity for not just you, but for the hospital."

But when he says that, all I'm hearing is Abbot-Fritz. I'm only a second year attending. They saw my last name and that's why I'm even in the running. It sucks as much as it's incredible. Welcome to my life. Never knowing if something you're getting is earned or gifted because your family name is famous and you're worth a bazillion dollars.

But...

"Wow."

That's where I end because something catches my eye. Or

should I say someone? Nope, there are two people who catch my eye. The first is my brother, Kaplan. The second is the stunning raven-haired beauty sitting across the table from him.

What the absolute motherfuck is Kaplan doing eating lunch with my girl?

He must see me because he smirks right at me before turning back to her and saying something. I stare. I watch. I clench my fists as he throws away the remains of her lunch and helps her up with his hand. Why is he touching her?

What the fuck is going on?!

"Luca, did you hear me?"

I flash back to Alvin just as Kaplan and Raven leave the café, his arm over her shoulders. He spins her around in his arms, cups her face in his hands, and says something that has her hugging him. HUGGING HIM!

"Luca!"

"Yes. Great. Awesome. I'm beyond excited."

I turn back to Raven and Kaplan just in time to see him kiss the top of her head and then she blows him a kiss as she walks away. I'm done. Toast. Never in my life would I have expected this. Alvin Grosspooper is still blathering on but who gives a fuck? It's not like I'll actually win the Treesprite Grant. Kaplan is walking toward me, all smug grins and knowing smirks until he's just about to pass me and throws me a wink.

My head flies around just as Raven exits the building.

"If you'll excuse me, Alvin, I have to be going."

And with that, I bolt past my boss, straight for the exit, and out onto the street. My head whips left and then right and then left again, and I spot her, hunched into her large black coat that matches her hair as she fights the Boston November wind.

Before she can escape, I race after her and grab her arm, hauling her into an alley and slamming her into the wall. She's riled and fiery and full of hate I intend to play around with. Because fuck all if I'm not just as mad.

"What are you doing in my hospital? With my brother?"

She gives me some back and forth. But it comes down to one thing…

She lets me kiss her.

That is until she pushes me off. "You wanna know so bad, go ask him yourself. I have to get to work."

She attempts to shove me away. To run. But once again all those cautionary directives about patience and keeping my dick in my pants are like balloons of wasted, hot air. Instead of attempting to play the game where I automatically lose, my hand grasps her arm and I yank her back, slamming her body straight into mine and then back against the wall.

My face gets right up in hers. "Oh no, Little Bird. You're not going anywhere just yet."

"Fuck you, Luca. You ruined us. Years ago, so I've moved on."

"Bullshit you have," I spit, my hand gripping her hair by the roots, forcing my face right in hers. "You couldn't have moved on because I never did. I never did, Raven. It was impossible. How could there be any other woman when you were all I could think about?"

"Bullshit! You fucked those other women!"

"I never touched any of them!" I scream. "You, Raven. Fucking you! Do you not get that? Do you not see? Do you not understand all that I risked? All that I gave up so you'd have the goddamn world knowing I could lose everything? I haven't been with anyone since you!"

"I'm not yours anymore," she cries.

My mouth hovers over hers. "Little Bird, you'll always be mine."

My lips crash onto hers, devouring her, holding her captive as I consume her inch by inch, morsel by morsel.

"You are inked on my body. Penned on my soul. I fucked up

and I hurt you and I'm sorry, but don't pretend you don't need me as much as I *need* you."

Her hands dive into my hair, ripping as hard as she can at me and *yes!* Give me all the pain, Raven. All your hurt. My teeth scrape along her bottom lip, sucking it into my mouth before I turn my head, deepening our angle. The taste of her mouth has me groaning, rocking the steel pipe in my pants into her like a teenager with no self-control.

I'm an addict who has gone four years without a fix.

This woman drives me crazy. It's not enough to just possess her. I need to *own* her.

Our tongues thrash, fighting. She climbs up on her tiptoes, trying to get closer, but there are too many barriers between us. Unzipping her coat, I press my chest against hers and she moans when she feels how hard I am. She's wearing a black dress and I hike her leg up my hip so I can grind right into her pussy.

"I fucking hate you."

"I know," I pant into her. "But you want my cock more than you hate me." My hand slides up the stockings on her legs and when I find lace along her thigh held in place by satin straps, I groan, ripping my lips from hers. "Thigh-highs? Garters!" My hand climbs higher and Christ, her panties are the tiniest scrap of lace that barely covers her. "I bought you these, you little tease. You were wearing this while having lunch with my brother?"

She has to know how much that infuriates me.

"Yes. And I'll be wearing them all through rehearsal this afternoon too."

Something inside me snaps. It's not logical. I know it's not, but my dick is doing all the talking for me now.

I cup her pussy in my hand. "This is mine, Raven. I already told you no one else can see this." I fist the lace in my hand, my thumb thrusting up into her. She moans, her head falling back against the brick as she rocks into me. Her pussy so wet, she's already dripping on my hand.

"You gonna rip these too?" she snaps mockingly, only to gasp as I take my thumb out and thrust three fingers in instead.

I wasn't going to, but now I sure as hell am.

Just as I tear them from her and shove them in my pocket, a car horn honks in the distance and our bodies jerk slightly apart. We're in an alley, barely ten feet from the street. If someone looked in, they'd see her coat acting as a barrier, but it wouldn't be hard to discern what we're up to.

I pump my fingers into her, slower now, sliding in and out while holding her thigh tighter against me. "I'm not stopping," I tell her, staring into her obsidian eyes ringed in aqua. Her lips part as I keep going, finding her clit now with soft circles that I know drive her wild.

She sinks her nails into the back of my scrub top, but her gaze flashes over toward the street, and I see it. Rational thought attempting to creep back into her pretty head and I sure as hell can't have that. Fuck patience and fuck keeping my dick in my pants. That might work for other women, but not this one. This one needs to feel me. Needs to see the passion I have for her.

She needs to know she's the *only* one and I'm not going anywhere ever again.

I silence her thoughts by sticking my tongue back down her throat the way I'd love to be sticking it in her pussy right now. I fuck her mouth like this, the way my fingers are fucking her, slow, even, ravaging. And finally, when her eyes are closed and her mind is giving itself back over to me once more, I quicken my pace, building her higher.

She whimpers, her hands fumbling with my scrub top, lifting it so she can scratch at my chest and abs. Her fingers scrape across the flesh just below my left axilla, by my heart, and I shudder at what her hands are unwittingly touching.

She's angry and frantic and she does likely hate me, but there is no denying what's happening between us. Her leg wraps tighter around my hip as she rides my hand. My mouth hits her jaw, her chin, her neck, nipping, sucking, tasting, eating at her.

I'm going to ruin her once and for all the way she's ruined me.

She comes on a wet rush, her creamy channel convulsing around my fingers as she bites down into my shoulder to stifle her moan. Spasm after spasm takes over and I have to hold her up as her body bucks and jerks, locked between me and the wall. Her small hand grabs my dick through my scrubs, squeezing me so hard, stars glitter across my vision and I hiss out a wheeze. But before I can groan or attempt to catch my breath, she's fumbling with the drawstring of my scrubs and tugging my aching cock out.

A cold blast of air hits me first before her hand takes over, coating me in warmth, and my face falls to her forehead as I pump into her hand. What is it about her touch that utterly destroys me? I suck her cum off my fingers, and she watches, eyes narrowed and breathing shallow. That fist grips me tighter and I smirk at her attempt at hurting me.

She forgets I like a little pain with my pleasure and my girl is the queen at toeing that line.

I jack off into her hand and *fuck* that's so good. But it's also not nearly enough. I'm so turned on right now I can hardly think. Obviously, since I'm about to screw Raven blind in an alley right beside the hospital I work in. I want to spin her around, press her palms into the bricks, and squeeze her tits while I fuck her from behind, but the notion of anyone seeing her in any way keeps my position held firmly and before she can argue or fight, I line my cock up with her weeping pussy and drive it home.

Sweet mother of *Christ*, that's insanely good.

"Shut up, Luca. Don't talk."

I grin, biting at her bottom lip. I hadn't realized I had.

"You always liked it when I talked. Remember? I could play with these tits"—I give one of them a firm squeeze, gliding my thumb over her hard nipple—"and get you to come just from my dirty mouth and a few good nipple flicks." I do just that and she hisses out a feral sound.

"I hate you. I hate you so goddamn much." That last word is a moan as I start to slide out, only to slam back into her. Hard. Quick. Frenetic. I grab her hip and grind into her, rolling my hips in a circle so I catch her clit, then do it all over again.

"But God, Raven, do I love you."

Her hands are in my hair. On my chest. Scraping and scratching and pulling and tearing. My hand is all over her too. In her hair. On her tits, rubbing across her nipples and hating the barrier of clothes between us. I need her naked, beneath me, over me, wrapped around me.

My lips and teeth suck on her, my tongue licking anywhere I can reach. All the while my hips gyrate, filling her up, pumping and grinding and thrusting, the angle shallow, but I make it work for us. Taking her hard right here, out in the open, against a fucking wall like the animal she makes me.

The world around us recedes. It's just her and it's just me. As it always was every time I was inside of her. All of me tethered to her.

She moans, her nails digging in deeper, trying to mark me.

I chuckle as I move, hitting her spot. Watching her blissed out face.

There is no slowing down. There is no stopping. There are zero fucks to give in this moment because I need to own her, and she needs to be owned. She's so wet and so tight and feels so fucking good.

"Harder," she cries into me, her hand gripping my arm, her nails slicing into my biceps, but that's all she's got as she starts to convulse, squeezing me with every muscle inside her as she comes on me, coating my dick. It's the most mind-bending sensation of wet heat and I follow her over the edge, grunting and growling and swearing into her, taking her mouth as I do because I need to taste her as we come. And come. And come. I swear it's never-ending and that I've never come this hard in my life.

The moment she sags against me, she instantly stiffens.

Don't do it. Don't regret it.

Her eyes blink open, and she pulls back, staring straight at me.

"Don't regret it."

She's still silent, but her face…

"No, baby. Don't do it."

Her eyes glass over and then she's shoving me off her, tugging down her dress and zipping up her coat. I tuck my dick back in my boxer briefs and tie up my scrub bottoms. All the while my eyes are locked on her.

"Raven?"

She's not saying anything, and silent Raven has my heart thundering.

I cup her jaw in my hand and the look in her eyes nearly breaks me. They're so vulnerable and lost. Begging me closer and pushing me away all at once.

"You're leaking out of me. We didn't use a condom."

I nod, feeling bad about that, but I won't apologize either. I figured that would happen and now I regret tearing her panties. But I'd be lying if I said I didn't like that part of me was inside of her. I don't even care that we didn't use a condom because this is her and this is me and this is us and she's worth every risk and consequence.

"I don't exactly keep condoms in my scrub pants. I'm clean, though. I swear it to you, I am. You're the only one… you're the only one I've ever gone bare with."

She clears her throat, emotion battling all over her face. "I have to go."

"Have dinner with me tonight."

She shakes her head in my hand. "I have to go."

I hold her jaw a little tighter. "If you have to go, I will let you. But know this, I'm only doing that because I know you have to get to work, and I can see you need space. But don't overthink this, Raven. Please, don't do that. I want you. Only you. Always. I will wait and I will fight, and I will try to be patient, but don't run from me. Love me, hate me, burn me, blame me, I don't care. But don't run from me anymore."

"I have to go."

And with that, she does run. Out of the alley and away from me. My heart sinks to my feet, only for my blood to boil back up.

Because I'm an asshole who just watched my girl run from me after I frantically fucked her in an alley and she told me she hates me, I thrash my way through a children's hospital. I have surgery. A rather unpleasant surgery that I intend to work a goddamn miracle on.

Glioblastoma in a fifteen-year-old that was caught serendipitously. The kid was playing football, took a hard hit to the noodle, and ended up having a CT scan that discovered the tumor. It's still relatively small but aggressive and that's where my mind needs to be.

On this kid and saving his life so he can graduate high school and play professional ball, since that's what he told me his dream is—I always ask kids before surgery what their dream is because it gives them something to focus on and fight for. I digress. My mind needs to be on this kid.

Not on Raven. Not on my asshole brother who feels like he's playing me.

I cover my hair with my scrub cap, don the shoe sleeves, and hold a mask up to my face before storming into an OR I have zero business storming into. Except my thieving, conniving, underhanded brother is in here.

"What the hell were you doing having lunch with Raven today? Are you trying to steal her from me?" I bark out and all heads swivel in my direction save for one. Kaplan doesn't even twitch a muscle as he continues to stare down into... a tiny baby's open chest. Shit.

I'm seriously losing my mind, and this is not who I am.

"Bovie that small bleeder," he says to some resident beside him, who eagerly springs into action. "Luca, did you know that the heart I'm currently operating on is about the size of a large walnut and weighs approximately twenty-five grams?"

"I do now."

"This little guy has hypoplastic left heart syndrome and since you're not a total moron, I know you appreciate the severity of such a condition. And given the size of the child and the size of the heart, you have to imagine that my total and complete concentration is required."

Yeah. I'm a dick.

"Kap... I'm going into surgery on a fifteen-year-old's brain in ten minutes. Please, just tell me now so I can get my head straight."

"No. Which incidentally is something you should have already known. I watched both of you lose your absolute minds in heartbreak that night at the Vineyard and I did the only thing I could think of to help you both. I befriended her. I listened when she cried, and I planted tiny seeds that you were just as miserable as she was and stalking her all across the planet because you couldn't handle what had happened between the two of you even if you knew it was the way it was supposed to be. She is in Boston because I spoke with the board of the Boston Symphony Orchestra and demanded they make her a better offer than any other orchestra out there who was wooing her, which they all were. I also helped facilitate a job for her in this hospital as a quasi music therapist. One, because it's what she's passionate about and I like making her happy. Two, because you work here, and I knew your paths would eventually cross. I am helping you, little brother, and I am helping her. Now shut your mouth and don't screw up the gift I'm giving you and get out of my OR."

Damn. I'm such a fool. "I can't hug you right now, but I think you already know, if I could, I would."

"Pansy-ass."

I chuckle. "I love you, Kap."

"Love you too. Let today be the day we both save some lives."

Amen to that. And as I walk out of my brother's OR and head for my own, I'm grinning like a lunatic. No more running. Time to catch my Little Bird and make her mine for good.

21

Ducking into Dunkin' Donuts, I race for the bathroom, feeling Luca's freaking cum dripping down my inner thigh. I suck in a sob and lock the door behind me, peeing and cleaning myself up. It's a single bathroom and I have nowhere else to look but at the giant mirror across from me that's broadcasting my reflection.

"You look like you just got fucked in an alley."

I groan, my face falling into my hands.

I can't believe I did that. That I allowed him to do that. That once again I'm sans panties and my hair is a mess and yup, that's a nice red mark on my lower neck. A tear falls down my cheek. Thank God for birth control. Oddly enough, I didn't need him to tell me he was clean or that I'm the only woman he's ever been bare with. Somehow, I already knew that.

Luca Fritz might have hurt me, but he'd never *hurt* me.

"Hot mess, girl. You are one hot mess."

That La Perla bag had been taunting me like the devil she was and even Jesus's mother couldn't stop me last night from opening it. I had a glass of wine or three and peeked inside. Then I tried everything on and this next morning I picked out the panties, garter, and thigh-highs he bought me because they made me feel sexy. Knowing he had gone to the store and picked them out himself, picturing them on me when he did. I felt beautiful and confident in them and that's what I was aiming for heading into my interview.

Now, I feel... I don't know what I feel.

I told him I hated him. And his response... *"But God, Raven, do I love you."*

I shudder, shaking. More tears fall and I can't make sense of them.

That look in his eyes as he begged me not to regret it. As he told me he would give me space. *I want you. Only you. Always. I will wait and I will fight, and I will try to be patient, but don't run from me.*

How do I reconcile this?

How is this the same man who stared directly into my eyes and told me he didn't love me? That he didn't want me. Who told me to move on because he had.

Flushing the toilet, I stand up, pull down my dress, and head for the sink. I wash my hands and then run my fingers through my tangled hair before applying some concealer from my purse onto the red mark he gave me and removing the mascara stains from beneath my eyes. But I still don't look like me.

Someone knocks on the door, and I exit, heading back out into the cold November day. I need to be at rehearsal in a half an hour now and my plan had been to walk. It's not too far from where I am, but I'm running out of time.

And my hands are shaking.

And my body is too.

Making a decision, I duck into a bar on Huntington. It's a college bar, dark and aggressively reeks of stale beer and crappy cologne, but I don't care. "May I have two shots of..." I pause. What won't stink on my breath? "Fireball?" I begrudgingly ask because I have cinnamon gum in my purse, and I can play it off well enough.

"You got ID?" the bartender asks and after I show it to him, he pours me my two shots. I slam them both, toss him some money, and then race out, as I hear the T rumbling up the street. Somehow, I didn't miss it, I climb on, and shove two sticks of gum into my mouth while not making eye contact with anyone.

I've just had public sex in an alley beside a children's hospital.

A strange sort of smile curls up my lips. I did some wild things with Luca Fritz that summer, but I have to say, this takes the cake. *Don't regret it.*

Do I?

How can a human regret two mind-blowing orgasms all within the span of ten minutes?

In truth, I could go down the dark and slippery path of self-doubt and what this all means, but frankly, I just don't have the mental energy for it. It doesn't have to mean anything I don't want it to. I got off. He got off. He said some stuff. I'll pray like hell I don't think about it until tonight when I allow myself a five-minute mental freak-out.

There.

Hopping off the T at Symphony Hall, I rush into rehearsal, grateful things haven't started yet. The performances we had done before were a special charity event, lasting four concerts in total and raising a lot of money for Dana Farber. But now we're back into regular symphony mode. Well, holiday symphony mode since Thanksgiving is a little more than two weeks away.

"Hey," Catarina greets me without looking up, her eyes fixed on her oboe.

"Hey." I head for Azrael, unzipping her from her case, and sag in relief. This is what I do. This is what I know. God, I wish I were wearing panties right now. Or pants since I have to spread my damn legs and stick a cello between them in front of a hundred people.

"Jerimiah wishes you luck today. I saw him before I came in."

I glance up. "Why do I need luck today?"

"You know we're playing through all the pieces once and then Friday Antonio is letting us know who he wants for his solos, right?"

My hands freeze. As do my insides. "No. I didn't know that."

She laughs lightly. "Like you have anything to worry about."

"Uh-huh," I whisper absently, though my heart is thundering. I never had an ounce of stage fright until I moved to London. I could have played for the Queen before that without an ounce of nerves, but then I entered this amazing school filled with amazing artists and whether I like to admit this or not, my confidence and faith in myself had just been rocked. Severely rocked.

I was suffering once again from a case of I'm not good enough and it carried over to my music. I quickly learned people in these types of situations, these types of schools are not out to be your friend. They are your competition. Your frenemy. They sling anything they can at you to make you doubt yourself all the while doing it with a smile and an "I'm just trying to be helpful" song.

The "you keep your friends close but your enemies even closer" type.

Two months in, I was throwing up before even simple performances and that included most of my classes. It got to be so bad, I was petrified I'd never be able to play in front of anyone again.

I knew I needed to do something about it, so I started with psych classes. And my world changed. I also secretly met with a therapist there once a week. I thought I was completely over it.

Not even batting an eye about performing toward the end of my time in London or when I was traveling after. Then I moved back here and started with this symphony, and I don't know what happened.

It's not anywhere near as bad as it was when I first started school, but I hate that it's back at all. However, right now, I'm not as nervous as I would be. Could have something to do with the two shots of Fireball warming my belly. Or the two orgasms before it.

"Why are you making that face?"

"What face?" I respond far too quickly, my voice higher than a cheerleader at a pep rally.

"And is that..."

"What? What are you doing?" I squeak when she stands up, walking toward me with large, purposeful strides. Her black pixie hair is spiked today, and her brown eyes are lined in black, giving her a beautiful evil devil look.

"Is that..." Her voice trails off as she gets closer, her inquisitive eyes lasered in on my neck. My hand flies up, clapping over the spot I know she already saw, and a triumphant grin breaks out across her face. "Oh, it is. Oh, it most certainly is. You have a hickey on your neck the size of a quarter that you did a shit job of covering with concealer." She waves a hand around my face. "And you're... I don't know. Red. Tussled. You totally had sex with someone, didn't you? Hot super orgasmic sex by the look of you."

"You can't know that!" I practically screech. "Maybe I just used my vibrator."

"And it gave you a hickey?" I get a "who the hell are you kidding" face.

I'm seriously going to kill Luca for that. Him and his damn mouth. That stupidly hot, dirty mouth.

"It's fine," she tells me. "Sex is natural, and everyone does it. And the people who don't and are of age, seriously need to. You don't need to be embarrassed. I'm proud of you for getting some. Hopefully, it'll help you relax. You're damn tense, woman. But who was it? Who put that sexed-up muss all over you? Do I know them?" She leans in and whispers, her eyes tracking over to the partially open door. "Was it Antonio? I heard he has a magic penis if you're into those and can move past the halitosis."

"No. It was definitely not Antonio."

"But it was someone. And by the look of you, they gave it to you good." She fans her face. "Damn. I'm loving this. Details. I'm gonna need *all* the details."

Frantically, I glance toward the door, my eyes wide. "We're not doing this. We have to go out and play in a minute."

"Then you have exactly one minute to tell me absolutely every last detail. I may not be into penises, but I can appreciate the sport, if you know what I mean. Come on," she whines. "Don't hold out on me. You're redder than blood splatter in the snow right now."

"What?"

She waves me away. "I was watching *Law & Order* reruns before I came in. Unlike someone who has hickey giving, dopey smile inducing, orgasmic sex."

I shake my head, debating if I should tell her I just had regular bed sex or dirty alley sex when Quill comes busting in. "Bitches, it's playtime!" She freezes when she sees us. "What? What did I miss?"

"Raven had sex."

"Catarina!" I smack at her shoulder.

"Oh, please. It's just Quill. Quill wouldn't talk shit if she had a mouthful of it. Would you?"

Quill shakes her head, her blonde chin-length bob swinging around her. "Absolutely not. Not a peep out of me. So... sex?" Her eyebrows bounce up and down suggestively before she shuts the door behind her. "Are we talking good sex?

Like life-changing, vagina-ruining, toe-curling, I can hardly walk now sex? You're dealing with two taken ladies. Let us live vicariously some."

Ugh.

I fall against Catarina. Never in my life have I had girlfriends. I had Rina, but she's older than I am by several years. When your parents are spies and you grow up with a family of billionaires, you learn that trusting people is a dangerous game to play. Plus, when you spend all your free time playing the cello, you're not exactly hanging out at the mall with your besties. I was an emo orchestra nerd. And I was okay with that. I mean, at least I never gave it a ton of thought before.

But now... now it might be nice to have someone who doesn't know my life and isn't intimately ingrained in it to talk to. I open my mouth to start spilling my guts, when there's a knock on the door.

"You're needed on stage," someone calls out.

"Later," Catarina demands with a pointed finger. "You'll tell us later?" This time she's checking.

"Later," I promise as we grab our instruments and head to practice.

Entering the stage area, I take my seat beside the other cellos, who give me that grin that doesn't touch their eyes and could never be considered a smile. They don't like me, and I understand it. I'm twenty-two and came in as first chair and was immediately given a solo. You don't win over love and affection that way.

Antonio stands at the podium, calling us to the piece already set up on our music stands. "Winter" by Vivaldi is typically a piano piece, but it's been reconstructed for the entire orchestra.

He finds me, staring for a moment before he begins moving his arms, starting the piano first before bringing in the violins, flutes, oboes, and clarinets. The piece continues and I play along until it grows to a mournful juncture and then Antonio cuts out all other instruments and then it's just the cellos. All four of us, but I know what this is and so does everyone else.

My eyes close and I force my breath to remain even.

It's just rehearsal. Just notes. Play, Raven. You were born to play.

We play for three measures and then percussion enters in, and I breathe a sigh, still hating that I'm reacting this way, yet oddly grateful I downed the two shots after what happened earlier with Luca. I don't even care. Whatever it takes to make it through this.

One song morphs into another and then he breaks us up by instrument groups, having us each play leads on various pieces.

Five hours later, I'm entering the back room to store my performance cello I keep here and find Catarina and Quill somehow already waiting for me along with... flowers.

"These just arrived for you," Quill says with a smug grin. "And this time, they have a card."

"Oh?" I stare at the bouquet. White roses and I nearly laugh. Is he waving the proverbial white flag? Never. Luca Fritz never surrenders.

"Did you read it?"

"No," Catarina replies primly, perched on the edge of the counter. "We were waiting for you, but the temptation was killing us. Good thing you came in when you did. I'm assuming these are from the hot sex guy?" Her fingers rake over one of the roses, caressing the petals.

"Likely, yes."

"And is hot sex guy *the flowers* guy?"

"He could be."

"Do you ever answer anything directly?"

I grin. "I was trained not to." They think I'm kidding. I'm absolutely not.

"Oh my. The plot thickens." Catarina is having such a difficult time holding in her curiosity, she's practically vibrating.

Licking my suddenly dry lips, I make my way toward the huge vase of white. At least two dozen and all perfect. I inhale their fragrance, smiling stupidly despite myself. I grab the card from the holder and open it.

"My love for you is a puzzle... for which I have no answers. I can't control it... and now I don't care. I truly, deeply love you." - Padme Amidala

I crack up before I can stop it, my eyes thick with tears once more. He freaking sent me a Star Wars quote. So Luca, it's ridiculous. And that quote, those words. I sigh. This man.

"What? What does it say? Who is it from?"

I hand Quill the card and she reads it, her jaw agape by the end. "Um. Wow. Just... yeah, wow."

Catarina snatches the card from her hand. "Who is Padme? That's a total chick name and I know you're not gay."

"Padme is the mother to Luke and Leia Skywalker."

They both shake their heads in unison as I take another inhale of the flowers.

"You mean like in Star Wars? I don't understand."

"Yeah. Me neither."

"Sucks to be you then." I wink at them.

"You're not going to tell us?" Catarina is incredulous, but I can't. I might have been ready to open up about all of this before, but now... I don't know. What would I say? Luca is famous. A billionaire. And anything between us would be construed wrongly. I'm not ready to share that, especially when anything I would share is suffused in heartache.

"I've sort of reunited with someone. Someone who I... someone who I was in love with once. And then he broke my heart and now..." Now I hate him. Only somehow that doesn't feel right to say anymore.

"And now?" Quill prompts.

"And now I don't know."

"This mysterious man is the one who has been sending you

flowers for years. Even though he broke your heart and is back in your life and bed, but you don't know what it is?" she surmises, a touch incredulous.

I stare at the flowers. "I don't want to get my heart broken again." I gave him all of me once, but that wasn't enough. What if it's not this time around either?

Catarina wraps her arms around me from behind and Quill joins in on the other side of us and somehow, I'm crying. I can't remember the last time someone held me or hugged me like this, not including my father, because it's different. Octavia gives me love and comfort and support, but I've never cried on her shoulder the way I am now. Certainly not about her son and the number he did on me.

"Do you want me to take a bat to him until his lungs bleed?" Catarina asks.

A croak of a laugh sputters out of me and I pull back, wiping my nose and eyes with the back of my arm. "No. Not yet."

"It's a standing offer," she tells me, winking.

"That goes for me too. We know it's not easy for you here, but we have your back. With anything."

"Thank you. I am so grateful for your friendship and understanding." Because there isn't anything else to say to that. It's everything. These women are my friends, and this is not The Conservatory.

I get another two simultaneous hugs for that as they squeeze the life from me.

"Anyone want to take these home?"

"No," Catarina says, her voice firm as she pulls back, touching one of the roses with delicate fingers, her expression one of reverence. "These flowers... this time you're keeping them. No excuses allowed. They are the essence of love and so is this card. Whether he broke your heart in the past or not."

I stare at them, at the card still in Catarina's hand, and I take it back from her, holding the thick card stock tightly in my palm.

"Okay. These flowers I'll keep."

Because I fucked Luca Fritz in an alley today and he told me he loved me. Always. That he wants me. Forever. And then he sent me flowers with a line he knows only I'll get. It was designed to make me happy. To have me smiling and laughing. To make me feel loved.

Even though looming in the back of my mind, I know he's done and said all of this before. And I'd be a fool to believe this time is different.

22

Today is a day that by the end of it, it will be a miracle if I haven't thrown up at least twenty times or martinied myself into a stupor. The hospital is busy, teaming with a vibe and a buzz that feeds the hum rushing through my system. I'm excited beyond words about this, but my nerves are also getting the best of me.

What if the kids don't like me?

What if I don't do a good job with them?

"You're fine," Kaplan says without so much as a glance in my direction. I didn't even have to say a word, but somehow, he knows. That's Kaplan for you, I guess. He always seems to know. He shifts, adjusting my cello on his shoulder because he wouldn't let me carry it myself. Even though I do that every single day of my life.

My mother wouldn't like it, was his reasoning.

"You didn't have to walk me up, though. I know you're busy," I tell him as he presses the button for the neuro floor. A floor that is not his.

He doesn't reply, just crowds me to the back as other people get on with us.

"I got a text yesterday," he whispers, leaning down and catching my ear so others can't hear.

I blink before tilting my head up to his. "What does that mean? From who?"

"The older brother of an old friend of mine is coming to Boston this February for a quick trip. I haven't thought about her, the old friend that is, or her brothers in... Anyway, I'm walking you up."

I shake my head. "I have no idea what any of that means."

"Neither do I. I have no idea what it means."

"You're being cryptic as hell."

"I know. But when it comes to this particular old friend, I can't help it."

"Ummm..." I think about this. "Okay." Yep, that's all I got. "Well, if you ever figure it out, I'm here for you."

"Love you too, babe." He tosses me a wink and then the doors part. His hand meets my lower back as he guides me through and onto the floor, swiping his hospital badge even though I have one now too. "Don't show fear. Whatever you do, listen, make eye contact, treat them as their own human being and not a disease or condition, but above all else show no fear."

I pat Kaplan's shoulder as we reach the common room at the end of the hall, taking my cello from his back and placing the strap over my shoulder. "You'll make a great dad one day."

"Shhh," he admonishes, feigning panic as his head whips dramatically around. "There are ears in this place. And they hear everything. Don't speak such blasphemy." He gives me a wink. "Knock 'em healthy, babe." He drops a kiss on the top of my head and then saunters off, every single nurse and patients' mother doing a double take as he passes.

The room is already loaded with instruments stuffed into the corner as if someone dumped them in. I cringe and go at it, getting the room set up and ready. I have an hour before the kids come and it ends up taking me that entire hour to get the room set up exactly how I want it. Hospital lights are harsh, so I brought in lamps with color changing light bulbs that through an app I have, will pulse and change colors to the beat of our music.

I also set up the small area rugs on the floor, one for each kid, and chairs set in the back in case any of us—including myself since I play the cello—will need to sit.

When the first knock comes on the door, I practically squeal, holding in my desire to jump up and down and clap my hands like a twelve-year-old. A swell of fresh nerves fight their way into my bloodstream, but I tamp it all down as I open the door, allowing six kids to enter, filing in one by one. Some are hooked up to oxygen through nasal cannulas. Some have IVs going. A couple are bald—shaved heads with stapled scars in different places.

All staring at me and then at the room as if they're not quite sure what they just walked into or what they signed up for.

For a second, I can't catch my breath and it has nothing to do with my nerves. These kids are all around Stella's and Layla's age. I don't know their situation or their diagnoses, but theirs is a visceral sucker punch. I quickly recover, a new sense of warmth and purpose spreading through me.

Three nurses hover by the door, making sure their charges are okay and as they should be.

"Everyone pick a spot. Don't worry about the instruments yet and if you'd rather sit in a chair, just let me know." I turn to the door. "Do you want to stay?" I ask the nurses.

"Nope. We'll be back in an hour and a half. Just hit this button"—one of them taps her finger on a small keypad that has a red button on it—"if there's a problem."

"Got it. Thank you."

I get a good-luck grin from each of them and then they shut the door, leaving me alone with the kids, who have all taken seats on the floor, even the kids with oxygen tanks and IV stands beside them.

"I'm Raven Fairchild," I start, taking a seat in the one remaining spot, sitting cross-legged. "I am a cellist by trade and currently play for the Boston Symphony Pops Orchestra. Couple rules before we get started, okay?"

They groan collectively and I can't help but smirk.

"Come on. They're not so bad." I shift a little, rocking back and forth so I can get comfortable. "This is a safe place. That means we don't laugh at anyone. We don't judge anyone. We show respect to our fellow musicians. Everyone has a different way of expressing themselves and that's cool. That's art. That's music. So I will not tolerate talking shit about anyone."

I get some giggles now for my swear, which was obviously my intention.

"That is also the last time I will swear in here and that's another thing we can't do because I don't want to hear about it from your parents or nurses." I feign horror and the resulting smiles tell me they're starting to warm up to me.

"So, we just play music? That's it?" a girl with huge brown eyes and a shaved head with a giant stapled scar by her temple asks.

"What's your name?" I ask her.

"Genevieve, but everyone calls me Gen."

I nod. "Gen, that's one of the things we'll do for sure. If you're interested in learning how to play an instrument, I can help with that. If you just want to jam out, I can do that too. If you want to listen to a song and talk about it after, that's cool with me. This is your space more than it's mine. Let's go around and introduce ourselves and then I thought we'd play a game. You in?"

They tell me their names and I drag a chair out of the corner and open up my cello case, setting myself up. Their eyes are curiously glued to my instrument and then my phone as I bend, start the app, and hit play. Music streams through the speaker of my phone and the light morphs in sync, transitioning between red, pink, blue, purple, green, yellow, and orange.

I get a couple of oohs and aahs and cools from them.

"Who can tell me the name of this song?" I ask once the song is about halfway through.

Beth raises her hand like it's school and I nod in her direction. "Lady Gaga's 'Alejandro.'"

"Perfect." I hit pause and the lights return to normal. Then I get myself ready and start playing "Csárdás" by Vittorio Monti. It only takes me a few measures before their eyes light up.

"Hey, she stole that," Marcus grumbles indignantly.

I shake my head, coming to a rest. "She didn't. She had permission to use it or it's not under copyright anymore. Trust me on that. Want another one?"

"Yeah," Cindi exclaims, playing with the tubing of her IV that's attached to a port in her chest.

"This one might not be so obvious." I hit play and music filters in through the room, the light show starting again, and I can't help my smile as all of their faces glow with excitement.

"Oh, that's 'Memories' by Maroon 5."

"Yup." I point my bow at Tom.

I hit stop and start playing Pachelbel's "Canon in D minor", which is traditionally a cello piece, so it really soars through the room. The kids stare intently at my cello, listening closely, and once they hear the similarities between the chord progressions, I start getting some nods.

"Wow. Weird."

I stop playing and set my cello aside, rejoining them on the floor. "It is, right?" I tell Gen. "There are tons of other classical pieces out there that have influenced modern music. Classical music is my jam. I perform it. I write it. I live it. I breathe it. And at my funeral, they'll be playing it. But it's not what speaks to everyone, and I get that. I thought I'd play something I wrote and then how about you each take a shot at making something else out of it? Anything you want. Something that gets you going. That you connect with. We'll record it and then play it in my app, so the lights dance with it. Sound fun?"

I play for them something I wrote years ago and then each kid goes for an instrument and then it's all a lot of noise. Pounding of drums and banging of piano keys and clomping of xylophones. Once they're satisfied with their masterpieces, I have them each playing it while I record it and the lights flash along to our symphony.

The hour and a half fly by and when I call an end to our session, I get some groans of disappointment, which kind of makes me want to weep happy tears. This has been one of the best mornings of my life. I stumbled upon psychology as a way to help me overcome my own inner demons, but the reward of helping others—especially children—is like nothing else.

"I'm here next Friday with you since I'm on this floor only once a week. Think about what you might want to do, and I'll leave the instruments here so you can come and play them during the week."

I open the door and halt in my tracks. Luca is down the hall, talking to another doctor. Crap. I had been hoping to avoid him today. After what happened Wednesday, I'm not yet ready to see him.

Cindi sighs deeply beside me. "He's so hot."

I snicker. "You mean Dr. Fritz?"

"Yup. All the girls on the floor are obsessed. And that includes the nurses," Tom mutters derisively. "And the moms."

That I believe.

"You're just jealous," Gen snaps.

"Whatever," he grumbles.

I try not to think about all the nurses and moms on the floor who ogle him. As if he knows we're talking about him, his gaze cuts in our direction and his eyes lock with mine. A smirk hits his gorgeous face and like a Pavlovian response, my heart instantly reacts, racing around in my chest.

"Oh my God. He's totally staring at you. I'm shipping this like so hard while being completely jealous." Cindi nudges me in the back. "Do you know him?"

"A little," I lie. "Who is Dr. Fritz talking to?"

"That's Dr. Grosspooper," Tom declares, and I nearly choke on my own saliva.

I break my stare and flip around to all the kids who are huddled in behind me since I'm blocking the doorway. "I'm sorry. What did you just say?"

"Dr. Grosspooper," he repeats, his expression neutral. Not even a crack of a smile.

"No. That's not his name."

"Sure is," Marcus promises.

"*Grosspooper*?"

"Don't believe us? Here. Melissa?" he calls out to one of the nurses approaching us. "Who is talking to Dr. Fritz?"

Melissa's head flips over her shoulder, smiles a little too brightly at Luca, and then flips back to us. "You mean Dr. Grosspooper?"

I can't stop my incredulous laugh and now I feel like one of the kids. "You're messing with me, right?" I ask her.

She shakes her head, but she's biting into her lip as she suppresses her smile. "That's his name. Ask any of the kids, residents, or nurses on the floor. Right, guys?"

"Yup. Totally. That's his name," they all reply.

Oh boy.

"All right, everyone, time to get back." I step to the side, letting the kids pass. "Thank you! I can't wait for next week."

I get some waves and thank yous as everyone passes. Tom winks at me like a teenage flirt. Then I go back in and grab my cello, hoping that Luca will have moved on by the time I go to leave. No such luck. He's still there, talking it up with... Dr. Grosspooper.

With no choice but to head in their direction, I can only pray Luca doesn't stop me. First, I don't want to talk to him. I'm not in the mood for our back and forth or fighting. Or hot and sexy stuff. Second, I won't be able to hold my shit together if I have to say the other doctor's name.

How does a man go into pediatrics with a name like that?

It defies reason and logic. Kids live for an easy pass at teasing.

My head held high, my eyes on the prize—the two giant twin exit doors—I manage to put one foot in front of the other. Even though I feel Luca's eyes all over me. But he has no clue what today is. Other than my first day here, today is also selection day. In a very *Hunger Games* sort of way. Who gets solos for the winter holiday performance and who doesn't. And while I'd love nothing more than to scream I volunteer as tribute, I'm just not that brave yet. I'm working on it. I'm getting there. The mind is a tricky field of monstrous thoughts and I'm still tiptoeing along.

I make it ten steps down the hall before the pull becomes too much. The stare too intense. The sensation of the man too alluring.

In a moment of weakness, my gaze flashes in his direction and he's right there. Talking to that Grosspooper guy while staring at me as if he's picturing me naked. Grinning as if he knows what the inside of my pussy feels like around his dick.

"Raven," he calls out. "Hold up a minute. There's someone I'd love for you to meet."

Oh no, he motherfucking didn't. The amusement in his voice tells me he is a man with a master plan.

"Who's this, Luca?"

The man sounds like a caricature of a British aristocrat from a Disney movie and now I have no choice but to slow my escape and join the two men who have taken up the majority of the hall, forcing all others to shift their current around their island.

Shame I can't pull a *Miss Congeniality* on Luca... solar plexus, instep, nose, groin.

I think he can read my inner musing because his conceited grin only grows.

"Your balls are in danger, Doctor," I rumble in his direction.

His hand somehow meets my ass under my cello, giving it a squeeze before it lands firmly on my back shoulder. "Alvin, this is Raven Fairchild. Cello savant and our new musical kid guru. Raven, Alvin is the chief of pediatric neurosurgery."

"It's a pleasure to meet you, Alvin." I smile brightly at him, thinking it's a bit strange that Luca didn't call him doctor or introduce him using his last name, but then again, if my last name were Grosspooper, I wouldn't want anyone using it either.

"Oh," Alvin exclaims, giving me a long once-over. "Yes. Lovely. Brilliant. We're so happy to have you here with us."

I almost snort out a laugh. If this guy is English, my father was never MI6. "Thank you. I'm delighted to be here."

"Raven studied at The Conservatory in London," Luca continues. "Her father's home country, she felt compelled to return there. I'm sure the two of you could exchange stories about London. That is where you said you were from, right?"

Alvin Grosspooper grows pale. "Just outside of it, yeah. Brilliant."

I throw Luca a side-eye, only to feel his hand squeeze tighter against my shoulder.

"I'd love that, but some other time perhaps. If I don't get going now, I'll be late for rehearsal."

"Oh yes. Of course. Wouldn't want to hold you up and make you late."

Judging by his expression, I think Mister Fake English is relieved by that.

"Well, I have to be going now. Patients to see and all that. Cheers." And then he scurries off.

I turn on Luca, dropping my voice. "You know he's not English, right? And if he is, he's putting on one hell of an accent to cover another."

"Yes, but we haven't been able to prove that yet, so..." He shrugs simply, his eyes all over me, his impish smirk still curling up his lips.

"Is his name actually Grosspooper?"

Luca bursts out laughing, shaking his head. "Anyone who isn't NPO (nothing by mouth) gets an ice cream from the cafeteria on me," he calls out. "That includes all staff." There's a round of cheers and clapping, but before I can take in the scene around me, he's grabbing my hip and pushing me back a few steps to make room for a passing gurney. "I see my kids and nurses got you."

Ugh. I knew it. "They definitely did, and it seems they deserve those ice creams. What's his real name?" I cover my hands with my face. "God, what if I had called him that to his face?"

Luca chuckles, pealing my hands away from my face. "Now you know why I didn't introduce you to him using his last name. His real last name is Grosspotter. On this floor, and I suspect the entire hospital, he's either secretly referred to as Dr. Harry Potter or Dr. Grosspooper."

"I... I love that actually."

"It keeps the kids smiling and laughing. How was your first day?"

"Brilliant. Top-notch," I mock Dr. Grosspooper.

Luca cracks up, shifting me even closer to what looks dangerously like a supply closet. "You have no idea how hot it makes me when you mock my superiors and bond with my patients. Can I buy you lunch? Take you home with me after?"

"No and no. I have rehearsal. I didn't lie even if your boss does."

"He's a great doctor. Just a bit of a douche with a secret, is my guess. Anyway, if you won't let me get some nookie, you'll at least let me drive you to rehearsal, right?"

"Nope again." I shove Luca off me and head for the huge double doors that will lead to my freedom.

An arm wraps around my waist, yanking me into an empty patient room. He pushes my cello to the side as his mouth hits the back of my neck. The skin beneath my ear. I shudder, my eyes closing of their own volition. "Look out that window."

"Uh-huh." I can't manage to open my eyes while I'm reminding myself how to breathe and push him away at the same time.

"It's sleeting, Little Bird. I'm not letting you wait outside for the T in this. You'll be soaked and frozen through in minutes. And think of the pretty cello on your back."

Crap. I didn't realize the weather had turned. The news said not until tonight, so I didn't bring an umbrella with me. Welcome to November in Boston.

"I'm done for the day as luck would have it since I've been on since midnight. I'm driving you."

"Luca—"

"No arguing. I'm driving you."

"You're—"

"Not only a god in the sack but a hero among mortals and I'm helplessly in love with you?" He finishes for me, though that was clearly not what I was about to say. He kisses my neck, just beneath my hairline, holding my ponytail up. "I know. And lucky for you, I love it when you praise me."

I jab a backward elbow, hitting him straight in the flank. "If I let you drive me, you are not to speak."

Another kiss that has my whole body shuddering, and my nipples hardening. "I believe I've already heard this same warning before, and I didn't listen then. What makes you think I'll listen now?"

Reaching behind me, my hand glides up his thigh until I grab his hard dick through his scrubs. He moans, rocking into my touch. Then I squeeze. Hard. He hisses out a breath, his movements now paralyzed as he grunts in pain. "Fuck." I squeeze harder. "Okay. I'll behave. Shit." A wheeze. "Release. I'll only drive you. Promise."

"Good boy," I purr, releasing my grip and patting his dick before stepping out of his touch.

He spins me to face him. "You think that's turning me off, but it's not. Strong women who know how to handle my dick are my Viagra." Luca presses a kiss to my cheek. "Did I mention they're also *only* named Raven?"

I roll my eyes while fighting my grin. I hate how easily the man can make me smile. Even at his childish antics. "You're making me late, Fritz."

"Then let's go, Fairchild. I'd hate for you to be late on account of my dick and its kink."

Six hours later, my concern over vomiting hasn't abated. Luca dropped me off and true to his word, he didn't utter a peep in the car, though I could see him struggling with that. Any chance he could get away with it, his eyes were on me. He drove me, dropped me off in front, and helped me get my cello out of his trunk. I thanked him, and that was it.

The man makes me feel like an exposed wire near water—charged and ready to electrocute anyone who comes within touching distance.

But right now, I have much greater concerns than him.

I'm beyond exhausted. My back hurts. My nerves are frazzled. And I know what's coming next as I'm being called into Antonio's office. The last person here to learn their solo fate. Antonio had us play through the entire holiday arrangement and then one by one brought us into his office. We're talking a hundred people.

Quill saunters past me, giving me a sympathetic look. "Do you want me to stay?" she asks.

I shake my head, letting her know I've got this. "No. Get on home to your husband."

She smirks cheekily. "We are anyway. See you back there." I get a wink and I reach out and grab her shoulder, letting her know how grateful I am. After the flowers, my relationship and trust with them have soared.

I knock on the office door and immediately Antonio's thick Italian lilt rings out with, "Come in."

Sucking in a breath, I open the door and walk in, taking a seat when Antonio gestures toward the chair. His face is stuck on music sheets that I doubt he's reading because... why would he? That's simply a bit weird. But whatever. He's wearing his glasses and doing this all-empowered thing, so I wait him out.

Finally, he puts them down and leans back in his large leather chair, appraising me. "You are exquisite, my Raven. Every time I listen to you play, it is as if the music is making love to me."

And what on earth do I say to that?

"Thank you."

"You came to us with the highest recommendation from the most prestigious music conservatory in the world. I gave you your solo for the charity concerts and you did not disappoint."

"Thank you." And now I feel like a broken record as I sit in this chair, spine straight, hands held tightly in my lap, eyes on him.

"*Mia bella*, I would like you to take first chair, as well as two solo performances in the holiday concert."

And now I've lost my breath as I stare incredulously at him. *Two solos?* I'm a half-beat from passing out. "You would? Two solos?"

He chuckles as if this should have been a foregone conclusion. "*Ma certo*. Of course," he translates. "You are the star of this symphony, no?"

"There are many talented performers."

"Ah. Yes. But none of them are you. You are the brightest star in the night sky. I also happen to know of several large donations that have been made in your honor."

The Fritzes. The most generous human beings in the world. It warms my heart how supportive and loving they are, but... I hate that Antonio knows about it. I don't know what to say, so instead I just sit here. I've already said thank you enough and it feels as though he's leading up to more.

"You will do two minutes in Fantasia on Christmas Carols and three minutes in O Holy Night."

Two solos. Five minutes. I shift in my seat, uncrossing and recrossing my legs. "Thank you." I inwardly cringe at my incessant repetition.

He chuckles lightly, taking his glasses off and tossing them onto his messy desk. "You are in love? No?"

"What?" I sputter out, totally taken aback by the change in course.

He shrugs dispassionately. "When I interviewed you for this position, you had told me you were single."

"Yes." At the time, it was a totally inappropriate question, same as this conversation.

"But then I find you with a man on your opening night. The same man I saw you with at the bar the very same night. Is he behind your mystery flowers?"

"Antonio..." My voice dies off.

I have no idea what to say. I do not want to sleep with him, and I do not want to give him the wrong impression. Nor do I want to earn something I do not deserve simply because he wants to fuck me. Or because I bring in donation money from a prominent wealthy family.

"I am single, but truly, I don't see how my personal life is pertinent to my work here."

"It was Luca Fritz, yes?" he continues as if I didn't say a word. "I recognized him. Impossible not to."

Clearly, the man is not taking the hint.

"Luca is an old family friend as are all of the Fritzes. I know their weight in this city and I know their wealth. But I do not want to be considered for something I have not earned."

He gives me a satisfied grin. "Nor I. My father was a famous conductor in Italy. It took me many moons to climb out of his shadow. No matter. I offer you this anyway because your playing gives anyone who hears it chills. *Magnifico*. Your talent has us all shining like stars." He sits up, pushing himself in closer to his desk and setting his hands over his discarded music sheets. "But, *mia bella*, should you ever find yourself in a place where you are single once more, I would love to take you to my bed where we can make music of our own."

Wow. That's... insanely cheesy and a little creepy and yup. "I will keep that in mind."

He nods, grinning at me as if he's so pleased with himself. "We discuss your solos more on Sunday. Special practice at ten."

"I'll be here."

"Good night then, Raven."

"Good night, Antonio."

Rocked to my core in too many ways, I exit his office, falling against the wall and trying to catch my breath. Two solos. Not one. *Two!* I can do this, though. I can. I *know* I can. I conquered my anxiety once. I can do it again. Time to make this thing my bitch.

ngry, loud gangsta rap pulses through my ears as I push myself a little faster, picking up speed. "So if you're at the show in the front row," I sing. "I fucking hate you, you bitch ass ho." I snicker to myself at my changeup in the lyrics. It's actually helping. Maybe I should have started twisting lyrics like this four years ago. "A crazy muthafucker from tha street, bitch I'll be your freak in the sheets."

Yeah... I gotta work on this. That's been done.

I'm in my final mile, knowing I can't outrun or drown out my thoughts completely but giving it my most valiant effort anyway. And nothing says zero romance or zero fucks to give like N.W.A. They turned misogyny into an art form. Because stupid fact, if I'm not freaking out about the upcoming solos, I'm freaking out about Luca.

And any time I try not to think about the solos or him, that all seems to backfire on me, and I think about them more. Especially Luca. Especially about the alley and the flowers and the hospital the other day. I still can't decide which way I come out on this with him.

Come. Right. More gangsta rap.

But if I go any louder, I'll burst my eardrums and then I'll really be screwed. *Screwed*. Ugh!

I don't know how to stop this or what to do about him. The deep, gnawing pain he caused in the darkest depths of my desolate soul. The way he's storming his way back into my life with the subtlety of a bull in a china shop. The way I seem helpless to stop him from doing that. The pathetic thoughts plaguing my mind.

I can't stop them, no matter how loud I listen to music or how much music I play or how early I force myself to bed or how hard I work out.

I'm curious about him. I have many questions I'm desperate for answers to. I want to know about the last four years of his life that I missed. I went from needing to know every thought that passed through his mind to avoiding everything that ever had anything to do with him to this.

I didn't know he worked at Children's *and* Brigham and Women's. That must mean he does both pediatrics and adults. But why? Why did he do that when he had been so set on adults? And his shoulder? It's obviously healed, but does he ever have any residual issues from it? Is his darkness completely gone and was I truly the reason for that?

But the worst question of all... the one I keep cycling back to... Argh! Enough! I need to stop doing this to myself.

The cold November wind stings my face and arms as I pump faster, my breath shooting out of me in white plumes. Up ahead is my building and just as my feet hit the exit of the Commons, someone's hand forcefully grabs my arm, trying to pull me back in. A scream hits the air and I spin around, flip the trigger on the small can I have poised in my hand, and spray with everything I've got.

The man bellows out in agony, releasing me as he staggers back a few paces while swearing and clawing his face as if it's on fire. It likely is since I'm spraying him with a man-made form of the active ingredient in hot peppers, oleoresin capsaicin, right into his eyes.

Only... "Luca?!" Oh my God! I just sprayed an entire can of pepper spray into his face.

The can slips from my hand, clanging on the ground as I run over to him, grabbing his arm and dragging him back a step because he's blindly getting dangerously close to the edge of the sidewalk and the street.

"What the fuck? You maced me? Ow! My face is on fire."

"It's pepper spray actually. Mace is illegal in Massachusetts without a proper permit. But who grabs someone when they're running in the park?"

"I called your name. Twice! Who runs in the park before dawn?"

"Someone with pepper spray. Are you okay? Can you see?"

He's still wiping furiously at his face, now using his sweat-drenched shirt to aid his efforts and if I wasn't terrified that he was blind or that I did some serious and permanent damage to his retinas, I'd be ogling his abs. Wrong time, I know, but damn, you haven't seen these things.

"My face feels like it's been blasted with a grenade and a blowtorch at the same time. Fuck!"

"I'm so sorry. You scared me and my dad always taught me to act first and ask questions later."

"Spoken like a true double-oh-seven."

"Are you following me?"

He chuckles, but there is zero humor to it. He moves his hands away from his face, blinks, and then winces, clenching his eyes shut again. "You're the one running before dawn. And on a Saturday no less."

I frown at the accusation in his voice. When I first moved to London, I kept up that routine. I told myself it was easier to run so early because then I got it out of the way or because I had a full day and no other time for exercise, but the truth was, I was heartbroken and running that early made me feel close to him in a way I told myself was quasi healthy because it involved exercise. Then it just became part of my life and I stopped thinking about the reasons behind it.

"Come on." I take his arm, giving him a jerk so he'll let me lead him. "Let's get some water on your face."

"I'm shocked you're not throwing a parade at my pain right now."

"Don't tempt me." I look both ways as we cross the street. Thankfully, it's early, so there isn't much traffic. "Walk, Luca, we need to get you inside and your eyes washed out."

"I thought you weren't going to ever invite me into your apartment."

I throw him a look he does not see. "Do you want me to let your face burn off?"

"Only if you'll nurse me back to health."

I roll my eyes as we hit the sidewalk, my hand locked on his arm, helping him since he can barely see. "Good morning, Dr. —are you okay, Dr. Fritz?"

"Morning, Greg. Yes, I'm fine. Just startled my lovely Little Bird here, is all."

I smirk, shaking my head as I lead us through the lobby and toward the elevator.

Greg is right beside us, pressing the button for me while staring at Luca, terribly concerned. "Can I get you anything? A cold compress or some water?"

"No, I'll just go up to my place to take care of it. I'll be fine, thank you."

"Your place?" I parrot, my eyebrows knitting for approximately one second before I realize just how stupid and naive I am.

The man owns the building. Of course he lives here. I just haven't seen him since I moved in. I come and go at strange hours, and he does too. Honestly, I truly didn't consider it. No one I told I was moving here or living here mentioned anything other than it's Luca's building. I took that to mean he owned it, not lived in it too.

The doors part and I help him on, all the while glaring. "You tricked me."

"I did not. You never asked where I live. Now punch in 3-7-0-0 into the keypad."

"That's my birthday."

"Yup. It sure is."

I enter his code and the elevator doors close. He falls back against the wall, holding his shirt up to his face once again, and I stare up at his profile. Tussled dark hair wet with sweat, abs cut from steel, gorgeous, indented V dipping into his track shorts. And... is that—

"If I told you I lived here, you wouldn't have agreed to move in."

"Because you knew I wouldn't want to live in the same building you do."

He shrugs up an unconcerned shoulder. "Next time do your homework. Your father raised you better than that, Miss Act First And Ask Questions Later. Speaking of, I happen to know you never mentioned a thing to him until after you signed the lease." He squints one eye open and glances down at me, only to immediately shut it once more.

"I just wish you had told me."

"And I'm glad I didn't because now you live here and so do I. All's fair in true love. After you, beautiful." He waves me out of the elevator into a foyer that's obviously part of his apartment. He clearly has the entire floor to himself. "I need to go wash my face. Make yourself at home and no running out. I want to show you something after my eyes are no longer melting from my face."

"What if I don't want to see it?" I call after him as he walks down the hall straight into what is likely a powder room.

"You do. Besides, you owe me after this."

He has a point.

"It better not be your dick."

He doesn't reply, but I hear the water running, and though I'm tempted to go snooping around his home, I'm also too afraid to do it. Nothing worms a man into your heart or out of it completely like their home can. It's already not starting off well for me. It smells clean in here. Like his cologne and wood polish. And from what little I can see from the foyer, his furniture isn't all black leather either, which is a shame.

I was hoping for a dingy black leather sectional with stinky sweat socks hanging off it and opened, empty pizza boxes scattered all over the floor. No such luck. I see cream and dark wood and gray and I refuse to go any farther.

"You ready?"

I spin around to find Luca smirking expectantly at me.

"You thought I'd run."

That smirk grows into a grin as he steps closer to me, towering over me with his height, forcing my gaze up. His poor eyes are bloodshot as hell and the skin around them is red.

"I thought I'd have to chase you, yeah."

"You're always going to have to chase me if you ever want to catch me."

"Challenge accepted." He holds out his hand to me. "Let's go."

"So... it's not your dick?"

He laughs, but his hand is now holding mine and he's leading me through his ginormous place. I mean HUGE, and no, that's not a euphemism for—

"Not my dick, but that's certainly on the menu if you're interested. I have four bedrooms, Little Bird, and I'd happily christen each one with you."

I snort, rolling my eyes to the sky and then back. "Right.

Like you haven't already done that with at least half a dozen women in each room."

He stops right before we reach a random set of curved stairs off the main room and stares intently down at me. "Raven, at some point you're going to have to believe me. Trust that the words I'm telling you are true. I've never brought a woman here before. I haven't slept with anyone. Since you, there has been no one. They call me Dr. Playboy, but I am not the playboy the world thinks I am. I don't fall in love every week. I'm not breaking the heart of some model or actress or socialite. I play a role and I go to events and there are women who are photographed with me. It's all a lie. In four years, my heart hasn't beat once for any other woman because it only beats for you."

That's when mine starts to hiccup.

He kisses my knuckles and then directs me up the stairs. They wind and twist and then he's unlocking a bolt attached to a glass door and suddenly we're on the rooftop of the building. But it's unlike any rooftop I've ever been on before. For one, it's entirely enclosed in glass. For another, it's a lounge with couches and a pool table and a freaking bar and televisions— yes, that's plural because there are three over the bar—and a foosball table and a pool.

And that pool is big. We're not talking Olympic size, but we are talking lap size and it's on a freaking roof!

"Luca..."

That's all I've got.

"If it weren't freezing outside right now, I'd press this button"—he points to a button on the wall—"and retract the glass."

"The roof opens?"

He laughs at my incredulous gasp. "As do the walls."

All I can do is shake my head. "Was any of this here when you bought the place?"

"The pool was and there was lounge space. I added the rest. This rooftop is actually why I bought the building two years before I moved back here, and the renovations took just as long."

Staring out at the Boston skyline, The Common and the Garden, I can't stop my astonished grin. "It's incredible." I spin back to face him. "But what if you hadn't gotten an attending position here?"

He gives me a look that says, don't you know who I am? "I'm an Abbot-Fritz, baby. For better or worse. I was promised two hospital positions before I even came close to finishing my residency."

"I'm proud of you. Not for any of this"—I pan my hands around the space—"but for all that you've accomplished. All you worked your way back from."

His face lights up like Times Square at midnight. And before I can brace myself for it, he launches himself at me, picking me up off the hardscape and jumping us straight into the pool. Our bodies go tumbling into the water with a hard *splash*, water flying every which way as we sink down to the bottom. He kisses me briefly under the water before he grips my hips tighter and pushes up with his feet from the pool floor. We emerge with a sputter and a gasp, all breathless laughter.

His mouth claims mine once more, grinning against my lips as I spit some water into his that he tries to spit right back into mine. I shove him away before he can, treading water and kicking my feet up, swimming away from him.

"You could have at least given me the chance to take my sneakers off." I hold one up, out of the water. They're absolutely ruined. Heavy as hell and soggy against my feet. And my socks. Ewwww.

"I'll buy you another pair."

I splash water at his face. "No, thanks."

"But I want to."

"I have my own money, Luca. I don't need yours."

I rip off my ruined sneakers, one by one, tossing them over to the stone hardscape. Then my shirt, leaving me in just my sports bra and running shorts.

I spin in the water, swimming away from him toward the edge of the pool, staring out the glass as dawn crests above the Boston skyscrapers, painting the eastern sky with pinks and purples. Luca comes in behind me, his hands on the wall on either side of mine, locking me in, his chest to my back.

"Your pool is heated."

"So is the hot tub."

"No kidding. I never would have guessed that."

His teeth nip at my shoulder, and I spin around in his arms, wrapping mine around his neck. "You're still wearing your shirt."

His eyes hold mine, but something flickers in them. Something I'm not sure I've ever seen on this man before. He rips his shirt over his head and tosses it away. His sneakers are next and now he's just in his shorts and—

"Luca..."

I gasp, my hand covering my lips. I can feel his nervous gaze on me, but I can't remove mine from the left side of his chest as it hovers above the water.

Tremulous fingers glide through it until I'm touching his warm, wet flesh. Right over black ink. "A bird that you set free may be caught again, but a word that escapes your lips will not return," I read.

"It's a Jewish proverb."

I know it is. My mother told it to me once when I was just a child. It was a warning to watch what I said because I had told a lie about eating a second cookie. So simple and so benign and yet now it's imprinted on him. For me. For us. I glide up along the script to the small black raven, hovering on a perch right above the quote.

Right over his heart.

A tear hits my cheek and I force my gaze up to his. "When did you get this?"

"On your birthday two years ago. When you were out at a club, dancing with my sister and Grace and being hit on by every man who saw you. I was there. I flew in for it, knowing you were coming home. I watched you smile and laugh and dance your heart out. I watched you dance with other men and... I was happy you were happy. But I was so miserable in my own skin I couldn't stand it. I needed you with me, so I did this."

I shake my head. He was here on my birthday? I never saw him. Had no clue he was even in town. My fingers tickle along the bird and he shivers against me, his eyes laser focused on me.

"You were never temporary. You were always permanent. I'm sorry if I had you believing otherwise. I chose you. I swear I did. And my heart stayed yours. Forever."

I swallow. So many things exploding in my head, but now I'm onto something else. His scar. It's all healed up, no longer pink, but white and rippled and slightly indented. So different from how I saw it the last time.

"Does it still hurt?"

"Every now and then I get a twinge in it. I had another surgery on it about a year after to clean up some of the scar tissue inside."

God, all this man has endured and look at him. A successful surgeon. Just as he always wanted to be. And I'm successful too. A first chair cellist for one of the best symphony orchestras in the nation, slotted for two solos in the holiday Pops performance. But even though we have all this success, something has always been missing from it.

It's been incomplete.

And with that thought, a familiar pain twists inside me.

He cups my face, forcing my eyes back up to his, so intense, my breath catches. "You think I abandoned you. Betrayed you. And maybe I did to some extent. But all I knew at the time was that I was saving you. I gave you a life. I saved you from yourself. The woman who was willing to sacrifice her life for mine. I couldn't let you do it. I could. Not. Let. You. Do. It."

Our foreheads meet and I bite my lip, holding in my sob. Water drips down my face from his hair as he holds me up, and right now, it feels like we're in our own world, high above the city, encased in glass, bathed in warm water.

"Do you not understand how much that shows my love? I let you fly away from me, knowing other men would be diving right in to take my place the second they could. Knowing I might never win you back after the words I said to you that night. The things I did. I did them because I could not let you squander a once-in-a-hundred-years talent. Because your passion and love made me a better man and I had to be better for you."

"I would have given up that world for you."

"No, baby. You couldn't have. Think of where you are now. All you've accomplished. You were young and we were in love, but I was old enough to know better than to let you do that. I'm so sorry I hurt you, including traveling to watch you play and sending you flowers. I didn't know that made things worse. Everything I did was to catch you again, my Little Bird."

"Luca... It's been so long since we've been anything. And even back then, it was so brief."

"Does that make it any less real?"

No. It doesn't. I can try and fool myself by saying it does, but what's the point?

"The last four years apart were not because I questioned if you were the one. They were because I knew you were. Now I just have to get you to believe it too."

24

Luca wraps me up in a big, warm towel and does the same for himself, but I can't stop myself from shivering. I don't know if it's the cold or the man or the words he said, but my body is trembling, and my mind is rattling. I don't want to be this girl.

The one holding onto a grudge.

I listened and I heard everything he said.

He's said stuff to me before. Stuff that swore love and promised forever. And I believed him then. With my whole heart. He promises he meant it, that the way he hurt me was to save me, and part of me knows that's true. But it doesn't erase what's already been done.

Or my lessons learned.

Luca seems to be all in. Ready to go from zero to sixty in no time flat.

We did that once and it didn't end well. I've been left one too many times by people who claimed to love me. Not again.

What sort of disservice would I be doing to myself if I threw caution to the wind and gave him everything I had? I don't know. I just know my heart isn't ready for that yet. It's slow to trust, slow to believe, and slow to forget. My yearning for him weakens me and that's not something I can allow to happen again.

"Can I show you around?" he asks as we step back into the main apartment. I nod, words not exactly my friend in this moment. "You're thinking a lot."

"I am."

"Good or bad?"

"Both."

He gives me a sideways look but doesn't push it. Something I appreciate as he leads me from room to room. An office, a media room, an exercise room, a game room that he swears is for when Stella comes over, a library loaded with books, a crazy amount of Star Wars paraphernalia, and a wood burning fireplace, and an empty room save for an area rug and a large baby grand piano.

"What's this room?"

"What I hope will one day be a music room."

I look up at him, staring into his green, heart-stopping eyes that hold on so tight, expressing every thought with a visceral directness. He's not embarrassed, not an ounce of hesitation. He made this room for me, and he wants me to know it. But it's unfinished and unfurnished, something I also know is for me.

He wants me to make it my own one day.

Pulse racing, I step into the room, staring around, picturing it filled with instruments. There's a gas fireplace in here and I can see it all. Practicing my cello by the fire while the snow falls outside, Luca in his library or media room or even his office, though I doubt that. That office sees no action because if Luca is working, he'll do so sitting on a large, comfy sofa with his feet kicked up and his laptop on his lap.

We knew each other so intimately once, but it was so brief. Yet somehow, we still seem to know exactly who the other is.

My nerves frazzle, fear gripping my voice as I start to shiver all over again, teeth chattering.

"Are you cold?" His arms wrap around me from behind, his chest to my back, his body heat somehow making my shivers worse.

"Yes."

Without another word, he spins me in his arms, hugging me, holding me to him, my ear against his pounding heart, and I know I'm not the only one scared of what this all means. Of where it will lead and where it won't.

"Let's do something about that."

His fingers twine with mine and he leads me out of the music room, through a great room and past a kitchen and dining room, along several other closed doors, all the way to the end of this mammoth place to his bedroom.

I stop here, my arm extending until he feels the jerk of my immobility. He turns back to me with a wry smile. "I'm just getting you something warm to put on."

"I'll stand here."

"Do you want a shower?"

"I can go downstairs and do that in my place. In fact..." I swallow thickly, staring around his bedroom, at his dark bed, so neatly made that we could destroy in seconds. "I should do that. Go, that is."

"Let me give you something to put on first. I don't like that you're soaking wet. It's cold."

I'd roll my eyes and say something snarky, but he's in his closet in the next second and I don't get the chance. Or maybe it's because my snark is trapped somewhere in the back of my throat. Luca returns holding a huge Patriots hoodie for me.

"Close your eyes."

His eyes pulse with heat as he stares at me. "You know I've already seen, tasted, felt, and fucked every inch of you, right?"

And just like that, a brushfire blows through me. My face

burns as I walk into his room if for no other reason than I need a little distance from the man and his searing gaze. With my back to him, I toss his hoodie on the bed and pull my soaked sports bra up and over my head. In one quick motion, I pull his ten-sizes-too-big hoodie over me and then remove my shorts and underwear, my skin practically sighing to be rid of the cold, wet garments.

I spin around and swallow my tongue at the sight before me. Luca is standing exactly where I left him, his eyes scorching a trail over me, his thumb gliding along his bottom lip as he devours me without touching me.

My breasts swell, my nipples already hard as pebbles and my empty core floods with heat, becoming impossibly wet. I need Luca Fritz more than I am willing to admit. Even to myself. Especially when he stares at me like this.

"You are without a doubt the sexiest thing I've ever seen. Knowing you're completely naked beneath my sweatshirt." His voice is low and rough, my belly dipping along with it. "The second I walk you home and return here, I'm going to jerk off to you looking just like this."

Holy hell.

"Show me."

"What?" He blinks at me, his eyes widening even as his body takes space-erasing strides in my direction. I take a step back, the backs of my knees hitting the bed behind me.

"Show me how you're going to jerk off to me." I stare at that tattoo on his chest and then slowly shift my gaze up to his. "Do it, Luca. I want to watch you get off to me."

He groans, his head falling back as his hand absently rubs at his engorged cock, very visible through the thin, wet lining of his shorts. In one swift motion, he lowers them to the floor, his cock springing free, and dear God, I forgot how perfect this man is. Every inch of him. Muscles cut from stone, smooth, tanned skin, large, thick cock.

I lick my lips and he moans, grabbing himself at the base and giving it a good squeeze. "I can smell how turned on you are, Little Bird." He moves into me, close, but not quite touching, his black eyes blown out with just the tiniest ring of green around them. "Touch yourself." Hand on my hip, he lowers me until I'm sitting on the bed. "Lie back, slide the sweatshirt up, and make yourself come while I watch and jerk off to you."

Panting, I fall back onto his bed, hiking my feet up until they're resting on the frame of his bed, and then I let my thighs fall open. He steps between them, hovering over me, his hand still on his cock, though it's now still.

He's waiting.

My heart beats into a hysterical rhythm as I raise the navy fabric up my thighs over my pussy, higher until my breasts are exposed before removing it completely. My stomach quivers as my hand comes up, cupping my breast and pinching my nipple. Palpable lust licks at me, matching the hunger in his eyes, which are locked on my movements.

Slowly, he starts moving his hand, sliding up his firm length and rubbing his thumb over the head of his cock that's already glistening with precum. He uses it as lubrication and I lick my lips, wanting to taste him on my tongue, the words tumbling from my lips making his dick jerk in his hand.

"Baby, I'm drooling right now at the sight of you. I'm already barely hanging on and then your wicked mouth says something like that? Fuck. Touch your pussy," he demands, pure dominance. "Rub your clit and then slide two fingers inside yourself. Do it. Show me how greedy that pussy is for your touch."

My back arches as I pinch my nipple harder, my other hand moving into action, doing his bidding. A slave to him. To his look and his dirty mouth that makes me so hot and impossibly wet and more turned on than I ever thought possible. Knowing I'm the one doing this to him is a high unlike any other.

My fingers start rubbing at my swollen clit, making warm tingles shoot across my skin. Gnawing on my bottom lip, I glide my fingers lower, circling my opening.

"Good girl. Look at you. So wet, you're dripping down into your ass. All over my bed. You have no idea how badly I want to taste that. All of it. Fuck yourself, Raven, before I lose my mind here."

"I want to touch you," I tell him, pushing my fingers inside and moaning because hell, it's impossible not to. "Take you down my throat. Have you inside of me again."

"Picture it, Raven. All the dirty, filthy things you love me doing to you. Are you watching me? You see how hard you make me? All for you. Only for you. I'm going to take your ass next time. Do you remember that? How much you loved having my cock inside your ass?"

"Yes," I cry as I pick up my pace, lifting and squeezing and punishing my breasts as I hike one leg up onto the bed, butterflying my knee out. I'm so desperate to close my eyes, but I won't dare. I can't stop staring at him. His face drunk with desire, with need. His cock, heavy and hard, angry as he strokes it, cupping his balls with his other hand. What we're doing... watching, directing, yearning... it's so insanely intimate. Filled with so much trust, it makes my head spin.

He grunts, moving faster, and I match his pace, fucking myself with two fingers and finding my clit with my other hand. His hips rock forward, canting in my direction, and I'm so close. My legs shake and my body fills with a curling warmth that starts deep in my core, slowly spreading out.

"Luca, I want you to come on me."

"Fuck," he hisses. "I'm so close. You need to come with me. Tell me you're there."

"I'm there," I cry out. "I'm there."

"Fuuuck!" he bellows, cum shooting out of him and all over my belly and tits in thick, white ropes. The second it hits me, I come so hard, I'm seeing stars. My back off the bed, my eyes snapping closed as euphoria explodes through me until I'm boneless and spent. Panting and dizzy.

The feel of his hand startles my eyes open, locking straight on his smirk. "So damn hot, Raven. You are a fucking goddess," he praises as he rubs his cum into my skin before bringing his wet, sticky fingers up to my lips. I lick them, savoring his taste, and he takes my fingers into his mouth, all too happy to lick me clean. "Damn, I love how dirty you are." Bending forward, his lips fuse with mine, tasting himself on me and forcing me to do the same with him. "Any way I can convince you to stay here with me all day?"

"I'm supposed to have breakfast with my father."

"Shit. Then let's get you dressed back in my sweatshirt and downstairs before he finds me and kills me. Do you need a ride? I can drive you."

"No. I'm borrowing my friend's car."

"Raven—"

I shake my head and with a frown, he pulls me up off the bed, kissing the corner of my lips before he helps me into his sweatshirt the way you would a small child, arm by arm, then kisses me again, this time with so much passion, my toes curl. He runs and grabs himself a dry T-shirt and shorts.

"I'm not ready yet, Luca."

He stares into my eyes, his gaze bouncing back and forth between mine as if I've just said something vital to him. "I can be patient. Do I have to keep my dick in my pants?"

"Are you asking if you can fuck other women? Because the answer is no."

He chuckles. "That is most definitely *not* what I was asking. But that goes for you as well. No one else, Raven. I'll wait and I'll give you whatever you need, but the only people we touch are ourselves and each other. So... that's a no to me having to keep my dick in my pants?"

I fight my grin. "I'd say yes, but clearly we're not very good at doing that."

"Not with you, baby. I never will be. But I can do patience. For you, I can do anything. Just being with you again like this, *for now*, is enough."

"And if I said you had to keep your hands to yourself?"

He groans. "I can try, but I'm already thinking of ways to get back into your pants, so let's not have that be a make it or break it rule." He smirks, taking my hand and leading me out of his bedroom, toward the front door, grabbing my phone and AirPods on our way.

I don't say anything, still reeling from the confessions in the pool. At what we did after. We step onto the elevator. My sneakers and wet clothes are still scattered between his pool and bedroom, but I'll deal with that later.

He walks me to my door, waits while I punch in my code to unlock it, and then hovers by the entrance. His hand still holding mine, he jerks me to him, straight into his chest, and kisses me senseless. Full tongue. Tons of heat. But his hands stay stranded in my hair, not wanting to push me.

"Can I see you tonight?"

My heart pounds unevenly as I shake my head. "I have practice."

"You're going to be thinking about me in the shower when you wash my cum off your body."

"Are you going to jerk off to that?"

"Damn straight." Another kiss. "Despite being pepper sprayed and feeling like my eyes were going to melt out of my skull, this has been one of the best mornings of my life."

I laugh, pushing him back and shutting the door in his face before I kiss him again. Or drag him inside. Or invite him back into my heart as a full-time resident. But all I can think is *me too*. And that's what scares me the most.

25

"You sure you're good with driving a stick shift?" Catarina asks, her eyes wary as she swings her car keys around her finger, her body hiding behind her front door, likely naked since I know her woman is behind her.

"I can. A friend taught me when I lived in London." I pat her bare shoulder. "Don't worry. I won't hurt your baby and I appreciate you letting me borrow her."

The cold keys to her Jetta fall into my hand. "I don't do this for just anyone. She's my first love. I practically gave birth to her."

"And I'll stroke her like a lover."

She points at me. "You better. Care to tell me where you're going again?"

"To see my dad."

"But there's more to it than that. I can tell. Call it a lesbian's intuition, but we have a sixth sense for these things."

I shake my head. "That doesn't even make sense."

"You're deflecting."

I sigh, leaning against her doorframe. "It depends on how

you look at it. My life has always been a bit on the strange and unusual side. That's all."

"Are you going to explain what that means?"

"Yes, but not this second."

"Are you meeting up with your secret boyfriend for hot sex?"

I do my best to hold in my blushing. "Definitely not. In my case, man-given orgasms tend to leave a trail of destruction behind."

"You should try batting for my squad. We'll change your world."

I grin cheekily. "I have no doubt. Too bad the only vagina I want to touch is my own. I'll pick you up for the show. Thank you." I blow her a kiss and then I'm gone, heading west, listening to Bach and realigning my thoughts.

I haven't told many people in my life about my relationship with the Fritz family because it's a difficult one to explain. My father works for them, and I grew up in the staff house behind their massive mansion. But they've never treated me as the help's daughter. They treat me as their daughter. As their sister and friend.

That's not even including Luca because how do I explain that one?

So much of what we went through that summer feels private to me. It was a moment in time with lasting reach. Tentacles that have permanently wrapped themselves around me. Every encounter with him felt like a dream and I was living for the hope of it. For the hope of us that was crushed.

He was the broken bad boy, and I was the quiet good girl wanting to break free.

Now I don't know what we are other than still tangled in each other's web.

But it's not like he's any old guy I can chat up my friends

about. He's Luca Freaking Fritz. Billionaire. Playboy. Notorious bachelor. Famous as can be.

How do I explain to them that I'm already breaking promise after promise I've made to myself and all within a matter of weeks? I allowed him to fuck me in an alley and come all over me while he watched me masturbate. I have no clue what I'm doing. What I'm ready for and what I'm not.

All I know is that I need space. And time.

Before I cross that irrevocable line and I'm lost to him forever—the way I thought I was once. I told myself it wouldn't matter what he had to say. That his excuses were meaningless after everything the last four years did to me. But what he told me in the pool... his actions in the last couple of weeks... his tattoo...

The ride out to the compound is mercifully traffic free and I pull around the main house to the back where I grew up, staring at the staff house that's a mix of single rooms that utilize the common areas, including a shared kitchen and small one or two-bedroom apartments.

My dad, mom—until her death—and I lived in a two-bedroom, but when I moved out, Dad chose to switch to one of the one-bedroom apartments, making room for the head gardener and his family to have the two-bedroom.

So, it doesn't quite feel like home.

Hell, I practically spent more time in the main house playing with Rina and occasionally Grace than I did back here.

Stepping out into the November sunshine, I enter the house, head up to the second floor, and knock on my dad's door. He opens it not even two seconds later, a cup of tea—ever the Brit—in his hand and a smile on his face that pulls one of my own.

"You're late."

I roll my eyes, kissing his cheek as I walk past him. "Three minutes."

He shuts the door and I take a moment to look around. Oddly enough, I don't come in here often. Any time I ever came to visit or even when I moved back, I was staying in one of the extra rooms in the house. It's small, barebones, and so clean you could likely eat off the floor, just the way he likes things.

Clean. Utilitarian. Organized.

His whole life has been like this, and I wonder if it's a trait he picked up in the military. I never asked him because he doesn't talk much about his life growing up or his life in the British military and certainly never about his time with MI6. Then again, my father never talks a lot about anything. He was an orphan. Spent time bouncing between foster homes and the streets until he joined the military at sixteen.

Then he met my mother on an assignment.

Then he got shot and Dr. Fritz was in the right place at the right time and saved his life.

Dr. Fritz convinced my father to retire and move to the States to play the part of estate manager and chief of security. But my mother didn't retire. She spent as much time in Israel as she did with us, only to die.

My fingers find the picture of her in a silver frame sitting on top of his console table. I look so much like my mother, but with my father's eyes. "I'm not sure I trust my memories of her anymore," I tell him, an ancient sadness creeping back in as it does every time I think of her. "She was never around much and even when she was... she'd leave again. I don't know why she always did that." *Even when I begged her to stay.* "I don't know her favorite color or flower if she even had one. Hell, I don't even know how she died." There have been so many times in my life I wished I had my mother. Even when she was alive, I remember wishing that. Wanting to call just to hear her voice and not being able to.

It's a horrible thing feeling abandoned by someone you love. Someone who has sworn to love you always. What Luca said to me today in the pool... about my feeling as though he abandoned me—

My dad clears his throat from somewhere in the kitchen, ripping me from my dark thoughts. "Come sit down."

I take another second before tearing myself away and joining him at the table. It smells wonderful in here, like cooked meat mixed with something savory, and I already know what he's made for me. My suspicion is confirmed when he sets a large plate in front of me with two fried eggs, sausage, hash browns, tomatoes, baked beans, and a biscuit.

English breakfast, my favorite.

"Thank you. This looks delicious. I'm starving and this will last me all through rehearsal."

"Your mother had been away from us for two months when I got the call," he starts and my fork freezes in midair, my eyes growing wider than the plate before me. He nods at my fork. "Eat or I stop talking. You're already too thin."

I'd snort at that if I could find my voice or muster any humor. Thin is not something I've ever been. I'm curvy with big boobs and a good sized booty. I just happen to have a narrow waist. I take a bite of my food, forcing myself to chew and swallow, though I'm not sure I taste any of it.

He smiles, but it doesn't touch his eyes. "As I said, she was away for two months. Not uncommon for her, but I hadn't heard from her in over a week and she had always made a point to check in with me somehow every few days. So when she didn't, I knew something was wrong."

Tears build in my eyes. I can't even begin to imagine that level of fear. Not being able to reach your loved one, not knowing if they were okay while you're home taking care of your oblivious child. And then getting a call to say they weren't.

I clear my throat, forcing down another bite so he'll keep going.

"The Israeli government didn't tell me much. I didn't expect them to. The English government wouldn't have said anything either if the roles had been reversed. But I had an old mate still inside MI6 and I called in a favor."

"Dad…"

"Do you want to know?"

I drop my fork, choosing my coffee instead, and think about this. Do I want to know how my mother died? Doesn't change the fact that she's dead, but…

"Yes. I want to know." I stare at my father, my hand gripping the wood table in one fist, my coffee mug in my other while my food sits forgotten. I can't manage another bite. My stomach is in knots, my heart pounding so hard, it's racing through my ears.

He leans back in his seat, still holding his teacup, his gaze going to the window, lost, almost as if he's picturing it in his head. "She was infiltrating a terrorist organization in Yemen known for its exportation of arms throughout the Middle East and Russia. Somehow they discovered her true identity."

"So they killed her."

"Yes. It wasn't pleasant, but I won't give you more details than that." His head turns in my direction. "I never told you because, in theory, you were at risk. Just being our daughter, you were at risk. I kept you in the dark about so much throughout your life, thinking I was protecting you. Physically and emotionally. The lives your mother and I chose… well, you were just a little girl. So sweet and innocent. All you wanted to do was play music and make people happy. You're an adult now, but what I told you, however vague it may seem to you, you should not go around repeating it."

"I won't," I promise.

His features soften and he takes my hand, pulling it away from the table. "You should know that your mother loved you endlessly. Every time she left you, she cried and I'm positive you are the only thing that woman ever shed tears over. It would break her every time you'd beg her to stay. She would call, sometimes in the middle of the night, and you'd be asleep, but she would have me sit in your room just so she could hear you breathing through the phone. She had been contemplating retiring, but her love and commitment to her country compelled her. She was trying to make the world a safer place for you. I think that's the only way she was able to leave when her heart was always here with you."

Tears fall down my cheeks and I squeeze his hand.

"I never felt like I was enough to make her stay."

He frowns. "That's my fault. I didn't tell you enough. I was an orphan growing up in foster homes or on the streets, sleeping under bridges. Your mother was raised by parents who had also been Mossad. Neither of us had the easiest or most typical upbringing or chosen professions. Then we had this perfect little girl, and everything shifted. You must understand, all we can do in this life is our best. We make choices and live with the outcomes. And sometimes, we get it wrong. I did, and I'm sorry, Raven." His eyes bleed into mine. "Your mother was made to lead a certain life. And that is not a reflection on us or how much we loved her or how much she loved us."

I blow out a breath. A knot I hadn't realized was residing in my gut loosens, making me feel lighter. I knew she loved me. But I was a little girl, and I didn't understand anything beyond my mommy leaving me, even when I asked her to stay. I wish I had told my father this years ago, but I've kept so much inside myself for so long. A secretive girl growing up in a secretive world. Burying myself under forced optimism and smiles. Relying on the sun to always be there. Even if it was hidden.

It wasn't until Luca broke my heart and I went to The Conservatory that much of my insecurities and fears and doubts resurfaced. In the form of heartache. In the form of anxiety. In the form of unresolved feelings about my mother.

You can't fix what's broken if you don't try. But now...

today... between this morning with Luca and now with my father... something in my soul feels nourished.

"Do you regret leaving that life behind?" I ask after my contemplative moment.

He shakes his head, releasing my hand and leaning back in his chair, crossing his legs at the knee. "No. I understood your mother's convictions, but I was never the same after I was shot. I love my native country and I'm proud that I served them, but having you and moving to the States and working for the Fritz family has been my life's joy. I've gotten to watch you grow up and become the woman you are now."

Setting down my coffee, I wipe my face with my napkin, breathing out a shuddered breath. "Thank you for telling me."

"It's something I should have done a long time ago. Now you need to eat."

I roll my eyes but pick up my fork all the same. For a few minutes, we're quiet. Me eating, him sipping tea. Both of us lost in our reverie. "Luca called me this morning."

"He what?" I nearly choke on the bite of eggs I was swallowing.

He gives me one of his rare grins, clearly amused by my reaction. "Yes. He and I have already chatted a few times since you returned home. But this morning, he wanted me to know that he still loves you and is working toward a second chance. He wanted to make sure I had no objections with this."

I'm about to throw up all over this table. "That's what he said?"

"Well." He chuckles. "He said other things as well. Made me promises he swore he'd never break."

Christ, Luca. "Did he ask you for my hand in marriage too?" I mutter sardonically, but my eyes bug out at my father's expression. "Dad, I was kidding. Tell me he didn't."

"No. He didn't. But he made it clear to me that him pursuing you wasn't a short-term game."

I fall back in my chair, my hands covering my face. I don't know how I feel about this. About Luca calling my father, almost as if he's asking permission. "Did you know Luca lives in the same building I do?"

He laughs now and my hands fall to my lap. Sitting back in his chair, he brings his teacup up to his lips, taking a small sip while giving me a "don't be ridiculous" look. "Of course I knew. I know where every Fritz family member is, practically at all times, and that extends to their loved ones and significant others. I have trackers on their phones and depending on the situation, on their person as well."

I shake my head. "Why didn't you say something to me?"

He raises an eyebrow. "I made it clear I wasn't happy with you moving into his building. But I had spoken with him prior to that, and I knew what he was up to. Besides, would you not have moved there if I had?"

I don't know. That's what's bothering me. I'd like to say I wouldn't have, but I don't know.

"Darling girl, you're exactly like your mother. Headstrong. Stubborn. You were always one to do what you wanted regardless of what I said or any rules I set."

"Those months he and I were together, you never said anything until you realized how deep we were in."

"Are you asking why I never put my fatherly foot down or why I didn't kill the young lad when he hurt you?"

I giggle a little, shoveling more food into my mouth because it is delicious, and I do need to eat before I go to Symphony Hall later. "Maybe. Yeah."

He sighs, getting up and refilling my coffee for me and placing his cup in his sink. He stands there for a moment, staring out the kitchen window. "My answer is simple. And it's still true now. It's because I knew he loved you more than he loved himself."

MY FATHER'S words this morning haven't left me all day. His story about my mother. He told me he knew the moment he saw me brokenhearted that he had an inkling of what Luca had done for me and then Luca confirmed it when my father flew him back to Minnesota. My father was grateful for what Luca did. Not that I was hurt, but that he had put me ahead of himself and was sending me to London. It wasn't easy to hear. Any of it.

This entire day has had me in a bit of a haze, which is why when I arrive at my door, I nearly smash straight into Luca, who is setting a large bag down. He looks up, seemingly as surprised to see me here as I am to see him. A point he proves when his hands fly up in the air, his expression adorably contrite.

"I'm not stalking you. I figured you'd be out, and I just got home from a B's game. With Brecken, Carter, and Kaplan." He laughs, running a hand through his chestnut hair that's just a touch too long on top as it flops back down onto his forehead. "Okay, so now that you know I wasn't with any women tonight and that I'm not stalking you, here." He lifts the bag and hands it to me. "It's your exercise stuff—washed because it would be gross to bring them back to you the way you left them—and new sneakers. Your old ones were just that and they were never going to fully dry."

"You washed my exercise clothes and bought me new sneakers?" A warm, fluttery feeling fills my chest. A heavy, sweet ache that seeps deep into my bones.

"Yes..." he says slowly, tilting his head. "I can't tell from your expression if you're pissed or not."

"Not."

Relief washes over him and he tucks his hands in his

pockets all the while staring at me in a way that tells me he's doing that, so he won't be tempted to touch me. I smile.

"What's that smile all about?"

"You. This."

Now he's smiling too. "You're a runner."

I shrug. "Some asshole spent a summer dragging me out in the wee hours of the morning. Kind of stuck with me."

"I'd tell you that I don't like you running that early, but clearly you can handle yourself."

I giggle, falling against the wall beside my door. "You called my father this morning." I'm trying for indignant and failing miserably.

He matches my pose on the other side of my door. "I did. Did he tell you what we spoke about?"

I nod. "Some of it."

"Good. I told you I was trying for patience, but that doesn't mean I'm not constructing a battle plan."

"I think you might already be winning."

"Yeah?" Now that smile lights up his face, his green eyes sparkling.

"Yeah, but don't get ahead of yourself. One battle doesn't win a war."

"I already told you. All's fair in true love."

We stare at each other in the dimly lit hallway, energy crackling between us like kindling waiting for a match.

"Will you play for me?"

"Now?" I ask incredulously.

He rubs at his mouth. "I meant sometime. I know you had practice today and are likely tired."

Except I don't want him to leave. I don't want this to be it for tonight. I'm confused and conflicted, and my head and heart are a mess. But I know that for sure. I don't want him to go. Which is why he needs to.

"It'll bother my neighbors if I play now."

"The walls in this building are nearly soundproof."

I shake my head. "How much money are you losing by having me live here?"

"Little Bird, money is meaningless without having people to spend it on and share it with. I love that you live here. I love that I know you're somewhere pretty and clean and safe."

I laugh lightly, my hand propping on my hip. "You're crazy."

"For you." He straightens, his hands still in his pockets as he rocks back and forth on his heels, looking so boyish and handsome and sexy I could die. "Good night, Raven."

"Good night, Luca."

My heart thunders. We've done this exact same dance before.

He leans in and presses his lips to the corner of my mouth, and I wonder if he's having the same thought I am. Without another word, he's gone, strolling down the hall, and I unlock my door. But right before I go inside, I glance over my shoulder and find him staring at me, his expression so thick with burning intensity, my breath lodges in my lungs.

He winks, blowing me a kiss.

It'll be different than last time. That's what that looks says. *And no way in hell am I giving up now.* That's his promise as he steps onto the elevator and I go into my apartment, my bag of clothes and shoes he brought me in my hand. My heart trapped somewhere on the floors between us.

26

In order to understand women, you have to know how they work. How they think. How they feel. But most importantly, how they want to be treated. Those were the words Rina spoke to me this morning on the phone as she gave me a list of books I should purchase.

I'm expected at the compound for Sunday dinner in a little more than two hours, but I haven't been able to pull my sorry ass off the couch. I've been reading what I would consider smut, but what Rina promised me is solid romance. A Bible and a rule book.

All I know is that it's fucking hot and it's making me fucking hot, and I can't stop reading it, which means dinner tonight with my family might be an interesting affair. Especially when I already know Raven won't be there and I can't sneak off with her and live out some of these scenes.

For years before I met Raven, I believed the only things about me that a woman wanted were my dick, my credit card, and my name. But Raven always wanted more than that, not really caring about the latter two. She wanted my mind. My heart. My soul. I told her secrets I don't even tell Landon and I tell that fucker everything.

Speaking of... I pick up my phone and press his name on my recently called list.

He picks up on the second ring with, "You better not be canceling for tonight."

"I'm not. I'm calling you so I don't call her."

He breathes into the phone, saying something to someone who I know is either Elle or Stella and then he's moving, followed by a loud creak and the sound of a door shutting. "Do you want me to blather on about bullshit or do you have something more specific on your mind? Because we both know blathering is not my strong suit."

This is why I called my brother. "How are the plans for the new house coming along?"

"Good. Stella wants to take Elle out to see the property next week. Convince her to help us plan it and eventually move into it with us."

I whistle through my teeth, tossing my e-reader onto the couch beside me and kicking my feet up on my leather ottoman. "That's a big step, Lan. You all in like that."

He grunts, hating it when I call him Lan, which is obviously why I did it. "I didn't think something like this could happen twice."

"Don't do that. You deserve this. You deserve Elle. She's absolutely perfect for you. And for Stella. Any woman who can put up with your surly ass and a teenage girl is good people in my book."

"What if I'm pushing her too fast?"

"I find your lack of faith disturbing."

He chuckles but recovers quickly. "Thanks, Darth, but I'm actually serious here."

"Then you slow down, but I don't think that's the case.

Besides, the house won't be done for months. It's not like you're asking her to move in tomorrow."

He's quiet for a second and then says, "Dad told me about the Treesprite Grant. Congrats. I know what that means to you."

My head falls back against the soft leather of the couch, my eyes closing. "They only chose me as a finalist because my last name is Fritz and my mother's maiden one is Abbot."

"Possibly, but it's still one hell of an honor."

"I haven't won anything."

"Not yet. But you very likely could. What would you do then?"

What *would* I do then? Would I move to Brazil and then Ghana for two years? Leave Boston, my jobs here, my family... Raven? Can I even say no to something I want as badly as that grant? "Has anyone ever turned it down?"

He snorts into the phone as if that's the most ridiculous question he's ever been asked. "No. Never. It's the neuro equivalent of a Nobel Prize. You'd be making a huge difference in two parts of the world that need it. Other than Raven, that's all you've been talking about for four years."

I swallow thickly. "I'm finally starting to get somewhere with her and then this happens." I shake my head. "They won't pick me anyway. They just like having my name in the running." Right?

He laughs as if he can hear my unspoken question. "You sound like a robot. Tell me what the fuck is up, or I'll beat it out of you when I see you later."

"I'd love to see you try. You're younger than me by six minutes and I'm physically superior in all the ways that count."

"Bullshit," he snaps. "You sit to pee."

I groan, running my hand over my face. "That was one fucking time, asshole, and only because I was too sick to stand."

He chuckles, ripping one from me. "So you say."

"You're a punk-ass ho."

"Never claimed otherwise, but it still riles you up every time I mention it. If you recall, I'm the one you threw up on before you sat like a lady to pee. Tell me more about the grant."

Thank God for my brothers. For my family. I have no idea what my world would be like without them.

"I've decided not to think about the grant yet. There truly is no point if I'm not going to be winning it."

"Solid reasoning. Elle is trying to teach Stella how to cheer. It's the sexiest and scariest thing I've ever seen."

I rub at the grin on my lips. "I should have come over for brunch this morning," I tell him. "Hung out there with you and watched football instead of reading steamy romance novels all day."

Now he full-on belts out a laugh and simply hearing my brother laugh like this... hell, I can't think of anything better. It has me smiling like a damn, sappy fool.

"Let me guess, either Rina or Oliver got to you."

"Rina, though I know Oliver reads this shit with Amelia."

"Says it keeps their kink kinkier."

"I believe it after reading some of this stuff. Do you think Raven reads romance novels?"

He clears his throat. "You could read some to her. On the phone since she likely won't want to see your pretty face."

I bolt upright. I could do that. I could totally do that. It'll be like romantic sexting, if there even is such a thing. "You're brilliant. Later, bitch." Standing up, I start to pace a lap around my library, picking up a Luke Skywalker figurine and tossing it up in the air before catching it, repeating that as I move. I think about how she looked last night when she caught me in front of her door. The smile she had. Her dazed, googly-eyed look. The way she told me I'm starting to win her over.

Yeah, I'm gonna need to see her if I'm planning to woo her

with sexy romance novels and what Rina referred to as all the feels. Whatever the fuck that means.

I don't even know if Raven's home or if she'll knee me in the nuts if I show up at her door. Might be worth it to admire the fire in her eyes—the woman is damn sexy when she's ready to kill me—but I don't want to fight with her. We've fought and yelled enough in the past couple of weeks.

And yesterday, last night... something is shifting in her.

I need to make her fall in love with me again. Or at least admit she never fell out of love with me. Bonus, my girl likes a little dirty with her wooing.

Before I can talk myself out of it, I press her number and hold my breath as it rings through. Just when I'm about to hang up, her silky rasp comes through the phone and instantly I'm hard.

I glare down at my troublemaker. Really? The woman only said, "Why are you calling me?"

"Because I miss you."

"That's nice. I'm hanging up now."

"No. Wait. Don't." I clear my throat. Shit. "What are you doing?"

"Not going to the compound for dinner tonight, if that's what you're asking."

"It's not. So... tell me."

She sighs and that's when I catch a funny sound. Like splashing water.

"Are you in the bath?"

She's quiet for a beat before responding, "Yes. My back hurts after my practice today and I thought a bath and smoking a joint might help."

"I have a Jacuzzi."

"So do I if I turn on the jets in the tub."

Dammit. I forgot that point. "You smoked a joint?" I don't

know why I'm incredulous. Weed is legal in Mass, and I've certainly smoked and taken edibles on occasion, but Raven…

"It helps relax me. It's not too heavy, which I like."

She's so damn cute, I could die. "Take a picture for me."

"What?" she sputters.

But now I'm grinning like a devil. "Take a picture of yourself in the bath. I want a visual. Or we can FaceTime."

"Nooo. No FaceTime. And I'm not taking a picture of myself in the bath for your voyeuristic enjoyment."

I fall back onto my sofa, tossing Luke onto the couch beside me, my hand sliding down my jeans so I can grab my aching balls. "The old Raven would have done that. She was brazen. Fiery. A lot naughty."

She laughs into the phone, and I miss her so much. The way her eyes light up when she smiles. The way her hair tumbles down her back when she's truly laughing. The way she makes this tiny, contented humming noise when I hold her against me. How she is the most breathtaking thing I've ever seen whether she's sans makeup and covered in sweat after a run or dressed for a night out.

"Are you trying to peer pressure me into a dirty picture?"

"That would be assuming I'm your peer. We're in an entirely different generational bracket, baby girl. But yes, I'm totally trying to pressure you into sending me a dirty picture of yourself in the bath. If you want, I'll send you a dick pic in return," I tease.

She giggles lightly and I hear more water splashing around. Is she touching herself in there? Naked. Wet. Soapy. I need to see her.

"If you do it, I'll read you some of the romance novel Rina has me reading so I can learn to speak woman better. She said it helped Brecken immensely."

"She had him read *Twilight*. Is that what she gave you?"

"You mean that book about the vampire? No. Thank God. I

don't think I could do teenagers. This is a very adult book with very adult themes."

There's a sound on the other end that I'd swear is her attempting to stifle her giggle, but it breaks through anyway. That is until I hear the ping that indicates a text coming through.

"To help with your adult themes," she tells me and then I pull the phone away, practically drooling at the image that comes through.

It's Raven in the bath, her black hair piled on top of her head that's leaning back against the white porcelain tub. Her eyes are closed, and her beautiful, delicate neck is elongated. The drool-worthy tops of her breasts are swallowed up by bubbles, keeping her pink nipples from view. She's a tastefully erotic tease.

"I'm having this blown up and framed. Maybe done in black and white because that would be stunning. You are a goddess. Can I come down there? Read to you in person?" Maybe make you come in the bath and then spend the rest of the night inside you?

"You want to read romance to me while I take a bubble bath?" she deadpans as if she's not sure what to do with that.

"Yes, but only because it makes me more of a man and not less of one. It's not like I'm reading a Shakespearean sonnet or anything. We can call it smut if that makes it less romantic for you."

"If you bring flowers or chocolates, I'm going to drown you in the tub. And then eat the chocolates because chocolate is my favorite and I think this joint gave me a small case of the munchies."

"Is that your threatening way of saying yes? And getting me to run out and buy you chocolate?"

She doesn't respond, to the point where I pull the phone away from my ear to see if she's still there.

"How about this?" I venture. "You tell me the code for your front door. That way you don't have to get out of the bath, and you don't have to say yes or no."

More silence and then, "It's 1-2-3-4-5."

"Are you fucking kidding me with that? 1-2-3-4-5?"

"It was good enough for Spaceballs. Come on, Spaceballs is a riff on Star Wars."

Jesus. This woman. "I know it's a riff on Star Wars. I've only watched it ten thousand times. But we're changing that code to something less obvious," I tell her as I scoop up my e-reader from the sofa and jog into my kitchen, opening up cabinet after cabinet until I find what I'm looking for—the stash of candy I keep here for Stella—and then I'm out the door before she can change her mind.

"It's not obvious because no one other than an idiot would pick it."

"You're not an idiot, Raven."

She puffs into the phone. "No, I'm a genius. It's not obvious because it's so obvious."

She might have a point with that.

"Still, I don't like it." The elevator dings and I step on, punching in the code for her floor. "I'm not hanging up unless we get disconnected."

"I'm nervous."

"About me coming over?"

"About my two solos. For the holiday show. The holiday show is big time, and my solos are five minutes long, Luca. I'm one of six people who got solos, the only one who got two. That's it."

"I'm not understanding," I admit.

"I... I have a history of stage fright. Performance anxiety. Whatever you want to call it."

I stand here, staring at the metal doors, shocked out of my mind. "Since when?"

"Since I started at The Conservatory, and it was kill or be killed and everyone there was so talented. I don't know. My self-confidence was in the toilet and all of it combined started this."

"Baby..." I'm at a loss. "What can I do to help?" Because I feel like a large part of that is my fault.

"I worked at it, and it was so much better, it was nearly gone. Something about moving back here and starting with the symphony triggered some of it again, I guess. I know it's nonsensical. I know I'm talented and worthy. Now it's more like something that's ingrained in me. I can't help it. My body just reacts now every time the spotlight falls on me."

"Wow. I..."

"The bath and the joint are helping. It just feels like a lot so soon into starting with the orchestra, is all. I'll battle through it and hopefully in a few months, it'll fade away like it did before."

Raven is a big name in her industry for such a young woman. Probably because she is such a young woman. She's a savant. No kidding around. I wasn't lying about the once in a hundred-year talent.

"Does anyone else know?"

"Nooo. No one else knows."

"Thank you for telling me. For trusting me with that." I'm smiling while I ball up my fists. It's a strange mix of emotions, to say the least. Then again twisted emotions seem to be my thing with her.

"Mmmm."

The elevator door opens, and I speed walk down the hall.

"Raven... I think you're amazing and I'm so insanely proud of you for earning those solos. I just don't see how it's possible someone like you has a fear of playing for others. Tell me so I understand."

I shift my phone till it's wedged between my ear and my

shoulder and then I punch in her stupid ass code. The keypad beeps and lights up to green, the lock disengaging loudly.

"God, you're really here." She laughs the words. "I might need to rethink this."

"Too late," I tell her as I hit end on my phone and enter her bathroom that's only illuminated by the soft glow of candles. Raven is in the tub, covered with and surrounded by white suds, her face, neck, and upper chest the only parts of her that are visible, but man. She's flushed and wet and oh so naked beneath.

I take her phone from her hand, set it down on the shelf by the head of the tub, grab a stool from the corner, and park myself beside her. Her guarded expression has me not kissing or even touching her.

"Tell me why you're anxious about performing a solo."

I set the Snickers and the e-reader on the floor and drop my forearms onto the rim of the large tub. It's warm in here, the lavender fragranced air balmy, and I slide up sleeves before dropping my face onto my arms so I'm closer to her. She still hasn't answered me and I'm not sure she will, so I take over for her.

"You're one of two people who know the extent of the dark thoughts I had after I woke up in the ICU after I had been in a medically induced coma and intubated for five days only to subsequently be told that I might have permanent nerve and muscular damage and never operate again."

"And look at you now."

I grin at her, reaching out and brushing a few wet strands stuck to her forehead back. "And look at *you* now. That first night I watched you playing, it was as natural to you as breathing. Even if it stole mine. I never expected you to tell me how anxious playing in front of an audience makes you."

"Because it's not something I can tell people. You're a

doctor. You know what that kind of pressure to be perfect is like."

"I think people would find you inspiring, but I get what you're saying. You mentioned you did something that helped?"

"Yeah. It's why I started taking psych classes in London. I told my friends and professors there I was interested in music therapy and wanted a backup plan, and part of that was true, but I was also there as a way to help self-diagnose and treat myself. I also did therapy once a week."

"Sneaky woman. It helped?"

"Absolutely. I gained techniques for how to deal with it. Visualizations, deep breathing, pep talks, things like that. I've restarted all that now that it resurfaced, and it does help. I just hate that it's something I'm battling again."

"You never fail to leave me in awe."

She rolls her eyes at me, taking a handful of bubbles and blowing some of them at my face. I swat them away, doing the same back to her, causing the water to slosh around the tub.

"I'm serious, you little brat. You've never been afraid of tackling something others would run from. So I already know you won't do that now with these five-minute solos either."

"No. I won't. It's not the woman my mother and father raised me to be." Her fingers reach out, running down my cheek, painting me with water. "Are you really going to read a romance novel to me?"

"I was planning on it."

"What about dinner tonight at the compound?" Her teeth sink into her lip as she dips down lower, the water now coming up to her chin. Vulnerability and uncertainty play across her features, and I wonder if it's because she wants me to go or she wants me to stay.

But she gave me the code to her door. She sent me that picture of herself right here, naked in the tub. She told me about her performance anxiety. She's such a beautiful paradox, she never fails to challenge me while keeping me on my toes.

"Can I stay here instead? Have dinner with you?" I'd stay forever if she'd let me.

"I don't want to upset your mom."

My fingers glide down her face, across her cheek, retracting her lip from her teeth. "I'll tell her I'm with you—"

"No," she interjects sharply, so bothered by that, she practically leaps from the tub, not even caring that I can now see her breasts. "Don't do that. It's too soon. I don't want anyone to know, Luca. Hell, I don't even know what we're doing and—"

I pinch her lips closed with my fingers, shushing her and pushing her back down into the tub. "I won't tell them I'm with you. I'll just tell them something came up." Even though I frown as I say that. "So can I stay?"

"Start reading and we'll see how it goes."

"Do you miss London?" Luca asks, taking a sip of wine and then setting his glass back on the floor. We're having a picnic in my apartment, eating food Luca picked up from a pub down the street and drinking an expensive bottle of wine. The gas fire hissing right beside us is the only light source other than a few candles we have burning. It's insanely romantic and I think that's his ploy, to romance the hell out of me until I have no other choice but to give in to him.

Spoiler alert: It's totally working!

"Parts of it. Living there felt like home somehow. Maybe because my dad is from there or because the staff house never really did. I don't know. I loved the city. The history. The shopping. The vibe of the pubs and nightlife. I don't miss the weather so much. Or how ancient my flat was. And definitely not how expensive everything there was."

"I like London and I love Rome and Paris and Barcelona and yeah, all of Europe. But Boston has always been home for me. I always planned to come back after my residency. If for no other reason than Landon and Stella were here, as well as my parents. But Boston is in my blood."

"That's because you're freaking royalty here. Hell, you're royalty all over the world."

"I wouldn't mind it if I wasn't. If the things I got in this world I knew I was getting because I earned them." He pauses here, his eyes tracking to the fire as if something else is hitting him.

"What?"

He shakes his head. "It's nothing. Work stuff. Being famous and having a famous name isn't all that great sometimes. Especially when a certain raven-haired goddess is so slow to trust me when I tell her I never touched ninety-eight percent of the women I'm photographed with."

"Ah, but it's those pesky two percent—"

"That I never slept with and never plan to touch them or anyone other than you again? Yes, I know."

I chuck a fry at him, and he ducks, catching it in his mouth and chewing it up with a bright, cocky grin.

It's been the strangest, most wonderfully unexpected night.

When I finally started to turn into a prune, Luca helped me out of the bath and sat on my bed while I got dressed. All the while reading a freaking second chance romance book to me. He didn't touch me, though his gaze certainly lingered, and his dick was visibly hard through his jeans.

Then he ran out and grabbed the food and now here we are. Sitting on the floor even though there are plenty of places we could sit to eat. Talking.

He's been feeding me bites of his dinner and I've been feeding him bites of mine and it all seems so natural. The way it did four years ago.

We say our hearts break. That they never fully heal. But I think that's only because that's where we feel the physical pain the most.

Right in the chest.

But it's not our hearts that break. And they do fully heal, or maybe just lose interest in remembering. It's our minds that bear the brunt. That remember. That scar. That are slow to forgive. Not our hearts. They hold on when they shouldn't and then they're quick to fall again.

Because staring at Luca, at the permanent half-grin he's had on his face this entire night whether he's aware of it or not, has my heart wanting to jump back out of my chest and into his. Where it feels like it belongs. It's my head that's repeatedly throwing buckets of ice water on it. Only... with each passing second, those buckets get smaller and smaller.

Since I pepper sprayed his face and he still showered me with words of love and longing.

Since the second he showed up at my concert, his green eyes wide and practically unblinking as if he was afraid of missing a single damn second of seeing me again.

Since I left him that Post-it note and swore to love him forever.

"Did I lose you?" he asks, snapping me out of my reverie. I realize I've been staring into the fire, and I turn back to him, my focus adjusting.

"Just lost in thought."

"Good or bad?"

"I'm not sure," I answer truthfully.

Leaning forward, he places his lips on mine. Soft. Deep. So good, his kiss leaves me dizzy and full of wonder. He tastes salty like our food, and I lick my lips, savoring it.

"Are you done with dinner?" he mumbles against me before sitting back.

I take in the spread of mostly eaten pub fare between us and nod.

"Perfect. Take off your clothes."

"W-what?"

Luca climbs up onto his knees, gathering up the remains of our dinner and throwing everything into the take-out bag it came in. "Take. Off. Your. Clothes." His eyes meet mine. "Do it, Raven. Now."

I shake my head, sitting up fully, spine straight. "I never said we were having sex."

He laughs like I'm adorable. "I didn't say we were."

"But you're telling me to take my clothes off."

"Yup." He stands, bringing the to-go bag with him. "You better get started on that by the time I return with dessert, or I'll do it for you. I'm fine either way."

I stare after him. His self-satisfied smile makes me want to say something cutting. The dirty demand still hangs in the air, there for me to play with in my mind. Taking off my clothes isn't a big deal. The man has already seen me naked not just tonight, but a hundred times before, and physical modesty certainly isn't an emotion I battle with often.

But this is different and both he and I know it.

This is me baring myself for him. Not him going down on me in my bedroom while I'm still partially dressed or a quick fuck in an alleyway or even masturbating together because I asked for that. It's as if he's throwing down the gauntlet. If I do this, if I get naked for him, I'm allowing him in. I'm opening myself up to the possibility of us again.

Am I ready for that?

No. Yes. Argh! I hate thinking. I do it too damn much and what good or happiness has it ever brought me? I pull my sweater up and over my head, tossing it over by the couch. Then I scoot my butt left and right, wiggling out of my jeans.

"Panties and bra too, Little Bird. Don't think that take off your clothes is a technicality to leave them on," he calls out from the kitchen, doing God only knows what over there.

"Bastard," I grumble, and his warm, happy chuckle has me fighting a grin as I remove my bra and panties. "The floor is cold," I complain just as he steps back into view carrying a blanket. "Ugh. Get out of my head and stop reading my mind already."

"Not a chance." His eyes instantly grow dark and hooded when they find me, poring over every inch of me. "Spread your legs."

My heart ricochets around my chest.

"I thought you said we weren't having sex."

"Do it."

Heat floods my skin and suddenly I'm no longer cold. I lean back on my hands, which pushes my tits out toward him, and spread my bent knees.

"Good girl. Now don't move."

"Are you going to paint a picture?" I tease, but something in his eyes has my heart beating faster. The way they vacillate between playful, curious, and excited.

"No. I'm going to take one."

I bolt up, covering myself. "The fuck you are."

He grins, walking over to me and setting down a cloth bag from his hands that I hadn't noticed him holding before. "Relax. They're just for me."

"Until someone hacks your phone, Mr. Celebrity, or somehow stumbles upon them."

"Do you trust me?"

"Luca!"

"Do. You. Trust. Me?"

"No!"

"Woman, don't play games and tell me the truth."

Damn him. "Yes. I trust you. Ish," I tack on because I'm like ninety-four percent there with him.

"Then know that I will never allow anyone to see something that is only meant for my eyes. I was planning on keeping your face out of them anyway. And one day, when you fully trust me again, you won't even think to question the things I do with you." His hand meets my shoulder, and he pushes me back, uncovering my hands from my chest. "Now, back into that position."

This is it. After tonight, I can't pretend I want nothing to do with him. I can't go back to hating him. I can't pretend my heart doesn't sprint every time he walks into a room, or my body doesn't crave to run up to him, jump in his arms, and kiss him senseless.

"I'm scared."

His eyes meet mine. "It's just pictures, baby."

"No. I'm *scared*, Luca. You can't hurt me again, okay? I mean it. I won't... I won't be able to take it if you do that."

His hand dives into my hair, his forehead pressing against mine as he stares straight into my eyes. Into my heart. "You're my endgame. My no matter what. I'd burn down the world for you. You and I are meant to be. You stole my heart and never gave it back. All I want to do is return the favor."

"We're the tortoise and the hare."

"What?" He chuckles against me.

"We did fast, and we lost. Maybe this time we should try slow so we can win the race?"

"There is no finish line for us."

I angle up and kiss him, cupping his jaw in my hand. "I trust you."

"No more ish?"

"No more ish."

Another kiss and then he sits back, picking up his phone from the floor. "Good because the picture you sent me earlier tonight got me thinking. I've never done that with anyone. Taken pictures. Videoed anything. As you said, Mr. Celebrity and I'm not a dumb fuck. I'd rather not end up in the tabloids for a sex tape or blackmail or whatever. So this is me trusting you too."

My breasts feel heavier. My nipples tighten and my pussy grows impossibly wet.

"What if I'm just using you for your money?"

Leaning down, he bites my nipple. Hard. "Are you?" Two fingers push inside of me, and my head falls back on a moan. *Click.*

"Yes."

He smacks my breast, making it jiggle. *Click.*

"Your skin. Glowing like this against the fire. The light and the dark playing against you. You are fucking art."

"Luca," I whimper as he drags his fingers in and out of me, so slowly I feel like I'm going to die.

Click.

I open my eyes to find him snapping a picture of his hand between my thighs. Wet with my arousal. I didn't think this was something I'd ever find as a turn-on, but knowing he has these images of me on his phone. Knowing he'll look at them later and get hard, seeing us, remembering this...

Luca slides his fingers out, painting my lips with them, and then sets his phone down. In my next breath, he picks me up, dropping me onto his lap. "Hold on."

I wrap my arms around his neck and then he lays the blanket down on the floor where I just was before he shifts me back onto it.

"Close your pretty eyes, beautiful. Time for some dessert."

He pulls a red silk scarf out of the bag and brings it up to my face, covering my eyes and tying it tight behind my head. My hands tremble as I tentatively touch it.

Click.

I can only imagine what I look like and that drags a moan from my lips. Blind, my hearing and touch senses are heightened. The soft cashmere of the blanket beneath me. The hissing of the fire. The warmth it lets off.

But I don't hear him. Not even his breathing.

"Luca?"

"Relax."

Gently, he lowers me down until I'm fully laid out on the blanket, his fingers the lightest touch as they trickle across my face, over the scarf, to my lips.

"Open."

Oh Jesus. What is he doing?

"The way you're trembling and your breathing is all over the place, I'd think you didn't believe that I love you and would never do anything I didn't already know you would enjoy. Relax. We'll do this your way and go slow. Other than right now, which is going to be my way, but I promise you'll love it."

I laugh, the tense coil wrapped around my heart untethering something only to be replaced by a lightness I haven't felt in I don't even know how long.

"We good?" he asks.

"I'm good. You good?"

"I'm staring down at a blindfolded naked woman who has no idea what I have planned for her. I'm fucking fantastic."

"Not helping my nerves."

His lips meet mine, stealing my breath as his tongue plunges inside my mouth. "I'm going to eat you for dessert. Now be a good girl and lie still for me while I do that."

She settles on the blanket, her chest rising and falling with each ragged breath she's taking. My touch is cagey, and she's unable to anticipate it, or what I have in store for her. It's making me edgy with excitement, my cock straining so hard through my jeans, I think the fucker is ready to take on my zipper himself in order to be set free.

Staring down at my phone, I absorb the picture I just took of her. It's dark, but with the firelight dancing on her skin, it's nothing short of erotic art.

"Fuck, your beauty is so much, it's almost paralyzing. How is a man to think when you look like this?"

"You'll have to try. I'm waiting with my legs spread open."

A wry grin hits my lips and I lean forward, kissing over her thrumming pulse at the base of her neck. She sucks in a breath and holds it in as my hand cups her breast, so full and glowing orange in my hand. I can't stop myself from taking another picture. Already knowing I'm going to stare at these for hours after this night is over. Hopefully, I'll get to do that with her, but I think the jury's still out on just how far I've come tonight in my winning Raven back and making her mine scheme.

I have been bereft for four years, watching her from afar. Knowing she's made for bigger and better things than myself. I made a choice and that choice cost me. It cost her too. Dearly. But in the end, we are not flawed by our choices. We are stronger for them. Together.

I hope.

Returning to the bag, I pull out a few items, set them on the floor beside me, and then remove my shirt. Opening one of the jars, I dip my finger inside and then paint her lips, smearing them black.

Reflexively, her tongue juts out, licking at them, and I shove my finger in her mouth so she can suck the rich chocolate sauce off me.

"Good?"

"Mmmm," she hums appreciatively.

I pry my finger free of her mouth and do it again, this time spreading the chocolate over her nipple. I take a picture and then suck it into my mouth, causing her back to arch, her elbows digging in deeper into the blanket and floor.

I do the same with the other nipple and then set the sauce aside, picking up a chocolate caramel instead. "Take a bite," I tell her, rubbing it against her lips.

She opens and bites into it at the same time I pull it away, causing a string of caramel to cling to the candy and then break, sticking to her bottom lip and chin. My mouth cleans up the mess, my tongue and teeth scraping up the leftovers as my clean hand coasts down her stomach, pausing just below her belly button.

My lips fuse with hers, eating at her, tasting the creamy, sweet chocolate. "Do you want more?"

"Yes."

"Good girl. Open."

I place another candy in her mouth, this one a fudge truffle, followed by some chocolate sauce. The way she looks right now nearly does me in, the image so much better than any I conjured up in my head when I was purchasing everything.

I plunge my finger inside her just as she swallows the candy and I suck in a sharp breath. So ready for me. But not yet. I circle my thumb over her clit, staring down at my hand. What is it about touching her? Her stomach muscles quiver, her body shaking. So close and I've barely played with her yet.

Just as she swallows, I squirt whipped cream onto her stomach. "Luca! Ah! That's cold." She laughs, her body jolting, trying to dodge the cold cream.

"Hold still," I admonish.

"I can't," she shrieks, laughing harder.

"You're messing up my masterpiece."

"Screw your masterpiece."

"That comes next."

Giggles flee her lungs as I continue to spray pillows of white all over her belly and now breasts. "Promises, promises," she gasps, arching, her head falling back as I spray her nipple.

"You told me no sex."

"I am a woman. I reserve all rights of sexual intercourse and that includes changing my mind."

Woman is right.

"This'll shut you up."

I squirt whipped cream into her open mouth, making sure I get all around her lips. Then I take a picture. First of her belly and tits before she fucks it all up and then her face because between the cream and the blindfold, she's unrecognizable.

Her hand comes up, wiping the excess away and tossing it in what she assumes is my general direction.

"Missed." I reach over and remove her blindfold. One, because I want her to see. Two, because I miss her eyes and crave their dark, heady look when she's turned on.

"You total—" She glances down, tilting her head as she does her best to read my messy scrawl. "Luca's?"

"Yup. Mine. In case you were unclear." I dive in before she can say anything, licking as much of the white mess off her as I can. She falls back to the floor, lost somewhere between laughter and moaning.

"Don't I get a turn with that?"

"Not a chance, baby girl." Seconds before I go into a diabetic coma from all the sugar, I grab the damp towel I have still in the bag and clean her up with it. "Had enough dessert?"

"No way. I'm just getting started with mine." She shoves me down, climbing on top me and straddling my thighs. And damn. This view.

"Can I get your face now?"

"It won't go anywhere?"

"Never."

A nod.

Grabbing my phone off the ground, I unlock it with my face and snap another picture of her from above me.

"Lift your hair with your hands. Yeah. Like that." *Click.* "Fuck, you're so hot." With her hands holding her long, inky strands up, she starts to rock her naked pussy against me, grinding herself along the border of my jeans and abs. "That feel good?"

"Mmmhmm."

Fuck pictures. I switch to video mode and hit record. I can't decide where I want to look. At my phone as if I'm watching something I shouldn't or at the woman getting off on top of me. I want to take off my jeans. I want to slide inside of her and record the look in her eyes when I fill her up. I must tell her that because she rises onto her knees and undoes the button and zipper of my jeans, pulling my dripping cock out.

Licking her lips, she stares down at me, wrapping her hand around my length and then pumping up and down before lowering her body until she's doing the same with her pussy.

She doesn't push me inside her. Instead, she's playing with me around her opening, using my tip to rub her clit.

"I want those eyes, Little Bird." I get her flush of half-mast heat, the curve of her smile, the soft parting of her lips as she moans. "Fuck. Look at you. The way your tits move." I reach up, grabbing one. "Harder. I want you to come on my cock like this."

Sweat clings to her forehead as she picks up her pace, the feel of her slick pussy soaking my cock while her hand holds me against her has me practically seeing triple.

"Luca," she moans, her head falling back, her hair tumbling behind her as she angles her hips forward, seeking more friction, more contact.

"Good girl. That's it. Right when you start to come, I want you to put me inside you."

"So close." Whimpers tumble from her lips, her grip on me tightening, her pussy leaking all over me. Her movements grow less coordinated, more frantic the closer she gets. My hand holding the camera is shaking, trying desperately to keep this going.

"Now, baby. Put me inside you now."

Shifting her weight, she positions me back to her opening and sinks down. Streaks of white light fill my vision and I emit a guttural groan. Her pussy is so hot. So wet. So tight. It flutters around me, holding me in, and I have to grit my teeth and clench my ass cheeks so I don't blow my load this second.

"Fuck, Little Bird."

I pinch her nipple and thrust up and that's all it takes. She detonates, coming on a cry, her pussy squeezing me so hard, I wheeze, choking on my breath.

"Keep your eyes open. Don't you dare shut them."

They lock with mine and I record her falling apart all over me, my name chanting from her lips as I continue to fuck her, thrusting up and pinching her nipple. She collapses forward, her hands planting themselves on my chest, and it takes everything in me not to come with her as hot blood pumps through my veins, edging me closer.

Setting my phone down, I wrap my arms around her, dragging her face up to mine so I can kiss her. Still inside of her, I start to move slowly in and out of her like this, our mouths fused in a sloppy kiss.

I brush some of the sticky hair back from her face and find her eyes. "My favorite place to be is right here with you. Looking at you. Inside you." My lips layer with hers. "I love you, Raven."

"Then how about you put your money where your mouth is?"

"Huh?" It comes out as a bemused chuckle, only to turn into a raspy groan as she climbs off me and stands up.

"Come fuck me in my bed. Not against a window. Not in some alley. Or even on my floor. Show me what your love feels like from the inside four years later."

I don't have to be told twice. I stand up, kick my jeans off the rest of the way, scoop her up in my arms, and walk us into her bedroom. Pulling back the blanket, I set her down, slide in on top of her, and then cover us both with the blanket.

"Hi," I whisper to her, staring into her eyes like this, consumed by her and cocooned under the blanket.

"Hi."

I brush my nose against hers. "I've missed you."

"I've missed you. So much."

A rush of euphoria sweeps through me. The woman has an unsettling power over me. She owns my soul.

"I tried like hell to get over you for four years and no matter what I told myself, you were always there. In my head. In my heart. We made a lot of mistakes, Luca."

"I'm not sorry I let you go. I'm only sorry for how I did it. What happened to us after. Still, I can't help but wonder if I was wrong to make the decision for you. Something I never considered at the time. I knew what I was doing, and I felt it was the only thing to do. That my residency and Minnesota would have stifled you. That our love would have grown stale and bitter. But I never considered the possibility that it would have adapted. Taken on a different color or texture or flavor."

I loved her enough to let her go, and that loss nearly destroyed us both.

She licks her lips and nods, contemplating my words while something unreadable crosses her features. "I didn't listen. I only knew what I wanted and was blind to the rest. I would have loved you, Luca. And I would have found a way to love Minnesota and that life. But thank you for recognizing that I needed to live for more than just you. I needed to learn how to live for myself."

She snakes her legs around my hips, and I give myself a stroke before sliding back inside her. I rock slowly, feeling every inch of her, making sure she feels every inch of me. My hands intertwine with hers, raising them above her head as I adjust us, deepening the angle. I've never felt such a blinding need to be as deep inside someone as I do with her.

It's almost tormenting. A strange desperation.

"There is nothing like being inside you."

"Words, Luca. I want action."

I nip at her lips, grinning against her. "You want action, Little Bird? Throwing down the gauntlet like that will have me doing things I'm not sure you're ready for right now."

"Like what?" she challenges, growing breathless.

"Grab that bottle of lube from your nightstand."

She lets out a small laugh. "What makes you think I have lube in there?"

"Because you like your sex toys well lubed."

She sighs, but it turns into a hiss when I reach between us and start rubbing her clit. "What do you plan to do with it?"

"You have a choice," I tell her on a groan, sweat running between my shoulder blades as I ramp up my thrusts. But if this is going to happen, I need to pace myself. She feels too good. "We can use your toy on your clit while I fuck your pussy. Or I can take your ass."

"Oh God," she moans, her voice growing louder the closer she gets. She's already starting to grip me, and I know if I'm going to do this, I have to do it now.

"I can't decide."

I emit a strangled laugh and begrudgingly slide out of her. My wet dick smacks against my abs in fury for taking it from its home. But I want her like that. I've been dreaming of doing it again for four years. And I haven't. Not with any other woman since.

Reaching into her nightstand, I find the bottle of lube I knew would be there and throw her a cocky grin. She laughs, lying flat on her back as she watches me. I open the bottle and squeeze some into my hand and then all over my dick. "Come here."

Using my clean hand, I shift her to the end of the bed and hike her knees up. Her eyes are wild, a little nervous if I'm reading her right as my lubricated hand starts to play with her forbidden hole.

"Rub your clit, baby."

She does, one hand going to her clit, the other going to her breast, and I wish to hell I had brought my phone in here with me so I could take a picture of her like this. My finger slides inside her ass, pushing past the barrier of muscles and then back out. Over and over, I repeat this until she's relaxed and well lubricated.

"Ready?" I ask, leaning forward so I can plant my hand in the bed up by her face.

"Yes," she whispers.

Lining my cock up, I slowly press in, my face inches from

hers as I do. Her legs stay bent, but then climb up to my shoulders and *fuuuuck*. "You okay?" I grit out, clenching my teeth as I finally work myself fully inside her, her muscles doing unbelievable things to me.

"Yes."

"That's two yeses. Give me something else."

"Move. How's that?"

I grunt and gasp. "Raven Fairchild, I'm going to marry the fuck out of you one day."

Her teeth go into her bottom lip, and I don't know if it's from my declaration or from my cock being buried in her ass. Pulling out slowly, I pump back into her. A little harder this time. Spots dance in front of my eyes and if this is how I'm going to die, I can't ask for a better way to go.

"Good?"

"Good. Keep going."

My gaze falls to the place where our bodies are connected. Her fingers on her clit. My dick, wet and glistening, sliding in and out of her ass. Christ. I pump faster. Deeper. Harder. Gripping her hips, I lift them higher off the bed and start to pound. Her tits bounce and sway, her neck arching as her eyes close.

She loves this. I know she does. My beautiful dirty Little Bird has never been shy about sex and what she wants from it. Her confidence, so undeniably sexy, makes it impossible to think straight.

"That deep enough for you?"

"Put your fingers in me," she moans.

I just about come right then. I slide two fingers inside her, moving them in tandem with my thrusts, and that's when she starts to lose it. One hand gripping the blanket. The other wildly rubbing her clit. She's screaming and moaning and writhing. And I can't take my eyes off her.

I need to feel her come on my fingers, around my cock. And I need to feel it now.

I tell her that just as I pick up speed, giving her everything I have until I can't take it a second longer and come on a bellow, shooting myself into her ass. She follows me over the edge, screaming and cursing and ripping at me. Tsunamis of pleasure barrel through my body, taking over my senses.

All I know is that when I open my eyes, somehow, I'm on top of her, my chest against hers, her legs now around my waist. "Are you okay?" I ask her again, unable to move.

"I think that was the most intense orgasm of my life."

"Ditto."

That's all I've got and for a few minutes, we lie like this. Breathing each other in. When feeling has returned to my legs, I kiss her temple and pull myself up and out of her. She winces and I cup her cheek.

"Baby. Are you hurting?"

"No. I'm fine. Really." I pick her up off the bed and she lets out a small squeal. "What are you doing?"

"Taking you to the bathroom."

"Caveman, I can walk."

I meet her eyes in the dark bedroom. "I want to carry you. I like taking care of you." I set her down on the open toilet and she gives me a look. Not quite embarrassed, but not happy with me either. "Welcome to intimacy and unconditional love, baby girl."

I kiss her forehead, wash my hands, grab a towel for myself, and then leave her, shutting the door with a click behind me. Wiping myself off, I go back into the family room to clean everything up. And once that's done, I shut off the fire and pick up my phone. By the time I return to the bedroom, Raven is already there, under the covers.

I get in too, wrapping her up in my arms and dragging her to me until her head is on my chest. "Can I stay?"

"If you leave after that, I'll kill you."

I laugh, stroking my fingers through her somewhat tangled hair.

After a quiet minute, she says, "Hey, Luca?"

"Yeah?"

"I love you."

With that, she settles in, getting comfortable and falling to sleep on me almost instantly. A smile unlike any I've ever had hits my face. I send up a silent prayer. Begging that I can keep her like this, with me always. Hoping that this time, nothing can come between us.

Before dawn can crack its eyes open against the night sky, mine snap open. For a moment, I'm disoriented until I feel the tickle of hair on my chest and the warm, soft breaths of the woman wrapped around me like a vine. I hate to move. Hate to leave. But I don't have a choice on either of those.

I slide her hand off my chest and creep out from beneath her. She moans before I make it even a few inches, rolling over, and I puff out a sigh of relief until she says, "You sneaking out?"

"Yeah," I tell her, smiling at how she hugs her pillow against her naked chest. "I have an early shift and two surgeries to prep for."

"Have fun with that."

I chuckle. "What time are you done with stuff today?"

"I'm at Children's at ten and then I have rehearsal until Antonio dismisses us, so probably somewhere around six."

"Wanna go to a charity dinner with me tonight?"

"Absolutely not. That sounds awful."

I grin. "It is. But you'll be with me."

"Tempting, but I have symphony friends coming over tonight."

"Can I meet them?"

"Absolutely not," she repeats, but this time I catch her smile. "Maybe soon, though."

Leaning down onto the bed, I press my lips to the space between her shoulder blades. "I love you."

"Yep. Heard it all before."

Reaching under the blankets, I squeeze her bare ass. "That the best you got for me?"

"I might love you too. You know. Like a little."

I squeeze again. Harder.

"Or maybe a lot."

"That's what I thought. Talk to you later?"

"Yeah, yeah. Stop being so needy and let me go back to sleep."

With a grin, I leave her room, getting myself dressed and then doing an awesome walk of shame back up to my place to get showered and ready for the day. But as I open my phone—anxious to see some of last night's picture and video action—I pause when I find the text stream with my siblings in full swing. Even at this hour.

Kaplan: It was one meal. Don't you think you're overreacting?

Rina: No. Not even a little. You should know better by now than to second-guess a nurse's intuition. Something isn't right.

Landon: I didn't like her coloring if I'm being honest.

Rina: See!

Carter: Okay. Say you're right and something is wrong. What do we do about it?

Oliver: She'll blow us off if we try and say something.

Me: What's going on? What did I miss?

Kaplan: While you were busy with your 'other things' last night, which I assume means you were with Raven and acting like a ten-year-old not telling us, Mom didn't eat much if anything and was quieter than usual. And apparently her coloring is off according to our resident cardiologist.

I frown, reading that over twice as I step off the elevator into my apartment.

Me: She will blow us off if we say anything. Unfortunately, that's how Octavia Abbot-Fritz, Boston's queen and lover of appearances, rolls. **Did Dad notice?**

Carter: If he did, he didn't say anything or let on about it.

Kaplan: Which is why I think it's nothing more than an off night. Dad would be all over that.

Oliver: That's what you think or that's what you want to think?

Kaplan: Don't get all cryptic with me, baby brother. I'm just saying Dad wouldn't let that shit pass.

Landon: Likely not, but women notice stuff we don't evidently because Elle just read my texts over my shoulder and nodded her head, agreeing with Rina.

Oliver: Yeah. I just asked Amelia and she's on board with Rina too.

Carter: Grace as well. She's off today and volunteered to go over there and check on her. Talk baby showers or something.

Rina: I can go over too this afternoon. I'm only on till three.

Me: Good. Glad Gracey Lou Freebush and Rina Bina are on it. I'm with the women and nurses on this. I don't like it.

Kaplan: Report back to us after you go. Will I see the rest of you losers at the charity thing tonight?

Oliver: We'll be there.

Landon: Same.

Carter: I have the limo set to pick Kaplan and Luca up at six-thirty.

Me: See you then.

Doing my best to tuck my worry in, knowing Rina and Grace will check in on her today, I get myself showered and out the door. I wanted to watch the video again, but that will have to wait until later. Still... last night... my smile is uncontainable as I park in my spot in the garage at Brigham and Women's hospital.

My girl loves me.

She forgives me. At least I think she does.

Hopping out of the car, I hit the button to lock it up, but before I can make it to the elevator, someone calls my name. I turn to find one of the other neurosurgeons, Will James, jogging to catch up with me.

"Hey," he says, clapping a hand on my arm. "Glad I caught you."

I shake his hand. "What's up, man? I feel like I haven't seen you around much."

"I've been cutting back on hours. Spending more time with my grandkids. But I wanted to mention that I heard you're a finalist for the Treesprite grant. Congratulations."

My eyebrows hit my hairline, but I quickly rein in my shock. I didn't realize this was common knowledge. "Thank you. It's an honor to be considered."

We head toward the elevator, pressing the button. "I'm not sure if you knew this, but I won that grant once."

I pivot to face him right before the doors open and we step on. "No. I didn't know that. When did you win?"

He chuckles at my expression. "Years ago," he emphasizes. "I think I was just a couple of years older than you are now. It was an incredible experience. Changed my life. Made me a much better doctor, I can tell you that."

A strange cocktail of excitement and apprehension swarms through me as we're carried up into the hospital. "How so?"

"Well, for one, you make an incredible difference. I was in Argentina and then Kenya. The cases I saw in both places are unlike anything. Some of these people don't have access to clean water or proper shelter. So the care you provide goes so deep. Things like post-op care are a huge consideration. And some of the things you'll see have been undiagnosed and untreated for years, sometimes decades. It's a once in a lifetime opportunity, that's for sure."

I shake my head, floored by this. "I've wanted this for years," I admit. "It's why I applied, even when I was still a resident. I just never thought I'd be considered, let alone a finalist."

He shrugs, leaning back against the back of the elevator. "I hadn't either and then it happened. And I'm not you, if you know what I mean. I'm happy for you and I hope you get it. I still go on medical missions once a year for a couple of weeks because of it. You should find out soon, right?"

I nod numbly, staring up at the numbers as they glow from one to the next. "Couple weeks, I think."

The car starts to slow. "I wish you the best of luck with it." He smacks my shoulder, righting himself. "Let me know if you have any questions. I'm happy to help."

The doors part and with that, he steps out. Before I can think twice about it, I race out after him. "Will? Hey, hold on a second."

He pauses, turning to face me.

I glance down at this left hand, holding there for a moment. "Were you married when you went?"

He chuckles and something in the sound has me looking up at him. "So that's why you looked so forlorn. You've got someone?"

I nod. "Someone I don't want to leave." *Again.*

"Yes, I was married. But Kara wasn't working, and we hadn't

yet had the boys. She came with me. Volunteered in the clinics so we could be together. Is something like that an option for you?"

"No."

He bobs his head as he considers this. "I would have gone anyway. That was the plan if Kara couldn't make it work with her visa and volunteering."

I shake my head, my hands meeting my hips. "How could you have made that work?"

"Because we love each other," he says simply, as if the answer should have been obvious. "It would have been difficult, but we had made a commitment to each other and at the end of the day, it was only two years of being apart. I would have come home when I could, and she would have come to visit me."

How can he be so cavalier? We're talking South America and Africa. Not exactly around the corner. They make London look like a cakewalk. His words hit me harder than I expect them to. All of this has.

I think about the commitment I made to Raven. The wedding wasn't real, but I had promised her a lifetime. Then I broke it. Broke her. I couldn't do that to her again. And I don't think she'd understand if I told her I was going, but we'd stay together.

We're too new. Hardly even back together.

But the idea of this grant... of changing lives like that... of practicing that sort of medicine...

"I almost hope they don't pick me." I'm not sure I mean that. I want this grant so badly, I've been consumed with it. Like a kid who loves basketball and dreams of the NBA. Realistic for very few and I never considered they'd be interested in me for this. This could be the greatest opportunity of my life.

He gives me a sympathetic look. "Well, if they do, you and this woman will figure it out. If she's the one, you'll figure it out."

"Yeah. Thanks," I say absently. Will walks off and I'm left standing here, lost in a flurry of indecision. What on earth would I do if I got this grant?

30

"It's a Monday night," I object when Catarina enters my apartment holding a bottle of tequila and a bottle of margarita mix—the kind that already has alcohol in it. "Right. Monday. Margarita Monday."

"That's a thing?" I ask Quill, who is right behind her, carrying... more tequila. Oh boy.

She shrugs. "I have no idea. I was just told to bring tequila, so I did. You better have Mexican food and a lot of guacamole. Otherwise, all this tequila will burn an ulcer into my stomach."

"Boo," Catarina hisses out from the kitchen. "We're young and hot and not boring. Woo-hoo, Margarita Monday."

"Is she already drunk?" I whisper to Quill as I shut and lock the door.

"I don't see how since we Ubered here together after rehearsal. I'm still pissed it ran as late as it did. I'm starving."

"I'm not drunk. I'm having a girls' night. So put on the music, mix up the drinks, and let's eat."

I head into the kitchen, unloading the takeout that arrived moments before they did.

Pulling out a few glasses, I get started on the drinks, while Quill and Catarina attack the food. "My girlfriend called me old," Catarina says as she starts dishing herself up a plate.

I freeze midpour and turn to look at her, a frown on my face. "When? And how old is she?"

"She's twenty-five. Three years younger than me."

My eyebrows crease, as do Quill's. "I'm not understanding," she admits.

"I play classical music for a living and no longer wear slutty club dresses. I don't know." She shrugs up a shoulder as I finish making her drink—extra strong because clearly she needs it— and hand it to her. "I just figured by being with someone, living with them, I could just be myself and they'd love and accept that. I hated having to go to clubs to pick up women. I hated first and second and even third dates because I always felt like I had to be the best version of myself to get to a fourth date and for them to like me."

"Doesn't everyone feel like that? Isn't that why people hate dating?" Quill asks and I nod in agreement because yeah, dating sucks.

"Precisely. I think Talia just wants us to be more fun. We stay in a lot."

"You could have brought her here tonight," I throw out. "Had a girls' night like that. I could have invited a few of my friends too."

She shakes her head. "No. I wanted this to be just us. Maybe another night, though we'll all go out. You'll bring your friends and we'll be young and wild."

Both Quill and I scrunch up our noses at that, and Catarina laughs, cocking an eyebrow at me. "Quill I get. She's a married woman, but you're like twenty-two. How are you not out doing all those things?"

I make myself a plate of enchiladas and quesadillas and

beans and rice and then head over to my round dining table that's between the kitchen and the living room. "I like to think of myself as an old soul." Now I'm getting dubious eyebrows from both of them. "I don't know. In London, I was either heart-broken or it was all work with very few breaks. I was getting two degrees and had no real desire to meet a guy. Now I'm back here. All my friends, who are more like family, are all with people."

"And you're back with the guy who broke your heart." Quill says it like a statement as she sits beside me, taking a sip of her drink.

"I guess. It's complicated, but it's also not. Being with him is more natural than I would have ever guessed after what we went through."

"Which is..."

"More complicated than I feel like getting into while I'm eating." I take a bite of my food to drive my point home.

"Incidentally, how do you afford this place?" Catarina asks as she stares around my apartment. "I realize that might be a tacky question, but you don't have a car and I've heard you mumble about spending Uber money in the past. So..."

"I, um... I know the owner of the building."

"Girl, could you be any more cryptic about shit in your life?" Quill teases.

"For real." Catarina laughs, polishing off her drink and getting up to make another.

"My world is—" I'm cut off when there's a knock on my door.

"Expecting more company?" Quill quips.

"Um. No." Wiping my mouth with my napkin, I get up and head for the door. "Who is it?"

"Me. Open up."

His tone has me unlocking and flinging the door open in the next second. Luca is standing right in my doorway, his hands braced on either side of the frame, his body angled in. But his expression is as despondent as his tone was.

"Hey. You okay? What's wrong?"

He shakes his head for a moment, his green eyes clinging to my face. "Rough day. I just wanted to see you."

Without hesitating, I wrap my arms around his waist, tucking my face into the jacket and shirt of his silky tux, breathing him in. He emits a heavy sigh, his arms encircling my back, holding on tight. I know Catarina and Quill are likely watching, and though I had been reluctant to share him with anyone, it's a bit too late for that now.

I thought about him all day. Thought about what we did last night. And I'm not even talking about the dirty stuff. I'm talking about how hard this man made me fall for him again. His complete and utter devotion to me. To us.

"My mom isn't doing well," he murmurs against my neck, placing an open mouthed kiss and nuzzling in deeper as if he can't get close enough. "I'm not sure what's up with her, but Rina and Grace were there today and said she's more tired than normal and seems to be eating less."

I draw back, my chin dropping to his chest so I can look up at him. "Could it be from the chemo?"

"No. She finished that a couple weeks ago, so I doubt it."

I cup his slightly stubbled jaw in my hand. "Maybe it's just a cold or something. Is she going to get checked out?"

"I don't know. I was with my brothers tonight at the charity thing and we planned to go over there tomorrow night. Talk with her more about it." He licks his lips. "I'm scared," he confesses.

"I know, baby. I'm sorry." I squeeze him tighter. "I'm glad you're going to see her. Would it be all right if I went over tomorrow morning for a visit?"

He chuckles, the humorless sound rumbling into me. "You don't have to ask to go see my mom. She's practically your mom too and I think that would be good for her. She might listen to you if you suggest something."

"Okay. I'll go in the morning then."

Without another word, he leans down and kisses me. His lips are firm, almost demanding, maybe slightly panicked, and I can't help but feel there is more going on in his head than just his mom. The way he's holding me, as if he's afraid he'll never get the chance again, makes my heart beat just a touch faster.

Catarina blows out a catcall behind us and I grin into his lips. Luca just kissed me in front of my friends without realizing it.

A point he proves when he glances up past my shoulder and finds Catarina and Quill at the dining table, and his eyes widen in surprise. "Shit. I forgot you were having friends over. I'm sorry."

"Don't be. They didn't hear us."

"They saw us kiss."

I wink at him. "They sure did. Good thing you didn't cop a feel. Did you eat? Do you want to come in?" I ask when he pulls away, giving his arm a gentle tug. I don't want him to go. Surprisingly, I want him to meet my friends. "It's fine. It's just Margarita Monday and these are my music people."

He smiles, a touch of dawn hitting the darkness in his eyes. "Margarita Monday, eh? Didn't know that was a thing, though it sounds fun. But no, I already ate, and I won't interrupt."

"We don't mind," Catarina yells across the apartment. "She's told us practically nothing about you. Please, come in and give us all the details. I'm a lesbian, but that kiss was enough to make me bi curious."

I giggle lightly, turning to glance over my shoulder. "Bi curious?"

Catarina throws her hands up. "He's hot."

Quill's jaw is practically unhinged, and Catarina is now

grinning like the cat who ate the canary. "It seems you don't have a choice now."

"You're okay with that? Me coming in and meeting your friends?"

I stare up into his eyes. Him looking at me like this. Showing up here tonight the way he did... "Yes. I'm okay with it."

"I'm telling them you're my girlfriend."

"We heard that!"

I ignore Catarina. "Is that what I am?"

"Fuck yeah, you are."

He gives me another kiss, this one no less deep or intense. Part of me feels like I should still hold back. Keep myself in check. But the rest of me knows it's too late for that. I told him I loved him, and I meant it. There is no holding back after that. It's only forward with a prayer I don't get hurt again.

Twisting so his arm is around my shoulders, he shuts the door behind us and then goes to meet my friends. "Hi. I'm Luca." He extends his hand, first to Catarina and then to Quill, who still hasn't managed to pick her jaw up off the table. "It's nice to meet you both. You must play with Raven. What instruments?"

"You're Luca Fritz." That's Quill and shit. This is why I didn't tell them. This is why I hold so much of that side of my life back. That starstruck look. "Luca Abbot-Fritz."

"You sure about that? I could be Landon."

A laugh explodes from my chest before I can stop it. I realize people have mistaken them for the other. Hell, the first night Elle met Landon, she thought it was Luca. But if you know them, they're so insanely different, it feels almost impossible not to notice the difference.

"Landon is seeing someone who is not Raven. He's also a single dad."

Luca glances over at me with a bemused expression and

then back up at her. "Both of those things are correct. And my brother would be in a lot of trouble if he were seeing Raven. I staked a claim when she was barely legal."

I pinch into his side, and he drops a kiss on my head.

"Well, well, and my, my." Catarina leans back in her chair, taking her margarita with her, her food all but forgotten as she fans her face. "Hot. That's all I have to say. The looks he gives you, kitten, could start a forest fire in the middle of a rainstorm. I like it."

"So, *you're* the flowers guy?" Quill sputters. "All these years?"

I get another quick glance. I'm guessing Luca doesn't quite know what to make of these two. "That was me."

"The rumors were true then." Quill practically gasps. "A billionaire prince who broke your heart was sending them. Oh my God! I cannot believe it was Luca Abbot-Fritz, Raven. Do you know who he is? I know you recently moved back here, but..." She claps her hand over her mouth.

"Well, it's been a pleasure meeting you both. I'll let you get back to your night."

"No," Catarina pipes up. "Don't go on account of Quill's crazy. She's English and royals and gossip are their national sport. You have to understand how her mind works. You're like the Prince William of Boston to her right now."

Quill nods, still all starry-eyed.

"I'd say that's more Kaplan. You know. Eldest and all that. I guess I'm more Harry since I got the crazy raven-haired American."

I shake my head, shoving him off me. "Time for you to go, playboy."

"Yes, actually. Now that we know who Raven has been keeping a secret, we can talk about you once you leave. Drill her with questions."

I roll my eyes at Catarina and force Luca toward the door.

"Have a wonderful evening," he calls out to them as I shove him out into the hall, shutting the door behind us so we have some privacy. "Lovely friends. A bit interesting, but fun."

"Kiss me and shut up."

His lips crash down on mine once more, his hands up in my hair, holding me to him. We kiss like teenagers, a lot of tongue and lips and soft moans with a hint of grinding for a minute or two before I pull away with one last soft kiss.

"You okay?"

"A lot better now. My head is just full of a lot of things."

"Don't worry. She'll be okay."

His face casts down with a grim frown. "I hope so."

"Rebellions are built on hope."

A smile lights up his face, eclipsing any heartache previously there. "Did you just quote Star Wars to me? I fucking love you, Raven Fairchild. Thank you."

"For what?"

"For all of this. For always showing me there is sun behind the clouds, even when I can't feel it or see it." His lips meet mine once more, soft and sweet, and then he's walking down the hall. "Will you come up after your friends go?"

"Yes."

He blows me a kiss and then he's gone and I'm back inside, staring warily at my two friends.

"Luca bloody Fritz?!" Quill cries out the second I shut the door.

I shrug at her, grabbing my mostly empty margarita from the table and making myself another. Clearly, *I'm* going to need it.

"But. He's—"

I hold up my hand, stopping her. "I've known him my entire life. His whole family actually. My father is their house manager and chief of security."

"So. He's not some bloke you randomly met four years ago and are having another fling with?"

I shake my head, taking a sip, the tart of the lime and the heat of the tequila hitting me just right. "No. But now you understand why I don't like to talk about it either."

"I'd be broadcasting that, so not really." Catarina laughs, running her hand over her short, spiky hair before holding it out to me. "But we won't say anything to anyone. Will we, Quill?" She glares meaningfully at our English friend.

"No," Quill agrees quickly. "We won't. I promise. I'm just... wow. I'm in total shock. This is Boston and those chaps are practically everywhere. And gorgeous. I mean, so gorgeous. But, and I don't mean this the way it's going to sound, but Luca is known—"

"As a playboy? I know."

She bobs her head, glancing at Catarina and then back at me. "Yes. Right. That. But the two of you obviously looked—" Her phone chimes with some sort of notification. She picks it up and her mouth falls agape for the second time tonight before she quickly schools her features and flips it back over, face down on the table. That doesn't stop her cheeks from turning fifty shades of red room.

"What was that?" Catarina questions.

"Nothing. It was nothing."

"No. It was clearly something. What?"

"Luca," she practically whisper-hisses, visibly growing more uncomfortable.

"Huh?" I'm not following.

Catarina's hand shoots out and grabs Quill's phone. "You have Google alerts on the Fritz family?"

Now I understand why she was turning red. "I just like following them, is all. They're not the only ones I have that with," she presses sheepishly. "You said it. I'm English. We love our gossip."

"You just got an alert on Luca?" I surmise.

She sags a bit before rushing out, "It's a picture of him tonight with a woman on his arm."

"Let me see," I demand, snatching the phone from Catarina. And sure enough, there is a picture splashed across some celebrity entertainment website of Luca with freaking Priscilla Barnes looped around him so tightly she's practically growing on him. The caption reads, 'Is Boston's billionaire playboy finally off the market? Luca Fritz at the Healthcare for the Homeless charity event looking very cozy with Pricilla Barnes.

I snort out a laugh and hand it back to Quill. Shockingly, seeing that image... nope. Not an ounce of jealousy. He came here tonight right after that event. He came to see me because he's had a long day and needed me. He's told me over and over that these pictures are a lie. That he's not going home with these women.

That he's not the playboy they portray him as.

That he loves me.

And I believe him. I trust him.

Something shifts inside me. Something deep and soul-quenching as it rises from within me like a geyser. All these years, he really has been waiting on me to fly back home to him.

"It's bullshit," I tell them adamantly, never more sure about anything in my life than I am about him.

"Absolutely," Catarina agrees, slamming her hand down on the table, causing our plates and glasses to clatter.

"Most definitely," Quill chimes in now, her smile returning as she sits up a bit straighter. "He looked at you the way Harry looks at Megan."

"And that's a good thing?" I confirm.

"Absolutely a good thing. But I will say, he was still wearing his tux just now."

"So?" I shift in my chair.

Quill taps her phone's now dark screen. "This picture couldn't have been taken more than an hour or so ago and it's already online. You clearly prefer to keep your relationship with him on the quiet side and I'm afraid that might be rather difficult with a man like Luca Fritz. Just be careful, is all. It's only a matter of time until they catch on to you and it's out there."

31

Since I left Raven's over an hour ago, my mood has slipped considerably. I received an email from the Treesprite people informing me that I should hear about a final decision the Monday after Thanksgiving and that I'd have only seven days following that to accept or decline.

I don't know how things got this far.

I filled out the damn form in a roomful of other neurosurgeons, all of us joking about it. Wouldn't it be amazing if they took us? Yeah, right, no one gets it. I hear they're only taking doctors from Europe and Asia right now.

That's how it all went, despite my lusting after it, and now... now I'm a finalist.

I spent the following I don't even know how long researching for the hundredth time all that this grant does. The lives it changes and saves. The doctors you help train and teach. The impact I could have, not just on a local level, but on a global scale if I got this.

I think about that woman and her child. The way she was pleading with her husband to let them go in and get the child help. The fear crippling him at the idea of them being deported and forced to leave their child if the hospital called it in. I wanted to help them. I wanted to save them.

It would be the experience of a lifetime just as Will said. But it's so much more than that for me. How do you turn something like that down? You don't according to Landon and he's right. You don't. But then I think of my mom, and I think about Raven and...

"Luca?" Raven's sexy rasp rings out through my apartment.

"Back here," I reply because I've been in bed staring up at the ceiling, waiting on her while my thoughts tumble me about like a boat in hurricane waters.

"Hey," she says, her voice softer. "Did I wake you?"

"No."

I hear her moving about my dark bedroom. The blanket on the other side of the bed is peeled back and then her body is beside mine. Warm. Soft. Smelling incredible. She's not naked and I'm glad. I wanted her up here with me tonight. I wanted to sleep holding her. I don't want everything with us to be sex, which might sound ridiculous to say and even think, but it's true.

I want her for so much more than that.

"You okay?" she asks, her head hitting my chest, her ear against my racing heart.

"I don't know." I should tell her about this. About the grant. But chances are I won't get it and what's the point of upsetting her needlessly? We're so new and she'll lose faith and trust in me in a nanosecond. Thinking I'm racing off to leave her again. I can't do it. I can't tell her. I blow out a breath.

"Is it about your mom?"

"Partially?"

"Is it about me?"

Partially. "No."

I kiss the top of her head because I don't like doing this to her. I'm not a dark person, but when darkness creeps in on me, it comes fast, and it comes hard, and it's a sticky fucker. She knows this about me better than most.

"Is this about those pictures with you and Pricilla?"

A mirthless chuckle rumbles through my lips. "No. It's definitely not about that."

But…

I roll on my side, shifting her so we're face to face on my pillows. It's pretty dark in here, but I can still make out the outline of her face. See some of the sparkle of her eyes as they catch on whatever lighting is here.

"Did they bother you? I'm sorry. I should have mentioned it earlier, but my head wasn't on her or that at all. She was at the charity thing talking with me and she likes to touch. Likely because she knows cameras are there. I removed her hand from me the following second. I swear I did."

"Luca—"

"No. Let me finish because I don't even know if this is out yet, but I gave her a lift home. She lives here in the building as you know, and she asked for a ride, so she didn't have to Uber alone. Carter, Kaplan, and I took a limo, so they saw us pull up in front together. They took pictures, Raven. Almost as if they were waiting for us."

"I know."

"I didn't touch her."

"I know."

"You do?"

She laughs, reaching out and cupping my jaw. "Where did you go when you came into the building?"

"I got on the elevator with her, and I punched in your floor while she went up to hers."

"And after that?"

"Here."

"And do you have Pricilla hiding in your closet or bathroom?"

"Huh? What? No."

"Luca, relax. You're all wound up. I know you're not doing anything with her. You've never so much as looked at another woman when we've been together. Even back then. I never once was worried that you'd cheat on me."

I sag, releasing a breath I didn't realize I was holding. "I don't look at other women, Raven, because as far as I'm concerned there are no others."

"I will be honest. I never imagined I'd be able to trust you again, but these past few weeks you've done more than just tell me that I can. You've showed me. I trust you, Luca. And I want to do this with you."

My forehead presses to hers, my lips next. "Can I tell the world you're mine?"

"Not quite yet if that's okay. It's not you. I just don't particularly want what happened with Amelia to happen to me. You, Oliver, and Kaplan have always been the media's darlings. Landon they left alone—at least when it comes to his dating life—and Carter is a grizzly with them and until Grace, very uninteresting with his dating life."

"That's because he always brought his dates to his place. Never out."

"Well, the media, this town, likely even the world are obsessed with you. You saw Quill tonight and she's my friend, married, and harmless."

"Eventually, people will see us together and I'm going to want to tell them you're mine."

Her fingers coast through my hair until they reach the back of my head where she holds me against her. "I know. Just not yet. We have to get through my dad and your parents first."

∿

"DID you tell them we're a thing?" I ask Raven, speaking into my car's Bluetooth as I sit in Tuesday night rush hour traffic heading out to the compound.

Her husky laugh comes through the phone that instantly has my cock jerking in my pants. The woman isn't even in the car with me and we're not talking sexy, yet the sound of her laugh gets my dick hard. One day my dick will write a tell-all memoir about my obsession with Raven Fairchild and title it *Fucked From The Start*.

"I didn't have to. Evidently, some cocky asshole took it upon himself to do that for me."

I smirk. "I told them Sunday night that I had other plans, but I believe it's fairly obvious at this point that the only thing that can drag me away from Sunday dinner with my family is you."

She puffs. "My dad called me this morning."

"And?"

"And the two of you need to stop having early morning tea chats on the phone."

I chuckle, running a hand through my hair as I inch along I-90. "It's not every day."

"Luca!"

"Your dad is easily the coolest guy I've ever known. And if you ply him with enough caffeine, he tells you stories. Raven, did you know your father jumped out of an aircraft into Iraq during Desert Storm and rescued ten American POWs and there was nothing reported about it in the press?"

"Yes. Did you know Jerome was one of those men he rescued?"

"Jerome, Jerome? As in my mother's security detail?"

"One and the same."

I lean back against my leather seat, floored.

"My father doesn't mess around with your family, Luca. He hires the absolute best and only people he trusts with his life.

Do you know how many threats your family had against them last year alone?"

I glare at the screen of my car as if Raven's face is there and I can give her my WTF look. "Um. No."

She laughs. "Sixty-four."

"The fuck?!"

"You're a family of famous billionaires. Women have broken into Kaplan's apartment. Oliver's ex stalked him and Amelia all over town before threatening them. Grace's ex is a douchebag. Rina was kidnapped and held against her will in a junk house in Harlem. Landon's family was harassed morning, noon, and night after Reese died and we're not even talking about what Elle's family just put them through. You have paparazzi following your every move. How are you surprised by this?"

I stare out the windshield, dumbstruck. "I... I don't know. I never assumed it was like that." That's obviously naive of me. We just do our thing and live our lives and clearly that's because of our security team and men like Morgan Fairchild, former MI6, and his group of "don't fuck with us or we'll fuck you up" people.

"Well, now you know."

"Shit. I owe your father a cup of tea in person. If I send him some Earl Grey from England, do you think he'll like me more?"

"Can't hurt," she replies, and I hear noise in the background. Voices.

"You just getting in?"

"I sure am."

After what she just told me, that has me breathing a sigh of relief. Because if we're getting threats like this and someone finds out she's mine... Now I know why she wanted to wait. More than just the press.

At least I know her dad would kill anyone who ever dared to hurt her and no, that's not an exaggeration. He'd kill anyone who dared to hurt her. Yeah. I'm gonna buy the man some English tea. I'm all gangbusters on that trip until I hear a thick Italian accent come through the phone. Louder and likely closer than the fucktwat should be.

"That sounds perfect. Yes. Thank you, Antonio, I'd love that."

"And what exactly would you love Antonio to do that sounds perfect?"

She laughs. The woman laughs at my angst.

"Work on my solos tonight."

"Alone?" I practically spit across my windshield.

"Yes, Luca. Alone. I'm the only cello with a solo. But he knows about you and it's not like that. Just as I knew those pictures of you with Pricilla weren't anything, this isn't either."

Fuck. This means she's telling me I have to trust her. And I do. It's him I don't.

"Fine."

I won't show up at Symphony Hall tonight. I won't show up at Symphony Hall tonight.

"I'm coming over when you get home and sleeping with you."

"Is that a promise, Doctor Playboy? Do I get the full Luca Abbot-Fritz treatment?"

I practically growl, my dick getting harder because he knows what that voice is. That's her sexy, you're gonna get some voice and my guy is ready, front row for that action. "Anything you want."

"Good because I might want to play a game tonight."

Shit. I groan. I can't even stop it. "What kind of game?"

"The one where you punish me for staying late with my boss."

Motherfucker. I just leaked into my boxer briefs and now I'm getting off the exit for my parents' compound.

"I'm spanking your ass tonight, Little Bird, and then eating your pussy. From behind. And then fucking you. Again, from behind."

"Promises, promises. I have to go. See you tonight."

She disconnects the call and if I didn't want to save all my batter for later shenanigans and not get arrested for public indecency, I'd whack one off before pulling into the driveway. As it is, I'm the first one to arrive, which was sort of my plan since I missed Sunday dinner and feel just a touch guilty about it.

Parking my car, I hop out and then head for the front door. My father cuts me off before I get very far. "You're early."

"Yeah. So? That a crime?"

He glances warily over his shoulder and my blood pressure climbs.

"What are you hiding from us?"

He shakes his head, clasping my shoulder and leading me through the massive downstairs to the back where his study is. "Nothing," he says as he shuts the door. "I'm hiding nothing. But your mother is upstairs resting before dinner, and I don't want to disturb her."

"So you're aware there's something going on with her?"

"Suddenly you're an attorney?" He levels me with me a look before he goes about pouring us both a drink. My hand wraps around the crystal cylinder, pulling it to my lips. He can tell I'm not amused. "Luca, your mother has cancer. Recurrent cancer. I don't know what you and your brothers and sister were expecting, but it's serious stuff."

I swallow and choke on the liquid as it burns a path down the back of my throat. "We know. We're not stupid."

"But you assumed she'd have surgery, a round of chemo, and then dance around Boston again?"

"Something like that," I admit, which likely makes me sound foolish. I'm a doctor. One who deals with cancer on a daily basis. I know its ins and outs better than most. But this is my mother, so yeah, it's different.

"She's tired. She's anemic. She's not hungry. But she's fighting because she knows she has to. You guys coming in here and demanding things from her isn't going to help."

I take another pull and think about this. Because what he's saying...

"We're just worried."

"As am I. But don't think for a second I haven't noticed every nuance of every move she makes. I study her, Luca. I would be the first one to drag her into the hospital if I felt it was more than what it is. I made her promise me she wouldn't hide anything either."

"We can't lose her, Dad."

"And you think I can?" He downs his drink in one large gulp and for the first time, I'm seeing what my mother's cancer is doing to him. All this time, we've been so consumed with how it's played out on her. On us. But we haven't considered him, and how foolhardy is that? She might not have started out as the love of his life, but she sure as hell ended up being that.

"Do you want me to call off the brigade?"

"Just have them tone it down some. I promise, if there is cause for concern, I won't hold back."

And with that declaration, I text all my brothers, who are headed this way at this very moment. My dad is right and it's difficult to face as adults and doctors and nurses, but yeah, he's got this.

"Raven was here this morning."

I grin. I'm such a hopeless fool, but I grin all the same. "I know."

"She and your mother talked for a couple of hours. Told her that you're winning her heart over again."

"Winning? That means I haven't completed the job yet."

My father smirks the smirk of a man who's been married

for more than half of his life. "Son, take it from me, you've never completed the job. We're always winning but will never have won. The fact that you're winning means you're in the game and she's letting you believe you have the upper hand. You never will. You should go into it knowing that now, but she's letting you think you do and that's winning."

"You think she'd marry me if I asked her to? I mean for real this time?"

"I think she'd likely break your nose if you tried."

Probably. Is it strange that that's not a deterrent?

The door swings open with a knock and Landon comes in, eyeing the two of us, and then goes to make himself the vodka that he prefers.

"Do you have any idea how big Thanksgiving is going to be this year?"

My father and I exchange glances and then I stare into the back of Landon's head. "You're talking to us about holidays and guest lists?"

He takes the chair opposite us, sipping at his drink before resting it on his knee. "I'm just saying, it's weird, right? In the last six months, we went from Rina being the only one of us coupled up to all of us being in that boat with the exception of Kaplan."

"Grace always came for Thanksgiving here if she wasn't working," I argue.

"Yes, but now she's coming as Carter's. Not as Oliver's best friend."

"True. Does this mean I get to invite Raven?"

My father stares down into his bourbon. "She's invited every year, Luca. This is the first year in four she'll likely accept, though."

"Thanks for the kick in the nuts, Dad." I reach over and smack his shoulder. "I never can get enough of those."

"That's what I'm here for. But truly, it's just adding on Amelia, Layla, and Elle. Nothing too crazy."

"Will Mom be up for that?"

My father hits Landon with a look. "Your mother wouldn't miss Thanksgiving with her family for anything."

"It's less than two weeks away," I say, suddenly realizing the date with a note of panic. My drink somehow clangs on the table, my hands in my hair as I stare down at the carpet.

"What's all this?" my father asks.

"Treesprite," Landon supplies for me. "He's freaking out about it because he's dying to win it, but he has no idea what he'd do if he did."

"Ah. I see. Well, I won the Heartstrong grant when I was a new cardiothoracic surgeon. That had me in India for a year."

"Mom came with you for some of that and that was before you had Kaplan," I mumble before picking up my glass and finishing it off.

"And you don't feel Raven would be willing to do that?" he surmises.

"He doesn't feel he can ask her because she just started with the symphony and the hospital, and they've already been down this road once before."

I point at Landon, who has decided to be my voice when it was always the other way around. Falling back in love and forgiving himself has changed him completely. He's the man he used to be before Reese died and nothing—I repeat nothing— makes me happier. Still, it's a weird role reversal.

"Luca, love and commitment mean being there for the other person. Sometimes it's not always easy or convenient. Sometimes it's a sacrifice. But wouldn't that choice be hers to make?"

"I don't know. She's so headstrong, Dad. She follows her heart and—"

"And you made that choice for her once. She was young and it was likely the right call given where she is now, but she's not a kid anymore. You love this woman and talk about marrying her. That means you owe it to her to give her the choice, Luca. To respect her headstrong mind and heart. Whatever they decide."

I didn't give her the choice the first go around. I decided for both of us. Wrong or right, I did that. My father's right. If I get this grant, I have to give her the choice.

32

It's the Wednesday before Thanksgiving, so like the crazy people we are, Grace, Rina, and I are shopping through Wholefoods. It's the equivalent of going to the mall on Black Friday in here. It's packed with holiday pick-up orders and last-minute shoppers. We're the latter.

Stella and Layla had the idea of inviting all of the staff to have Thanksgiving with us. Typically, the Fritzes give most of the staff the holiday off to do their own thing, but this year, Octavia and Dr. Fritz extended the invitation to holiday dinner.

We're talking a lot of freaking people coming for a meal.

The garden room in the back of the house that is beside the ballroom is being set up as we speak with tables and food stations galore. But to add some crazy, Stella asked if each of the Fritz people could bring a dish to help with the cooking.

Stella, Landon, and Elle are making all the breads.

Oliver, Amelia, and Layla mashed potatoes.

Grace and Carter are thinking of doing apple and pumpkin pies.

Rina and Brecken get sweet potatoes and squashes, and I volunteered green bean casserole—my favorite—and brussels sprouts. Sophia, the house chef, is making two turkeys, stuffing, cranberry sauces, gravy, and who knows whatever else. But for the first time in four years, I'm looking forward to Thanksgiving.

It was sort of easy to not feel homesick over missing the holiday when I was in London since they don't celebrate it there. Still... I knew what I was missing. Family. Food. Love.

"To marshmallow or not to marshmallow? That is the question," Rina muses as she stares down at the bags of white puffs on the display in front of us.

"My vote is marshmallows," Grace tells her. "But that's just me. Carter has gone back to policing my sugar and junk consumption, so I'm at the mercy of others."

I snicker. "Like you don't have a stash."

She glances around as if Carter's going to jump out of the neighboring cereal aisle and bust her. "I've had to hide gummy worms in my shoe boxes and eat them either after he's gone to sleep for the night or when he's not home. It's so pathetic."

"You're a better woman than I am," Rina states flatly. "I'd just tell Brecken to fuck off."

"Different beast," I say, picking up two bags of marshmallows and dropping them into Rina's cart. "You're making four of these. Do two with and two without."

"Smart. And remind me why we're all doing this again?"

"To feed us commoners."

"No, that's not my issue," Rina smarts as she goes about grabbing maple syrup and brown sugar by the gross. "But why do I have to cook? Stella told me I can't get catering. That's just awful. I'm subjecting everyone to my poor cooking skills. It's a wonder Brecken doesn't have irritable bowel syndrome after suffering through a few of my meals a week."

"You?" I point at her, my eyes wide. "I haven't cooked in forever other than what I could make for myself in my tiny flat in London or in the community kitchen in the staff house. Most of the time I was eating cereal or soup because it was cheap, and London is not. We're using Luca's kitchen because it's huge, but Stella is putting a lot of faith in us."

Grace is beet red, her face cast everywhere other than at us.

"What?" Rina snaps. "What are you hiding?"

She nibbles on her bottom lip. "I might have ordered two of the pies."

Both Rina and I gasp.

"What? I am not a freaking baker, okay? I just like sweets. I ordered the pumpkin and chocolate cream pies. I'm making the apple. That has to count. We're talking three damn kinds of pie here and I'm a fucking resident. Carter made a test pumpkin pie that was so awful, it was inedible. I won't subject people to that. I just won't."

I hold up my hand as I load my cart with canned cream of mushroom soup. "No judgments. I have zero judgments and honestly, I'm grateful. I love the hell out of pie."

Rina bobs her head, her hair up in a tight bun, and she's still in scrubs from her shift. "Ditto. You're doing a service. Do you think they'd know if I scooted back over to prepared foods and bought them out of squash?"

"Probably, but I'll carry that secret to my grave," I promise.

"Me too." Grace nods solemnly.

We walk along, Rina and Grace going back and forth on the merits of adding clove in apple pies, when I blurt out, "Has Luca seemed different to either of you in the last couple of weeks?"

The two of them pause midaisle, nearly causing a traffic jam and getting a couple of snarly comments from a woman behind us. We let her pass us and then Grace turns to me, her eyebrows pinched together, her lips pursed. "Different how?"

"I don't know. Not distant exactly, but more pensive. I can't put my finger on it, but he just feels... off to me."

"Off," Rina echoes. "I don't know. I haven't noticed anything, but then again I don't see him a ton during the week. Could it be about my mom?"

"Maybe." I stare down at my cart, at the pile of food. "I feel like it's more, though. He's clingy, but he's also not talking as much as he used to. And his moods feel... darker, I guess." I exhale a heavy breath, scrubbing my hands up and down my face. "Maybe I'm just crazy and reading too much into things. We're new at this and yet we don't feel that way."

"It's like you two skipped over the getting to know each other phase and went straight into serious town," Grace quips. "Carter and I were the same way. We've known each other our whole lives and then suddenly our dynamic completely changed and we had to learn how to get to know each other as a couple."

"Right! Yes. That's how this feels. But we did some of that dance four years ago and now here we are, back to this, and everything is great. I mean, pure magic. We can't get enough of each other, but..." My hands grip the handle on the cart as I stare pointedly at my friends. "I also feel like maybe he's keeping something from me."

Rina throws her hands up. "If he is, I have no clue what it could be."

Grace shrugs sheepishly. "Me neither."

"Maybe I'm just—" I get cut off when all three of our phones ring simultaneously. "What the hell?"

"Carter?"

"Oliver?"

"Luca?" I answer. "What's going on? I'm with Grace and Rina, and they're getting calls from your brothers."

"My mom is in the hospital. She passed out in the shower this morning and Dad rushed her in by ambulance. They're doing all kinds of tests, but I'm headed over there now."

"Where? What hospital?"

"Brigham and Women's. She's in the Shapiro Tower Pavilion."

"We're on our way. Can I bring anything?"

"No. I'll see you soon." He disconnects the call and I've never heard him like that. His voice a concoction of scared little boy and all business doctor.

Grace and I both grab Rina's hands and without saying anything, the three of us abandon our carts and run for the exit. Grace drove Carter's car and the three of us pile in.

"Did Luca or Oliver tell you any details?"

I shake my head as I buckle up. "No. Just that Octavia passed out in the shower and Dr. Fritz rushed her into the hospital. She's on some tower pavilion."

"It's the private floor at the hospital," Rina whispers, her voice cracking slightly at the end as she types furiously into her phone. "Oliver told me the same thing. I don't think anyone knows anything right now. I'm texting Brecken."

"In this traffic, avoid Charles Street and take Storrow Drive. It'll be quicker because we can loop around and if it looks like it's backing up, we can get off and cut over."

Grace wordlessly does as I request. I've been trained for this, and they both know it. They know about my parents. "Carter said Landon is bringing the girls over to the compound to stay with Sophia there since he doesn't know how long he'll be gone for."

"Fuck! Just fuck! I knew something wasn't right. I knew it. And now this."

I reach forward and squeeze Rina's shoulder. "You're not helping yourself and you won't help anyone else if you lose your mind now."

"She's right. You don't know anything yet," Grace asserts, weaving us onto Storrow. "She could have just vasovagaled in the shower. Let's wait and see."

"Grace, how often do you go against your nurses' intuition?"

"Never," she replies solemnly. "But Octavia also perked up a bit last week."

Rina shakes her head. "Or she was putting on the Octavia Abbot-Fritz facade so we wouldn't worry."

"Maybe," I agree. "I'm no doctor or nurse, but couldn't it be something simple like anemia?"

"Could be," Grace concedes.

"Or it could be something worse."

"My lovely pessimistic, friend. I know you're an ICU nurse and are used to the worst, but what you don't see with your eyes, don't invent with your mouth."

She snorts. "Thank you, Yoda. Don't tell me Luca is rubbing off on you."

"That's actually a Jewish proverb. Not Yoda. And it's true."

"She's right, Rina." Grace weaves in and out of lanes around traffic. "I know you go to the dark side—pun intended—quickly, but you and I have both been around this shit enough to know it can be something very simple that caused this."

Rina sinks down in her seat, her blond head falling back. "I know and I'm sorry. I don't mean to be a bitch or snap at you guys. I'm just so scared, I can hardly think or take a breath. She's my mom."

"We get it," I tell her. "We more than get it. Octavia is all we have too."

Rina nods and none of us speak again until we reach the hospital and find Elle and Amelia flying toward our car. "We just got here," Elle cries. "Oh my God, do you know anything?"

Amelia puts her hand on Elle's arm. "Remember what I said in the car? You gotta breathe and calm yourself down. We will not help Octavia or anyone else by panicking like this."

I smirk at Amelia. She is undeniably calm. She's been through worse than this and is the guardian of a teenager, so she knows what she's doing. But it's good she's here. Because even though I've been trained to be calm, trained to be in control and think versus feel…

My insides are a motherfucking mess.

Amelia draws Rina in for a big hug, whispering something into her ear that none of us can hear, and my smirk grows. Because look at this. This group of women who band together to support their people. This family that is so strong in their love.

They are billionaires. They are famous.

But no one else knows them as this.

The family that would walk through fire for each other. The ones who only allow others who follow that motto into their lives.

I shoot up a silent thank you. Not a prayer. A thank you. Because love and trust like this don't come easy. And are never a given or foregone conclusion. But Octavia Abbot-Fritz and her children deserve every ounce of it.

I hold on to Rina's hand and then we're all going for the elevators. Only, we have to check in at the main desk. Get clearance for going up to this special pavilion. And then be escorted there because evidently, they don't mess around with security.

The dragging minutes in between us doing all this and getting to the floor feel like hours and our already frazzled nerves are on their last straw. I don't even know if I'm making sense at this point. All I know is that I can't handle this. I'm trying. I'm trying for strong and brave because that's all I know, but I already lost one mother.

I can't lose another.

The doors part and we're greeted by a nurse with dark hair and a kind smile. "You must be the Abbot-Fritz family. I'm Kelly. Please, come this way."

"Is my mom okay?" Rina immediately asks.

"We're running some tests and some of them aren't back yet." She glances at Rina. "You're an ICU nurse, correct?"

Rina bobs her head.

"Good. Okay. Her CBC showed an elevated white count around twenty-two thousand, as well as a left shift."

"She has an infection," Rina interjects.

"Yes. We're running blood cultures and have started her on antibiotics and fluids because it appears she's also a bit dehydrated. An infection isn't uncommon during or shortly after undergoing chemo. Her immune system is greatly compromised. But her EKG and chest X-ray are good. No obvious indication of a PE (pulmonary embolus) or pneumonia and her vitals are holding."

Rina squeezes my hand, her palm clammy against mine. "Thank you," she whispers as we're led around, only to find six Fritz men, including Dr. Fritz Sr., speaking to two doctors in the middle of the hall. There is a large nurses' station off to the side with a couple of people there working on computers, but other than that, the floor is empty and quiet.

It's so unlike any hospital floor I've ever seen.

I'm guessing this is a very private, very exclusive floor in the hospital.

The Fritz men turn as one, spotting us. My eyes lock with Luca's turbulent ones, much of the color drained from his face. He's not alone in that. His brothers and father appear as though they've aged ten years in the last hour.

I walk straight for him, releasing Rina so I can wrap my arms around him and hold him close to me. His face hits my neck, and he breathes me in, his body trembling against mine. He kisses my neck and then pulls me in front of him, my back to his stomach. All the Fritz men are cocooning their women, holding on tight. Kaplan and Dr. Fritz embrace Rina as Brecken isn't here yet.

"We're still waiting on one more, but please continue, Frank," Dr. Fritz says to one of the doctors.

What appears to be the lead doctor pushes the bridge of his

glasses up his nose as he takes in each of us. "Sure. Of course. As I was saying, we're still not sure as to the source of the infection. I've ordered an abdominal CAT scan, which they'll do shortly, and we're still waiting on some lab results, but we should know more by tomorrow."

"Can we go in and see her?" Rina asks.

"Yes. She's resting comfortably and the floor is yours. There is also a lounge in the back, and you have access to a concierge who will see to anything you need."

"Thank you," we all manage to mumble, shell-shocked and scared.

"Where is Breck—"

"I'm here," he calls out, sprinting down the hall. "I'm sorry it took me so long. Traffic from the financial district was awful." He throws his arms around Rina, who immediately starts to lose it against him. "No, baby. Shhh. It's okay. Don't cry."

Tears line my eyes that I instantly swallow down.

"I was bringing her in this morning," Dr. Fritz murmurs, his voice distant. "She had been doing better all week, but last night, she didn't eat much, and she was weak. I told her I wanted her to get some imaging and blood work done, and she refused the emergency room. Too public, she said. She didn't want news of this to get out." He emits a deep sigh, his hands on his narrow hips. "We had an appointment with her doctor and then..." He trails off and clears his throat. "Well, now that we're all here, I think it's safe to say that we won't be doing Thanksgiving at the compound tomorrow." He runs a hand through his thick salt-and-pepper hair, much the way all his sons do when they're scared or frustrated.

"We'll do it here," Grace suggests. "We have the floor to ourselves, and it doesn't have to be anything special. But it's not Thanksgiving without Octavia and this is where I want to be."

"Same," everyone agrees.

Dr. Fritz sighs, but there's a small hint of a smile on his face all the same. "Then this is where we'll do it. No doubt Octavia will complain. She won't relish us making a fuss over her, but she'll just have to get used to it."

"I'll take care of bringing in food," I offer.

"I'll help," Elle jumps in, tossing me a grateful smile as she leans against Landon.

"Me too." Amelia places her hand on Oliver's chest and stares up into his eyes. "We'll take care of everything. You focus on your mom." Oliver leans down and places a soft kiss on her lips.

"I guess we're doing a hospital Thanksgiving then." Dr. Fritz shakes his head, his eyes bouncing down to the floor. "Just don't tell your mother. We'll make it a surprise for her."

33

____

"**I**s this Raven Fairchild?" the woman with an unknown number asks into my phone nearly the second I step outside the hospital. It's late. It's dark. I'm exhausted. My bones weary. My muscles aching. My mind a funhouse of crazy, both physically and emotionally. The last thing I want to deal with is spam bullshit.

"It is. Who's this?"

My voice might come out a bit terser than it would typically, but I'm desperate for a shower and six hours of sleep before I have to return to the hospital. I left Luca there. He refused to leave, as did his brothers. Octavia slept most of the time we were there, waking very briefly and only sipping on some ice water. She wasn't pleased we were all there standing vigil.

She told us to go. That she was fine.

That's when Grace and I climbed in her bed beside her and told her we weren't going anywhere just yet, so she better get used to it. I only left once she fell back to sleep and Luca was passed out on a pull-out sofa, snoring beside Landon. But if I'm going to pull together a Thanksgiving feast, I need real sleep in a real bed first.

"I apologize for calling at this hour the night before Thanksgiving. I realize our timing is impossible. My name is Maia Dawson. I'm the personal assistant for the band Wild Minds. We spoke about a month or so ago."

Holy shit! "Yes," flees my lungs. "I'm so sorry. I didn't recognize the number."

She laughs. "That's how we like it, right?" Another laugh. "I hate to press this upon you without much notice, but the guys have an unexpected break in their schedule and can be in Boston to record next Thursday. I realize the timing might not be the best, but does this work at all for you?"

"Yes. Absolutely. I can do Thursday. My first holiday Pops performance is that Friday night, though."

"Not a problem. The guys and their producer, Eden, feel they should be able to lay down your part of the song in one day, but if we run over, we can always work around your schedule. We are very excited to work with you and are willing to do whatever it takes to make this easier for you, given the rush bomb we just dropped."

"Maia—I hope I can call you Maia—I'm just floored they want me. Thursday should be perfect for me."

Her giggle mixed with a hint of twang hits all my senses. "You can call me Maia, Raven. Kaplan has gone on and on about you and we've also heard your playing. You're incredible and we're so grateful you've agreed to record with us."

"Thank you!" I might have just peed my pants. A little. Not a lot. But WILD MINDS! "You had mentioned that they'd send over the song for me to familiarize myself with. Is that still a possibility?"

"Yes. Hold on a moment." I hear some noise and then, "Keith?"

"Yeah, Pandora?" comes through the phone in the background. *Pandora?*

"I'm on the phone with Raven Fairchild. Do you have anything of the song you want her to record on?"

"I think so. If I don't, Jas definitely will."

"Email it to me, would ya?"

He grumbles something I can't hear and then she's back on the phone. "We should have it for you by tomorrow or first thing Friday as well as further details about where and what time we're recording."

"Perfect. That's perfect. Thank you."

"Wonderful. We can't wait. We'll see you next Thursday."

And with that, Maia Dawson, wife of Keith Dawson, drummer for the band Wild Minds, disconnects the call. I scream. I mean, hell yeah, I do. I don't even care. I'm smiling when I don't feel as though smiles should be something I rock right now. I want to race back into the hospital and jump on Luca. I want to tell Octavia that I'm recording with a world-famous rock band. I want her to smile the way she smiles at me when she listens to the track.

I want the only woman I have considered a mother for the last fifteen years to be okay!

A SOUND WAKES me out of a heavy sleep, my mind disoriented, my limbs sluggish. "Hello?"

"Shhh. It's just me. Go back to sleep."

"Luca?"

A warm chuckle. "You expecting someone else?"

"Santa told me he was flying in for a pregame warm-up in my bed."

My blankets shift and then the heat of ten thousand suns moves in beside me. That is until the swat on my ass comes. "Tease." His hands hit my tits, his arms around my back, and then I'm being dragged into his chest. "Want me to fuck the Santa out of you?"

"I want you to get some sleep. What time is it anyway?"

"Two. I haven't bunked with Landon since we were twenty-four and Reese died. Doesn't quite have the same feeling. I couldn't sleep there. I kept getting up and checking on Mom and her lines and the monitor. I was driving the nurses and my father nuts."

Shit. The things this family has been through.

"Do you want to get married tomorrow?"

I still in his arms, my eyes snapping open so wide I can see the sun before it even comes close to rising over Boston Harbor. "Luca." That's as far as I get.

"I'm sorry. I'm so fucked up right now. I feel like I could lose everything I love at any second. She's septic. Did I text you that? They think she's septic and they can't figure out why. They added on a second antibiotic and her CBC is shit. My mom is really sick, Little Bird."

I cup his hands over me. "I know."

"I'm scared."

"Me too."

"I couldn't do this without you. You know my family. My life. My heart."

"That's because they're mine too."

He blows out a breath into me. One that says my words hit him on a deeper level, but he's just too damn wrecked to bring its meaning deeper into his mind.

"Sleep, Luca."

He's already there before I can even close my eyes.

I wake up to a kiss on my neck, hands kneading my breasts, something hard and thick rocking against me. "Mmmm. What are you doing?"

"What does it feel like?"

"Cuddling," I tease.

"We are cuddling till I'm inside of you. Then we're fucking."

"It feels good. What time is it?"

"Five. Come shower with me."

Five. That means he only got about three hours of sleep. Part of me wants to tuck him back under the covers and force him to sleep, but I know him. His mind is restless. Teeming with toxic energy. I've been wanting to ask him if something is wrong for over a week now, but never quite found it in me. I don't even know why. There's been this mounting unease sitting heavy in my gut because something just feels off to me.

He was distant. Here but not, in his head so much it was like every time he looked at me, something else sprang into his head that called his focus and put a frown on his lips. It's why I asked the girls about it yesterday. I was looking for a little girl talk. A little help and for about the thousandth time since I was seven, I wish my mother were alive.

Whatever has been heavy on his mind, I certainly can't ask him about it now.

Dragging him out of bed, we slink toward my bathroom, quiet but attached, his chest against my back, his hands moving my hair so he can kiss my neck.

"I'm supposed to work tomorrow," he murmurs while I go about turning on the faucet to hot and brushing my teeth. I rinse my toothbrush and hand it to him. He smirks, taking it from me. "I should have one of these here. Feels silly considering my place is ten floors up."

He's right. "Do you want to go upstairs and get ready?"

"No. I'm going to shower here with you and then I'll run up and change my clothes."

"Luca—"

"Shhh. Naked. Shower. Inside you."

I get a smack on my ass, but if he's going to talk like a caveman, I'll treat him like one. My panties hit the floor, followed by my tank top, and then I'm in the shower while he's still brushing his teeth. "Mmmm," I groan. "So good." My head falls back into the spray as I bring my hands up through it, arching my back and sticking out my tits.

Not even two seconds later, he's on me, and I hold in my triumphant smirk. Then I remember nothing about right now feels like a win and this isn't some hot quickie.

His mouth comes down on mine, kissing me like I'm his only source of air and he'll die without me. The grip he has on my hair is borderline painful while his raw intensity, his unhinged passion have me pulling him closer.

"Need inside you," he murmurs into me and before I can formulate a response, he's lifting me and pressing my back into the tiles. In one swift move, he thrusts in to the hilt and then holds still. I gasp out a breath. It's 5:00 a.m. and I just woke up and while I knew this was coming, damn, I'm *full*.

He slowly rocks into me, holding me up with one hand under my ass, his other on my breast as his mouth explores mine. But there's an undercurrent of desperation. I like it as much as it terrifies me. I've never been kissed this way. Not even by him.

"Raven," he murmurs into me, and I open my eyes to find his on the place where our bodies meet, his expression serious, eyebrows creased. I know his darkness. I've seen it. Luca has so much light and passion inside of him. So much love. It's why whenever he's hit by anything that rattles him, threatens him, challenges his heart, it hits him harder. I also know I'm one of the few he really shows all of it to.

He pushes in. Out. In. Out.

Then he's back on me, his lips bruising with the force of his kiss. Slowly, he starts to pick up his pace, understanding how time is not on our side moving him along. His hard cock throbs inside me and I moan, clinging to him as he sharply thrusts up while rolling his hips. Stars dot my vision and I squeeze him tighter with my legs, wanting him closer.

"Hold on," he tells me and unleashes his magnificent cock inside me. Hips pounding. Wet skin slapping. Moans and yeses and cries and pleas. It's so much. He's chasing away his fear and anguish inside me and I let him, matching him, showing him I can take anything he's got to give.

His pounding grows harder, more frantic, the back of my head hitting the tile. He doesn't stop to ask if I'm okay. If I want it gentler, slower, easier, and I'm grateful he doesn't. Deft fingers find my clit and I shake, feeling my orgasm rise and rise and grow and, "Ah!"

"That's my good girl," he purrs, and I lose it on him as if every nerve in my body just caught on fire. He comes with me, groaning and biting at my flesh, clinging to me. We ride it out together until all that's left is the sound of our ragged breathing and the water slapping against the tile floor.

I slide off him, kiss his sternum, and then direct him into the water. We take turns washing each other's hair. Bodies. And then he's kissing me, telling me he'll see me later. But it isn't until after he's gone and I'm getting dressed that I realize. His eyes... he didn't look into mine once all morning.

"Never have I ever or never will I ever..." Kaplan runs his hand through his hair like this shit baffles him, but on such little sleep and with all of our heads fucked up, we've taken drastic measures. "Fall in love with one of my brothers' girls."

"Both," we all shout out, lifting our glasses. "Drink."

He does quickly and then shrugs up a shoulder. "You players think you know so much. Maybe I'm just drinking to throw you off my game. Maybe I've been as pathetic as you poor bastards all this time."

"Oh yeah," Carter challenges. "You suddenly looking for love in all the wrong places? Planning on snaking one of our girls?"

"Maybe. Definitely not." Kaplan half-smirks, his eyes casting down, staring into his now empty shot glass as he pours another. "Next."

"Never have I ever or never will I ever go to a sex club."

"Both," we all yell once more, growing louder by the second.

Oliver frowns. "You think I'm so boring I'd never go to a sex club?"

"Fritz," I counter. "You're a fucking Fritz. Any of you motherfuckers dare walk into a sex club in this city?"

"Not a chance. That shit would hit the papers in seconds." Landon laughs. "But then again…"

"Yeah. We know." I smirk, rolling my eyes. "If you did, you'd go as me."

"Not anymore, dicktwat," Kaplan practically growls at me in warning. "You better not be seen out with any other women besides Raven either."

"You're right," I agree, holding up my hand. I love how protective Kaplan is with Raven. How they have a friendship as strong as they do. "My girl would either demand she come with me or cut me off at the stem. But I did in Rome once. Before I fell for my crazy American, English-Israeli goddess."

"We know." Oliver starts cracking up, practically falling off his hospital grade chair. "You had no clue it was a gay sex club. Or so you claim."

Now everyone, including me, is laughing our asses off. "I learned a lot about ass play in the five minutes I was in that club before I left. But Oliver, baby brother, drink that shit."

"Fuck," he hisses, doing just that and then wiping his mouth with the back of his hand. The second he sets his glass down, Carter instantly refills it. "Amelia is going to kill me for this. I'm going to be hammered before the food arrives." Sophia decided to take the pressure off everyone and is having a Thanksgiving meal of sorts sent in. It's just not here yet. "Why are we playing this again?"

"So we stop thinking."

Brecken points at Landon. "What he said."

"It feels more like a bachelor party, though I can't imagine this is the one any of you envisioned," Kaplan quips as he passes the bottle of Blanton's straight from the barrel. I have no idea where he managed to get this bottle, but last I checked, it's impossible to find. It's raw, uncut, and aged fifty years. But I guess if you're going to get fucked up in the hospital on Thanksgiving, this is the way to go.

Last night, Rina told Brecken she was ready to get married. That life is too short to waste not to be married to him forever. He got down on one knee, told her he loved her and that he'd spend his life making her happy.

Now she's rocking his diamond on her finger.

"Not exactly, but then again I'm a bit old for strippers and it wouldn't have exactly had the same effect with five assholes needlessly there to protect their sister's honor surrounding me," Brecken mutters dryly, swigging from his shot glass even though this isn't shot bourbon.

I clap my hand on his shoulder, giving it a shake. "Nah. All we would have done is very methodically show you what happens if you don't treat Rina right."

"My balls are shaking in their briefs," Brecken deadpans. "I took one look at that blonde and was a total goner."

"Aw," Oliver coos. "You're getting to the sappy drunk side of this rodeo."

I snort out a laugh. "I'm sorry, whose girlfriend is known to the world as their fiancée and is still wearing their great-grandmother's ring as a placeholder?"

"I didn't say *I* wasn't pussy whipped," he retorts. "But Brecken likes to effuse his softer, more feminine side when he drinks."

"How do you think I won your sister over so easily?" he jests.

We break out into another fit of laughter because nothing was easy about how he won Rina over.

"I guess now we'll have to plan an actual bachelor party since you're finally engaged to our sister. To that!" Glasses in hand, we each take down our drinks before refilling them. Again. It's not even ten in the morning.

"When are you getting married?" Oliver asks.

Brecken stares down at his glass as the six of us sit in one of the empty patient rooms. It's weird on this floor. It's just us, our security—since the front of the hospital is mobbed with the press even on Thanksgiving—and the doctors and nurses.

"I don't know. I was planning to propose today anyway at the compound before all this happened. Had the damn ring in my pocket when I got here yesterday. I was tired of waiting. Life's too fucking short. She just beat me to it, which makes it easier."

"Truth," we all agree.

"Part of me wishes we were able to do it here today, but we don't have a license and I understand that it's not the right time. Especially after the news we got this morning. I'd never interfere with that. I'll just have to marry her when all this is over and Octavia is home and doing well. Hopefully planning it with Rina gives her something to look forward to."

That's another reason we're drinking. Mom has to go in for surgery tomorrow. The CAT scan found a small abdominal perforation that led to an abscess. They want to give the antibiotics some time to bring down the infection before they go in and repair the issue.

None of us are doing well. Obviously, since we're getting shift-faced.

My father is blaming himself for not bringing her in sooner. Rina has been crying and on the phone with her friends a lot.

Mom has been sleeping nearly nonstop, but she told us point blank she did not want Stella and Layla here because she didn't want the girls to see her this way. Amelia and Landon were one hundred percent in agreement with that. It would be too upsetting.

Elle and Amelia decided that they would go to the compound and do Thanksgiving there with the girls. Make it a girl party or something. Landon and Oliver are visibly torn, wanting to be with their girls, but I don't think any of us are leaving again until Mom comes out of surgery and is recovering.

Rina walks into the room and takes the full glass from Brecken's hand before drinking it herself. She drops onto his lap, curling into him. His arms immediately encircle her, holding her close. "I told Mom we're getting married. That I wanted to do it at the compound. Maybe a Christmas or early January type of thing. Small!" She glances over at me. "We'd have to do it soon if you're leaving in March, right? I still can't believe you didn't tell me about it. That Dad had to this morning when I mentioned weddings and timelines."

I refill my glass and take my third shot of the morning. "Rina, chances are I'm not getting this grant. And besides, how can I leave?"

"Mom will be better by then," Carter maintains, his weary eyes closed as he lies back on the bed, his hands behind his head. I don't think any of us managed more than a few hours last night.

"I know." Because I don't know what else to say. The last thing I want to talk about, let alone think about, right now is that grant. But it's nearly impossible not to. Especially whenever I'm with Raven because I hate keeping this from her, but needlessly starting a fight or upsetting her feels cruel. It's not a conversation we have to have yet. Hell, it likely won't be a conversation we have to have at all.

"I'm gonna go check on her." Without waiting on my siblings, I peel myself up and off the sofa and amble down the hall. My dad and Morgan Fairchild are off in a corner talking, their heads close and their expressions serious. I don't know if it's about security or everything else.

My dad confides in Morgan the way I confide in Landon

and my siblings. My dad being an only child and a man who doesn't trust easily has Morgan. That's about it.

Just as I reach the threshold of her room, I pause at the sound of voices.

"You feel that?" Grace asks and I peek in, checking to see if she's talking to my mom or someone else. My mom is awake, her hand on Grace's bump being held in place by Grace's. She's in bed with my mom, though she likely shouldn't be, but on the other side of her is Raven, who is also tucked in. I didn't even know she had come.

"Is that..." My mom's weak voice trails off.

"That's your grandson kicking. I felt it for the first time the other day."

My mom visibly starts trembling, her eyes shining over, and Grace starts with it too, a tear hitting her cheek in no time flat. Raven holds my mom a little tighter, sinks in a little closer, and I watch her hold my mother like that, my chest clenching.

"Does it hurt?" Raven asks, placing her hand on top of my mom's over Grace's belly as she rests her head against my mom's shoulder.

"No. Feels more like bubbles right now." Grace sniffles, wiping at her face.

"Carter kicked from the moment he could until he broke my water."

"Oh God," Grace groans with an exaggerated moan and my mom attempts a smile. It's not her real smile. She's in pain and she's exhausted.

Raven sits up a little straighter, staring down at her, and I wish I could see her expression. "Maybe if I play, that will help the baby settle down? Fall asleep?"

A tear falls down my mother's face and I just about lose my mind watching it, choking down my own emotions. This woman, who somehow manages to continuously rebuild me brick by cracked brick, loves my family. Loves me. I need her to stay with me. But... how do I ask that of her? If I win this grant, how do I ask that?

A familiar block of ice settles in my gut.

My mother cups Raven's face in her hand before it falls limply back down to the bed. She can't even answer her. She just nods because it's pretty damn obvious the music is for my mother and not for my growing nephew.

Grace gives my mom a kiss on the forehead as she climbs off the bed and frowns. I bet she still has a fever despite the medications they're giving her. Raven too climbs off and goes for a chair in the corner, her cello already beside it.

"Hey," Grace says to me as she leaves the room.

"She has a fever?"

"Feels like it. Not terrible. They gave her Motrin an hour ago, but she's refusing all other pain medications."

I twist to glare at her. "Since when?"

"Since this morning. It's killing your dad to watch her in pain like this, but she said she was sleeping too much on them."

I shake my head, my hands meeting my hips. "She won't heal if she's always in pain."

Grace places her hand on my shoulder, giving me a squeeze just as the first notes of some song fill my mom's hospital room. "Now you know why we've been distracting her. Why we had Raven bring her cello."

"Gracie Lou..."

"I know. But Octavia Abbot-Fritz is nothing if not a fighter. She'll be back to planning our weddings and interfering in our lives in no time."

I sigh, feeling sick and hollow. "Not much of a Thanksgiving, is it?"

"Not much, but at least we're together. Rina told her that she and Brecken are engaged, and Carter and I are going to tell her that we're naming the baby after her and Oliver. Every piece helps."

I flip back to her. "You are?"

She smirks. "Owen. We're using the O from their first names because we honestly couldn't come up with anything else." She snickers. "I want to watch their faces at the same time, so I made Carter promise we could tell them both together."

I reach out, placing my hand over her belly. "Owen Luca Fritz. I like it."

She laughs, smacking my hand away. "Nice try. I'm going to go take a nap before I fall asleep standing up. Or worse, have a seizure. Let your mom get some rest too. Raven's got her for now."

"She's got me too," I murmur to myself as Grace heads for one of the empty patient rooms at the end of the hall. I head into the room, take the seat on the opposite side of my mom, and grab her hand. It's ice-cold and I immediately start rubbing it between mine.

My mom's tired green eyes meet mine and she gives me a soft smile. The one she used to when I was little, and she'd stand in the corner watching us play or read or even watch TV. I used to call it her mom smile. It was content and grateful, and I wonder if that's what she's feeling now or if it's the music doing that. Or if Octavia Abbot-Fritz is still putting on the brave show for her kids.

Raven is playing something that is giving me chills. Her eyes are closed, but the emotion on her face is stealing my breath.

"She's trying not to cry as she plays 'Kol Nidrei' for me," my mom whispers, shifting in the bed with small, tense movements so she's closer to me. I lean in, helping her out.

"I don't know it."

"It's what's played on Erev Yom Kippur, the Jewish High Holy Day." My mother clears her throat. "Raven might not remember this, but it's the first piece she mastered, and she played it for her mom over the phone shortly before she died."

Shit. "I'm sure that's not—"

"Shh," she hushes me, shaking her head. "She's playing it for me now because it's one of my favorite pieces. But I also know it makes her feel closer to her mother."

I'm choked up beyond words and my face falls against the bed, against her arm as I continue to hold her hand.

"I'm glad she gave you a second chance."

I grin against my mom, swallowing hard. "Me too."

"Don't worry, Luca. It's like I already told her. I have no plans to go anywhere anytime soon. My Rina is getting married. My Grace and Carter are having my grandson. My Oliver is in love. My Landon is too and finally happy again. And you have my Raven. I will live to see it all, including Kaplan one day finding love or at the very least married to a woman of my choosing."

I let out a small laugh. "I love you, Mom."

"Me too, baby. Now I'm going to rest while our girl plays for me."

I kiss my mom's hand and sit up, finding Raven watching us, tears all over her face.

"I love you," I mouth to her.

She bobs her head, closing her eyes once more as she continues to play. But I can see it. I felt it last night and this morning in the shower too. She knows me. As I know her. Our souls are connected as one.

She knows there's more going on with me than just my mom.

35

The wait for Octavia to come out of surgery was interminable. And when she came out, other than her being alive, the report wasn't great. More infection than they saw on the CAT scan. Larger bowel perforation. More bleeding than they wanted. Not out of the woods yet with getting the infection fully under control since it's in her bloodstream.

They didn't return her to the floor the Fritz family had taken over.

They put her in the surgical ICU (SICU) and that's where she's been since Friday and today is Monday. But the SICU has different rules and we've only been able to see her in small shifts for small periods of time. None of us have slept more than a few hours here or there. I'm not sure we've eaten much either.

But slowly, steadily, she is improving and right now, that's all I can ask for.

My father hasn't left Dr. Fritz's side unless he's in with Octavia and most of the others are bouncing in and out of the SICU waiting room. I've been bringing them coffee and tea and food. Staying as busy as I can because if I don't keep moving, I'll start thinking and if I start thinking, I'll start crying and if I start crying, I won't be able to stop.

I've gone to practice, working on my solos because I don't have a choice. Plus, again, I need the distraction. I also haven't seen much of Luca. Passing texts and phone calls and him sneaking into my bed or me doing the same in his for a few hours together even if we're sleeping.

But it's Monday and with the world restarting after the holiday weekend, I find myself at children's hospital for my music therapy group on the neuro floor. Normally my neuro day is Friday, but the cardiac floor asked if I could switch with them and I'm grateful for it. I'm hoping to see Luca, even if it's just for a couple minutes.

"What are we playing today?" Mac, short for MacGyver—I'm guessing his mom was a fan—asks. Nearly every week it's a new group of kids, which is both fantastic and a bit stressful since I have to try to remember new kids and faces, but Mac was here last week.

Part of me just wants to say "fuck it, play whatever the hell you want. I'm too tired and emotionally drained to come up with anything better," but I obviously can't do that or Pricilla will throw me out on my ass before the words even finish tumbling from my lips.

"How about music trivia?"

"Music trivia? What's that?" a girl whose name I've already forgotten—*Cara? Clara? Sara?*—asks.

"I'll hand out a sheet of paper and a pencil to each of you and then I'll play a song. You tell me to stop when you think you've got it and write it down. The one with the most right answers wins."

"Wins what?"

"I brought fidgets." I dig through my bag and pull out the small bag of prizes I have in there.

"Cool. Yeah. Let's do it."

"I wanted to hear you play again," Mac states with a look in his eye that is all flirt and an attempt at seduction. Sixteen years old, he's creepily closer in age to me than Luca is. I shudder every time I think about that.

"I can play the songs for trivia instead of pulling them up on my phone, but that will make it harder."

"Sure will," he quips, earning a couple of snickers from the other guys in the room.

I pop a reprimanding eyebrow at him. "Can you hold in your hormones, or do you want me to get your nurse so you can go back to your room and hang out with your mom?"

"How about you call Dr. Grosspooper instead?" someone else suggests.

Dammit. I'm never going to live that one down. It's been passed along from group to group. "Nice one. Now let's play before we run out of time."

The hour and a half drags on, but it's fun all the same. The kids get really into the trivia, razzing and laughing and smiling, and that's obviously the point of this. To have kids in the hospital undergoing the worst of the worst remember what it's like to be a kid and not a patient. Even if just for a short time.

I say goodbye to the kids, haul my cello up onto my back, and head in the direction of Luca's office. I texted him about five minutes ago and haven't heard back. If he's in the OR or with a patient, I'll just leave him a note on his desk and go on to rehearsal. But as I round the corner, a loud popping sound followed by shouts startles me, throwing me out of my groggy thoughts.

A gathering of about twenty people or so stands in the hall that leads to the attendings' offices. They're popping bottles of sparkling cider and have balloons and flowers and even a cake. For a moment, I think it's someone's birthday until I hear rounds of congratulations and we're so happy for you and you must be so proud, and we knew you'd get it.

I can't get close enough to see who they're talking to, and I stop one of the nurses who, like everyone else, is all smiles and clapping hands. "Hey," I say to her. "What's going on?"

"Dr. Fritz won the Treesprite Grant. It's unbelievable."

I blink at her, my breath feeling as though it's been frozen in my lungs. "Treesprite Grant?"

She must misinterpret my question and befuddled expression for excited incredulous because she says, "I know, right? Amazing. I can't believe he'll be gone for two years, but wow, it's such a tremendous honor."

Two years? All that frozen breath flees my lungs and suddenly I feel like I'm melting from the inside out. My face is hot. My muscles screaming at me as they tighten up. Glancing over into the epicenter of the chaos, I spot him. Luca is smiling, laughing, and talking with Grosspooper, who is shaking his hand and clapping him on the back.

They hand Luca a glass of the fake champagne and suddenly they're toasting to Dr. Luca Fritz, winner of the Treesprite Grant. But all I can think is, I knew it. I knew there was something he was keeping from me, and this is it. It doesn't even take a rocket scientist to understand why he did. Even a simple musician and music therapist can figure it out.

He's leaving for two years.

And he didn't talk to me about it. Not once.

Shaky legs barely hold me up as I run out of here, heading for the exit. I need to get out of here. I can't breathe. All I smell is hospital. All I hear is them congratulating him. All I see is his fucking smile that feels like the ultimate betrayal. A stab in the back. Or more aptly the heart.

I knew I shouldn't have trusted him.

I knew I shouldn't have let him back in.

My heads spins, my hand pressing into the side of the elevator, so I don't pass out. But the moment the shock of the cold late November air hits my face, reason starts to seep back into my clouded brain, and I take a calming breath. Shifting over to the side of the building, I sit on a stone ledge, set my cello down beside me, pull out my phone, and make the call.

Kaplan picks up on the second ring. "Hey, babe, you okay?"

"Tell me everything about Luca and the Treesprite Grant."

Within seconds, I'm learning all about the grant and foundation. All the good it does in the world. How rare it is to be accepted into it. How after Luca went back to Minnesota, he became obsessed with helping people who didn't have proper access to healthcare. Donating money and applying for grants that would allow him to make a real and direct impact. It's the opportunity of a lifetime for him. Of that I have no doubt. Can I blame him for picking something like that over me? Over us?

I think about my job. My life. My goals.

I can't go with him—not that he asked me to. But I won't offer it either. I love him, but I can't be that eighteen-year-old girl again. The one who lost sight of herself because of a man. The one who never felt she was enough to make people stay. Tears hit my cheeks and if I thought I was all cried out after the weekend I've had, I was wrong.

Two years.

What does that mean for us?

Was I always just the filler? The in-between girl until he found out if he won this grant? Was he even going to tell me? Finding out from a random nurse that my boyfriend won this grant is not what I saw coming.

God, how did we end up here again?

In a place where division is imminent. Where we're dancing between two worlds, never quite lining up. I think back on my time in London. On what those four years were like. I had fallen in love with the right man at the wrong time. Instead of trying to compromise or work through it, he ended it. A ruse for my own benefit, he swears.

How has this become our modus operandi?

Time ticks by as I sit out here. I know I need to go. That I'll be late for rehearsal if I don't. But I can't go. I can't leave. Quickly, I shoot off a text to Catarina, asking her to let Antonio know I'll be a little late, and then I rise, grab my cello, and enter the hospital again.

The burning in my chest fueled by the mess in my head is enough to carry me back up to the neuro floor, down the hall, and over toward his office. I don't know what I'm going to say. What I'm even feeling about this. I'm proud of him and devastated by him. I was living in a fantasy world. But now I'm being torn from it, straight into the harsh reality that maybe, just fucking maybe, we aren't as meant to be as I thought.

I know, going in, there is a very real possibility that I could lose everything. Again.

The crowd is mercifully gone, the party all but over save for a few straggling balloons and half-eaten cake out in the main area that the offices feed off of. His door is closed and once again, I realize I don't even know if he's in there. He knew I was here today in the hospital, but as I glance down at my phone, reading the message from Catarina telling me no problem, I realize Luca never texted me back.

Familiar pain threatens to suffocate me. Drag me back down. Hold me hostage.

This is going to hurt something fierce.

Sucking in a sharp breath, I rap my knuckles on his door, but there's no answer, so I try the nob. It turns, unlocked, and when I push inside, I find Luca sitting on his couch, thighs spread, head in his hands.

I shut the door behind me and that seems to jar him out of his reverie because his head snaps up and his lost green eyes lock on mine. He licks his lip, and I can see the struggle playing out across his face. This is not the man in the bar who intentionally broke my heart. This is a man who is dismantled from the inside out.

I know the feeling.

"Congratulations," I tell him, meaning it.

"I didn't think I'd get it. I truly didn't."

I blink at him. "How do you feel about it now that you did?"

He doesn't answer and I hate how indiscernible his features are. How quickly he can shut it all off. How easily he can hide things from me.

"How long have you known it was a possibility you'd win?"

He sighs, his gaze falling back to his hands before he reluctantly answers, "A few weeks."

Wow. That's...

"And in the few weeks you've known about this, that you might be moving to another country for two years, you didn't think to mention it at all? Like hey, Little Bird, I know I've been promising you the world, telling you that I love you and need you and that you can fucking trust me again, but oh, by the way, I'm possibly headed to Brazil and Ghana?"

"I didn't think I'd get it," he repeats, and it makes me want to bash his handsome face in. "We were just getting back together, and things were great. Maybe that makes me selfish or an asshole as you so love to call me, but I didn't want to rock the boat unnecessarily."

Rock the boat? This is punching holes in the side of the hull and sinking it.

"You still should have told me about it," I snap, setting my cello down on the ground like I'm gearing up for a fight. "That's what couples do. They talk. They tell each other things. They don't hide important pieces of themselves and their lives from the person they claim to love. Christ, Luca. For someone so smart and so talented with a scalpel, you suck at relationships."

His hands scrub up and down his face and then back

through his hair, messing up what was already a disaster. "I know. I was... scared to tell you. Scared you'd push me away before I got my second chance with you."

I glare and he throws his hands up, exasperated.

"I didn't know what to say. I've been after this grant for years. I didn't want to start a fight or have you upset when in all likelihood, I wasn't going to win it."

"But you did win it!"

"Because I'm a fucking Abbot-Fritz, Raven," he barks, shooting off the couch and stalking toward the window. His hands white knuckle the frame on either side as he looks out at who the hell knows what. "That's why I got it."

"Shut up, Luca. Just shut the fuck up with self-deprecating bullshit. Especially when you know it is bullshit. Maybe your name played a factor, but a foundation like that isn't going to give a grant as big as that one to someone who isn't qualified. I'm proud of you. So proud. You fucking deserve it. But I shouldn't have had to hear about it from a nurse in the hall!"

His head falls. "I know. I'm sorry, Raven. I truly am. I was going to tell you tonight after rehearsal. I didn't know you saw all that."

I shake my head, staring into the back of his. I suck in a deep breath and ask, "When will you leave?"

"I don't know what I'm doing yet."

"When. Will. You. Leave?"

"Middle of March."

Four months. Well then. I take an inadvertent step back, bumping into the door, my hand hitting the nob. There's that.

He laughs mirthlessly. "There's what?"

I hadn't realized I said that out loud.

"Does walking away make it easier for you to do this?"

"What exactly am I doing?"

"Telling me that you love me and that you're proud of me, but that you're not coming with me."

My body physically reacts, tremors rolling through me and churning up the already bubbling acid in my stomach. On a ragged breath, I whisper, "I'm not going with you."

His grip on the window tightens. "I know. I wanted to ask you to. My father told me I should give you the choice, but I wouldn't beg you to even if that's what I want to do. I know you can't come, and I didn't want to put you in that position again." He sighs. "You could ask me to stay."

I shake my head, my hair flying. "No. I can't."

His head whips in my direction. "What if I want you to?" he snarls through gritted teeth.

I want to. I want to run to him and throw my arms around him and beg him to stay. I want to beg him to choose me because suddenly those old feelings that no one ever had before are resurfacing even if they aren't truly founded in reality. And yes, I'm still furious with him for keeping this from me. Even though the gut-wrenching pain at the idea of losing him again far outweighs my ire.

But I can't do it.

"I won't ask you to stay for me." I fumble through my thoughts... what I want, what I *need* to say to him. "The only way you can know if something is real is if you give it your all." My eyes meet his. "I gave you my all. More than once. But I won't do it, Luca. I heard all about that grant just now. I know what it means. I won't be the one to hold you back from something as incredible as that just as you refused to be the one to hold me back from The Conservatory."

For the first time in four years, I understand with perfect clarity all that he did for me. What it cost him to make that choice. He did choose me even when it felt as though he didn't. Sometimes choosing someone is letting them go. Is walking away. Even when it kills you to do so. He loved me enough to do that for me and I will do the same for him if I have to. But I will not make a decision he'll be forced to live with. It has to be him, and I can't make it easier or allow him to use me as a cop-out.

His eyes search mine from across the room. "It's two years, Little Bird. I'd be gone for two years, only returning very sporadically and not for any real length of time. I want this grant." He laughs mirthlessly. "I want this grant so fucking bad that I've been trying to talk myself out of wanting it since I heard I was a finalist. But the distance... it'll be so much. And it's not as though I can fly about the world to secretly watch you play. Or that you can just fly in for a weekend. We're talking South America and Africa. Remote parts of both. We barely made it those four years without each other and they were torture. I'll be straddled between two worlds, not knowing the next time I'd be able to talk to you, let alone see you."

And I'll be missing something I deem vital. Him. My hands shift, pressing into the door, holding me up. "I know."

He frowns. "But you still won't ask me to stay?"

I shake my head again. He made a choice for me, and I still don't know if he was right to do what he did. I'm here and I'm happy and yes, part of me is grateful for what he did for me. I became my own person. My own woman. Stronger and inde-pendent. But could I have still become all of this without London? Could I potentially have been more than I am now because we wouldn't have had those four years apart? He saw London as my end all be all, whereas I saw potential hidden in different shadows.

I'll never know what would have been. And I won't do that to him. I won't make a decision for him that forever alters his course. He said so himself. He's wanted this grant for years. Then there's also the paralyzing thought... what if I ask him to stay and he doesn't?

"Are you ending it with me then?"

"Is that what you want?"

"Fuck no, it's not." He tears away from the window, bolting

over to me, his hands on my hips, his face right in mine. "If you won't tell me to stay, then I want you to tell me that if I go, it won't matter. That even with the distance, we'll do it anyway."

"Can we?"

"Is your heart no longer mine?"

"My heart has been yours since I was a child. Tell me a truth here. A grown-up one. The only thing I've ever wanted in this world from you is your love. And yet no matter how fast I am to give you mine, I continuously feel yours is a trial I have yet to win. Another broken happily ever after. Is that what this will be?"

His forehead meets mine, and he growls, "No," against me. "No. My heart is yours. It has been yours since you were eighteen and I found you playing your cello in my family's garage. That hasn't changed. It never will." Softer this time, more desperate. A plea. "I want this grant, Raven. And I want you."

I hold him against me. Tighter. Desperate. "I'm so proud of you. You amaze me. All that you've come back from. Grown from. I want to see you do this. I want to watch all that you can become as a doctor. As a man." I cup his face in my hand, feeling the bristles of his stubble against my palm, holding in my sob. "But I can't be a go-between."

My body seizes in on itself and I rip myself away.

Grabbing my cello, I flee his office without looking back at him. Without waiting for him to say anything else. If he tells me he loves me, I'll crumble like a stepped-on chip. I can already feel my strength dwindling. My desire to go back on my word and beg him to stay. I'm burning strength the way a drunk burns brain cells. That's already how I feel, and I hate that I'm back here. That we're back to this place.

Worse yet, I honestly don't know how this will turn out for us.

36

———

The door shuts behind her and I collapse against it only to slam my fist into the wood. It doesn't splinter and it doesn't crack because the fucker is made out of solid wood. All that means is that my fist stings something fierce and that only seems to fuel my rage more. When I received the phone call this morning, I wasn't expecting it. I had been checking my email, searching for the blanket "thanks for your application, but unfortunately, it's not you" letter.

Instead, I got the phone call telling me I'd won the grant and before I could even begin to process the man's words, there were knocks on my door. The hospital had already been notified and Grosspotter as well as the entire department were there, practically throwing me a parade.

Hope and desire have dragged me into dangerous places before, but this might be the worst of them yet. I want this grant. For so much more than just the prestige or experience of it. When I think of the lives I could impact... I *want* this grant. Raven and this type of work are all I've been focused on for four years.

Ever since that night in the alley. I wanted to help them. I wanted to save that child. And I would have done both without involving the hospital if that terrified father had given me the opportunity. I tried to relay that.

I failed.

He shot me in a moment of panic—I saw it all play out in his eyes—and then my life was forever changed. One moment. One rash decision. That's all it takes sometimes. I'm a Fritz. A man with endless money and endless resources. But what did he have? What did his family have?

I have so much power to fix things. And that's what this grant was meant to do for me. Idealistically help change the world to be a more medically balanced place—even on a small scale, piece by piece. There is a fountain of people out there who do not have access to healthcare or are afraid to access it for one reason or another, and I was determined to change that.

Then Raven came back into my life.

Then I won this grant.

And now...

"Fuck," I hiss, clenching my eyes shut and picturing her. The way she looked at me cuts me deep. I saw it all splash across her face with the subtlety of a drive-by shooting. The familiar glimmer of betrayal in her eyes. The sadness in the furrow of her brow. The steadfast determination in the hard set of her mouth.

I saw it all that night in the bar four years ago too.

But then... then she bled outwardly for me. Today, my Little Bird was trying to hold it all back. And that alone has my insides revolting. How much can I hurt one person? How many times can I test her trust, her love, before I lose them both for good?

Would I stay if she asked me to? Would I throw away this grant, this opportunity just like that? Conversely, can I truly go and leave her here? Would there be anything to come back to if I did?

My fist pounds again, thumping as hard as my heart does in my chest.

She called this my Conservatory and she's not wrong. Four years ago, I made the choice for her to go, knowing what it would mean for her life.

What have I done?

I can't let her walk away from me like that. Even if I don't have all the answers yet, I can't let her walk away.

Ripping the door practically from its hinges, I race out into the main room and then the hallway, searching left and right. Shit. I'm such a fool. My badge hits the keypad and then I'm slamming my hand into the elevator button. Fuck! How many minutes did I let go by? Dammit, she could already be at rehearsal, and I can't go barging in there. Can I?

No. She'd kick my ass for that and rightfully so.

The elevator finally opens and after stopping on practically every goddamn floor, I sprint out of the hospital, heading up toward Huntington. The icy wind bites at my face and the bare skin of my arms. Scrubs in thirty-five-degree weather isn't ideal, but I hardly register it as I reach the street and see the Green-line stopping, Raven getting on.

I fly out into the street, narrowly missing getting hit by a car. Horns blast at me as I reach the center island of the street, yelling out for the T conductor to wait for me. I climb on, panting for my life, and wince when the guy asks me for my T-pass. Shit. I don't have a fucking T-pass because I never ride the fucking T.

I'm an asshole, entitled Fritz. I drive or Uber or hell, have someone drive me.

"Here," I tell the conductor, watching as Raven heads toward the back of the train, her large cello perched on her back, oblivious to any commotion I've created. Pulling out my wallet, I hand the guy a hundred and tell him to keep the change. He stares at me like I'm crazy, but smartly doesn't stop me as I weave in and out of people to get to her. "Raven!" I call out as two massive dudebros who look like they live in the gym stand in my way, gruffly being dicks for no other reason than they can be about moving so I can get past them.

Her head whips around, her cerulean eyes wide as they lock on mine. She's so fucking pretty, my breath catches and I inadvertently smile.

"What are you doing here?"

"Trying to get past these two Gamorreans."

"What did you call us?" one of them barks and I nearly roll my eyes.

"They were Jabba the Hutt's security. Look them up." I meet his eyes. "Do you really want to do this?" The look in mine tells him he doesn't and finally he relents an inch, allowing me to push him aside and thrust through the narrow pathway as the T shakes and ambles along the street.

"That's Luca Fritz," someone murmurs, but I don't care enough about being recognized to remove my eyes from Raven's. She's standing in the center of the aisle, staring at me, nervous indecision warring across her pretty face.

When I reach her, one hand slips around her waist, the other up along her face and into her hair. "I wasn't done talking."

She shakes her head. "Not now, okay? Not here." She nervously glances around, noting the people staring at us. "I have rehearsal. I can't talk about this—" I silence her with a soul-stealing kiss. Right here on the T in front of everyone who is likely snapping pics or taking videos. Who cares? She's mine. Let the world fucking know it already.

"What if I go?" I breathe against her.

"Then I'll be here."

"What if I stay?"

"Then you have to do that for yourself. You didn't want me to resent you. This is your Conservatory, Luca. I get it. I understand it. But I won't do to you what you did to me. Every choice we make has consequences. And even now looking back..."

I know what she's saying. Was I right to do what I did? She's here and she's happy and yes, part of her is grateful for what I did for her. At least I hope it is because... she's so much. She became her own person. Her own woman. Fiercely strong and independent. Her talent recognized and revered. But could she have still become all of this without London? Without the Conservatory? Part of her will always wonder.

She grazes her fingers over my face. My lips. My heart. "A bird that you set free may be caught again, but a word that escapes your lips will not return."

My hands meet her face, and my lips are on hers, bruising in their ferocity. She kisses me back equally as intense. I don't want to let go. I'm terrified this could be it even if we say we'll make the two years apart somehow work. It's two years. Life can change on you in an instant. Think of all that's possible in two years.

All you have the potential to lose.

"Luca." She sags into me, gripping my shoulders as the train jostles us about. "I don't want you to give up—"

I silence her again with my lips. "Raven Fairchild, shut your beautiful mouth and let me tell you that I love you. That I don't know what I'm going to do just yet. That I have so much to think about. I didn't think I'd get this. I promise you, I did not. I assumed they liked my name among the finalists and that would be that. So, I just need a little time, baby. That's all I'm asking for. But don't... do not give up on me."

Raven's gaze burns into me, tears clinging so delicately yet so boldly to her eyes, refusing to fall. A noise cuts through and it takes each of us a moment to realize that it's a camera clicking and that no one is talking. That the only sound besides the blood rushing through my ears is the rumbling of the train on the tracks. We have a very public audience. An audience that is filming us. Photographing us.

In my moment of panic, I didn't think, and I didn't care.

Hell, I still don't. But Raven does. I know she does. She doesn't want to be plastered across some trashy magazine calling her my girl of the week or speculating about her.

I cup the back of her head and press her into my chest, doing my best to shield her. "Christ. I can't stop fucking things up with you. Can I?"

"How are you this famous?"

I chuckle, my lips in her hair. "Fuck if I know. Carter and Landon especially think it's absurd. Most of the time, I just ignore it."

"This is going to be everywhere."

"I know. I'm sorry. Clearly, I keep finding new and inventive ways to make your day brighter."

She giggles into me; her fists clenching my scrub top and thank God. She's still here. She's still holding on. She's not running from me.

"I want you, Raven. This is not me choosing something over you. Please know that. I'm not abandoning you. No matter what I do, we'll figure it out. Together."

A nod. That's it.

The T comes to a stop and with it the shuffling of people all around us. I shift us to the corner, keeping my back to the car and her tucked into my chest, hidden from view. The T starts to move again, and I hold her the entire ride up to Symphony Hall, both of us holding our tongues.

I walk her inside and kiss her again before I'm forced to leave. But right as I turn to go, she grabs ahold of me again, dragging me back. "Find me when you've made your decision and we'll talk more then. Until then I need time of my own. And space."

I don't want to agree to that. I need her now more than I

think I ever have. I need to feel her close and know she's not slipping through my fingers while I work this all out for us, but I understand her asking this and I nod.

I leave her here, my heart thrashing violently from within me.

I return to the hospital, round on a few patients, smile through the congratulatory texts and phone calls and pats on the back, grab my stuff, and head around the block to see my mom. My mind is still spinning, my thoughts stringing me in a hundred different directions.

Right before I enter the building, Kaplan and Landon are walking out.

"She's sleeping," Landon says by way of a greeting. "Dad is with her now, but they ran all kinds of tests and things today and she's wiped. She's back up on the floor, though, so that's a good thing and they said depending on the results of her scans and tests, she might be able to go home the day after tomorrow."

"Thank Christ for that. Maybe I'll hold off on visiting her then. Go in later or first thing tomorrow. I'm working here tomorrow anyway."

"Probably a good idea," Kaplan agrees. "She's going to have a long road ahead of her, but she'll get there."

"Let's hope this is the last major scare she gives us for quite some time," Landon intones.

No kidding. "I won a major grant today and could possibly lose the love of my life. Anyone up for a burger and a beer?"

"Raven said she wouldn't stay with you?" Kaplan stares at me as if I just grew horns before his eyes. "I spoke with her today. Told her all about the grant. I assumed she was asking so many questions because she was either planning on going with you or sticking it out with you."

"She hasn't said either way about sticking it out with me, but she's not coming with me."

"Shit. What will you do?"

"I haven't decided yet if I'm going to accept it or not. What? Why do you look so shocked?"

"I don't know. Because the Treesprite Grant isn't something you turn down."

"Thanks, Kap. Very helpful."

"Just keeping it real. Was Raven okay? Poor girl is so blindly and foolishly in love with you." Kaplan shrugs when I flip him off. "I just feel like she could do better."

"You mean like you?" Landon quips.

"That's the most disgusting thing I've ever heard in my life. No. Not me. But definitely someone else."

I punch his shoulder. Hard. "Thanks, brother. Always appreciate the love and support."

"Fine. How's this? You went four years without each other. What's another two?"

I shake my head as we fight the wind, heading up toward Mission Hill and the pub across the way. "Not helping. And not possible."

"Then I guess a burger and a beer it is. On me. At least until you figure the rest of your mess out."

37

"Oh my gosh, do you see all that press?! I'm going to pee. I swear to Christmas, I'm going to pee." Layla squeals from the back seat of Kaplan's car, bouncing up and down against the restraint of her seat belt. "There are so many of them out there!"

"You better not pee. Do you have any clue what the leather you're sitting on costs?"

"Land Rover Range Rovers are for suckers," she replies, and I snort into my Starbucks. "But for real. I kinda need to pee and I'm excited, so bladder control issues are at hand."

"Do the Kegels. Live the Kegels," Stella tells her and again, I can't fight my laughter, even with a stupid grin or a sip of the crazily caffeinated coffee Kaplan bought me.

"Do you think they'll interview us? I hope so."

Kaplan shakes his head. "We're not going to see them. We're going in through the garage for a reason. You can hold your bladder for ten more minutes."

Thank God we won't see them. I've had enough press for one week. The video and pictures of Luca and me on the train caught like wildfire. Somehow my face wasn't too visible in any of them, but the press is all over Luca Fritz declaring his love and kissing a woman in public. They've been stalking our building without knowing it's me and now they're out front of the hotel too. Obviously for different reasons.

"Ten more minutes!" Layla cries.

"Darlings, I talked your caretakers into letting you skip school for this. If urine hits my seats, I'm cutting you both out of my will."

"I'm in your will?" Stella asks, perplexed.

"Baby girl, I got one niece and one nephew on the way. Having a will seems stupid given how much your grandparents and daddy have stashed away for you, but life sucks balls sometimes and it is what it is."

I roll my head over my shoulder to find two beautiful faces full of bemused, blinking eyes. "You lost them."

"I tend to lose all women once I open my mouth. That's not what they're interested in from me."

I smirk at him. "Then maybe you shouldn't be such an untouchable, gruff bastard with them."

"If I wasn't, all of my mystique would be gone and then women would think they had a shot with me. Could you imagine how awful that would be?" He gives an exaggerated shudder.

A thunder of amusement hits me strangely and I tilt my head, finding his profile. "One day, Kaplan—"

"Oh my Saggingballs, we're here," Layla hisses, cutting off my train of thought.

"Language," Kaplan tries to admonish, but I'm no backup because this is when my nerves kick in. And hard. I'm shaking so badly, I'm about to spill my coffee all over Kaplan's leather.

He pulls his bazillion-dollar car into a special spot underground in the hotel and then we climb out. His arm snakes around me, twisting me to face him as I grab my cello. "You're not breathing, babe. Breathe."

"You breathe," I snap back.

"Okay. Feisty it is. But you still require oxygen to profuse your cells and you're not taking any in."

"That's because all the oxygen around me tastes like panic and espresso."

"Nonsense. You're a cello prodigy. Tell me who you are."

"It's Britney, bitch."

Kaplan cracks up, to the point where he nearly topples over onto the concrete floor. "You'll be just fine," he wheezes, holding his side like he has a stitch. "Fuck. You crazy, beautiful woman, you'll be just fine."

"Kaplan, I'm clearly psychotic right now. So far from fine."

He's trying to contain his laughter, reaching out and gripping my side. He steadies his expression. "Only if you don't think you are. They called you. They want you. Not the other way around. You're the rock star, babe. Remember that when you walk in there and own the room. But the truth is they're just people. Good people at that."

"All I know is that I get to babysit for Baby Cora and Adalyn Diamond," Layla squeals with an excited clap before she launches into some kind of dance, moving her arms and hips. "I don't care if you're Britney or Christina, just play that cello you're holding and let's do this."

"What she said," Stella agrees with a half-hearted shrug because though she's along for the ride and the fun, music and babysitting aren't her scene the way books and cooking are.

"You've got this."

I'm not exactly given the choice as Kaplan steals my cello from my back and walks it to the elevator here in the garage. We hit the button for some floor and then security comes to join us, checking Kaplan's and my IDs, and then we're flying up to the top floor of the posh Boston hotel. For a moment, I think about my building. About Luca's penthouse, but I quickly shut that all down.

I haven't talked to Luca since Monday and today is Thursday.

I've resisted the urge to call or text him like he's a mosquito bite. Itchy and tempting as hell, but a few good scratches and then I'm bleeding. God, the man has me so twisted up, I don't even know if I'm making sense. What's going on with us is not helping my already tormented nerves. Today I am playing a song that will be recorded onto an album that is produced by one of the world's biggest alternative rock bands. Tomorrow night is opening night at the Holiday Pops, and I have two solos. Octavia is finally home and resting, but weak as a newborn lamb and has a long recovery road ahead of her.

The last thing I needed was to throw more Luca Fritz crazy into my head.

Every time I open our text messages, I stare at our last words. Start to type. Then immediately delete them. I told him I need space and time and I do, so I'm sticking to that. Even if I miss him like a missing piece of myself, complete with phantom limb pain.

The kicker? On a few occasions, I've seen the three dots bouncing, indicating that he's starting to text me, only to watch them disappear. It's beyond frustrating. And heartbreaking. I don't want to ask him to stay, and I don't want him to give up on this opportunity, but I cannot bear the thought of losing him again.

The elevator doors open, revealing only three doors on this floor, each labeled with a P and a number. "We're recording in presidential suite one," the security guy, a huge Black man with kind eyes, tells us as he guides us in that direction. He knocks once and then someone else, another large security man, answers the door.

We're ushered inside the palatial room decorated with dark wood floors, sleek gray rugs, and luxurious fabrics. The walls are adorned with artwork that appears every bit as expensive as this room. It's bigger than my apartment. By a lot, it seems.

"Welcome." A thin man with dark hair, dark eyes, and flawless mocha skin greets us. "You must be Raven. It's such a pleasure to finally meet you. I'm Marco Morales, the band's manager."

I reach out and shake his hand. "It's a pleasure to meet you."

"This guy I already know." He shakes Kaplan's hand. "Good to see you again, man. But who are these stunning creatures?"

"This is Layla and my niece Stella."

"Lovely." A noise pulls his attention over his shoulder. "Oh, and look at that. Right on time." Two little girls come running out of what I assume to be a bedroom, laughing with each other until they spot us and freeze, taking us in. The older one has long, reddish-brown hair and bright green eyes. The younger is blond with hazel eyes. Both so beautiful and adorable, I could die. "Stella, Layla, this is—"

"Adalyn and Cora Diamond," Layla supplies, her eyes as wide as dinner plates. "Wow. This is totally the coolest. And wow, I just love your dress." She points to Adalyn's purple flowery dress. "And your headband is amazing, Cora."

Cora comes bouncing over to us, but Adalyn stays back, watching us reproachfully.

The world already knows that Adalyn Diamond is autistic after the press relentlessly stalked them a few years back, but their father, Jasper, had warned us that she tends to be reserved when she first meets new people. Her speech is also delayed and on rare occasions, she has some issues with her emotional regulation, though he didn't feel that would be an issue with the girls.

The girls didn't even bat an eyelash at the warning.

"I think they are here." A man's voice booms through the room and suddenly I'm face to face with Jasper Diamond, Gus Diamond, Keith Dawson, and Henry Gauthier, the lead singer, lead guitarist, drummer, and bassist respectively for Wild Minds.

Now I know what Layla was saying about peeing her pants. I'm utterly flummoxed.

Introductions are made and I shake hands and say hello and introduce myself. At least I think I do. They all give Kaplan the bro hug as if they're ancient besties and I try to remember what he said to me. That they called me and that they're just people and that I need to own the room. But this is *Wild Minds*.

"Ady, sweet girl," Jasper says, kneeling down so he's closer to her height. She has to be about seven or eight, if I had to guess, and Cora I think is maybe four or five. I don't follow the lives of celebrity children all that closely. "These are my friends, Layla and Stella. They're here to hang out and play with you and Cora."

Adalyn meets her father's eyes—and wow, they look so much alike—and then reluctantly back to the girls.

"Do you want to show them one of the games on your iPad?"

"Can I play Minnie Mouse Obby on Roblox?"

"Oh! I love obbies," Stella pipes in. "I haven't played the Minnie Mouse one yet. Can you show me how?"

"Gus," she whispers, looking up at her uncle. "You want to play too?"

"Not now, 'little darlin'. Later, though. But you go on. Show Stella here how you kick butt at those obbies." Gus takes her hand, helping her along.

"What are you wearing?" she asks, taking Stella in, her tone one of pure delight.

Stella smirks and peeks down at her outfit. "Purple. I heard it was your favorite color. Mine is green."

Seriously? She's wearing purple to make Adalyn more comfortable? Just how special and sweet is Stella Fritz? But if anyone should understand what it is to be a famous kid, it's her.

Not quite the same caliber as Adalyn or Cora Diamond, but Stella is an heiress and quite well known in Boston.

"I want to play hair salon," Cora squeals and runs off laughing, back toward the bedroom. Adalyn takes Stella's hand, and she and Layla don't have to be told twice. They're already following after the girls and a second later, the bedroom door shuts.

"Don't worry," Kaplan says. "Both Layla and Stella have their phones. If there's an issue, they'll call."

"And I'll be sure to check on them," Marco offers. "I love playing hair salon." He gives me a wink and I grin, some of my nerves easing.

"I'm not worried about it." Jasper waves them away. "I'm just glad they're here. Vi is resting in the other suite and it's good for Ady and Cora to have other girls to play with."

"Is Viola okay?" Kaplan asks.

"She's fine. This pregnancy is taking its toll on her, is all."

"That's why Naomi didn't travel with us," Gus jumps in, referring to Naomi Kent, his wife and famous popstar. They just recently announced that she's pregnant with twins.

"Where are your boys?" Kaplan turns to Keith.

"With my parents," he answers, absently twirling a drumstick in his hand. "It's tough keeping an eye on those two on a normal day and impossible when we're working, so my parents offered to take them for a few days."

"Hey!" A beautiful blond woman comes out that I instantly recognize as Maia Dawson. "Perfect timing. Eden was just telling me everything is all set. Hi, I'm Maia. We spoke on the phone."

I shake her hand and smile.

"Honey, relax. This is gonna be fun. Do you want some water or anything? More coffee?"

I stare down at the cup in my hand. "No. I think if I have any more caffeine, I'll grow wings and fly."

Everyone laughs and I relax a little more. Maia and Marco usher us into what appears to be some kind of dining room that's been converted into a makeshift studio with all the furniture cleared out of it. There are instruments everywhere, various types of guitars and basses, and even a small drum set. Off to the side is a soundboard with two laptops and a tablet set up. Sitting in a chair in front of it with light purple hair is Eden Dawson, Keith's baby sister who is also dating Henry.

"I've heard you play," she tells me after we're introduced. "Your music is incredible. I can't wait for your cello with this song. It's going to be fucking epic."

We all go back and forth a bit. Talking music and getting to know each other a little.

"So tell me," Jasper starts, getting down to business. "I know you've read over the music. Do you have any issues with it?"

"No. It's beautiful. There was one part I wasn't sure on in comparison to the rest of the song, but I think I just need to hear it once and then I'll be able to lay my stuff down."

"Let me cue it up," Eden offers. "We finished recording their parts yesterday before we flew here." She presses a few things into the tablet and then the song comes through the speakers. I close my eyes and listen, thinking of the piece I've already played with a few times this week and how it will flow alongside the other instrumentals and vocals.

"Ah. Right there. That note you're hitting, Jasper. If I can, I think the cello hitting a lower note will work better. Otherwise, I'm afraid it will blend too closely."

His eyes widen and he peers around at his bandmates, who seem impressed. "Sure," he grants. "Let's try it out."

Hours later, with my back sore, my fingers numb, my wrist aching, we finish the song. And it's gorgeous. Eden was absolutely right with how the cello adds another layer of depth and emotion to it. I made some minor tweaks that they approved, and I was grateful for that. They weren't what I was expecting.

Kaplan had told me time and time again, but you never know. This is their music. Their song. They're entitled to be entitled about it.

"This is fantastic," Maia chirps as we listen to it one last time, making sure it's perfect. "God, I love the cello on this. It gives the ballad such a soulful presence."

"Totally." Eden's head moves to and fro, her eyes closed as she listens. "Would you ever consider doing more if we needed it? On a different song or different album?"

A laugh slips past my lips "Of course. Are you kidding me? I'd be honored. Truly. Anytime."

"Awesome." She starts talking with Jasper about something else and I stand, closing my eyes while twisting my back in one direction until it pops, followed by the other. But when my eyes open, they lock straight on someone standing in the corner. Someone unexpected.

Luca.

38

I came here under the strict instructions, **I need you to do me a solid and pick up Stella and Layla from a babysitting gig because I'm running behind with my patients.**

That was from Landon and that text came about two hours ago.

Imagine my motherfucking surprise when I showed up at the hotel, only to find my ID being taken and my name being called upstairs to the higher-ups? Security wouldn't tell me a thing. All I knew when I stepped on the elevator was that I was to secure my niece and quasi niece. Then Marco Morales and Maia Dawson answered the door.

I had forgotten about Raven's gig with Wild Minds.

Mostly because I heard about it in passing months ago and Kaplan hadn't mentioned a thing since. Neither had Raven. So I was feeling a bit bereft. A lot left in the dark and even more pissed off—I get I have no right after what I've put Raven through, but whatever.

Was I genuinely here to pick up the girls or was this a ruse to get me to see Raven?

Couldn't tell you.

Even now, I still have no clue.

An adorably pregnant Viola Diamond came waltzing into the suite, searching for her girls, and that's when I called Oliver to come and pick up Stella and Layla. The moment I heard those cello strings and realized the company, I knew there was no way I was going anywhere.

Irony? I had planned on doing all kinds of romantic things tonight with Raven.

Candles. Flowers. Chocolates—I knew those would be a winner. Dinner. Words—I had all the words planned. I needed everything in my arsenal of wooing, and I know this.

It had taken me a solid seventy-two hours to get everything straightened out with this grant. To figure out how everything would end up working and create a solid plan. A sellable plan. I can't remember the last time I slept. The number of times I had to talk myself out of calling or texting or running down to Raven's apartment is ridiculous.

But I wasn't going to half-ass this either.

She deserves more than that from me. She deserves everything, which is why I've held back.

Once Oliver showed up to collect our girls, Kaplan followed after him because I told his sneaky ass to leave, and now I'm the only one left. The man who has been watching her play and record with Wild Minds.

You have no clue how big my boner for my girl is right now.

Epic.

She's so hot like this. All sexy and genius and take charge. This woman... this is what I wanted for her. It's why I made the choice I made all those years ago. It's a very thin line. Between wanting to make the decision you feel is right in your gut for others and stepping back so they can take the reins and decide their own path.

Is there a wrong? Is there a right?

There might not be an answer to that, but regardless of the

controversy, there are consequences. Either way you go, there are consequences. That's what hurts us the most. The aftermath. Something that feels so right in the moment feels so very different days, weeks, or months after.

I can't help but wonder if the choice I made now, the one she refused to force me into, will feel different.

Her eyes lock on mine and she freezes midstretch, her expression blanking out, and I have no idea what to do with that. I had already talked with the guys while Raven worked with Eden, so right now, all I want to do is grab my girl and go.

Raven blinks and then turns away, and my gut sinks.

She thanks the band, Marco, Maia, and Eden and then collects her things. But the visible shift in her is clear. Her smile is gone. Whatever one she's forcing is just that, forced. I've drained the light from her eyes, and I hate the idea that that's how she's been since she found out about the grant.

"Are you my ride?" she asks, finally coming over to me while searching around for Kaplan.

"If that's okay. I sent Kaplan home. I was hoping we could talk."

A head nod. That's all I get, and it's not a happy one at that. I grab her cello from her back so she can't escape and then Marsellus, Wild Minds' main security guy, walks us to the elevator.

We thank him, but the moment the doors close, I turn on her, grabbing her by the waist because I cannot fucking stand this another second. "I've made my decision."

"Okay..." It's a hoarse whisper that has her nervously licking her lips.

"The only reason it took me so long to tell you was because I had to figure some things out. Make some arrangements. It's not because I wasn't dying every second of every minute to see you. You told me you wanted me to have everything figured out and then I should come for you."

"What arrangements have you made?"

"Hold that thought." The elevator descends quickly, but I don't want to have this conversation in the freezing cold garage or even in the car while I'm driving, so I press the button for the lobby. The doors part and I take her hand, pulling her through the lobby as I search around for an optimal spot. "This is why I wanted to have this conversation at home," I gripe. "Here." I shift us into a small alcove between the front desk and the bathrooms. It's quiet over here, unlike the sidewalk outside the building just beyond the windows. It's teeming with press, annoyingly similar to the front of my building, and who knew Boston had so many paps at their disposal.

"Luca, we could just talk about this in the car or back at home."

"No. I can't wait. I've waited three freaking days, Raven. I'm done waiting." I cup her face in my hands. "You caught me at a bad moment on Monday. I was there, feeling crestfallen and stranded in indecision, which is ridiculous. I know it is, but you've called me petulant in the past and well, yeah. I can be that sometimes. But in truth, how could I be stranded in indecision when there was no decision to make?"

"What do you mean?" She shakes her head, her brows creasing.

"I'm staying," I whisper into her. "I'm not taking the grant, Raven. I knew I wasn't going to. I was just... battling the disappointment of that. Trying to find another angle when there isn't one."

"But Kaplan said it's a grant you don't turn down. That no one turns it down."

A shrug. "Well, I did."

"Luca—"

"I'm not leaving because I cannot leave you," I tell her, cutting her off because I need to get this out. "I want the grant. But I want you more. I want to be here when Rina gets married, and I want to be here when Carter and Grace have their baby. I want to be here when eventually Oliver proposes to Amelia for real and Landon moves into his dream home with Elle. I want to watch my perfect niece turn into a crazy, hormonal teenager. I want to be here for my mom and my dad. But I cannot leave you. Not ever again."

Her chest rises and falls, each breath she takes deeper than the one before it. Her gaze dances back and forth between mine, almost as if she's waiting for a but, but there is no but to this. Not really. It's more of an adjustment to things.

Her hand hits my chest, over my pounding heart. "You won't regret it? Turning this down and not going?"

"I'm bummed. I'm seriously bummed. But the arrangements I mentioned, well, I am going. To Nicaragua actually, not Brazil."

"What?"

"Relax, baby, and let me finish. I wanted to have everything mapped out. This summer, I am taking a small sabbatical and I am going to work in a clinic that deals with primarily neuro cases. My plan is to go the week after the Fourth of July because I know the Pops do a special performance for that. So, I'm hoping you'll consider taking two months off after that and come with me. I was thinking... you could do some music therapy there. I spoke with the director of the clinic, and he thought the patients would be very receptive to that. If you don't want to do that or you can't, I'm still going, but it's only for two months. Not two years."

"Luca..."

"If it works out the way I hope it will, this might be something I'd do every year or every two years or however we can manage it. I'm also toying with the idea of setting up my own sort of foundation that will help support such ventures. My siblings said they'd be down to go and try something like that, but Carter obviously won't go until the baby is at least a year and I doubt Landon will leave Stella for more than a week or two tops."

"I... I don't know what to say."

"Say you'll think about this summer. But this summer aside, two years is too long to go without you."

Her arms wrap around my neck, dragging me in closer. "You're staying? This isn't some 'I'm going to tell you I want forever and then decide in two days I'm going'?"

Wow. I was seriously an asshole to this woman when I did that. "No. I'm staying, baby. I'm not going. I'll never do something like that to you again."

"Good. Because even though I wouldn't ask you to stay, I was dangerously close to doing it anyway."

Hearing her say that has me winded.

"I shouldn't have put that on you. I was... upset. Like I said, you caught me in a bad moment. I'll have those sometimes. This stuff with my mom. This grant. I've been a bit of a mess. But being with you, I've come to realize... I'm not broken, and I'm not healed. I'm not lost, and I'm not found. I'm not dark, and I'm not light. I'm not a disaster, and I'm not perfect. I'm just me. But together we're a flawless balance of all those things. A symphony only you and I can hear. I can't live without you. But more importantly, I don't want to try. Not ever again. I love you."

She smiles up at me, a smile that clenches my chest and robs me of my breath. "I love you too. I'm glad you're staying. Forget living without you. Life's too short not to live it with you. And yes, I think I'd like to come with you this summer if I can manage it with my current obligations. It'd be incredible to play music there. To help in any way I can."

My hands dive into her hair and I kiss her. I kiss her good, long, and hard. Full-on tongue. The way I intend to kiss her every day from this moment on. For the rest of our lives because you can bet your ass I'm marrying this woman—for real this time.

"Raven, you are the Obi Wan for me."

A burst of laughter flees her lungs, head thrown back. "That's horrible! How long have you been holding on to that one?"

"Four years. Never found the right time."

"It's so cheesy. Boston's notorious Doctor Playboy is such a closet nerd."

"But I'm your closet nerd."

"That you are," she tells me as I lead us back to the elevator and down into the garage. I help her into my car, shutting the door behind her, but it isn't until we're driving past the hotel that something occurs to me. Something that requires fixing, almost immediately.

Unfortunately, that'll have to wait a few minutes until we get home.

"I have tickets to tomorrow night." I glance over at Raven as we meander through Boston evening rush hour traffic. "We all do, actually, with the exception of my parents, who are devastated they can't be there. I purchased a balcony section for us and already told your dad he has to sit next to me."

She makes some kind of incredulous sound in the back of her throat. "That's insane, you know."

I smirk, dragging her fingers over to my lips. "My girl is a first chair cello for the Boston Symphony Pops holiday show and has not one but two solos. Do you think I'm missing that? Never. Plus, I have to bond with your father so he doesn't kill me in my sleep while making it look like natural causes."

"He's more apt to make it look like an accident. Fewer questions that way."

"Good to know. Even more of a reason to suck up to him. But for real, I'm so proud of you, baby. I know you're nervous about it, but we're your family and we'll be there cheering you on and loving you no matter what."

"Thank you," she whispers.

I continue to hold her hand until I pull into my garage spot, putting the car in park and turning to her. "Are you hungry? I can make us something or we can order takeout."

"I'm starving and whatever is fastest."

Hmmm. Perfect. "I'll order from the bistro around the corner, and we can go and pick it up. What do you want?"

I pull up the website for the restaurant on my phone and we place our order. I'm starving too. I feel like I haven't eaten anything in a week. Not since my mother was put in the hospital. Raven too looks a little thinner.

"How about we eat dinner by the fire and watch a movie? I think we could both use some relaxation time."

"If you buy me dinner and give me an orgasm, I'll let you talk me into a Star Wars binge marathon. I might even suck you off at some point while you watch."

I choke on my own saliva only to laugh. "God, how did I get such a bitch for a girlfriend? Seriously? You're the freaking worst, Raven."

Winking at her, I fly around the car, helping her out. A loud beep sounds through the garage as I hit the clicker and drag her into my chest and kiss the hell out of her.

"Wanna get married?" I ask once she's good and breathless.

"No."

"Wanna make a baby?"

"Also no."

"This age gap between us might be trouble."

Honestly, I might have a point with that. My siblings—minus Kaplan—are all settling down. Oliver and Amelia have Layla, even if she's not their kid. Landon has Stella, who is a freaking teenager. Carter and Grace have a baby on the way, and Rina just got engaged. I'm thirty-three and ready to settle down, with her, but the look on Raven's face tells me that the idea of marriage and babies, even with me, at this stage of her life gives her palpitations.

"I can wait," I promise. Maybe. I'm not very good at patience.

As if reading my mind, she says, "You'll have to discover a calmer, more patient zen inside you."

I swing our hands between us as we walk up toward the street. "Not likely."

Just as we turn the corner, I see them. Just as I knew I would. The paparazzi are unfortunately brutally relentless. I get it. Sorta. This is Boston and there isn't much action around here. Well, except for the Abbot-Fritzes evidently.

"Can we tell people now?" I ask as we draw closer. "And by people, I mean, can I kiss you in public and hold your hand"—I raise our joined hands up to my lips— "and take you out to dinner, so everyone knows you're mine?"

She blows out an uneven breath, clearly not having seen the guys hanging around the front of the building yet, and slowly nods. "Yes. I didn't like how they were speculating on who I was. I didn't like the things they were saying about the mystery woman. So yes. Let's do it."

"Thank fuck." I hold her hand against my lips and kiss her palm, her wrist. "I hated keeping my mouth shut about you."

A smile lights up her face. "We're really doing this? Like more than we were before, aren't we?"

Using our linked hands, I spin her around on the sidewalk, hauling her into me and cradling her against me. Her face tilts up, our eyes connected. "Forever, Raven. I mean it. I don't want to date you. I don't want to go slow and see how it all works out. I want a life with you. I want to wake up beside you every morning and fall asleep with you in my arms every night. I want marriage and babies and grandkids. I want it all."

"Luca! Luca! Is this the mystery woman? Miss! Over here. What's your name?"

Suddenly, we're surrounded by four guys, all yelling things at us, flashing cameras in our faces. I give Raven a look. The one that says she just agreed to be mine publicly and then turn to them with a smile I rarely afford the press. "This is Raven Fairchild. She's a cellist for the Boston Symphony Pops Orchestra. I've known her all her life as her father works for my family." My eyes meet hers again. "And I love her more than anything in the world."

I plant a deep kiss on her lips, holding her tight against me.

And after a few more seconds of questions and pictures, I wrap my arm around her shoulders, thank them, and then push us along the sidewalk.

She grimaces, glancing over her shoulder, no doubt seeing them working frantically on their phones. "Ugh. That's going to be everywhere within the hour."

"Yup. That's the price you pay when you date Doctor Playboy. You're stuck with me now."

"We'll see how it goes, Doctor Playboy. For now, take me home, feed me, and maybe I'll let you read me more of that second chance romance we started."

"I already know how it ends."

She quirks a brow at me.

"Happily ever after."

EPILOGUE

Raven

Eight Months Later

ON A PERFECT MIDSUMMER Martha's Vineyard night, with the sun setting over the western horizon—skies so pure, glowing in a pomp of pink and gold—I find myself walking alone on the beach. Waters of the bluest of blues crash along the shore, the best soundtrack despite the hint of music from the Fritz ballroom swirling along in the breeze.

The wedding went off without a hitch.

Some early panic by the bride turned into tears and laughter and a lot of kissing. I will admit, I shed more tears than I thought I ever would.

And now, with the party in full swing, I snuck out undetected, walking up toward the stone wall of the English garden that sits tucked away along the outskirts of the property. Needing a brief reprieve. Just a moment to myself to get my thoughts in order. Everyone in the world I know and love is in the ballroom, enjoying the reception, drinking, dancing and laughing.

And yet, for reasons I'm not entirely sure of, I couldn't help but wander out here. Lost in my thoughts.

It's been a long five years since I was here last.

They say that life is a never-ending circle. Everything that is old will one day be new again. Fashion trends. The food chain. Life. And in my case, love.

Five years ago on this very night, I was practicing my cello only to look up straight into the green eyes of the man I had been in love with my entire life. A man I never imagined would see me as anything more than the hired help. The house manager's daughter. The little girl he once saved from a near drowning.

That summer forever changed me.

Its aftereffects comprising both the best and worst days, weeks, months, and years of my life.

The breeze is warm and welcoming, swirling a sweet path along my skin and kicking up the ends of my hair. My heels are long since forgotten at the base of the steps, the sand soft and granular as I leave a trail of footprints behind me. I don't intend to go far. Just a moment to chase the dying sun before the fireworks explode from the barge fifty feet offshore.

It's been a long day. A sweet day. The best day. But a day that brought determined looks along with it. Obvious thoughts.

Which is possibly why I catch the faintest hint of celebratory cigar smoke and cologne on the breeze as it skirts in behind me.

He's there. Somewhere. Watching. Following.

I know he is.

Even if I can't hear him against the crashing of the waves along the shore. I feel him. I *always* feel him. The thrill of my pulse. The flutter in my chest. The delicious curling in my lower belly. My body a helpless slave to him.

That thought has me smirking despite my sudden need for a moment of solitude.

The crest of the waning sun sizzles into the edge of the deep blue ocean, bringing a hint of an extra breeze along with a smattering of clouds determined to block out the stars. But not on this night. It's been a hot day, one full of sun and joy. A light at what has felt like an interminable tunnel for a family who is no stranger to fear or heartache.

"Little Bird." His voice carries and a smile slips up my lips as I keep going, gliding along the fenced wall and then up into the gardens. Roses, jasmine, lavender, lilac, bushes and trees and tall grasses swath around me, consuming me in their fragrance. A deep inhale and along with the flowers, *him.*

Then arms from around my back, folding across my chest. "Don't struggle my wild, frantic little bird."

"I am no bird."

"Ah, but you will always be my little bird. A raven, so brilliant and strong, dark and unyielding. My father told me I will forever be chasing you. Never having won, but hopefully perpetually winning."

His mouth hits my neck. The skin beneath my ear. Kisses and licks and breath.

"How are the bride and groom?"

A smile against me. "Deliriously happy." Another kiss, his arms squeezing me against him. "My baby brother got married tonight." A laugh. "Explain to me why this feels so different than when Landon married Reese."

"Because Landon was barely out of college when he married Reese. You're all men now. Grownups." I giggle. "Well, sort of."

"And you? What are you ready for? What's your next adventure?"

"Tomorrow. And the day after that. And so on. I suppose Central America is in there too."

"But what else? What other adventure does your heart need? What else can I give you to make you feel complete?"

"You by my side, but why does this feel like you're building me up to something?"

"I might be." He spins me around, the frill of my skirts splaying out between us.

"Not interested," I shoot out when I catch the gleam in his eyes.

"You haven't heard me out yet."

"I don't need to. The answer is no."

We leave in a little over a month for Nicaragua. The symphony takes a small hiatus after the Fourth of July Pops concert, so the timing works out well. The hospital wasn't so jazzed about my taking this time, but Luca can be persuasive as hell when driven.

It'll be an adventure, as I said. One I can't wait to tackle.

I've been slowly brushing up on my high school Spanish and going through some things I want to do when I'm there. Luca is beside himself with the planning of it. We're going to take his family plane and Landon and Oliver are joining us for the first two weeks. They're donating all kinds of medical equipment to the clinic.

I don't think I've ever seen Luca as excited about anything as he is about this.

It's filling his soul in ways nothing else ever has.

"Do you know one of the things I love about you?" Luca murmurs in my ear as he dips his face toward mine.

"What?" I reply absently, staring out toward the dark sky over the ocean. Any second there are going to be fireworks and I don't want to miss them.

"That you fit so perfectly against me. Your body tucks straight into mine. Head beneath my chin. It makes dancing with you that much better."

Without music, he starts to sway me to the call of the

breeze. The feel of the night. How easily I get lost in him. How unimaginable I find the thought of being found again if it's with anyone but him.

I kiss his chin. "I love you."

"I love you more. But you're too far away."

I laugh. "I'm in heels. That tucks me right into you. I'm not normally this tall."

"Little Bird, you've always fit perfectly against me."

"It's my favorite place to be," I tell him honestly, glancing up so I can find his sparkling eyes and contented grin visible in the last remnants of twilight. I still can't believe Oliver got married today. The baby brother and wow, just how gorgeous are all these Fritz men in their wedding apparel. Casual in khakis, white dress shirts, and pale blue linen blazers.

Kinda preppy, but that's also kinda Oliver.

"You know, things are going to be different when we're in Nicaragua. My hours will be long. More surgeries. More community care."

I drag my fingers through his hair as he continues to sway us like a pendulum. "I know. I'm not worried about it. The work you'll be doing... it's so important. I love that we're doing this. I love that I get to be a part of it with you. See this side of you up close."

And part of me still feels bad that he declined the grant. I mean, don't get me wrong, I'm thrilled he's not leaving for two years. But I know what fulfilling this journey is to him. I understand what it means. It's not something I'd ever want to hinder or take from him. Not only is the work vital, but it nurtures his soul.

I guess that's when you know something is real. Forever. Binding.

When you're both willing to make the vital sacrifice in the name of the other. When what drives them also starts driving you.

"I'm not sure I can do this with you like this."

My head jerks back, my eyes searching. "Like what?"

"As not fully mine."

"Luca—"

"What if I need more?"

"What sort of more?" I retort with a challenging brow.

"You as my second self. My second half."

"You have one of those. His name is Landon. Looks just like you minus the freckle in his left eye."

"He snores."

A laugh bursts from my lungs. "He does not. You just don't like sleeping beside him any longer."

Luca takes my hand, twisting me through the night air of the garden just as the first of the fireworks hits the sky, illuminating it with a burst of blue and green, startling us with its sharp crack.

He pulls me back against him as we stare at the sky. "I like sleeping beside you. An addiction I'll never want to cure myself of."

"Luca. What are you doing?"

His eyes briefly meet mine. "I'm not asking you to marry me, if that's what you're worried about."

I was. A little. Or maybe a lot. But hearing him say that's not what he's doing...

"I want more than marriage, Little Bird. I've waited so long for you. All my life. This is where it all began for us. On this island. On this beach."

"Well, for me it began long before that. But you were so old, and I was so young."

He smiles at me, his lips against mine. "That first night when I found you playing cello, all I could think about was how I shouldn't be looking at you the way I was. Thinking about you the way I was. I think I fell in love with you the very first second I saw you."

"And now?"

"Now?" He laughs as more fireworks pop overhead, startling us with their loud boom. Crackles and fizzles and starburst. For a moment, we can't help but watch them. Lost in their beauty. In the wonder of it all. "Now I love you more than I did in all those moments combined. Which is why I'm not asking you to marry me."

"You're not?"

"No. I'm asking you to spend the rest of your life as my partner in crime. The woman who will forever keep me on my toes. Remind me that there is no end to our race. That I'll never have won you because I'll have to spend every second of this life working to win you. Always."

More cracks of fireworks, painting Luca's face in varying shades of rainbow as they float from the heavens. But his eyes. That earnest expression. That raw, impassioned need.

"I'm not asking you to marry me because marriage is a union," he continues. "A legal contract. A piece of paper. A term of negotiation. Raven Fairchild, I'm not asking you to marry me because I need you to be so much more than simply my wife. I'm asking you to be the mother of my children. The better half of my soul. The sense to my nonsense. The light to my dark. The perfect to my imperfect. The right to all my wrongs. My symphony. My music. My heart. My life."

"Luca—"

His hands press into my spine, dipping my lower back in until my body is aligned with his. The tip of his nose kisses mine.

"Tell me, baby. I know you're young and I know this isn't what you wanted just yet. I know a lot of that is because I did it all wrong the first time. But I don't know how to continue on as your boyfriend. I don't know how to pretend you're not the best part of me. I don't *want* to introduce you as anything other than my wife. You've been it for me for five years. Be it for me forever. Tell me yes and be my wife, my love, my passion. My forever."

No ring. No one knee. Just direct eye contact, as always with him.

Bodies wrapped as one. Hearts beating in sync. Fast and off-pace and creating a song only we hear.

My lips meld with his and I answer him the only way I can after a speech like that. "Yes. I'm forever yours."

That's it. Anything else would be a crazy lie.

I am young and I hadn't wanted to get married just yet, but he's right. Calling himself my boyfriend is laughable. He's more than that. He's always been more than that.

His lips crash to mine, closing the minuscule distance between us. Tongues and heat and passion and fire and endless love against the sparkling sky. On a night filled with memories. For his family. For us. For all that's yet to come.

EPILOGUE 2

Chapter 1 - Doctor Untouchable *Unedited and subject to change*

KAPLAN

I knew when this day started that it was going to be a fucking shitshow. Nothing good ever starts with a wakeup call from your mother asking you to meet her for lunch. Especially when you already know the reason for the lunch and have been dreading it, well, practically since the day you were born.

Then there's this call...

"All I'm asking is if you think she'll say yes?"

I clench my jaw and run a hand through my hair, my other gripping my steering wheel so tight the leather creaks. "Luca, how should I know?"

"Because you somehow know Raven better than anyone. You're like secret girlfriends. She tells you shit. Confides in you."

I'd smirk at that if my insides weren't being poked at with something hot and sharp. Honestly, I hope Luca proposes. I hope Raven says yes. I hope they live happily ever after and suck all the attention and limelight for themselves. Then maybe for once in my life I can stop having that pesky four-letter word thrown at me with the hope it'll finally stick to me.

Love.

The one thing everyone from my family to the press to the endless stream of money-hungry women lining up at the mention of my name try to shove down my throat. But the worst part, the part that has me mashing my molars is what's coming for me in the absence of love.

"I think she'll think it's too soon. You've only been back together a couple of months."

He puffs out a breath. "Rina and Brecken just got married. Oliver popped the question to Amelia for real on New Year's. Carter just did the same to Grace on fucking Valentine's Day."

"Feeling left out?" I quip.

"I just want Raven as mine. Truly mine. Wearing my ring and my last name. Forever."

"She's not going anywhere, brother."

"I know that. That's not why I want to seal the deal. I love her, Kap. This is what you do when you love someone."

I grunt, so beyond not in the mood for this. I grip the wheel tighter which I didn't even realize was possible. Soon my knuckles will split. "I'm ignoring you."

"You shouldn't. It's time, old man."

"I have enough on my plate without trying to deal with yet another gold-digger or entitled fledgling celebrity after more fame and headlines or a socialite looking to sit around in her designer digs and do lunch while we spend decades ignoring each other."

"There's that side of it. Or. You know. You could find actual love."

I blow out a silent breath, my eyes closing as I reach a traffic light. I knew this day was coming too. It's what happens when all of your younger siblings are happily hitched up to wonderful women and your mother is obsessed with love, marriage, and grandchildren.

But they're not me. Their path was always easier.

"Not interested," I tell him, opening my eyes again and shoving any useless frustration at this conversation down as the light turns green and I start to drive again. "How about you focus on Raven and leave me to handle my life. Raven is young. Give her time before you put a ring on it."

"I know. Maybe for her birth—"

"What the fuck?" I practically yell, coming to a screeching halt as a barrage of white that is absolutely not the snow currently falling practically lands right on the hood of my car with a thud.

"Kap? Kap, you okay?!"

"Luca, I gotta go." I disconnect the call, throw the car into park, and then get out right into the middle of traffic. The white starts to move, sliding across the hood of my SUV until it's on the opposite side from me. I slam my door shut and repeat myself. "What the fuck?"

"Oh my god!" the woman shrieks. "You stopped! Thank God, you stopped."

I blink at least a thousand times, trying to make sense of the mass of tule and silk and lace and unruly dark hair before me. "You flew onto my car. Didn't exactly give me a choice. What was I supposed to do, run you over?"

She's standing in the street, hugging the side of the hood so she doesn't get hit by passing cars, but her wild, frantic gaze is over my shoulder, anxiously watching whatever is there. Reflexively I turn to look, cars hocking and shooting around me, spraying slush and ice up onto my slacks, and find a cluster of people dressed in tuxedos and gowns standing at the top of the church steps, glaring down at us as if they're about to give chase.

"They followed me? I can't believe they followed me out!"

I flip back around to find the woman opening the passenger side door of my car and jumping in, piling her dress in along with her before slamming the door shut. "What the fuck?!" This time I bellow it at the top of my lungs. "What are you doing getting in my car?"

Opening my door, I nearly get sideswiped by a passing taxi, the driver yelling and cursing at me. Yanking my door shut, I throw on my hazards, and then turn on the marsh-mallow that's taking up half the front of my car.

"Get out!"

"No! I can't. You have to drive. Please. I'll pay you. Just drive before they come after me." Large, slightly watery, heavily made-up brown eyes plead with me, her hands directed toward me in supplication.

My head whips back around and sure enough, the guy, who I can only assume is the groom is shooting down the stairs, his fists balled up, an incensed scowl perched on his face. A couple of women follow him, staring straight at me as if I'm the asshole, and I turn back on the bride in my car, just as miffed as the dude she ran out on.

"Seriously," she cries. "You have to go now. If he gets to me, I won't be responsible for what happens next. The blood of many could be on your hands."

I level her with my no bullshit glare. The one that makes sane women cower. Not this one. She simply throws her hands up in the air, unnerved and at the end of her rope.

"Please, please, please drive us out here. Clearly, I'm desperate. Who throws themselves into oncoming traffic to escape their wedding if they're not?"

"Are you in some kind of danger or just crazy?"

A humorless laugh. "I'm possibly crazy, but not in the psychopathic, I need locking up kind of way. And I guess if you consider being chased after by my mother, my maid of honor who is also my cousin, and my lying, cheating, user of a now ex-fiancé who has been fucking said cousin being in danger, then yes, I'm in danger. So now that we've cleared up my morning from hell, can you drive, or do I have to hurl myself on another moving vehicle?"

I scrutinize her for a second. What I can see of her that is. Round face. Those big brown eyes as dark as the piles of hair pinned up on her head guilelessly imploring me in a desperate, slightly unhinged way. Glossy pink, pillowy lips. Curves for days. Large breasts with an ample amount of cleave spilling over the top of the stiff bust of her dress. Skin the color of the falling snow. Pretty.

For a runaway bride with smeared make-up and more layers than anyone should be wearing.

The groom is now edging toward the street, trying to find a safe path toward us amongst the North End traffic. He's shouting something I can only guess at along with a tall, willowy older-ish—she's had more work done on her face than the Ted Williams tunnel here in Boston—woman beside him.

"Please," she says again, this time as a strained whisper. "I can't face any of them right now."

"Screw it."

I throw my Land Rover Range Rover into drive and skid on the slushy road as I start to peel out, back into traffic.

Curves for Days sags back into the seat. "Thank you. Thank you so much." The relief in her voice is palpable. "I don't even care if you're a psycho who is going to take me back to his underground basement and make clothes out of my skin."

"Basements by definition are underground, and I think flying into a stranger's car makes you the psycho here. Not me."

"It's been a morning in case you missed that. I think I should be afforded a modicum of slack."

She rights herself, ripping a sparkly clip and attached veil from her hair, followed by pin after pin. They fall onto her lap and a wry, incredulous grin hits my lip. I just picked up a runaway bride who threw herself on top of my car to escape her fiancé and her mother and now I'm driving her... "Where are you headed?"

"Not to Scotland, that's for sure."

Huh? Whatever. "Fine then. I'm dropping you off on the next corner."

She shakes her head, her long, long silky hair tumbles all around her as her fingers massage her scalp. She moans, throwing her head back and closing her eyes in extasy. And hell in a handbasket, my cock twitches in my pants.

"Wow, that might be better than any sex I ever had with Tod. It's amazing how good that feels."

I throw her an impatient scowl trying not to think about the sound of her moan or how good whatever she just did feels to her.

"Sorry. I'm staying at The Newbury. You can drop me off there if it's not too much trouble or anywhere somewhat close where I can walk since I don't have my purse or my phone or even a damn coat." She lets out a cackle. "I just ran out on my wedding. Did you see my mother?" She points past me with something close to a dumbstruck, self-satisfied smile on her lips and an incredulous sparkle to her eyes. "She was furious. She didn't even care when I told her I overheard jackass mc jackass and perfect mc backstabbing bitch face fighting about their love." She frowns now, her face falling toward her hands.

"Did you love him?" I don't know why I'm bothering to ask

questions if for no other reason than I'm curious. And oddly, I want her to keep talking. Her voice... it's sweet and smooth and rich and warm—like caramel on a sundae.

She shrugs, her gaze going to the window, staring out at the passing landscape. "I thought I did. Or maybe more like I told myself I did?" She shrugs again. "I don't know. One of my stepfathers, Mitchell told me love is for pansy asses and suckers and my mother for once agreed with him."

Can't argue that.

"But I chose not to listen," she continues. "Always optimistic, glass half-full, blind to what's actually in front of me, Bianca. That's me. Oddly I'm more furious and hurt than heartbroken. But maybe that comes later? What are the stages of grief again?"

"Denial, anger, bargaining, depression, and acceptance."

Her gaze slingshots over to mine. "Wow. You just pulled that right off the top of your head. Are you a shrink? Because likely, I could use one of you right now. Or maybe a vat of vodka and fried food I could pretend is a shrink. Alcohol and carbs are medicinal, right?"

"No. I'm a different type of doctor."

"Hence the nice ride. One of my other stepfathers, Duke— he's the one who's currently married to my mother—has a car like this though his smells more like the ranch and less like sexy man cologne."

"Huh?"

She ignores me, as she continues to orate and fidget in her seat. "Incidentally thank you for stopping and not running me over. I figured it was a fifty-fifty chance I could die when I flew at your car but was willing to risk it given the alternative. I hope I didn't dent your hood."

"You didn't."

"Well. Thank you. Again." Her fingers toy nervously with her dress.

"You're welcome. You can relax. I'm not a psycho. I'll drive you to the hotel because as luck would have it, that's where I'm headed too."

"No way."

I nod in concession. "Way."

She smiles a crooked, shaky smile and something about that sparks something in me. A familiarity or a memory I can't place.

"It's like fate knew I was gonna need to run out on an asshole today or something."

I crack a hint of a smirk as I change lanes. "Or something. He cheated? That's why you ran?"

"Yep. The entire time he and I were together apparently, which was about two years. I had no clue. None. I don't know if that makes them exceptionally brilliant at hiding it or me insanely stupid for missing it."

I glance quickly in her direction before turning back to the slippery roads. "Them good at hiding it. You don't strike me as the stupid type."

"I launched myself into traffic and am now in a stranger's car after running out on my wedding," she deadpans.

Touché.

"Besides, it was two years. I mean, he and I were *living* together for the last six months I was finishing up grad school and yet somehow, I still missed it. I realize I was busy but come on. That's just pathetic. I wish I could go back in time and smack myself upside the head with a healthy dose of sense."

I have nothing to say to that, but luckily I don't have to as she continues on without missing a beat.

"I thought he loved me. He gave me this whole dog and pony show about how he loved me all through college but was always too nervous to make a move or risk our friendship, which is why it took him until fucking graduate school to make a move. I was gullible, I guess. Hopeful. I didn't have a lot of guys pounding down my door and certainly not ones who looked like Tod. I never imagined when he proposed six months ago that he was actually in love with my cousin. Or that the only reason he did propose was because he has to marry me."

My eyebrows knit into a V, and I briefly catch her eye. "Why does he have to marry you if he's in love with her?"

She shifts, staring down at the white of her lap. "His last name is MacMillin as in MacMillin Investments. Only as it turns out his father isn't much of an investor. His parents also have expensive vices. His dad's a gambler and his mom's a shopper. I don't know the details. I just heard him tell Ava, that's my cousin, that his family money is gone and the only way to save the company is to marry me." Another loud cackle, her hands flying all about, and I realize this woman is incapable of sitting still for a minute. "He genuinely thought that by marrying me I'd fix his family's wealth. Fool clearly did not read the prenup my step-fathers made him sign."

"Step-fathers?"

"It's complicated." She hiccups out a sob, her moods swinging faster than a newborn's, and I glance over at her as I try not to kill us on the congested streets. "I should have known he never actually loved me. The signs were there all along." She shifts and then I hear a ripping noise as she tears apart her dress.

"What are you doing?"

"Removing some of this nonsense. I can't breathe." She starts yanking at the back of her dress and then tugs at the bustline, more of her full tits spilling out and *Jesus*. If she doesn't stop doing that, I'll crash my car for sure from all the blood flow in my body rapidly shooting to my dick.

"Can you not do that?" I practically groan when she bounces in her seat and her tits do the same.

"There. Better." She sucks in a deep breath. "Do you have

any clue how tight my mother cinched my corset? 'It'll make you look skinny, Bianca'," she mocks who I assume to be her mother. "'Come on and suck in. You couldn't lose weight for your own wedding?' Ugh. I didn't even want this dress. I wanted something sleeker. Something that accentuated my curves, not hid them. She's the one who made me look like Cinder-fuck-ing-ella to hide my hips and thighs because she thinks the world has to be a size two or they're fat."

She starts to cry and dear god, what have I gotten myself into?

"I'm such a fool. They turned me into such a fool. I must look so insane to you right now, but I'm not. I simply trusted the wrong people. I know I shouldn't be babbling on like this and I'm positive you're likely annoyed with me, but I can't help it right now."

Shit. A strange woman in a wedding dress is having a break-down in my car and I have no clue what to do other than drive and keep my mouth shut. But as insane—yes, that word again —as it seems, the idea of her crying like this, being this sad over a loser guy like that hits me strangely. Almost... protec-tively? No. Maybe. I don't know. In a way that makes me want to right all her wrongs, which makes zero fucking sense given the situation.

She lets out a wet, mirthless laugh, her gaze casting over to me. "We were going to Scotland for our honeymoon." Her hands fly up in the air again, her voice rising with them. "Scot-land! Can you believe it? Scotland in fucking February."

"I'm not following," I admit.

"You're a hot, sexy guy with money. In my experience, guys who look like you and drive cars like this only have sex with model-hot women. I bet you like looking at them naked any chance you get, right?"

I open my mouth to say something only to close it immedi-ately. I can't decide what I'm supposed to focus on there. The fact that she thinks I'm hot and sexy or the way she just nailed my dating life down to a cliché. She's tall and young, but other than that there is nothing about Curves for Days that even remotely resembles the women I typically date or more aptly fuck—not that I've been doing any of that recently.

Despite her observation, I have a very valid reason for that.

"Um…" I try again, still incapable of an adequate response because I'm not about to get into my personal life with this woman even if in the ten minutes she's been in my car she's somehow managed the impossible. She intrigues me. If for no other reason than she has a nice rack and an interesting story.

Thankfully her question is rhetorical, and she continues blathering on without waiting on me.

"Most couples go to the Caribbean or Hawaii for their honeymoons. They go skinny dipping, snuggle on the beach together, and fuck in random, public places like the ocean. We were going to Scotland in winter. You get me now?"

"Not exactly." I glance over at her, taking her in for a moment now that we're stopped at another light by The Commons. She's a mess. Her wild mane of hair is all over the place. Her face painted in dripping black make-up. Her dress is ripped and huge and covers most of her and the front seat. I still don't know what to make of her while she spills her life story to me as if I'm Dr. fucking Phil and give a shit.

"Sweaters and parkas and heavy coats," she tells me, staring straight into my eyes as if the answer should be obvious. "He didn't want to see me in a bathing suit because he's disgusted by the way I look. I'm not a size two or a four and or even a six or eight. I don't look like my perfect cousin or my perfect mother. He said something to her about it today. 'You think I like having to fuck her? It's all I can do to get hard. I close my eyes and picture you.' That's what he told my cousin." Her face falls to her hands once more and she sobs into them. "He was always commenting on what I was eating. What I was wearing.

How often I was exercising. He was going to marry me, and I disgust him."

She shakes her head, her hair flying, and I catch a hint of vanilla and brown sugar, sweet and richly warm, enticing like a cookie straight out of the oven. Falling back against the seat, she wipes at her face, all the while I'm gripping the steering wheel again, enraged. I don't even know this chick, but what kind of man says things like about a woman? Uses a woman like that and to such an extreme? It's taking everything inside me not turn this car around, find that small dicked asshole and bludgeon him to death with one of the golf clubs I have sitting in my trunk.

"If I were a stronger woman, I would have done more than dump the bottle of water I was holding on his head and run. I would have kicked his ass and then plotted his death. Hers too for that matter. There were so many signs that I ignore over and over again," she continues, oblivious to my fury. "My mother pushed me on him. 'He has a good last name. Family money. He's interested in you. Marry him, Bianca,'" she mocks again, gesticulating all over the pace as she builds steam. "Now I'm in Boston and not Texas or California or Colorado and it's like... shit. What am I going to do now? We moved here last week so he could head up the Boston branch of his father's failing company. We don't even have an apartment yet, which now I see as a blessing. We're staying in the hotel." She snorts. "On me, of course. He had me book the room and it's on my credit card. God, I'm so stupid. So blind and stupid."

"To me it sounds like you dodged a bullet. You can do anything now, right? No apartment. Doesn't sound like you have a job here either. You obviously have money since that's what he was after. You're free. He's the one who's fucked. You're not marrying the loser. You should be out celebrating."

She doesn't say anything and that just pisses me off. I pull over into an open parking spot on the side of the road, throw the car in park, and turn on her. I give her a big once over. I still can't see much. She's not small, I get that. But fuck all to hell if her curves for days aren't sexy. She edges back toward the door, because yeah, we don't know each other.

And I'm visibly angry.

And I have zero business doing anything that I'm doing right now.

She blinks at me, those milk chocolate doe-eyes wide as tears drip from them.

"You are beautiful, and he is a loser. You hear me? Any man who treats a woman like that is a fucking loser. A waste of space and life. And your mother and that asshole should shut their mouths about your body. Nothing hot or sexy about bone-thin, sweetheart. Nothing."

She tilts her head, studying me for a moment, her eyebrows kitting together and crap. Here we go. She's two seconds from recognizing me and I'm not in the mood. I have enough of my own madness to deal with. My own family shit.

The last thing I should be doing right now is getting involved in her mess.

Without another word, I throw the car back into drive and head toward the damn hotel. I don't even know why I said all that to her other than I can't stand seeing a woman cry. Or hurt. A personal flaw I've been working on overcoming over the years. That's all that was.

But truly, she should know she's better off without him.

I pull up in front of the hotel and immediately the valet comes to open her door, icy wind and snow spilling inside and she shudders. But those big brown eyes are back on mine, a soft, sweet smile too, and something foreign inside of me shifts a little with it.

"Thank you again for rescuing me," she says tenderly. "I think you're right. I've been looking at this all wrong. I dodged a bullet today. And if I decide to stay in Boston, maybe fate will step back in, and I'll see you somewhere again. Then I can buy you a drink to thank you properly."

With that she launches herself across the console, drops a kiss on my cheek, and then flees my car, racing into the hotel, a flutter of white trailing her.

I stare after her, a bemused smile curling up my lips as my fingers find the slightly wet, sticky spot on my cheek she just kissed. A chuckle hits the air and I shake my head. I step out of the car, handing the valet my keys and accepting the ticket in exchange.

That was the strangest half hour of my life. As I head toward the entrance of the hotel, the same one she just fled into, I can't decide if I'd mind running into her again or not. And if I did, would I let her buy me that drink?

THANK you for taking the time to read Doctor Playboy and the first chapter of Doctor Untouchable. I am so very grateful!! I hope you enjoyed them and are getting excited for Kaplan Fritz, and if you are, make sure you snag Doctor Untouchable now.

If this is your first book in the series that you've read and would like to start at the beginning with Oliver's book, keep reading for Chapter one of Doctor Scandalous!

END OF BOOK NOTE

Thank you lovely reader for taking the time to read Luca and Raven's story. It was an emotional one. The most emotional in the series for sure and I wasn't sure how it was going to be taken. I sweated this one more than the others by far. When this series originally popped into my head over two years ago, it was Luca and Raven's story that came first.

Luca made a lot of mistakes. He was very flawed and imperfect. But in his heart, it was always Raven. I think that's what I loved so much about him. About their story. Their total love and devotion to each other, even when they tried to fight it or ignore it or pretend it wasn't even a thing. Love cannot be denied and I think that's possibly the theme of this book. That and appearances aren't always what they seem as Luca was anything but a playboy.

But in truth, to me, this story felt very real. The characters act the way we do. In the moment. And they didn't always get it right. Or did they? It's impossible to tell. Would Raven have been better off if she had stayed with Luca? I'm not sure that's a question we'll ever be able to answer. Our decisions have so much power and all we can do is hope to hell we're making the right one.

There are so many people to thank for this story!! My lovely beta team, Patricia, Danielle, and Kelly. Thank you so much! Without you, I would have been drowning in doubt on this one. To my beautiful editors, Ellie and Emily. You take my words and help perfect them.

To my absolutely gorgeous girls and my incredible husband. Words have not yet been invented to describe my love for all of you. Thank you for being my biggest fans and greatest champions. I love you endlessly.

And thank you (again) readers. You are why I do this. You allow me to tell the stories that live in my head and my heart and I am eternally grateful to you for that.

I hope you're excited about Kaplan's book. He is, as his brothers, unexpected. His story was so much fun to write and I know you're going to love it as much as I do.

XO,

Julie (J. Saman)

ALSO BY J. SAMAN

Wild Love Series:

Reckless to Love You

Love to Hate Her

Crazy to Love You

Love to Tempt You

Promise to Love You

The Edge Series:

The Edge of Temptation

The Edge of Forever

The Edge of Reason

The Edge of Chaos

Boston's Billionaire Bachelors:

Doctor Scandalous

Doctor Mistake

Doctor Heartless

Doctor Playboy

Doctor Untouchable

Start Again Series:

Start Again

Start Over

Start With Me

Las Vegas Sin Series:

DOCTOR SCANDALOUS

Oliver

I'm walking toward the gates of hell. And they charge for admission.

"Oh, Oliver..." Christa Foreman greets me with a slow once-over, her pastel-pink lips curling up into an impish grin. She's aptly named, because our senior class president was no joke when it came to strong-arming and manipulating her fellow classmates into getting what she wanted. "It's so good to see you. Wow. I mean, I see your pictures in magazines and on social media every now and then because I follow you, but you're way better looking in person than I remember from high school."

"Um. Thank you?" It comes out as a question, my head tilting in her direction.

"Sure. No problem." She licks her lips, her long, fake eyelashes batting faster than a butterfly's wings at me. "Are you here alone tonight?" She giggles as a flush creeps up her cheeks. She's married. Can we just say that? "I'm only asking because I need to know how much to charge you. I got stuck collecting money until the event coordinator can get her shit together." She huffs out a flustered breath, rolling her eyes derisively. "Anyway, it's a hundred per person. Should I put you down for one or two?"

And this is where I hesitate. Not over the money. The money is not an issue.

"Just give me a second."

Christa stares longingly at me, licking her lips. "Sure. I'll give you all night."

"Right." Because I have no idea what else to say to that. I don't remember Christa being so overtly interested in me when we were in high school. Then again, that was ten years ago, and I was most definitely taken. Which is both the main reason I don't want to be here and the main reason I came. But now I'm starting to reconsider everything.

I have nothing to prove by being here.

Not to *her*, her douchebag husband—my former friend—or anyone else.

I should just go. Maybe meet up with Carter, who I already know is going to our favorite bar, and get lost in a night of fun. Nothing about this hellhole will be fun. And in truth, I could really use a drink. A quiet one. It's been a shitful week. Too many patients. Not enough time. Oh, and finding out that your mom's cancer is back is always a winner.

I slip my phone from my pocket and shoot off a text to my best friend, Grace.

Me: Sorry, babe. Not gonna be able to make it.

The message bubble instantly dances along my screen. **Grace: It's not a choice, honey pie. Everyone is already asking when you're going to get here. Everyone.**

And instantly I'm tempted to ask if *she's* asking. In fact, my thumbs, who seem to have a mind of their own, start to type that very question until I tamp them down and rein them under control. Of course, she's asking. That's what she does.

She continues to hunt me down with terrorist-level determination, even all these years later.

She's likely giddy at the prospect of rubbing her picture-perfect life in my face without even caring that she's the last person on the planet I want to see tonight or any other night. Hence why now is the perfect time to leave.

Me: Don't care.

Grace: Yes, you do. Come on. I know you're already dressed for tonight. Carter sent me a text.

Carter. My traitorous brother.

Grace: Just come inside the hotel. Come up to the reunion. Have a drink with me. See the people you haven't seen since high school who will fall at your feet the way they did back in the day. Oh wait, they still do.

Me: You're doing a shitty job of selling it there, sweetums.

Grace: Everyone will think you're a pussy if you don't come.

Me: Nice gauntlet drop.

Grace: I thought so. Now get your ass over here!

I growl out a slew of curses under my breath, still seriously contemplating fleeing for the sake of my sanity, when I catch sight of a short, curvy redhead in a tight, backless black dress, higher than high heels, and fuck-me red lips that match her hair walking up to Christa. She's as late as I am, and before I know what I'm doing, a smile cracks clear across my face.

I know her instantly.

Even if it's been ten years since I've seen her. A guy never forgets the girl who gave him his first boner. A first-ever boner in class, I might add. We were twelve and she bent over to retrieve her fallen pencil when a flash of her training bra caught my eye. Instant erection.

I was pretty smitten after that moment, as you might imagine.

"Amelia," Christa greets her, her face now lacking any of the warmth it had when she was talking to me. "I had no idea you were coming."

What the fuck? You'd think in the ten years since we graduated from our annoyingly prestigious prep school that the rich girls would get over the self-created, mean-girl bullshit they had with the scholarship kids.

Amelia turns redder than her hair, and she takes a small step back before straightening her frame and squaring her shoulders. "Well, I'm here. Graduated same year as you. I even received the invitation in the mail. Must have been an error on your part," she finishes sarcastically.

"Uh-huh. It's a hundred-dollar entrance fee," Christa snaps, taking far too much pleasure in announcing that sum as she purses her lips off to the side, giving Amelia a nasty-girl slow once-over.

"A hundred dollars?" Amelia asks, though it comes out in a deflated, breathy whisper.

"Yup. Sorry," Christa sneers with a sorry-not-sorry saccharine sweet voice. "No exceptions. Not even for the kids who were on scholarship."

And that's it. Before Christa can say anything else that will make me want to throttle her, I walk over to Amelia, wrapping my hand around her waist. "Sweetheart," I exclaim. "You made it. I was starting to get worried."

Amelia jolts in my arms, her breath catching high in her throat as she twists to face me. Then she looks up and up a bit more because she's about a foot shorter than I am even in her heels. Suddenly, two sparkling gray eyes blink rapidly at me, and my heart starts to pound in time with the flutter of her lashes, my mouth dry like I've been eating sand all night.

"I'm sorry," she says, confused, her parted lips hanging just a bit too open for us to be selling this. "I think you must—"

I lean in, my nose brushing against her silky red hair that

smells like honeysuckle or something sweet and I breathe into her ear, "Just go with it."

She swallows audibly as I pull back, staring into her eyes and wondering how a color like that is even possible when she smiles and robs me of my breath. *Whoa.* That's unexpected.

"I didn't mean to worry you…" She trips up, biting into her lip like she's searching for a suitable term of endearment. Or maybe my name? I guess it is possible she has no idea who I am. We didn't exactly run in the same circles, and I just came up to her and wrapped my arm around her. "Oli," she finishes with, and I blow out the breath I didn't even realize I was holding.

"It's fine. I just didn't want to go in without the most beautiful woman in the world on my arm."

Amelia gives me that stunning smile again, this time with a blush staining her cheeks, and I marvel at how it makes her eyes glow to a smoky charcoal. Goddamn, she's fucking sexy.

"Wait," Christa interrupts. "You're with her?" She points at Amelia.

"I sure am," I declare without removing my eyes from Amelia's because those eyes, man. They're just too pretty not to stare at. "I'm a lucky bastard, right?"

"You're with him?" She turns that finger on me.

"So it seems," Amelia replies, her tone a bit bewildered, though there is a hint of amusement in there, too.

"But. You're. You. No. You're Oliver Fritz," Christa sputters incredulously. "And she's Amelia—" Her words cut off when I throw her my most menacing glare, already knowing the exact nasty nickname she's about to throw out. Why certain women feel the need to degrade and belittle other women, I'll never understand.

I slip two one-hundred-dollar bills from my wallet and toss them at Christa. "Have a good night," I say instead of what I'm really thinking. My fingers intertwine with Amelia's, and then

I'm dragging her past Christa, down the long corridor with the paisley rug and gold walls, toward the ballroom.

I guess I'm going to my high school reunion after all.

The second we're out of sight of Christa, Amelia yanks her hand from mine, stopping in the middle of the hall and turning to stare up at me. "You remember me?" she asks and then shakes her head like that's not what she meant to say.

"Amelia Atkins. You were in most of my classes from the time we were in sixth grade or so, on."

"Right. What I meant to say is, thank you for stepping in back there, but it really wasn't necessary."

"Maybe not. I'm sure you can handle yourself with women like Christa. But it felt wrong to stand there and watch that go down, doing nothing. I can't stand women who feel the need to hurt others just to make themselves look and feel better."

She folds her arms over her chest, giving me a raised eyebrow. "And yet you dated a woman who did exactly that all through high school."

Touché. A bark of a laugh slips out my lungs. "Can't argue with that. Hell, I dated that same vicious woman through college too. Adolescent mistake. What can I say?"

Still, at the mention of that particular woman, an old flair hits me straight in the chest. My fingers find my pocket, toying with the large diamond solitaire set in a diamond and platinum band I stuck in there tonight. It's *the* ring. The one I nearly gave to said woman who was screwing around on me with my friend, Rob. A lesson in betrayal I've never forgotten. It's why on certain occasions, I carry it with me.

A reminder to never get too close again.

"Sorry," Amelia says, withering before my eyes. "That was insanely rude of me. I don't even know why I said that. Christa got my hackles all fired up, and I just took them out on you instead of her, like I should have. Damn, some women seriously suck, right?" I can't stop my chuckle, though I think she was being serious. She stares down at the rug, shifting her stance until she's leaning back against the wall opposite the closed doors where the reunion is taking place. "Look, I wish you hadn't paid for me. Money and I aren't exactly on speaking terms at the moment. It's going to take me a while to pay you back. But I *will* pay you back. I just don't have that kind of—"

My fingers latch on to her chin, tilting her head back up until our eyes meet. "I don't care about the money. And I don't want you to pay me back." She opens her mouth as if to argue with me, and I shake my head, cutting her off again. "I mean it."

She huffs out a breath. "Well, thank you. That's very generous. But if this is how this night is already starting off, I'm thinking maybe I should just go. Hell, I shouldn't even have come here in the first place. I don't know what I was thinking. My sister talked me into it, and I thought..." She shakes her head. "Never mind. It's stupid."

I prop my shoulder against the wall so I'm facing her, folding my arms while I stare at her because I can't seem to help myself. "Why is it stupid?"

"You really want to know?"

"I really want to know."

Those big eyes slay through me, slightly glassy with emotion. "Because no one in there wants me there. You heard Christa. I was fooling myself into thinking that I could waltz in here ten years later and everyone who treated me like garbage growing up would finally see me for me. That they'd finally realize we're all on an even playing field now that high school is over. It was going to be like putting all my old bully nightmares to rest once and for all. Only, nothing has changed. I'm still the girl wearing thrift store digs who couldn't even afford to pay the entrance fee."

Wow. That's...

"Can I tell you something?" I ask.

Her hands meet her hips. "You mean something to rival the

way too personal verbal diarrhea I just spouted at a man I haven't seen in a decade?"

She's trying for brave and strong, and even sarcastic. But she's sad. I can see it in her eyes that bounce around my face, almost as if she's not sure she wants to know what I'm about to say. No one wants to be slammed back into their high school nightmare. She wanted to walk in there and make all those assholes eat their words.

I want that for her too.

I like Amelia. I always have. There was something about her that just got to me on a weird level I never quite understood. She was sweet and nerdy and quiet and reserved. So understatedly beautiful. Her hair was all wild with red curls. Her glasses a touch too big for her face. Her body small with her ample curves hidden beneath her ill-fitting prep school uniform.

And looking at her now, after hearing what Christa was saying to her...

In truth, I do remember people being that nasty. Though now I'm positive it was a lot worse than I knew about if Christa's reaction to her tonight is anything to go by. I only heard comments here and there that I didn't pay much attention to, nor did anything to stop. Even if I never directly contributed to it, by not stopping it, I was part of the problem.

That's on me. And it's not okay. I should have done more to protect her. I should have said something.

"Something like that. You told me yours. Now I'll tell you mine."

"Alright."

I step into her, bending down like I'm about to tell her a secret when really, I just want to be closer to her. Smell her shampoo that makes my cock jump in my slacks. Feel the heat of her body as she starts to blush from my proximity.

"I don't want to be here either. I got talked into it by my friend, Grace, and now here I am."

Her eyebrows knit together. "Why wouldn't you want to be here? You're a doctor. You were the most popular guy in our class. Captain of the football team. Everyone loved you. Still do, if the tabloids are anything to go by."

I suck in a deep breath, ready to tell her something only my family and Grace know. "My ex is not only in there with her husband, my former friend, but she's pregnant. Likely going to be delivered by either my brother or my best friend since she sought them out to be her OB. How's that for irony?" I roll my eyes. "The only saving grace I have when it comes to Nora is that she never knew I was about to propose. I had the ring in my pocket, ready to drop down onto one knee, but before I could do anything, she told me she was in love with Rob and that we were over."

Amelia sucks in a rush of air, her eyes flashing. Her hand shoots up, covering her parted lips as she stares at me with a combination of shock and sympathy. "God. That's awful."

"The real kicker of all that is I had made a lot of sacrifices for her. A lot. Nearly everything I wanted I had given up for her with the exception of medicine. But I chose NYU to be with her instead of playing ball at Michigan. I finished college in three years instead of four because she said the sooner I can complete med school and residency, the better. Then, on the fucking day I got into Columbia for med school and was set to propose, she informed me she had been cheating on me for the better half of six months."

Six. Fucking. Months!

"Jesus, Oliver. I'm so sorry. I never heard anything about that."

"That's because no one knows, so if you wouldn't mind keeping that to yourself, I'd appreciate it. The last thing I want is for that to hit the press next."

She reaches out her hand, touching my arm and giving me a squeeze. "Of course. I'll never tell anyone. I don't blame you for not wanting to go in there. It seems we both felt like we had something to prove by showing up tonight."

That's not the reason I came tonight. But Nora is the main reason I didn't want to go in. I've successfully avoided seeing her for years. In truth, I've been over her for a long time, just not over what she did to me. Most of my bitterness and resentment is on me. I should never have made those sacrifices for her.

I gave up pieces of myself I can never get back.

But Amelia deserves more. She always has, and she never got it. She deserves to have people look at her and treat her with the respect they never did. They owe it to her. Hell, I owe it to her. I don't want her to leave tonight the way she is now.

"I only wish it had turned out better for us," she continues. "But I think my carriage has officially turned back into a pumpkin and I should just cut my losses and head home. Tonight can't possibly end the way I had envisioned it."

Like a bolt of electricity flowing through me, suddenly I'm giddy with an idea that is quite possibly the most ridiculous idea in the history of ideas. Christa nearly swallowed her tongue when she thought Amelia was my date. So maybe everyone else will react the same way if that's what they see. Bonus for me—I'll have a hot as hell woman on my arm and maybe Nora will leave me alone.

More than that, I *want* to go in there with Amelia. I want to spend more time with her tonight. And if they don't like it or think less of me for it, well, I don't give a shit.

But Amelia being my date isn't enough. Not with my reputation. They'll just assume I'm using her, because ever since Nora and I split up... I've been somewhat of a player. A fact the media loves to report on. Hell, my face is splashed across the internet every other week, showing me with a different woman each time. Not in the last few months or so, but it's been the standard of my life since Nora. It's the way I keep from getting hurt again.

And the media reporting on it all? Well, that's the standard of all my brothers' lives. It comes with being a Fritz and living in Boston. We own this city. We're royalty. For better or worse, that's how it is.

But if Amelia and I really want to make an impact tonight... if I really want to make all those assholes who hurt Amelia choke, and Nora—who still calls me to tell me *all* her 'happy' news—realize that I've finally and officially moved on from her... it needs to be more than just people thinking I'm dating Amelia.

They need to know she's something special. Believe she's something special *to me*.

My fingers dig back into my pocket, locating that ring. Looking at her... plotting this insane idea... I'm hit with the fact that I know it will change everything. Both for her and for me.

A deviously crooked smile curls up at the corner of my lips.

Yeah. I have an idea, alright. And I think I can get Amelia to go for it. It's only for a few hours anyway. What could go wrong?

Want to know what happens next with Amelia and Oliver? Grab your copy of Doctor Scandalous now!

www.ingramcontent.com/pod-product-compliance
Lightning Source LLC
Chambersburg PA
CBHW031436160726
47994CB00005B/1747